I0750657

RAVENRY

BRAD LANCASTER

Library of Congress Cataloguing in Publication Data:
Lancaster, Brad
Ravenry

ISBN 978-0-9986435-5-7

Published by:
Saint George's Hill Press
17503 10th Avenue N.E.
Shoreline, Washington 98155

First Printing: 2021

This book is printed in Times New Roman font.

Printed in the United States of America

For my dear friend of decades,
MICHAEL HENRY BREHM,
who made sad versions
of this novel into
a paperweight,
a doorstop,
and the
butt of
many
little
jokes.

TABLE OF CONTENTS

BOOK ONE: TALE OF ENDINGS

BOOK TWO: TALE OF BEGINNINGS

SLEEPWALKING

As I walk,
Forest jokesters cawk and clack,
Hoary cedars their ravenries,
Towering evergreen nests.
Swooping from eminent heights,
Busy black beaks pilfer by day,
Food and joy, berries and salmon.
Hundreds convene in jesting rest,
Heedless of our empty stomachs.
All is one, everything connected.

As I sleep,
Their spectral namesake marauds.
Ebony feathers rustle dreamrealm.
From heights unimagined, Raven dives.
Slashes meaning from brainbones.
Strips carrion from unwary souls.
The sacred corvid roosts in dreams.
Minds weave its chimerical Ravenry,
Heedless of my fractured heart.
Everything connected, all is one.

Charles D Ravenhill, Ph.D.
Regent, U'mista Cultural Center
Alert Bay, British Columbia, Canada
July 2061

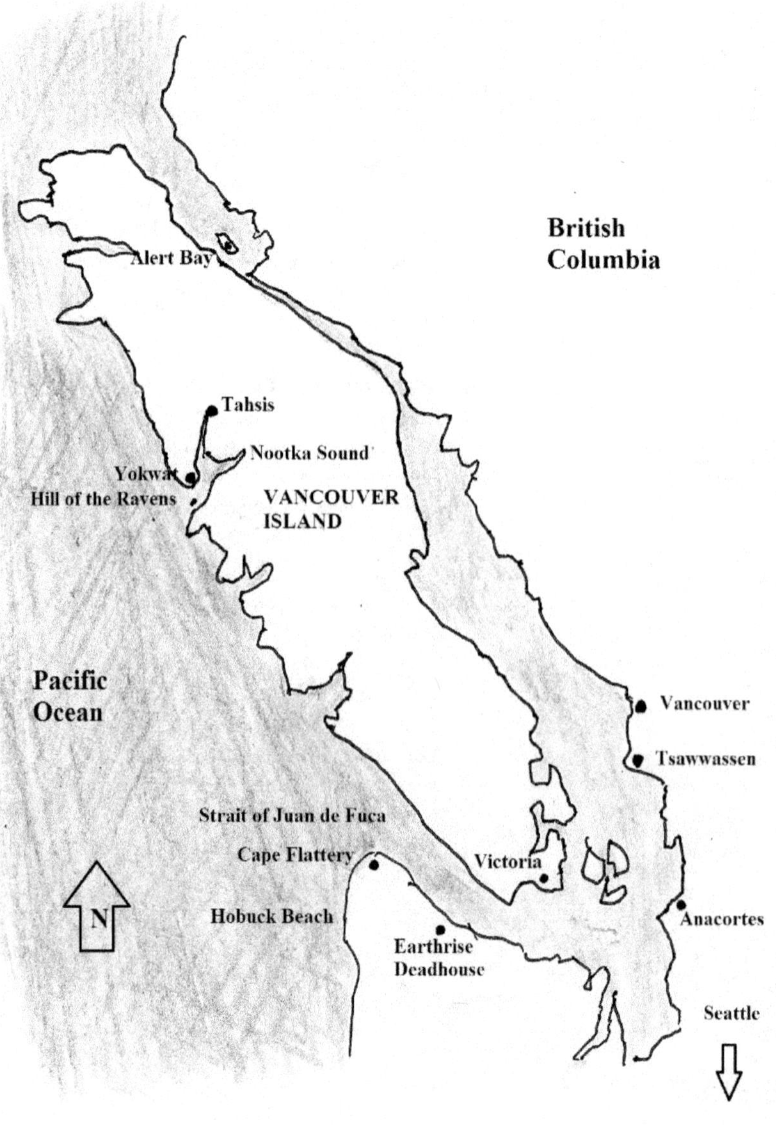
British
Columbia
Alert Bay
Tahsis
Nootka Sound
Yokwat
Hill of the Ravens
VANCOUVER
ISLAND
Pacific
Ocean
Vancouver
Tsawwassen
Strait of Juan de Fuca
Cape Flattery
Victoria
N
Hobuck Beach
Anacortes
Earthrise
Deadhouse
Seattle

Guide to Speculations

Noeforming. Minds in proximity intermingle. Long association produces similarity. What might eons of intimacy produce? Humans value individuality. Other species, longer lived, may not. Might a species that valued identicality make of tasting another's mind an art form, even a science? Might such creatures create a medium in which to store and share their art? Might aliens plumb the mentation of lesser species, as a perverse offshoot of their higher art? A zoo of minds? How would a species of identicality regard "noeforms" of inferior animals? As debauched aesthetics? As pornography? As abomination?

Null Space. In linear algebra, null space is a matrix the summed vectors of which equal zero. One might call null space a set of solutions to a problem that provide no solution at all. Might null space exist in the same sense that the four-dimensionality which humans experience exists? Might null space be a dimensionless dimension underlying all dimensions? Might its properties be utilized for instantaneous travel ("stepping through") or communication ("the We"). For defense ("null field")? As a weapon ("the Mastican envelope")?

Masticans. On earth, single-celled bacteria probably evolved first (prokaryotic micro-organisms). These lacked nuclei and specialized organelles. They reproduce by fissioning. Eukaryotes, a more specialized sort of bacteria, probably evolved later. Eukaryotes have a defined nucleus, organelles (such as mitochondria and golgi bodies), and reproduce both asexually (mitosis) and sexually (meiosis). Bacteria overmatch all other life forms on Earth, both numerically and in biomass. Humans are agglomerations of differentiated tissues of eukaryote-like cells. In alien ecosystems, might prokaryotes have out-competed eukaryotes? Might prokaryotes have adapted by engulfing rivals possessing superior adaptations, engrafting these innovations into their plasm, in a kind of self-aggrandizing phagocytosis? Might they have scaled themselves up to macro-organism size to accommodate their many kidnapped organelles? Might they have engulfed a rudimentary intelligence and found consciousness? Might such creatures live immensely long lives, replacing failed organelles as simply as humans eat? Might Masticans emerge from such an alien ecological history? Might such beings prefer trichotomy to dichotomy, trilateralism to bilateralism, if their appendages came in triplets rather than duplets, like us poor, flattened, left-right bilateral humans?

Raven. Raven is one among the spirit pantheon of the Amerind tribes of the northwest coast of North America. In some subcultures, Raven dominated the spirit world. Raven is godlike, possessed of superhuman powers and creative capacity. Raven tricks. Raven forces change. Raven transforms himself and circumstances. Raven hungers, tirelessly seeking food and ribald amusement. Raven cares, yet carelessly. Raven courses the metaphysical abyss, intruding seldom, but often enough. Of gods, humans know nothing.

Yet, if people spoke only of what they know, the world would languish in excruciating silence. Perhaps it is best that we sometimes mumble theological surmises, though we know we stutter nonsense as our lips move.

MAW. In exotic circumstances, when conditions mimic the timeless "instant" before the Big Bang, matter collapses into dimensionless singularity. Singularities occupy the cores of spiral galaxies. Singularities also form when high-mass stars explode as supernovae. The gravitational attraction of singularities is proportional to the mass that the singularity has collapsed into itself. At some proximity to a singularity, escape velocity from the object's gravity well exceeds the speed of light. So, no light escapes. That threshold is called an "event horizon," and the object itself a "black hole." Is it possible that, in the collision of two galaxies, the stars and dust of a large black hole, comprising millions, even billions, of solar masses, might be stripped of its host of accompanying stars and launched by gravitational perturbations into deep space? If so, one might encounter a starless, hungry horror like the "Maw."

ENIGMAT. What might a hyper-empirical species, completely lacking an innate sense for the divine, call an eons-long series of events which appear, in their concatenation, of intelligent, often hostile, origin? The aliens' best minds ferret a riddle wrapped in a mystery, ensconced in quandary, wetted with conundra, frozen in sphinxian silence, shaped as a question mark, lost in a labyrinth of doubtful arcana (apologies to Prime Minister Churchill). One might throw up all three hands, and call the phenomenon "Enigmat."

AMITY. Amity" is "friendly relationship." Its synonyms are friendship, friendliness, harmony, harmoniousness, understanding, accord, cooperation, companionship, amicableness, goodwill, cordiality, warmth, or concord. An antonym of "amity" is "enmity," which means "a feeling of active opposition to someone or something." Synonyms are hostility, animosity, antagonism, friction, antipathy, animus, acrimony, bitterness, rancor, resentment, aversion, bad feeling, ill will, bad blood, hatred, loathing, and odium.

BOOK ONE

TALE OF ENDINGS

PROLOGUE
OLYMPIC PENINSULA, WASHINGTON
2363 A.D.

Raven the Trickster toys with my family. From before time, she cackles and prods. Raven's mind lies dark as his feathers and purposes. The Mowachaht, my people, tell a tale. Raven fashioned humankind to salve its boredom. The Trickster pried open a primordial clamshell in which we sheltered. He cast us upon the beach. Since that day, we remain playthings of supernal forces.

For centuries, Raven has crushed the Mowachaht in the collision of cultures. The English, the French, the Americans, the Canadians, now the Masticans. Raven drives us Ravenhills somewhere, somewhere unstated. Raven holds hostage our sleep. He intrudes upon dreams. Raven weds us, buries us, grieves us, saves us. Raven approaches, ever the sublime narcissist—all day, every day, all Raven. I complain, but I lack comprehension. Who can trust perceptions, especially stress dreams? None knows Raven.

I am Daniel Ravenhill. RavenPod, my neurolinked family, asked me to recount these stories. I am told these tales by those who lived them. I speak beneath the stripped sky of the Mastican envelope. You may surmise that Odal and I are close. That is true, but was not always so. Odal has befriended my family for most of a millennium, though his goodwill was not always so apparent as now. You may have heard rumors of Earthrise Deadhouse; those are probably exaggerations or hysterias. We did live the old ways, the hoary, forgotten life skills. And I am, in fact, wedded beyond marriage and a bigamist. That much I avow.

Ravenhill suffering is soulish, mostly. Physical pains wash past, like desert gullywashers, greedily sucked by time's parched sands and thirsty winds. Fleshy throbbings are soon forgotten. Raven's torments endure. Our mirthful corvid demiurge pummels Ravenhills with pitiless thrashings that leave no welts. I am not addled. I sympathize with your disbelief. Some whisper about mental illness in the Ravenhill clan. Think me a trenchant animist, if you must. Or a wack job. But hear my story. It is your story too. I would not believe me, were I in your shoes. Mythology mumbles metaphor; religion reeks of suspect similes. Of gods, humankind grasps nothing. And yet, Raven comes. When she pleases. If it suits him. Raven is fickle, yet patient also. And, apparently, hungry, in some unfathomable sense. Ever departing, tickling deaf ears: Cawk. Cawk. Cawk. Cawk.

The Masticans aim to kill humanity. Though their omnicide may prove their own undoing, they enact their festering billion-year-old hatreds. Trilectical cognition dwarfs bilateral mentation, so they declaim. Bilateralism infests their galaxy, indeed many galaxies. Mastix must purge. The Mastican envelope will engulf humanity, and all other bilaterals, if we and our friends fabricate no way out. Masticans have enveloped thousands of bilateral species, as macrophages gulp viruses. All those bilaterals perished. I am not being gloomy. None escaped; that is the fact. How can we imperiled prisoners proceed? Without stars, trapped with our sun, no life on Sol's planets will survive. What paths lie open to creatures such as us and our alien friends? Is Raven for or against man? Does care lie beneath her untamed frivolity? We shall see.

To understand, you will need to hear Ravenhill stories. Some of us are here, noeformed in odd co-consciousness. The dead, the living, the alien, the fabricated. I recount stories from before my birth. I speak of worlds no human has visited. Those who lived these stories dwell in my mind, as do I in theirs. We are one, yet still many. We seek a path forward, a Mowachaht path, a human path, a Mastican path, a virulent path, a cyber path. We seek a common course, sufficiently capacious to accommodate us all together. We see that all things resolve into one thing, and whatever exists is connected. Appearances to the contrary delude. Unity in diversity. The core truth of philosophy, sociality, physics, and sex. And, yes, theology.

We have linked. For us, joinder is a marvel of collaboration and tolerance. But have we commenced a workable journey out of the Mastican chokehold? We have doubts. Grave doubts. Perhaps humanity will perish. We shall see.

For my part, I hear a dark whoosh. Black wings flap, traversing numinous interstices, bridging the epistemological abyss that segregates things cosmological from whatever may be otherwise. We noeformed few, and some human others, dangle from inky talons of eternity.

Metaphysical feathers rustle.

I hear avian chuckling.

Cawk. Cawk. Cawk. Cawk.

CHAPTER 1
ENIGMAT

IN THE GREAT ABYSS OUTSIDE THE SCULPTOR GROUP OF GALAXIES
JUST BEFORE THE TIME WHEN HOMINIDS EMERGED IN AFRICA

Odal and Haras plummeted toward the Maw, clutched in its inexorable grip. Wisps of gas cascaded from the starry backdrop. Stars decomposed, squealing X-ray profusions. An elongated red giant, stretched toward nothingness, erased into the oblivion of its dismembered quarks. Odal spun from leg to leg to leg in a null-field. Three eyes of his three primary lobes sipped the spectacle. A hiss of wonder leaked from Odal's pinnacle vacuole.

Haras inquired, "A thought?"

"I feel grief," Odal said. "A genocide of stars. In our hundred observations of singularities, I have seen no crush so potent," Odal replied.

Haras spun in agreement.

Haras wondered more at Odal's mind than the Maw. Odal, as a virulent Mastican budded to the purpose, experienced awe, not puddle-pang. Haras tasted Odal's mind. Putrid. Haras wretched. Odal's breaches of puddle etiquette were legend. But, of course, that was true of all two hundred virulents. A necessary evil, Haras, and all the trillion Masticans, now believed. But a billion years ago, Haras argued against succoring virulents. They would be unpredictable buds, he had worried. Yet, times, as do they ever, changed. Virulents were now the shock troops of phagocytic envelopment. Bilaterals would today be extinct in the Mastican galaxy, Omban. The puddle had virulents to thank for that outcome.

As an oddity of nature, Haras loved the Maw. It was hypertrophic, stupendous. The Maw gave "big" a bigger meaning, even to the Masticans, who moved stars and edited the biome of galaxies. But, as a common strain

Mastican, Haras tolerated the threat of the Maw only so far. Haras could feel fingers of numbing catatonia clawing.

Odal engaged the Maw with Haras. Part of his mind, however, lingered elsewhere. At this very moment, hundreds of light years distant, Qadax moved to extinguish the Nestles, a vegetable bilateral sentience, which Odal had studied, among other species, these last two million years.

Odal and Qadax had argued. Odal recalled.

"I must be there. I understand the Nestles," Odal insisted.

Qadax's vacuole pursed, then rippled. Strong censure. Qadax spoke in his puddle voice, "My bud, a Mastican, even a virulent, cannot permit attachments to bilaterals. If the We suspected . . ."

Odal interrupted, "But the We does not suspect. The puddle does not prefer to noeform virulents. We disturb them. The puddle cannot engulf our affections. Common strainers do not want to grasp what I have learned from bilaterals. The puddle seeks only safety and sameness."

Qadax responded, "The common strain created the Pathogene. We are its progeny. They have benefitted, as have virulents. The Maw begins its entry into Omban. The Maw will, in time, suck much of our cluster into itself. You must be there with him, to help Haras, to protect Mastix and the other trilateral worlds. We must know all we can know. It may be that no mere puddler can breach the event horizon of such a singularity without losing consciousness."

Odal marshaled his final argument, "We have restructured Omban galaxy group for the gravitational skew of the Maw. The move of Mastix and its sun proceeds. Relocations of a thousand other worlds will be complete millions of years before the Maw poses any direct threat to the puddle." Qadax agreed, but did not relent. Qadax could see he must share his darkest concerns with Odal, who would remain persistent to a fault.

Qadax said, "We have been battling the Enigmat relentlessly, Odal, for a billion years, and extinguishing bilaterals for more than 600 million years. The Nestles are last among bilaterals in Omban. Since we little understand the Enigmat, none can say what may be its response. We know neither where nor what the Enigmat is. Does it not seem too coincidental that as the We envelops the last bilaterals in Omban, the Nestles, on that very day that the Maw consumes its first stars in Omban? Absent our efforts, the Maw would consume our puddle world and its star. What stroke of primordial ill-fortune launched the Maw directly at Mastix? How was this coincidence arranged? What might the Enigmat contemplate?"

Odal spun silently, to show attention and respect. He mulled the puzzle.

Qadax continued, "And another worry. Assuming Mastix does in fact eliminate Enigmat's bilaterals, do you think the We shall continue to tolerate virulent oddness? Won't the puddle be done with us, and the Pathogene extinguished?"

Odal rested quietly on his tripod of legs, a cessation of spin. Odal mulled Qadax's disturbing speculations. Odal's pinnacle vacuole rippled, "I relent, my stirp."

Odal and Qadax noeformed. Though a youngster less than ten million years old, his mind was a clone of his stirp's billion year mind. Every petal of their consciousness blossomed to one another, for the mere joy of the sharing. By contrast, the noeform of the We swirled with compulsion. From a virulent perspective, common strain life was lockstep conformity born of gnawing puddle-pang, the neurotic, synchronous bleating of a trillion identical sheep. From the puddle's perspective, virulents were dangerously unpredictable. Pathogene, the virulent gamble, was the puddle's long, promising, but risky, experiment in intentional psychopathology. Among all virulents, Odal best tolerated solitude. His existence was a Mastican oxymoron.

So, Odal accompanied Haras to the Maw. There lay no solitude comparable to that just inside an event horizon. And no known event horizon so isolating as that of the Maw. Haras heard Odal slosh.

"Gurgles?" Haras asked.

Odal admitted, "The Maw daunts." Apprehension scratched Odal. Fear. It was typical Mastican far-from-puddle anxiety. Masticans suffered this distemper as a two billion year legacy of the bacteriological bogs in their evolutionary past. Thousands of millions of years of sentience had not erased the Mastican compulsion for togetherness. Every Mastican yearns for slack water brimming with bacilli, blooming with proto-Mastican bacteria. Masticans demand puddle consensus. Odal's body remembered, in its nucleic acids, the puddle swarm of cylindrical athrocytes besting all comers. Masticans plundered the genome of challengers, engulfing competitive genetic materials, then transducing their wonders into the puddle's collective cytoplasm. Masticans adopted what was best in opponent genetics and organelles.

Mastic fear of the Maw was well-warranted. Were the Masticans able to liberate all the energy frozen in every scrap of matter in their globular cluster, concentrate it in a single pulse, and slam that burst accurately on the Mawpoint singularity, it would make no difference. The object was simply too massive.

Odal admired Haras's fortitude. Odal was bred for threats. But Haras was a puddler. The elder's self-restraint impressed Odal. Odal could choose alone, if need be. He could consider possibilities inconceivable to puddler trilaterals. The Maw wrote the final paragraph of Haras's lifelong investigation of singularities, his largest and most dangerous exploration.

As they plummeted, gravity waves buffeted Haras and Odal. Their null fields shielded them. Such capsules had carried Masticans safely to the heart of stars. But, unless they stepped through, even the null field would prove no obstacle to the reality-ripping forces of the Maw singularity. Its gravity entombed Odal and Haras in a crude, but effective, coffin. As they crossed the event horizon of the Maw, the team would enter the most exotic and dangerous place in the then-known universe.

Haras said, "In ninety-three seconds the Maw crosses the traditional border of the Omban ellipse." This grand-daddy of black holes would hurtle through the Sculptor group, of which Omban was one globular cluster. The Maw would plough through Omban, gorging on millions of star systems. But with the mass of several galaxies, the Maw's gravitational tendrils would work havoc throughout the Sculptor group. A nightmare tangle of gravitational interactions promised disasters. Skal had worked out that dance a hundred million years ago, painstakingly, when the Maw's threat was first detected. Preparations to preserve the core trilateral star systems had been underway for many millions of years. Mastícans ferried valuable star systems out of the Maw's path. They precisely destabilized others so the Maw's havoc would exactly counteract trilateral meddling, leaving those systems in a semblance of their original state. Odal reached out with his mind to the We. Time dilation made their respective processing rates gibberish to one another. Odal relented. In a matter of a few hundred seconds, every object in his sight would be sundered. Each would occupy no volume, bear infinite mass, and become a dimensionless point in spacetime. Reality, there, changes costume. Life is unthinkable. But first came Odal's and Haras's plummet into wonder.

Qadax floated weightless against the galaxy-spattered backdrop of the universe. The regal virulent prepared to complete his 600 million years of labor. With the planning and research, the task had required almost all of Qadax's billion years since his artificial budding. Now, Omban and the Sculptor group of galaxies would be free of bilaterals. And with that extinction, Mastix would be free of Enigmat influence. So Qadax hoped. So he believed.

Qadax partitioned his mind, sequestering the virulence that puddlers found so offensive. He linked with the We. A trillion Masticans noeformed their minds to that of Qadax. His victory would now be theirs, quite literally. Qadax and the We became a homogeneous, stagnant pool of perfection—the Mastican We. The We recapitulated, in its victory slosh, its billion year game of chess with an indetectable adversary:

Probes confirmed what colonists confronted. Bilaterals polluted Omban. No corner of the globular cluster was unscathed. A plague of dimorphs infested puddle precincts. Ugly, violent, ignorant creatures. Diadic sexual reproducers. Semen-injectors, squirting haploid entries in a gamete survival lottery. No orderly mitosis. Willy-nilly. Helter-skelter. Unseemly genetic chaos, aslosh in bumping and sexual spasms. All bilaterals are perverse in form. Two arms, two legs only. Two-lobed brains, trapped in a sad caricature of consciousness. Dualities preoccupied bilaterals. Everything was up or down, right or wrong, left or right, black or white. Conceptual poverty left bilaterals vulnerable to metaphysical hallucinations, rampant speculations upon macro-beings, and every sort of subempirical surmise. Superstition prevailed among every such species. They had to fill their blanks somehow. Insupportable mental meanders sufficed.

Then came the shock, more than a billion years ago. Bilaterals, so stupid few could master interstellar transport, spread. Exploded, actually. Some agency planted or coaxed. The enemy, which came to be called the Enigmat, terrified Mastix. The We failed consensus. How might one frame an envelopment strategy to which all might consent, when the enemy is unknown and non-local?

The We ultimately resorted to desperate measures. It undertook Pathogene. It budded virulents, mutant trilaterals. Virulents tolerated independence in a manner no self-respecting Mastican could countenance. Cautionary voices warned of the danger of virulents, not only to bilaterals, but also to the puddle. The We reached consensus to clone virulents only after stringent safeguards were agreed.

Virulents turned the tide. Qadax, preeminent among virulents, adapted the null field for offensive use. Infested systems were encapsulated. No cosmic energy could breach null fields. None entered. None escaped. Life forms, even Masticans, would be trapped if enveloped. Enigmat transplantations increased. Qadax hatched the insidious ruse of Forms, by which to culture-strip bilaterals into passivity. Where cultures crumbled, bilaterals were ill-suited to transplantation. The Enigmat capitulated. The Sculptor Group of galaxies was cleansed, or will be so this very day. The We has declared it so.

Mastix took the fight to Enigmat. In an adjacent galactic group, the We had already commenced expeditionary incursions. One galaxy predominated, a modest spiral. There, bilateralism was rife. Infested planets were identified. Overcrowding crushed most bilateral species, too stupid to curb their reproductive urgency. The newest virulent, Odal, researched these species in the spiral neighbor. His reports, alleged to contain noteworthy results, have not yet been submitted for noeform. But soon shall be.

The We emerged from its rhapsody of conquest elation, more a song, a liturgy, than a report. A symphony in which ideas and conquests were notes. A billion years of stitching perfected its melody. A trillion voices in labyrinthine synchrony, diverse, yet absent dissent. Qadax hovered near the heliopause of Nest's sun, far beyond the orbit of its outermost planet, beyond its Oort cloud of unassimilated proto-junk. He directed a null field plasm into its cradle latticework. Qadax reported, "The Forms have ben regressed. What we might learn of Enigmat has been gleaned here at Nest. Is consensus firm? Shall I rid Omban of this last Enigmat incursion?"

Without hesitation, the We boomed, "Proceed."

The Maw's event horizon blotted half the universe. Haras sloshed. Odal noticed. "It is time, Haras." Haras brushed Odal's consciousness, leaning his teetering psyche on the crutch of the young virulent's aberrant stability. Haras's consciousness stuttered. Odal sensed Haras's gratitude for support, but also his disgust. That was the virulent's burden. To exist for a purpose with which one was not wholly sympathetic. Odal knew Haras could not understand. That the We might err was incomprehensible to a primordial puddler.

Haras detected Odal's odd thoughts, "The We errs and learns daily, young one. But in matters of will, the We cannot stray. The We wants what we want. It is us."

Odal decided to speak. 'What if the We *must* want what it does not want?"

"That is not possible, Odal," Haras growled. Haras's vacuole flapped fluster.

Odal partitioned his skepticism from Haras.

The two passed the Maw's event horizon. Distorted suns suffered their million-year death spirals. These screamed dirges in electromagnetic dissonance. Photons shattered. The Masticans plunged through transformations, layer after layer, each stranger than the last. Odal felt stress in his null field. His sense of time lacked synchrony. Odal decided, "We must step through now, Haras."

Haras consented. Odal spun to duck around spacetime, across a dimensionless intervening universe, and re-enter four-dimensional space just outside the Maw. As Odal passed through the rift, he heard a sound (which was impossible). A glottal plosive, Cawk, Cawk. It called to mind the guttural vocalizations of bilaterals at what they call "jokes." Then came the flutter of a wing in flight, then a sound of vacuole off-gassing. Odal's sensed digesting organic lipids. The smell of fatty acids, churning their esters and amides, slightly burned, tickled his mind (another impossibility). He saw, peripherally in one eye only, a hint of an aerial bilateral's beak, from which dangled a keratinous curved claw. A fleck of cell wall, hirsute with black filaments, drifted. The silhouetted beak snapped Haras, rupturing his null field like a bubble on a beach. A black wing veered from sight.

Then the heavens wore stars again. Haras did not step through. Odal felt the extremity of Mastix's plight. Something incomprehensible tickled a soft underbelly of his mind. Odal called for Qadax. But Qadax was occupied.

Qadax gave the command. Nothingness burst from the lattice, tracing the Nest heliopause. The Mastican envelope propagated at the speed of light. In some days, no stars but their own sun would trouble the Nestles, as the great black sphere of the Mastican envelope locked the Nestles in. Their sun would, given time, cook Nest and dispatch the Nestles.

Odal's terror roiled his cytoplasm. He partitioned his virulence, then brushed the We. The puddle pondered the Maw and grieved Haras. To Odal's perceptions of how Haras died, to Odal's odd sensations, to his forbidden suspicions, the We gave scant attention. How could the Mastican uni-mind credit the perspective of one deviant member in unimaginable distress on the fatal side of a colossal event horizon?

Odal urged the We to pause. He clamored, as only the young do, for attention. "Great Ocean of Knowledge, hear me. Within the Maw, I saw and heard things, impossible things. The We should investigate. Haras did not die. He was killed. Extremity invites caution."

The We trumpeted elegant silence. It showed respect for a gifted youngster. Acknowledgement without attention.

Odal could not let the many noeform his consciousness. Puddlers might learn the breadth of his deviance. Odal could be absorbed into the puddle as fertilizer, and Qadax as well. Perhaps all virulents would be sundered. The We might abruptly conclude its failed billion-year virulent experiment in alternative consciousness. The Pathogene itself could be terminated.

Odal quaked at the danger, not of the We, but of the Maw, of what he saw past its event horizon. Odal doubted that the Maw's trajectory was random misfortune. Did Enigmat provoke the Maw? Had Mastix provoked Enigmat? If so, all the puddle's preparations might prove vain. Or a trap of some exotic sort.

The puddle preened imperious. The successes of billions of years rendered the We incapable of self-doubt. The collective consciousness of a trillion trilaterals ignored Odal's sensations, discounted his fears as hysterical outlier melancholy. Never, except in trilateral mentation, had reality been so finely mapped. Of reality, no species drank so deeply as Masticans. Their communication was global and instantaneous. The breadth of their colonization astonished those few bilaterals who learned that much. The We was accustomed to its own accuracy. All comers found Mastican technology magical and incomprehensible. No other fathomed their insights, even when matters were meticulously explained. Mastican mentation was unique. It was mysterious. It decrypted the universe. To bilaterals, it proved maddening—and fatal.

Confirming a billion years of habit, Qadax echoed the puddle's fury. Mastix doubled-down on eons of deadly rampage. Envelopment of Nest was right. Every bilateral homeworld must be gulped. A trillion Masticans boomed consensus.

All, except one. A lone, ignored dissenter.

Odal, behind partition, hidden from the puddle, abjectly discounted by insuperable Mastican consensus.

Odal hesitated.

CHAPTER 2
YACHAKAS

NOOTKA SOUND
WHAT WOULD BE LATER NAMED VANCOUVER ISLAND
1565 A.D.

Tootoosch poked his head through the smoky entrance to the longhouse. Broad cedar roof planks were shoved aside to let smoke out and sunshine in. The days shortened as morning frosts of Burning waned toward blustery Rough Sea and snowy Elder. The bronzed, heavily-muscled Tootoosch scanned the longhouse interior with intense black eyes. Children played. Women cooked and sewed. A few, the oaf Shewish among them, slept. Finally, Tootoosch's eyes landed on his brother's son helping his mother hang dried salmon in the longhouse rafters.

"Yachakas, you little fleck of sandpaper. Today we chase flat rocks."

Little Yachakas, whose name meant sand shark or Dogfish, looked up with surprise.

"What?" he asked, wondering what his beloved uncle meant. Tootoosch stuck his arm further into the beam and plank building. Ornate halibut hooks dangled from his fingers. Dogfish squinted. A great smile lit his face. Yachakas would accompany his uncle in a great cedar canoe, and they would tempt halibut.

"Hali—," Dogfish clapped his hand over his mouth before he could finish. Tootoosch shot him a severe look, one which reproved the boy wordlessly. The youngster sprinted across the sunlight mottled interior, littered with debris and fish bones. Older women scolded and shook their heads gently in disapproval.

Tootoosch scuffed his nephew's head. "Boy, do not speak old green slate's name. You will alert him to our stroll today," Tootoosch warned. The hunter never spoke of his quarry. Dogfish nodded aggressively, now reminded that the Spirit of Halibut might be eavesdropping. Dogfish's careless mention of their outing could alert the halibut of Nootka Sound to danger.

"Uncle, how do you know when flat rock spirit might be listening?"

Tootoosch sighed. "More questions, young one?"

"I have many. About our life. About the old stories."

"That is certainly true," Tootoosch laughed, and walked on.

None in all the thirteen houses of the Mowachaht tribe fared so well with the Spirit of Halibut as did Tootoosch. Once he had brought to Yokwat, the Mowachaht's summer village, exposed to the open ocean, a grandmother of the halibut. Four men groaned lifting the fish from the water, and a great feast was held that very day to appease the spirits of the halibut peoples beneath the sea. The bones and guts of that matron fish were carefully returned to the water that they might take flesh anew and live once more.

"Follow me," Tootoosch commanded, and pointed to the spit of basalt which sheltered their little cove from the Pacific inclemency of Nootka Sound.

Tootoosch strode gracefully. Dogfish clambered clumsily. Blockish, black rocks tripped him. Thickets grabbed his feet. Nettles pricked him. Dogfish clamped his jaws. Nothing would convince him to shame himself before Tootoosch with whining or complaint.

The two wrenched loose cedar boughs. In the cold Pacific inlet, they scrubbed themselves. When red with irritation, and blue with cold, their lice drowned. Yachakas followed his uncle's incantations, appeasing the many spirits that crowded their watery world. Dogfish could have sung along. He had learned. Though clumsy, the young man's mind skipped, nimble and supple. His many questions annoyed some of the Mowachaht. Insistent probing had earned him his childhood name, Yachakas, which means dogfish. Dogfish are nuisance sharks. Their skins, once dried, are used as sandpaper to smooth carvings and polish mollusk-shell blades and points. Little Yachakas abraded some, counterpoint to a generally compliant crop of youngsters at Yokwat. He asked where the pole attached, the one that held up the disk of the world. If lightning was Thunderbird's pet snake, why did He keep so many pets? Women hissed at Yachakas. Such knowledge lay with shamans, not boys. Yachakas frowned, and yearned for the day he would receive his adult name. Then he would be a man of the village. He might get answers.

Tootoosch asked, "My son, have you touched Arima, who is heavy with child?"

"No, uncle. I have avoided her."

"That is good. Flying turtles hate the stink of pregnant women." The hunter winked.

"My son, have you walked past a bleeding woman?" Tootoosch raised his eyebrows, to indicate the sort of blood he meant.

"That too I have avoided, uncle."

Tootoosch handed Yachakas a tiny woven cedar ball, with a long string attached. "Bind this on. It will help us find flat rocks in the trees." Yachakas laughed with his eyes. He wound the strap around his upper arm. Inside the ball hid a fragment of a blind snake Tootoosch had killed, which scent masked human odors, so offensive to spirits.

Tootoosch thanked Ichtope, the humpback whale spirit, and Sky spirit for the good hunt they hoped to have. Dogfish matched his uncle's obeisances. As they paddled toward open water, elder in the stern, youth at the bow, the beach bustled. Canoes smoldered, blankets wove, and planks split. Children danced the Wolf whirl, awash in the Tlokwana's cultic imagination, preparing for the big party. Over all hung an unspoken pall, the crisis chief Qwistok suffered with whales. Because of that, Yachakas avoided chewing pitch. Gum bothered whales and salmon. No villager chewed when the winter's supply of food grew uncertain.

Tootoosch paddled briskly. Yachakas's eyes widened. The open Pacific, outside the shelter of the spit of Yokwat, might gulp a two-man canoe. If they hooked a large halibut, it might drag them miles before death frosted its eyes. This outing might sorely test Yachakas's endurance. His paddle bore Raven's image. The two sliced through swells. Tootoosch noted the fiery, nettled welts on his nephew's forearm. The boy met today's challenge with quiet confidence, and a bit of trepidation.

"You stroke well, little Dogfish," Tootoosch encouraged. Yachakas smiled.

The expanse of the sea stretched before them. These waters fed the people. The ocean was their highway. Snow, the mange scales of Sky Dog, whitened peaks and leaked down valleys. Fog burped from the kneecaps of Crane, lying in low smudges against shadowed shores. A profusion of steep, green islands dotted the thalassic seascape. Glacier-carved verticality made Yokwat spit a prize. Twice in Dogfish's short life the tribe had defended their summer village from insurgents paddling north. Prime village sites were few, and always claimed.

The broken necks of bull kelp flopped past in currents. Small crests atop swells splattered the paddlers. Seabirds played in the stiff onshore wind. This turbulence scared Yachakas. Tootoosch saw his nephew's back tense.

"You know Raven and Bear sought flat rocks, as do we today," Tootoosch probed. Of course Yachakas knew. Every Mowachaht heard these stories from infancy. Yachakas nodded, struggling to hide his growing alarm. Of all the Mowachaht legends, Yachakas best loved those of Raven.

Tootoosch settled into a cultic voice, the smooth talk of an oft-repeated liturgy.

Raven the Trickster was a chief of the Mowachaht. He asked Black Bear to go halibut fishing one day. Bear dug his toe into the dirt, staring fixedly. He fidgeted.

Bear said, "I will go, but promise you will do me no harm. You are clever and a trickster. I am just a stupid bear." Bear slobbered a bit from the corner of his mouth, like nervous brutes do.

Raven replied, "Why, Bear! What harm could I do to you? You are fifty times my size, and a thousand times as strong. Can I lift you with my wings? Can I pierce your hide with my beak?"

Bear found muddled truth in Raven's words. He fetched his paddle. Bear checked his hooks and lines. He grabbed octopus for bait. But Raven brought no bait. Bear wondered, but shrugged it off.

Bear took the bow, Raven the stern. They paddled far up Muchalat Inlet.

"We have gone far enough," Raven decided. "Throw out the anchor."

Bear tossed the stone from their canoe, and played out cedar bark rope until it bottomed. Bear rigged for halibut. Raven turned his back to Bear, fussed with his gear. Bear lodged the octopus tentacle on his hook. Both wetted their lines. Immediately, Raven caught a halibut. Then a second. Soon, the bottom of the canoe brimmed with Raven's catch. But Bear caught none.

Bear was embarrassed. How would he explain the outcome to the villagers? They would laugh at him. And Bear hated being the object of scorn.

Bear asked, "What are you using for bait, Raven, that you have caught so many of halibut's family?"

Raven smirked, "If I told you, you would not bait your hook as I have baited mine."

Bear, the dim hibernator, disagreed, "I would do anything to avoid being the butt of jokes, Raven." Bear tried to look cute, as coy as a slobbering bear can look.

"Alright, Bear," Raven sighed. "I have used my dick for bait. I cut it off and put it on the hook. Halibut love it, as you can see."

Bear's slack jaw dropped open. He wanted to avoid humiliation. But he also wanted to keep his privates. Bear protested, after thinking it over for a time, "If I cut off my ladysnake, how will I put it back on when we are done with halibut fishing?"

Raven's eyes danced their jig of amusement. He laughed, Cawk, Cawk. He pulled a lump of gum from his beak. "We paste it back on with this gum when we are done. That is how I do it."

Bear hesitated, then said, "Alright. Let's do it."

Bear lay back and parted his legs. Bear raised his shell knife to slice off his genitals. Bear entreated Raven, "Is this going to hurt?"

Raven responded, "Removing your holepoker will hurt, Bear, but not so much as returning to Yokwat fishless."

Bear sawed off his dingus. Bear groaned. Raven said, "Lay back your head, brother. Take a nap."

The bottom of the canoe filled with blood. Soon, Bear kicked twice, and died.

Raven paddled to shore. He put Bear's stiffening corpse beside a great fire he built. Raven covered the corpse with mosses. He poured water over Bear's bulk. When cooked, Raven ate Bear—fur, muscles, ears, claws, and all. Bear's winter fat burned, creating an oily cream that wafted deliciously. This, Raven drank, then belched. Raven gathered Bear's bones and hid them beneath a salalberry bush.

Raven paddled home to Yokwat spit. He turned the six largest fish so their heads pointed toward Bear's seat. Mowachaht situate their halibut in this manner to indicate who caught them. Raven began to wail. He crunched onto the pea gravel beach.

The Mowachaht gathered around Raven. Raven said, "Bear caught these six fish. The seventh was gigantic. Bear tangled his feet in the line, and was hauled overboard. He never surfaced.

The villagers puzzled. Did Raven speak truly? Or was this one of his many tricks?

Raven belched again. It smelled of bear grease.

Regardless, most believed Raven's tale. Some grumbled, certain Raven can craft a lie like no other. Raven deceives to amuse himself. All knew that.

Raven gave some halibut to Bear's widow, but kept the rest for himself.

And that is why, to this day, ravens laugh around Yokwat, but no black bears.

When Yachakas emerged from the story of Bear and Raven, he and Tootoosch had paddled far. They could no longer see Yokwat. They dropped anchor against the incessant shoving swells.

Their fortune was good. Several small halibut lay in the canoe. They would make a meal for the families of Yokwat. Two large bottomfish were tethered through their gills to the side of the canoe with cedar bark rope. Tootoosch bashed their tiny brain boxes.

As they paddled, Yachakas jabbered. "Why would Bear agree to cut off his dick? Did he not know that Raven plays practical jokes?"

Tootoosch shrugged. "Of the Spirits one can never know."

"And how could a raven eat a whole bear? How could he move the corpse to the fire? He is so little. The bear is so big."

"Size may not matter to Spirits," Tootoosch ventured.

Yachakas opened his mouth to voice more pestilential questions. Tootoosch raised a hand for silence.

Yachakas and his uncle turned the canoe homeward. An image of Raven splashed into the water on the boy's paddle. In and out, in and out. As the two neared the mouth of the Sound, a tiny island slid up aport. A knuckle of granite poking from the water, only five war canoes long. On the ocean side, it was precipitous. Landward, it sloped gently from the water. Scraggly firs clung to its rocks, rooting in quartz and feldspar dust, organic detritus, and a fertilizer of bird droppings. It was an unexceptional island, except for the ravens. Several score hopped and clacked and strutted, a wingding for avians. Usually, ravens gathered to quarrel over carrion. But no carcass was evident. The ravens were agitated.

Tootoosch paddled faster. Yachakas asked, "Why hurry, uncle?"

"Because that island is a Ravenry. The Spirits are strong, so it is dangerous. Those ravens potlatch with the Trickster himself," murmured Tootoosch. Dogfish knew he too should fear. But he did not.

Yachakas asked, "Uncle, has any man of Mowachaht claimed that little hill for his ritual place?"

Tootoosch shook his head. "I do not believe so, boy. It is far from Yokwat across open water. I would not return to that place. Raven will capture your dreams, make you crazy. I saw one raven shaking a rattle over a rotten log. The log writhed at the jester's croaking. I heard groaning, like cedars bending in gales."

Yachakas had not seen or heard these things. He held his tongue. At that instant, there germinated within Yachakas a seed, the sprout that would become a towering cedar of obsession in his clan. Monomania amidst polyanimism. Fixation dissenting from generalism. From among the hidden world's many divinities, Raven seized Yachakas. The Trickster disturbed dreams, drove desire, dug direction.

In the open sound, Tootoosch poked Yachakas, pointing behind them. A dark wall of cloud loomed. "The old man has farted." Legend had it that southeast winds, the violent sort, are flatulence of an ancient mythic spirit. Mink, it was said, could calm the old man's bowels. Tootoosch began the song of Mink. Chanting paced their paddling. Growing waves slid beneath them as the waters turned gray and turbulent. The smudge of Yokwat fires beckoned. But the storm rose. Yachakas's paddling stuttered.

Tootoosch turned again to story. "I will tell you again of your namesake, Yachakas." Dogfish nodded stiffly.

Three Mowachaht boys ventured into the woods, much farther than their mothers permitted. The boys were Yachakas, Spirit of Elk, and Small Clam Boy. This last was eldest son of the Mowachaht chief, and so, a person of great importance in the village. The boys spied a river, the Mowinis. They paddled up its meander.

Far from Yokwat, these bad boys met an ugly woman sitting on the river bank. Beside her sat a huge basket. She chewed gum furiously. The boys paddled up to her, over Yachakas's objections. She looked, to him, evil.

Near the bank, Small Clam Boy spoke to the hag. She whirled, blowing shaman dust over the boys. All sank to the bottom of their canoe. She leaned over them. Yachakas recognized her. She was Malahas, the Woman of the Woods.

Malahas took gum from her mouth, dripping with her spit. She smeared it on Yachakas's eyes, sealing them shut. She plucked him up and dropped him in her great basket. Then she gummed Spirit of Elk and Small Clam Boy. She dropped them on top of Yachakas. As she traveled, little Yachakas squeezed through the weave of her basket. He fell to the ground behind Malahas and felt his way to a big rock. Malahas did not notice.

The Woman of the Woods, when she arrived home, took a long pole and tied the feet of Spirit of Elk and Small Clam Boy to it. She hung them over her hearthfire and smoked them to death.

Dogfish pried the pitch from his eyes, and made his way back to Yokwat. He told the tribe his story. The mother of Small Clam Boy, the chief's son, was anguished. Tears gushed like spring streams. She bawled for four days. At the end of those days, she blew her nose and threw the snot on the ground. The muck lay there.

The next day, her mucus moved. It grew a little head, then some arms. On the third day, it was long as his mother's hand. On the fourth day, the snot child began to cry. His mother swaddled him in a corner of her cedar bark blanket, and tucked it away beneath a giant spruce, behind a clump of licorice fern. She told her husband, the chief, of the strange incident. The very next day, Snot Boy walked into the Mowachaht village. He had become a young man overnight. The chief adopted him, since his wife begged.

Snot Boy heard his mother crying. He asked, "Why do you cry, Mother?"

She said, "You were born from my tearful snot. Before I blew you from my nose, the Woman of the Woods stole my baby, Small Clam Boy, and killed him. She murdered also Spirit of Elk. Only Dogfish escaped. Woman of the Woods kept those poor boys up the Mowinis River."

Snot Boy made himself a bow of yew and two straight arrows, which he tipped with mussel shell. The next morning, Snot Boy's mother painted his face, and adorned his ears and nose with abalone jewelry. He was most beautiful. Snot Boy took his weapon, snuck out of Yokwat, and found Malahas, the Woman of the Woods, up the Mowinis. Snot boy hid in a tree above a quiet pool of the river. Malahas saw his reflection in the water, and exclaimed, "What a beautiful face!" But when she looked up, Snot Boy hid himself. He continued the ruse three times. The fourth time Malahas turned, Snot Boy showed himself. The Woman of the Woods was smitten.

She said, "Come be my husband, beautiful one."

Snot Boy answered, "I cannot, for you are ugly."

"What did your mother do to make you so beautiful, young man?" asked Malahas. Snot boy shrugged his shoulders. Malahas persisted.

Snot Boy relented, "Very well. I will tell you. She positioned my head on a flat rock and smashed it with another. Then my mother artfully remolded my head, and brought me back to life. She taught me her secrets."

Malahas frowned.

Snot Boy said, "I could do this thing for you, if you can find the courage. Once you are beautiful, then we can marry."

Malahas hesitated, but then found two stones of sufficient size. She laid her head on the biggest flat one.

Snot Boy lofted the other stone, but Malahas jerked back.

Malahas asked, "Are you sure you can make me alive once again after you have made me beautiful?"

Snot Boy sneered, "I thought an old woman like you would lose courage. Stay ugly. I will not marry you." Snot Boy stomped off. But the Woman of the Woods begged. She fell to the ground, groveling. Snot Boy waited, pretending to be undecided. Then he consented. The Woman of the Woods squealed with glee.

She put her head on the flat stone and closed her eyes. Snot Boy smashed her skull to bits.

Snot Boy walked to Malahas's house. He heard a man's voice calling. It came from the pot in which the old witch crapped at night. It smelled terrible. Snot Boy smashed the pot. Each piece of the broken pot called to Snot Boy, making a racket.

There was a voice at the door. There stood the Woman of the Woods. Her head was roughly pieced together. She roared her evil laugh. Snot Boy notched an arrow, and shot Malahas through her heart. Now she was really dead.

In the rafters of Malahas's house, over his head, Snot Boy found two desiccated lads of the Mowachaht. Dried, they dangled. Snot Boy laid the victims on the floor. He pissed on them. Their thirsty bodies drank up his urine. They regenerated.

When their senses returned, the three boys paddled back to Yokwat. Small Clam Boy's mother was most grateful. She kissed Snot Boy.

The entire village celebrated his valor.

Tootoosch and Yachakas neared the spit that made Yokwat cove. Their songs had sufficed. Mink had spared them. The storm lashed. Thunder broke, ricocheting off rock cliffs. But two fishermen rounded the jumbled rockery to Yokwat's safety. They had escaped Old Man's indigestion.

"Well done, Yachakas. You stroke well." His uncle offered praise freely. For that, Dogfish was grateful. He smiled, and splashed a little brine back toward Tootoosch. They laughed.

Yachakas, however, could not shake the ravens from his mind. Nor their hill across the open water. The island called to him, in the dark of night as he huddled beneath animal hides which warmed him near the communal hearth.

Qadax hung in his null field. He waited alone, a predatory ritual that had engaged him for hundreds of thousands of millennia. Pinpoints jewels of diamond, azure, sapphire, and saffron studded the regal black skirt of the cosmos. These waxed to a lustrous tangle as he peered down the spiral arm of this galaxy he had invaded. He probed with three sensitive eyes this galaxy's clustered core as he slowly rotated. After several million years of observation, the time was ripe. Such was Mastican patience, the puddle-norm.

Here, so far from anywhere, Qadax waited. Nothing of importance lay nearby on this dismal little arm of this unexceptional spiral, save a grubby little planet, infested with unexceptional bilateral consciousness. It was a blue water world engorged with breeding bilaterals. None of the monkeymind bilaterals grasped their peril. Mastix would envelope. As it had in Omban, Enigmat would withdraw. Most virulents concluded that the Enigmat's surrenders betrayed weakness. The puddle bootstrapped Enigmat cessation into a harbinger of inevitable trilateral domination. But now, as the Maw cataclysm hurtled toward Mastix, Qadax wondered, and Odal feared. Had withdrawal been weakness? Or Enigmat's astonishing patience, a hypertrophic state of repose beside which that of Mastix paled? Or mere toying? Or a component of a still-unrecognized Enigmat trap? The We could not entertain such ideas. Qadax, who could imagine, quaked. Odal, budded to independence, feared. Odal could examine that which even Qadax's expansive mind could not admit.

Odal tickled his stirp's mind. Odal's null field shimmered, and the young Mastican stepped through.

Qadax sought, "How goes the Maw rescue, my bud?"

"Linked or loose?" Odal inquired. Virulents preferred loose.

Odal reported, "Skal's calculations for a trajectory to rescue Mastix may need revision."

Qadax ground, "Skal can do his calculations alone, Odal."

"If Skal's plan works, Mastix, Treasury World, and the Planet of Remembrances will evade the Maw. Much of the rest of Omban will not," Odal recited.

"You have doubts," Qadax sensed.

"I do," Odal admitted. "Not with Skal's math or his diligence."

"The Maw?" Qadax surmised. His pinnacle vacuole rippled unhappily. Catatonia tickled the periphery of Qadax's consciousness. He shook off puddle-pang.

"No, stirp. Not the Maw itself. What I saw within the Maw. What killed Haras," Odal said.

"Yours was a queer apperception indeed. I have mulled it. I would give that moment more weight were it not for your insufferable obsession with bilateral mysticisms," Qadax chided. Then he mumbled, "That is probably my fault. . ."

Odal pinched his pinnacle vacuole between two digits. He would not speak if he was not to be taken seriously. Qadax's eye twitch told Odal to speak.

"What I saw in the Maw was more than a distortion of consciousness, stirp. What persists for me is this. I saw and heard admittedly impossible things. Then Haras died," Odal recounted.

Qadax spoke with strident insistence. "What you saw? This is a flaw in virulent protoplasm. This is why the puddle-mind exceeds that of virulents. The shared mentation of the puddle edits out eccentricities and larks. Sharing a trillion minds' experience levels observation to a quantum that simulates the noumena. The puddle sees reality as it is in itself—almost. Theirs is a simulacrum of raw objectivity. None but trilaterals share minds. No other compares to Mastican physics. What the We thinks remains a deadly intricate approximation of the world-in-itself. The puddle cannot take seriously eccentric, especially ego-centric, perception. That means the We cannot take *you* seriously, Odal."

"The We sees much, but not all," Odal responded.

"Explain."

"Mastix is a viewpoint. We see as we evolved to see. We see what we evolved to see," Odal reasoned.

“It is not so, my bud. The We sees reality. It has no perspective per se. Except in those tiny fragments the We occasionally encounters and incorporates every million years or so. Perspective plagues dimorphs. It is their ultimate downfall. Their linguistic, time-laden communication. Their cerebral bilateral paucity. Their minuscule lifespans. Bilaterals can manage nothing more than perspective, as you call it. The We calls it, not perspective, but inanity.”

Odal countered, “Bilaterals see their mental defects only with great difficulty. Perhaps it is so also with the puddle.”

Qadax crushed his vacuole. His cell wall rippled in displeasure.

“I am chastened, stirp. I withdraw,” Odal backtracked.

The two hung for a time.

Qadax softened, “Proceed, friend. I budded you to tell me things I am too old to notice.” Qadax would listen to his bud’s ravings. He summoned dispassionate equanimity.

“The puddle’s Enigmat strategy is misguided, stirp,” Odal said flatly.

Qadax puffed from his vacuole. “Never in a billion years have I heard such immodesty. You presume to judge the wisdom of a trillion puddle-mates over a billion years? You, a mere bud?”

Odal retreated again. “I err in service of the We.”

Qadax spun to gain full trilateral view of his bud. His vacuole pulsed with concentration. Qadax relented, “Speak your error fully. It was I who budded radicals into your neural plasmids.”

Now Odal puffed. Odal had always assumed he was a straight-up clone, like other virulent budlets. This new bit of constitutional treason left Odal feeling disconnected. If true, it might be that no other Mastican, virulent or puddler, could share his perceptions of the meaning of the Maw’s trajectory. To deviate was, in Mastican parlance, aberrant, even pathological.

Odal began to lay out his thought for Qadax. “Bilaterals defend themselves differently than we do.”

“Yes, yes. I am well-versed in the particulars of bilateral predation,” Qadax shot.

Odal continued, despite his stirp’s impatience, “We engulf a threat, neutralize it, then examine its corpse. Absorb its benefit. Bilaterals stalk. They observe, learn patterns. They teach themselves to think as does prey or an opponent. Then they strike.”

Qadax sank toward catatonia. “Dimorphs are dim-witted parasites. You cannot expect the puddle to imitate bilateral predation! Not with the Enigmat. No. We engulf. We digest. Only then do we absorb promising elements of prey.”

Odal spoke a bit more loudly, “Perhaps, given the way bilaterals respond to threats, they have surmised what the We is yet unwilling to recognize. Perhaps they know more of Enigmat than the puddle.” We know nothing of the Enigmat, after thousands of millennia. One cannot fight that of which one knows nothing," Odal insisted. "We know nothing of the Enigmat's *affections*."

"Again, your unconscionable fondness for bilateral mysticisms," Qadax hissed. "Affections supplant thought in impaired species. The Enigmat remains our most elusive opponent. It suffers no affections, bud."

Odal's pinnacle vacuole pursed. He spun once, then rested silent. Quiet reigned for a time.

"Speak, young one," Qadax resumed.

"To know what a creature loves is to understand it, stirp. The Enigmat is a bilateral enthusiast," Odal responded.

Qadax pinched his vacuole in disgust. "To confirm such sentiments would require noeform of bilaterals. That would pollute the puddle irreparably. Better that Mastix should be destroyed, and all trilaterals with it. This thing shall not be done." Odal recoiled at the vehemence of his stirp's rejection. His mind churned. The puddle would gag. Even his own stirp, hoariest among virulents, cinches his vacuole to the idea.

Then Odal felt tissues tighten in his membranes. The thing must be done. Perhaps no other than he could take that plunge. Odal chose. Even if it meant excision from the We, which would probably kill him, he must lunge forward. Even if he was to become fodder and an epithet, so it must be.

The bud partitioned his sentiments from Qadax. Then he lied, another Mastican impossibility. "I concur, stirp. Bilaterals disgust. Perverse slime." His words lacked conviction. But trilaterals lack a sensitive lie detection system. What use would it serve, given that all (except virulents) persistently share their entire mind with all others?

Qadax growled a liturgy aimed more at convincing himself, at soothing his puddle-pang, than at convincing Odal. "The Enigmat must be engulfed, forced into the open. I am redoubling assaults on bilateral homeworlds, pressing ahead with the envelopment of targeted planets in this new galaxy, the spiral."

Qadax spun before Odal, and commanded, "Go to this planet. Reconnoiter Enigmat's presence there. Make ready introduction of the Forms."

Qadax took Odal's silence for consent. Extrapolations danced in the bud's imagination, secure behind cognitive partition. Odal would act. But he would never be able to justify his tasteless, forbidden excursions to the We. Even to entertain such thoughts insured that the puddle would judge him certifiably insane.

The young trilateral settled toward certainty. There was something undeniably right about what he planned. Odal's vacuole relaxed.

The bud stepped through to the water planet.

CHAPTER 3
KUSHKU

NOOTKA SOUND
VANCOUVER ISLAND
1566 A.D.

For Yachakas and the Mowachaht tribe, Rough Sea waned toward Elder. Families lingered at Yokwat. There was murmuring. Chief Qwistok grew sullen, then surly. Tight lines etched his face. A month ago, in any normal year, the tribe would have packed the village. To songs of thanksgiving, the families would have slid north and east. Forty-five foot long, wide-beamed moving canoes would have paddled to Tahsis, deep on the inside of Nootka Sound, to the sheltered winter camp. There the people would wait out winter, safe from the violence of Pacific winter storms. But the thirteen family groups of the Mowachaht lingered in the deepening chill which gripped the summer village. Qwistok was in trouble.

No whale had been killed. That was a chief's job. To kill or conjure whales. But for Qwistok, no whales complied. No blubber was rendered. No new whale-tendon bowstrings were drying. The California grays were long gone. Humpbacks were few, to judge by spoutings. Not even a drift whale, dead of natural causes, snagged on Yokwat spit. Even a carcass would satisfy the villagers, including Qwistok himself, in his growing desperation.

The Nootka were, above all, whalers. Several men of the Mowachaht had opportunity, early in the season, to make a kill. All balked. It was forbidden that anyone should spear a whale before Qwistok harpooned his. And, strangely, in expedition after expedition, despite evident exertions and ritual preparations, Qwistok never saw, much less beached, a whale. There came whispers. *Is the chief unclean? Has he offended the Spirits? Has his aging mind forgotten the rituals that once led Whale people to his harpoon with such ease and regularity?* Men said nothing. Women exchanged nervous glances.

Qwistok had aged. Yet, he was not decrepit. His muscles bulged like a buck's rump. His eyes glinted like sunlight on ripples. In truth, Qwistok was just entering his prime as an elder statesman and leader. But no fresh whale bones bleached on the sand at Yokwat.

So, Qwistok turned to Spirits. The Shrine of the Lake. Qwistok led two assistants to the place. To the little hut full of skulls, and masks, and magical cedar statues of Mowachaht whalers. Qwistok undertook, once again, the ardors of calling drift whales to his shores. But he knew, as did the villagers, that he lacked the prime ingredient of the ritual.

Odal finished his survey of the water world's biomass. In a shallow orbit, he rotated slowly in the transparent ovoid of his null field. Below him, a blue and white world spun, tumbling masses of vapor obscuring alternations of blue seas and brown and green landmasses. A lone barren moon orbited the planet, tickling oceans to rhythmic undulations.

Odal's life-sensing organelles detected spillover energies. That could be evidence that Enigmat interventions perturbed the bipedal monkeymind species which would soon come to dominate this world. Flashes were greatest in a handful of locales. Odal chose the most intense of these as the hub of his forbidden investigation. The Mastican stepped across to a point on the planet's surface a short distance from a hunter-gatherer village.

Towering flora, a vaulting green canopy, loomed overhead. It darkened the small moss-bound clearing into which Odal emerged. Odal rotated, engaging the multiplicity of his sensory plasmids. Liquid water dripped from spongy lichens. A vacuole in the side of Odal's cylindrical body gulped a volume of atmospheric gasses. A noxious mixture, heavily laden with oxidants and tincture of biomass. Rotting branches and leaves emitted olfactory stimulants, jumbled together with the omnipresent texture of airborne floral gametes. The clearing teemed with simple life. Billions of living individuals—flagellators, and squirmers, and thousand-legged wrigglers and tiny hot-blooded scamperers—inhabited the surrounding grove. A more complex creature approached.

Odal mapped the contours and hues of his surroundings. He would blend his null field to its context. He would observe monkeymind bilaterals from within this blind.

Then, from behind a rough floral stalk four meters in breadth stepped a shaggy biped, draped in the hirsute epidermis of a quadruped predator. *A sexual injector*, Odal noted, dangling between the creature's two legs. It leaked yellow fluid. The hapless bilateral quaked, then shrieked again.

"Spare me, Woman of the Woods!" it screamed. Odal surmised an entreaty to a tribal demon. Odal projected a stasis field over the distressed animal. He levitated it closer, inspecting the specimen, frozen in space and time. The moment had come. The irretrievable step lay before Odal.

The virulent extended his mind, penetrating the boney shell which harbored the frantic parasite's bulbous nerve organ behind two panicked eyes. Gingerly, Odal mapped its contours, enumerated its neuronal connections, quantified the biochemical bath in which it floated. A sense of putrefaction spilled over Odal, almost a smell. *Distasteful little creature*, he thought. *So simple, utterly primal. And so terribly stupid.*

Odal impressed an image of the captive's mind securely behind a cognitive partition. The creature called itself Shewish, and this place Yokwat.

Odal sloshed. His cell wall quaked. There was danger that this forbidden act might also prove a fatal one. But, slowly, as minutes passed, Odal's cytosomal perturbations calmed.

Odal examined the paltry noeform of Shewish, handling it with the satisfaction bilaterals lavish on diseased carcasses. Odal felt puddle compulsion to cleanse himself. He would scrub fingers of cognition with lathered reason. He would eschew bilaterals forever. Before Odal could swear off humanity, in Shewish's dim mind, Odal tasted mystery, hints of a grand something Shewish barely grasped, jumbled together with his avalanche of superstition and silliness. Odal pondered the oddity. He could make no sense of it.

His scan complete, Odal finished blending his null field. Light bent around the null field, re-issuing in its original gestalt. Odal vanished, though the spongy detritus where he stood bore an impression of his null shell. Odal dissolved the stasis field that bound Shewish. The clock of reality began to tick once more for the noeformed bilateral. Witless, the creature crumpled onto the forest mat, littered with dried cedar fronds. Its respiration racked. The pitiful biped leaked lachrymal water from its eyes, and more yellow soup from its sexual injector.

After some minutes, Shewish peeked up. Seeing nothing of the Woman of the Woods, the little creature fled back along the path by which it had come. It flailed in lathered panic.

Yachakas was oblivious to Qwistok's problem. Dogfish's fingers twitched as he stared at nothing. The boy's mind lingered on the hill of the ravens, that knuckle of granite across the open waters. Finally, one afternoon curiosity overwhelmed caution. He snuck from Yokwat, and lingered in the sun of his island.

Whenever duties permitted, Dogfish paddled his boy's canoe across dangerous waters to that isle. He took care to avoid Old Man's flatulence. Yachakas was not stupid. And, so, he explored the islet and privately claimed it as his own.

Even the ravens seemed to accept his franchise, though as co-tenant, not owner. This ravenry belonged to Another. Yachakas wondered at the disk of the world, and marveled at the aviary antics of the raven jokesters.

One fateful afternoon, little Dogfish dangled his feet over the precipitous eastern edge of the igneous hillock. The sycophant rumble of surf mesmerized him. Yachakas had spent the night on his hill. Ravens cajoled downslope. A breeze, warm for the late season, blew in off the sea.

In the distance, Yachakas heard a wail. He squinted. Two canoes slid across the mouth of the Sound. Screams split the air. Yachakas shrank back into the scrubby trees. Perhaps the party would slide past his refuge. But the paddlers stroked straight to Dogfish's hill. Yachakas saw that one member lay in the trailing dugout; he did not paddle. The canoes landed on the landward, gentle side of the hill, and so could not seek Yachakas's canoe. Their cargo was a corpse, he could now see.

Then Yachakas saw the face. It was Shewish, the village oaf. Red lacerations crusted with dry, brown blood spattered his forehead. Livid purple tinged Shewish's eyesockets. Offloading Shewish, the man tried to dig a shallow grave. No bear would bother the corpse on this island. But the hill's soil was thin. They scratched a gash in the hillside, and buried Shewish in loose rock. Shewish's mother wailed. Red eyes spilled down stricken cheeks. Her sons seated their mother back in the canoe. The party left as suddenly as they had appeared.

When the party disappeared, Yachakas pushed off his canoe. He puzzled these events. Summer camp scuttlebutt would provide answers.

Yachakas ground onto Yokwat's beach. Pregnant Arima, hungry for conversation, waddled up to Dogfish.

"Have you heard?" she asked. Yachakas looked at her blankly. She longed to pull words from him, as a dog jerks hide from an elk carcass.

"Shewish is dead," she blurted. Dogfish raised an eyebrow.

"Yesterday afternoon, Shewish went rooting in the forest. He returned, talking crazy. The Woman of the Woods, he blubbered. Shewish climbed up the rocks of the spit, slipped, and fell. He landed flat on his head," Arima sniffed, "Shewish was always so clumsy."

Yachakas peppered Arima. His questions emptied her shallow bowl of knowledge.

The puzzle made little sense to Dogfish. Shewish's death was accidental. Why the family's flight? Why hide his corpse? Arima started to ask a question, but Dogfish walked away from her wordlessly.

Yachakas hunted and found Tootoosch. Out past the village longhouses, ducklings in a row. His uncle steamed yew branches for halibut hooks. Tootoosch engaged two ranking men of the village, Tyees, in serious talk. Dogfish stood silently. He knew better than to interrupt adult conversation. Tootoosch finished, then turned to Yachakas.

Dogfish said, "I have something to discuss, uncle."

"Later, Yachakas. Shewish has died, and his family made off with . . ." Tootoosch began.

"It is important, uncle," Yachakas interrupted. The elder nodded slowly. Tootoosch respected his beloved nephew's intelligence. The boy would not risk ire without good cause. The older man took Dogfish by the shoulder. They walked through the village to the exposed side of the spit, a hundred yards or so. Waves crashed on the steep pea gravel of the beach. Pebbles screamed, oooo-eeeeeiiii, ooooeeeeeeeii, as waves rolled them past one another. Foamy spittle polished the nuggets, then vanished into its interstices. Stripes of finer silicate sands laced the beach. Winter storms would flush those from the incline.

Yachakas began, "I spent last night on the hill of the ravens, the little island we saw when last we troubled halibut."

"I warned you not to go back there," Tootoosch scolded.

"I know, uncle. But it has become an important place to me." Tootoosch shook his head in disapproval. His brow wrinkled. Still, Yachakas's courage impressed him. The open water was wide. The older man said, "I do not approve. I will take this matter up with my brother." Yachakas sighed and looked at a crab leg, dismembered on the beach. He began to regret this conversation. He knew that if his father became involved, he would be punished.

Yachakas raised his eyes. He pressed on. "Shewish's family came to my island today. They buried Shewish under some rocks on the landward side of the island."

Tootoosch beamed toothily. Two incisors were badly chipped. He put his arm around Dogfish's shoulders. "Good, Yachakas. Good. You did well to come to me. Now Qwistok can summon whales."

Dogfish looked puzzled. Tootoosch explained, "You are too young to understand. All of your thirteen years, there have been whales. Qwistok is a great hunter. But this year, Humpback Ichtope has ignored Qwistok's prayers, his cleanness. So, Qwistok calls drift whales. However, he lacks one ingredient for an effective spell."

"Shewish?" Dogfish guessed.

Tootoosch nodded. "The family grieves. Shewish would have been proud to offer a final service to the Mowachaht." Yachakas raised an eyebrow. "Wander off that way. Say nothing."

Tootoosch told Arima, whose mouth would let everyone else know, that he and Dogfish were going to repair the Mowinis weir. "Come with me, nephew," he called to Dogfish. "We will lose a night of salmon, if we do not repair the fish catcher."

Wisps of distant cirrus clouds radiated like wild orange hairs from the sinking pate of the sun. A chill bit the air, and Yachakas saw the whiteness of his breath.

The two launched a vessel large for two, but adequate for a third man to sleep in, if necessary. They paddled around the end of the spit.

Open waters posed dangers in daytime. Only the foolhardy and parties of war undertook the open expanses at night. This evening's moon neared full. Its radiance made their transit less gloomy, like the embers of an evening's fire. The Old Man controlled his bowel. Waves were almost docile.

Yachakas wished the winds were stronger, once they unburied Shewish. He smelled. Yachakas gagged. The putrid mephitis of the grave scratched his brain. The two plopped Shewish into the center of the canoe. Dogfish wretched most of his evening meal onto raven hill, a gastric mush of salmon, nuts, dried huckleberries, and fiddlehead ferns. The ravens, invisible in the dark, clacked their thanks. The two shoved their canoe back into the Sound. They breathed through their mouths.

A considerable distance from Yokwat, Tootoosch and Yachakas hid their canoe. Dogfish yearned for the open ocean, windless as it had been, once they began the overland trek to the Shrine of the Lake. His back ached. Shewish's stiff legs, and his incipient rot, troubled Yachakas, both physically and ritually. To touch the dead sullied one before the Spirits. There was the smell and sticky fluids.

And something more. Shewish had become a spirit walking among Spirits. An object of dread. Now Shewish dragged Dogfish into the night woods. The dark rain forest pressed in. He slid on muddy inclines. He ducked swinging fists of Douglas firs. He wrenched his feet free from gnarled knuckles of cedar roots. These clutched greedily at him as he passed. Even steady Tootoosch felt terror. Eyes widened; whites shone. Covens of animal witches, otters who chase children with spears, bristling giants sporting fantastical fangs and claws, nightmarish creatures that kill men with shouts, crabby minks and chattering squirrels with tiny rattles and magical powers. The woods brimmed. And Shewish, the oaf, had seen Woman of the Woods. He died for that glimpse. The tangled vital opulence of the forest became a snare, once the sun abandoned the Mowachaht people to depredations of darkness.

Dogfish's lungs ached. He and his uncle scaled the last steep to the small lake. At the plateau, they slumped onto the muddy shore, leaving Shewish several yards away. Neither savored his morose, putrescent company.

A quarter mile across the water, fire flickered. Figures move along the shore. There stood a rough little building. Someone splashed in chill waters, chanting. Tootoosch put a hand over his mouth, telling Dogfish to remain silent. After their breathing slowed and bodies cooled, they took up their stinking burden. They labored toward the fire.

Yachakas recognized Qwistok in the water. His face had grown sallow. Exhaustion wound its vines about the powerful man. Qwistok chanted a prayer, waded four steps to his right. He uttered another prayer. Uncle, nephew, and their delivery caught Qwistok's eye. He ignored them, except that his chants grew louder. The two dropped Shewish by the Shrine.

Tootoosch and Dogfish nestled in spongy debris beneath a towering red cedar. The older man pulled his knees to his chest to warm himself and get comfortable. He, apparently, planned to sit for some time. Yachakas imitated his uncle. They watched Qwistok work his way, for more than an hour, round the circumference of the little lake. Assistants onshore followed his watery prayer dance.

Tootoosch broke their silence, whispering, "Qwistok came to the Shrine when the moon began to wax. Four nights he bathed continuously in the lake, scrubbing himself with branches. After each bath, he prayed in the Shrine to his Spirit guide, to Ichtope, to send the Mowachaht a drift whale. He sings to Ichtope our need and faithfulness. Then he fasted. Now every night, Qwistok walks around the lake, waist deep, praying. When Qwistok begins to mumble the songs, his assistants pull him from the water. Days, Qwistok sits in the Shrine, singing to Ichtope. His assistants beat drums."

Yachakas rose and peered into the small cedar shack of the Shrine. Firelight flickered. Eight leering skulls, a pelvis, and arm bones hung from the walls. Dogfish jerked back, afraid. He found himself panting.

He hurried to sit again beside his uncle, who said, "Those are the heads of great whalers. One you met, Toowinnakinnish, the old Hesquiat chief. Qwistok stole his head last year from his burial site."

Tootoosch continued, "Tonight, Qwistok will ask these dead men to send us a drift whale." Tootoosch fell silent.

Yachakas wanted more, "Then what happens."

"You will see, if Qwistok grants my request," the older man murmured.

The chief faltered mid-chant. He shook his head, and began again. The song trailed off. Qwistok's assistants splashed into the lake and pulled their chief to shore. Qwistok shoved their hands away, and after a minute, rose. He walked slowly to the Shrine.

"Greetings, honored Qwistok," Tootoosch said. Qwistok acknowledged Tootoosch silently.

"We bring what you sought." Tootoosch pointed toward Shewish's corpse.

A wan smile lit Qwistok's face. "You have done well, my friend. How can I reward you, hunter of halibut?"

"We would assist you in calling drift whales from the Whale people."

Qwistok nodded, and shooed away an assistant who hovered. "That is good. Sunrise at Whistling Rock. Go now. I must sing, and cajole my predecessors."

Tootoosch nodded. He nodded toward the corpse. He and Dogfish hoisted Shewish's chill body on their shoulders. They walked toward the outside beach. After an hour, Tootoosch lowered their burden next to a bush. He broke off a considerable dead branch, flattened its ends, and picked at the pith until he had a tube clear of obstruction. Rested, they again carried Shewish.

Pounding wound through the muffling forest. Yachakas smelled outside brine. Rotting drift logs and kelp mixed with Shewish's stench. Tootoosch pulled aside a large branch, and before them the dark Pacific stretched to the edge of the world's disk. Whistling rock jutted from the sand a half mile north. They plodded toward it.

Stippled night sky hinted purple. Wisps, dreams of clouds caught hints of dull red. Tootoosch cut a rope with his shellknife. He removed the blanket from Shewish. They rolled Shewish down the beach, removing one mat at a time. Then Shewish lay before them in a bloody bearskin, sprinkled with sand. Yachakas brushed grit and twigs form the dead villager's face and clotted hair. Tootoosch retrieved a large flat rock. Morning breeze fluttered off the water, as high clouds turned pink, then grew edges of white. Whistling Rock whined quietly as breezes tickled it.

Tootoosch grabbed Shewish under stiff arms. He dragged the dead man to the flat rock, and flipped the cadaver over, face down. The fleshy nose squished against the basaltic slab. Tootoosch stepped back and folded his arms. Yachakas looked up, recognizing that something was finished.

Tootoosch instructed, "Do exactly as I say. Ask no questions." That was not easy for Yachakas. He struggled against impulses that would send him into careening questions and unbidden action. Outside, Yachakas looked stoic enough. It was otherwise within.

In mere minutes, Qwistok emerged from the steep hillside behind Whistling Rock. His hair was freshly oiled and smelled of whale blubber. Qwistok's face and shoulders wore a dusting of sacred red ochre. He was alone. Qwistok carried a three foot long stake, and a large mallet. He slished though the fine sand to Tootoosch, handing his Tyee the stake and hammer. Qwistok turned his attention to chanting. The chief sang to a thundering ocean with outstretched arms.

Tootoosch situated the point of the stake at the back of the dead man's skull, near its base, and inclined the awl slightly. The halibut fisherman lanced Dogfish with intense eyes. "Hold the stake tightly. Do not move it. Do not flinch." The boy grasped the stake with both hands. His knuckles turned white. Tootoosch raised the mallet high above his head. He looked to Qwistok. Tootoosch thought, *One blow or bad luck.*

Qwistok's chant surged, then ended abruptly. He nodded toward Tootoosch, who stared at the top of the stake, then swung fiercely. With a clap, the stake drove through Shewish's cervical vertebrae, some soft tissues, and out his mouth. Tootoosch put his foot against the back of the corpse's head and jerked the stake loose. The hole oozed foul fluid. Tootoosch handed the ritual mallet and stake to Yachakas, and pointed where he should lay them.

"Do as I do," was all Tootoosch said to Dogfish.

They stood Shewish on the flat rock where he had been skewered. Tootoosch bent Shewish's arms, which offered considerable resistance, up and out toward the ocean. Tootoosch shoved the hollow branch, which he had fashioned the night before, into the hole driven through Shewish.

Qwistok moved up behind Shewish. The chief took care not to touch Shewish or Yachakas or Tootoosch.

Qwistok called through the tube, "Whale people! I too call you, along with Qwistok. I am Shewish, who is dead. I walk with spirits. I too know the Mowachahts' need and cleanness. Whale people! Rise up from your houses beneath the sea. Get in your canoes, which are your great bodies. Paddle with the giant oars of your flukes. Spit the sea into the sky from your blowholes. And send us one of your dead comrades, to dwell with the Mowachaht. With us, your dead comrade will drink all the sweet water he can hold! Whale people! We, the Mowachaht, will trade with you. Send us one of your beloved friends. I, Shewish, who am dead, will leave my people on the beach to live with you beneath the waves!"

Then Tootoosch tipped his head toward the sea. He and Yachakas began running with Shewish between them. They ploughed into the churning Pacific. They cast the remains of Shewish into the surf, holding up their end of the bargain with the Whale people.

Qwistok turned silently and strode toward Yokwat. Tootoosch led Dogfish the opposite direction, north up the outside beach. There they settled in a favorite place of meditation between two pillars of mossy basalt. They prayed and bathed and sang for two days, until, purged of ritual impurity from contact with Shewish's corpse, they could safely return to Yokwat.

After their purification, they slogged south along Nootka Island's outside beach toward Yokwat. Pea gravel squeaked. Tootoosch and Yachakas rounded the corner to the great arching beach that ended in Yokwat Spit. A mile in the distance, a commotion clamored. Yachakas ran. Tootoosch also loped. Both stopped and stared. Yachakas trilled his child's war cry. He ran toward the crowd, leaping and hopping. Smiles eased many faces.

Long black strips of skin peeled back from the carcass. A gray whale, long as a war canoe. Lines of women carried greasy chunks of white blubber. Dogfish saw smoke from the rock fires. Hot rocks boiled boxes of water, rendering adipose tissues. From seething tubs, the women skimmed melted fat. Sealskin bladders filled. There would be no feast of whale meat. That smelled. But sinews and bones and blubber and skin would serve the Mowachaht.

Most important, Qwistok stood above the scene, on the hump of the sheltering spit. The chief smiled and nodded. Yachakas made his way through the bustle to Qwistok. When he saw the boy, Qwistok dispensed with head rubbing, which is reserved for children. He thrust out his hand. He seized Yachakas's forearm.

Surprised, Dogfish returned the clasp. The boy smiled widely. *Welcomed as a man by my chief,* he thought. Something churned warmly in Dogfish's chest. A time in his life had passed. Another had begun.

The Mowachaht celebrated when the sun fell into the ocean. Tyees sat in a row. A great bonfire lit the steep beach. Boiling blubber wafted through the tribe. Their fortune was good. People leaned on one another. Babies snuggled. Their chief still called whales. The Whale people still listened.

The shaman screeched his scratchy song. A lyric of a soul released to benefit the Mowachaht. The odd melody of identity, of belonging. Of Kushku, a man young, a man of promise, a man of Raven's clan. The shaman wiped sweat and flicked drops toward the fire. He sat, and chanted.

Qwistok called, "Tyee Tootoosch must sit at my right this evening. And Kushku shall have my left. Come, sit, Kushku." Puzzled, the tribe peered hesitantly. Perhaps their chief had spent too long in the lake. For no man named Kushku dwelt among the Mowachaht.

Tootoosch wound through the group. He bent to Qwistok's lips. Tootoosch turned. He picked his way to Dogfish. He led his nephew to Qwistok.

Qwistok stood. "People of Yokwat. Meet Kushku, holder of the secret name Raven stole with the sun and moon when he pillaged Magician's House. You have known this man as the boy Yachakas. Boy no longer. Kushku has taken a place for himself, a ravenry island across the open water. That island shall be called Hill of the Ravens. Kushku alone shall wash himself there, to seek Spirits. Raven touches us through Kushku. See the drift whale!"

Many clicked their tongues and murmured approval.

Kushku saw Yalan smiling broadly. She looked straight at him, unblinking. He noticed, not for the first time, but now with a different sort of appreciation, how very beautiful was the chief's daughter. His squirter stirred.

"Mowachaht, welcome your Nuu-chah-nulth brother."

Men rose chattering. Many clasped Kushku's arms. Food was eaten. Songs were sung. As the moon rose, Qwistok stood.

"For Kushku, I tell of Raven making mankind."

A hush fell.

Raven stole the Sun and Moon from the Dark Magician. As Raven fled, he carelessly dropped them in the sky. That was good. Otherwise, he would have been too slow to escape Magician. As it was, Raven got scorched black.

With Sun and Moon in the skies, there was light on the plate of the lands. Raven saw the surface of the world lay under water. It was inundated by a great flood. Raven flew and squawked over Nootka Sound. Waters slowly receded. Mountaintops, then valleys, and finally beaches appeared. Waves still lap the island, hoping to recapture their former glory. In time, the land dried.

Raven grew dreadfully bored. The land offered no amusement. Raven ate his fill of flotsam. He gorged. Still, nothing pricked him, sated his curiosity.

Raven picked his way along the outside beach. He flipped rocks. He kicked logs. He wandered.

Then Raven came upon a giant butter clam shell. Tiny squeaks, squeals of fright, leaked out. Raven peeked into the mouth of the clam. There cowered many little creatures, terrified by gigantic Raven. His blackness lured, but terrified. His cawing laughed, but threatened.

Raven joyed. At last, something interesting.

"Come out, little animals. Come out!"

There came no answer. The clam shell shook with trembling.

Raven changed strategy. He pried the shell a bit.

"Come out now, all of you. I am going to step on your clam."

Creatures spilled from the mouth of the shell. They were like men, only strangely colored. All were male. Raven was delighted to see the creatures. The humans saw that Raven would do them no harm. Those few coaxed the rest out of the shell.

Men-humans thrilled Raven. He watched. He prodded. They leaked and defecated and cried and laughed and trembled and boasted. The men-humans thought highly of themselves, pointlessly. Soon, however, their antics repeated. Raven grew bored, even with the men-humans. An idea came to Raven. He would need to provoke the men-humans. He would challenge them. The avian spirit lifted his beak toward the moon he had stolen. He cawed. The earth shook.

"Come, little ones. We will adventure!"

Some men-humans approached. They climbed onto Raven's back.

Others cowered. Raven snatched these and threw them onto his spine. Raven flew north, to a beach with an abundance of chitons.

Raven deposited his passengers onto this new beach, not far from Kyuquot Sound. The men-humans frolicked. Laughter rang.

Raven pried loose a big red chiton. Now, if you have ever seen a chiton, you know that its underside looks like a woman's private places. A plump smile between two big red lips. When you pry one loose, it rolls into a tight ball. Raven, that Trickster, threw the chiton, with accuracy only a Great Spirit can muster, at the groin of one of the men-humans. It hit the man-human squarely. It rolled around his penis. Raven pried loose many more chitons. He hit the mark of every man-human, missing not one.

The men humans panicked. They struggled to pry loose the chitons from their dicks. Then they stopped. Strange little smiles spread across their faces. They panted. Their hips jerked. Then they slept. The chitons loosed themselves and crawled slowly back into the sea. When the men-humans woke, they wandered off. Never again were they seen.

But the chitons! Raven watched them. Days passed. They grew, they stretched. Something grew within. After a month, the chitons waddled to shore and parted their lips. Out came humans, both men and women! All had dark skin that tanned yet darker. Each had black, inky eyes, like Raven's own. Those Mowachaht, our ancestors, piled onto Raven's back. He flew south. Raven dropped them on this very spit, Yokwat. That very summer, they built the first longhouse of our people. They felled cedars. They split off planks. They raised houseposts. Some of these very posts and planks were those they made.

Raven began his game. He cares for us. When bored, he tricks and deceives and steals from and lies to us. For his amusement. And because he cares for the Mowachaht. Or so it seems.

Kushku became entangled in the chief's rendition of Raven's saga of creation. Questions ricocheted inside his skull. How can men have sex with chitons? Why were men-humans hiding in a clamshell? If Raven is so big and powerful, why is he so hard to find? Why is Raven bored? Are the other spirits like Raven? When I pray, why does Raven seldom answer? Is Raven our friend?

Yalan sidled off, her buttocks dragging Kushku's eyes with them.

Some matters came clear to the freshly-minted man-boy. Raven makes people what they are. Raven gave the Mowachaht their history. And Raven manipulated his life by tricks and torment and dreams. This very day, Raven made little Yachakas into Kushku of the Hill of Ravens.

And Yalan. His thoughts of Yalan confused.

Kushku heard inaudible chuckling. He looked around.

No one was laughing.

Kushku wondered.

CHAPTER 4
BOX

ABOARD THE GOLDEN HIND
OFF WEST COAST OF VANCOUVER ISLAND
DECEMBER 1578 A.D.

Expanses of British canvas, some edges tattered, strained in stiff storm winds. Seventy-two of Her Majesty's finest fought rigging as their wooden vessel, a mere hundred tons, ploughed through gray, ominous brine. A mountainous, angry skyscape in gray peaks and white escarpments churned past overhead. Salt spray whipped off bubbling crests of swells, wetting decks. These creaked, as roiling sea pummeled the hull. Aching cold, that damp hypothermia of the foggy North Pacific, sucked at the weary crew of *The Golden Hind.*

Francis Drake sought riches, but also a Northwest Passage. He would, to cap his long voyage, sail home across the mythic northern waterway. He would short cut to Mother England, tracking north, ever north. Francis Drake dragged his ship along by sheer force of will. Laden with pirated booty. Drake the navigational genius. Drake the privateer. Drake the autocrat. Drake the disciplinarian.

Murmuring rumbled below deck. Every morning, winds howled louder. Waves crested higher. Pervasive cold bit deeper into scurvied bones. Even the old seadogs grumbled. Drake had to make a show; he lacked choices. So, Drake finished the purge he had begun a continent away. So sad for his naïve, young assistant, John Slannery.

Good Queen Bess commissioned Drake for trade and exploration. The Queen herself, leaning from her velvet and gold throne, confided to Drake in a whisper, somewhat wistfully, "I would gladly be revenged upon the King of Spain for divers injuries he has upon Our Person inflicted." Drake, a seaman, but no less a politician, quietly amended his royal charter in invisible letters. He would pillage Spanish settlements and trade in the New World. Queen Elizabeth, for her part, would in the end profit 4,700 percent for every pound invested in Drake. The sum was sufficient. Her Majesty paid off the kingdom's national debt.

Shipboard, crewmen balked when the time came to kill Spaniards. They plotted. One of their number betrayed. Off the east coast of South America, a summer's dawn saw a yardarm from which Thomas Doughty and those of his sentiments dangled by newly-lengthened necks. Young John Slannery had also conspired with the mutineers. Drake, however, spared the boy, for the sake of his youth and fear of God Almighty. Few murmured. Prudence, and affection for one's own neck, advised silence.

The Golden Hind swept unopposed up South America's Pacific coastline, relieving merchants of their wares and wealth. Bullion and coins and pearls and gems filled the hold. The vessel's watermark disappeared below the waves.

Now, however, victories faded from memory. Frozen winds buffeted them. Off the drenched cedar-festooned coastline of a large island, the crew grumbled again. Drake needed to make an example. So sad for John Slannery.

Drake nodded to an officer, "Cut 'm down, Mr. McKinsey." The officer, a boy himself, gulped, "Aye, sir."

John Slannery's sea chest, a sturdy oaken affair with riveted steel straps and a skeleton key padlock hanging from its hasp, lay on its side, just out of reach of John's dangling feet. McKinsey righted the chest. He jumped up on it. John Slannery stared with lidless eyes, thrust out now upon his bloated cheeks. A purple tongue filled the gaping mouth. Blood vessels had burst, adding streaks of deeper red to Slannery's carroty curls. McKinsey sawed the rope that had dismissed his friend John. John's body fell in a lump on the deck.

Drake turned to the assembled crew. Over the wail of wind, he shouted, "In Her Majesty's Navy, we have two rules: fear God, and obey your captain. Look on the last of Doughty's mutineers."

Drake paused. The spectacle etched its ugly lesson.

Drake barked, "Organize a detail, Mr. McKinsey. Lash Mr. Slannery to his sea chest and throw him to the fishes."

McKinsey watched as his friend, now a corpse, sloshed over the crests of waves. The red mane was visible for a time, then vanished altogether. Young McKinsey wondered where currents would carry his friend John.

Drake released the crew to their duties. He ducked into his cabin. The prow of the *Hind* swung hard about. The winds drove them southward, now seventy-one in number, depleted from their original complement of eighty.

Drake scratched in the ship's log that an ensign, one John Slannery, had been tragically lost at sea. There followed a recommendation that the Slannery family be compensated for their loss.

NINETEEN DAYS LATER
TAHSIS WINTER CAMP

On the damp dirt floor of Qwistok's smoky longhouse, Kushku sat, legs crossed. Women danced, circling the fire. Yalan sat across the stage, her raven hair and eyes shining. Past the surging yellow licks of the circle's fire, Kushku and Yalan held one another, if only with eyes. Each remembered those few sacred hours stolen with one another deep in the woods. When they loved with more than a look.

A tear slid down Yalan's cheek.

Kushku released her eyes, and stared at a root in the floor near his knee. Qwistok's daughter tortured Kushku. Her breasts heaving. Her eager pleasure against his thrusting. Tears gathered on his lower lids, a silent lamentation. Beautiful Yalan. Yalan who moved him. Yalan the forbidden.

The screech of pipe whistles jerked Kushku from sullen pain. Old Ansinit whirled, lunged, jumped. He pounded the circle with his Tlokwana dance. Ancient songs poured from him. Dirges and reveries and mystic motion guided him. Ansinit's Wolf mask clung tenuously to his grayed head. The cedar twine slipped. Fangs decorated the mask's angry green mouth, set in an elongated black and red snout. Demon-yellow eyes hovered over the teeth. Over Ansinit's back, which curved beneath the weight of years, lay a Chilkat blanket, its abalone insets studding angular images of Ichtope and Wolf and Thunderbird. Young men scattered eagle down before Ansinit's gyrations. The longhouse floor grew white with drifts of warm snow. The gathered Mowachaht throng patted the black earth to the rhythm of a lone booming drum. The scream of whistles again split the air, and the growl of whirling leather bullroarers.

Qwistok pointed a finger. Over the pulse of song and drum, Homak, the medicine man, called. He sang tales of spirits and demons, of beasts and heroes. Raven's antics, eminent among the Great Spirits, rolled from the old man's tongue. The aviary prankster protected the Mowachaht. Finally, his cultic reveries delivered, Homak settled old bones back onto his seat. Ansinit resumed.

Kushku brushed a feather from his shoulder. This Tlokwana, this Wolf Dance, was given in Yalan's honor. Qwistok celebrated Yalan's adulthood, the last of his children. The chief invited nearby tribes. He lavished potlatch wealth upon them. The festivities and exchanges would last a week.

Kushku saw Qwistok's design. The old manipulator fished for a suitable husband of the gem of his clan. It was time for Yalan to marry. But she would not wed Kushku, though he was, by Qwistok's own admission, a sturdy and honorable young man, and a skilled hunter. Yalan would be tied to the son of a wealthy neighboring chief. She would be used to increase Qwistok's prestige and influence. She would leave the Mowachaht forever to bear children for a stranger.

Kushku turned his eyes to Qwistok, who sat in the most private corner of the longhouse. He again wore his fabulous Chilkat blanket as a cloak. Each year, now eight summers one after another, there had been whales. Sometimes many whales. Since that difficult autumn when Kushku and Tootoosch had rescued Qwistok with the gift of Shewish's body, Qwistok had grown wealthy. And famous. Canoes of whalers slid onto the beaches of Yokwat, emissaries from the Haida, or Bella Coola, or other far flung coastal peoples. All sought whaling wisdom from Qwistok. As Kushku surveyed his aging chief, Qwistok's eyelids fluttered with fatigue.

Ansinit also saw. His warbling song rose. A signal, as he signaled every winter. Boards were torn from the back of the longhouse. In poured "wolves," seven or eight of them, men of the village wearing wolf skins, their faces blackened.

Two bounded to Yalan, snarling. Pretending to bite her, they dragged Yalan off, exiting through the hole torn in the back of the longhouse. She feigned terror. Others were also bitten off, following Yalan with their wolf escorts. Yalan and the initiates would be spirited deep into the "woods" (which, by a feat of ritual self-deception, was actually an adjacent longhouse). There, the initiates learned spirit songs and dances. And they practiced ribald skits with which to later entertain potlatchers.

One Wolf man bounded toward Kushku, his cedar mouth wide to bite the young man off. Kushku recognized Tootoosch under soot and fur. His uncle handled him roughly, bustling him out the front entry of the longhouse. They ran to nearby woods up river.

When hidden, Kushku spoke, "Thank you, uncle. I do not think I could endure another year of instruction with the children. Especially not with Yalan there. Kushku diverted his eyes so as not to betray the emotion that sat like a boulder in his chest.

Tootoosch knew his nephew too well. He saw Kushku's pain. The older man shook his head. "Qwistok has grown muddled with years. His pride rules him. He forgets the boy who once spared him great shame."

The two stood silently. Kushku could not win Yalan. Yet neither could he release her in his heart. Defeat had not yet dug its fangs into his flesh.

Tootoosch broke the silence. "Qwistok has decided. Yalan is his daughter. He is chief, and it is his privilege."

Kushku hung his head. "It is difficult, uncle. I have so many questions about why this is so. Why is Yalan's voice unheard? Why is wealth so important to Quistok?"

Tootoosch shrugged. "It is our way." He grimaced with friendly eyes.

Kushku shook his head, and pushed his uncle's shoulder affectionately.

The silence again stretched. From a distant cedar came faint cawing. Forest whispers tickled their ears. They walked toward the tidal currents of Tahsis Inlet. They surveyed the gray water. Clumps of fog drifted on its surface. A light drizzle fell.

Kushku looked at Tootoosch. "I dream, uncle. Raven wakes me to confuse me. I have slept little."

"What does Raven say?"

"I do not know, uncle. I see my ritual place, the Hill of the Ravens. Yalan dances on my belly. Once, I cut off Qwistok's head with lightning. There are strange canoes."

Kushku blurted, "I must go."

"The winter waters. . ." Tootoosch cut himself off. He laid an arm across Kushku's shoulders and squeezed. "Perhaps you are right, nephew. Wash yourself. Seek Raven. Perhaps the Trickster will share something of his dark mind."

Kushku nodded to his soot-covered uncle, who scratched at his encrusted skin. The young man walked off toward the canoes without a word. As Kushku disappeared into the undergrowth, he called back to Tootoosch, "You could use a little washing yourself."

Both laughed.

Odal, invisible, trailed young Kushku when the young man abandoned the Tlokwana. Enormous spillover energies erupted. The Enigmat labored. *But at what?* Odal wondered. Kushku seemed a target. That itself was news. Never before had Odal sensed an Enigmat intervention so finely pinpointed. Or perhaps it was that trilaterals had never before so closely observed Enigmat activity among bilaterals. The complexity boggled Odal. Guiding cosmic outcomes by teasing individuals this way or that. Odal set himself to discover what interest the Enigmat had in this lowly Nootkan, Kushku.

Kushku paddled through heavy seas down the Inlet to Yokwat, lurching over crests and bailing his canoe. He forsook sleep, washing and singing through the night in the little pool near the summer village site. At dawn he braved the open mouth of Nootka Sound. When the bow of his dugout scratched into the lee-side gravel of Hill of the Ravens, exhaustion clutched him. Kushku wretched, but his empty stomach produced only bitter spittle. Wearily,

Kushku settled to routines of ablutions and chanting. He arranged rocks around him. For reasons he little understood, it mattered that the rocks were just so. Kushku wondered about that.

When Kushku, then younger Yachakas, asked about washing-rocks, Homak the shaman rolled his eyes and walked off.

On the afternoon of his second day, Kushku winced in a blinding cold drizzle. He could no longer feel his legs. Rain stung less. A rotating gray fuzz nibbled the edges of sight. Kushku closed his eyes. He slumped into the gravel at his right side. He lay there motionless. His tongue lolled from his mouth.

In stupor, skies clear. Kushku rises, refreshed. Then skies darken. A black wing blots the sun. Immense feathers extend to the horizon. Brooding clouds hover around the wing.

Cackling laughter shakes Hill of the Ravens. Lightning splits the sky. Kushku convulses. When he again stands, a proud Mowachaht warrior stands before him. A hatchet drops from the sky, crashing into the man's skull. Raven's claw reaches from gray clouds, seizes the man, and casts him north, across the waters.

Thunder throws Kushku to the ground. A scrubby man, possibly not Mowachaht, writhes nearby. He is trapped in a thicket of gleaming upright roots. Bizarre animals with human faces overpower the slight man. They make a woman of him with their lusts, and dismember him. They wear his bowels as a necklace. Death paints a dull glaze over his staring eyes.

A flash. The hair on Kushku's arms smokes. The disk of the world slides off its pole, fragmenting. Hill of the Ravens skips across Nootka Sound, as pebble tossed by a boy. From the fissure, bleached men burst, thousands, white as snow. They gnaw upon Kushku. A snow-man, in garments of blue and gold, offers Kushku a copper more beautiful than the most powerful chief might own. The snow-man grows great black feathers, then flaps off toward the steaming horizon. Kushku hears cawing, cackling.

A Mowachaht warrior sits silently, bobbing his halibut jig from a canoe the color of salmon sides, beneath two crescent moons, on a sea the color of inland turquoise stones.

A last flash strikes.

The world disappears.

A faint sound of flapping.

Cawk. Cawk. Cawk. Cawk.

Kushku opened his eyes. Water ran into them. Winds lashed. Drizzle swirled. Waves crashed against his islet. Rock shuddered. Kushku lay in the gravel, eyes half open. After some minutes, he shook his head. He tested his legs. He stumbled to his canoe.

A perfect circular depression in the gravel caught his eye. Curiosity pressed him to investigate. But wisdom overruled. He might again fall to visions. Kushku struggled over the crest. The island tamed bitter wind. Kushku sat.

Odal's brain plasmids shook off catatonia. He struggled back toward consciousness. Suppressed puddle-pang. Regulated cytoplasmic agitation and pressures. Partitioned and partitioned again. His cell wall stopped flapping. His pinnacle vacuole sphincter released a whistle of trapped noxious gasses.

Memory returned. Kushku had collapsed. Odal had noeformed him. That glimpse had cast Odal flailing into abyssal insentience. The trilateral touched bitter sound in his vacuole, saw a smell of Otherness, clenched an opulent concept of absolute vacuity.

As equilibrium crept back, Odal remembered. An asymptotic, sub-empirical impossibility. Bigness bigger than the bigness of all big things. Eternity—a bauble, a plaything. A mind impenetrably dark. Not evil. Inscrutable: dark light, an innumerable numeral. Odal grasped muddy clarity, an authoritarianism wholly anarchic. He touched the cosmic accident, and knew it the product of perfected purpose. Odal, tenuously, held in mind an idea possibly fatal to trilaterals, and yet life-giving. He knew what he touched. Enigmat.

Qadax's bud recognized the complex from a thousand planets, from Nest, even from this backwater world called Earth. But no trilateral had ever before tasted the thing. The sly conundrum waggled its whiskers one way from outside, another from inside. The Mowachaht called this under-ness, this beyond-ness, the Great Spirit. Exteriority penetrating interiority. Interiority suffering, yet welcoming, exteriority. Knowledge of the unknowable. A knowledge not of seizing, but of being seized. Knowledge that owned the knower. Odal lapped at a bowl of insanity.

Odal again stuttered toward insentience. He crammed Kushku's noeform behind partitions. Then Odal cordoned the noeform from himself as well. Kushku's vision bore danger. Odal would have to examine this gem of oxymoronic mentation one facet at a time. Odal feared.

Odal spun a few meters onto bedrock. With a thought, he brushed the gravel where his null field left its impression.

Sheltered from the brunt of the storm, Kushku ate. He drank rivulets pouring off wide rhododendron leaves. He slung a cedar blanket over his back. As the rain slackened, his head cleared. Fingers tingled, warming. Prickly pain banished numbness.

Kushku stood. The circular depression had vanished, though the tide fled. He bent to touch the gravel, wondering. From the water, a skeletal face grinned up at him. A bleached man. A snow-man! Like his dream. This one had no eyes, and hair the color of a cutthroat's jaw! Kushku fell back on his butt. He shut his eyes, fearing he again fell into visions. A song to Raven rose in his throat. But it sounded small against the sea surge and howl of winds. He closed his mouth.

Minutes wore on. No further apparitions arrived. Kushku cracked open an eye. He saw storm. His island no longer writhed. He looked suspiciously. The leering deathmask still scoffed silently from a shallow shelf nearby. A boy's corpse, half-eaten, rotting, water-logged. A young man with skin the color of eagle's down and hair like a sunset. The creature stared eyelessly at Kushku. Ropes lashed what was left of the man-boy to a box. But not a bentwood box. A box unlike Mowachaht boxes. A marvelous box.

The box and its rotting passenger shifted. The lot might wash from its precarious perch. Kushku waded the shallows. He dragged his find beachward. He grasped the dead man's arm. Fingernails sunk into waterlogged necrotic flesh. Kushku leaned back, leveraging his weight. Abruptly, he collapsed backward, splashing into a foot of water. He held a bicep and skin dotted with orange hairs. Kushku winced salt water from his eyes. He lunged, grabbing a rope that wrapped the box. The lipless, flame-haired snow-man slid from those lashings. Kushku watched the nightmare grin fade from sight through a forest of kelp. The body vanished into deep water.

Kushku pulled the box onto the pea gravel beach. With some difficulty, he cut the lashings with a broken mussel shell. He rolled the box over, inspecting it side by side by side. Panels of dark wood lapped strips of another sort, an odd, grainless wood, brown with reddish streaks. The color brought to mind beaver pelts. Water burbled from a small crack in the bottom.

The box had a humped top. Kushku's pushing and jerking would not open it. The hunter sat frustrated beside his prize. The box was his by right of the drift whale. But so far, its only gift was wet clothing and skinned knuckles. Kushku thought the matter over. He settled on a plan. He would remove the floppy part that hung from one side of the lid. It was made of the grainless beaver-wood. Kushku found a rock with a pointed end. He struck the floppy part. A tiny scratch shined like a salmon side. Kushku was astonished. Such hard wood, this beaver-and-salmon-wood! Kushku continued hammering. Such blows would have reduced any Mowachaht box to splinters. He tired of bludgeoning the snow-man box. The setting sun peeked through thinning storm clouds. Kushku began to lose hope. He considered smashing the wood faces of the box. His back steamed with sweat.

Kushku delivered a last fierce blow. The floppy part clicked, and fell off. Kushku jerked on another piece of floppy beaver-wood. It lifted. He strained at the box's lid. It swung open, like a berry-picker's basket top.

Little within the chest was familiar. He recognized odd moccasins, somehow like those interior tribesmen wore. There were clothes, but in colors of sky and snow and blood, sewn from a thin hide with tiny thongs. Kushku tipped some brine from the box. Filmy, waterlogged fragments of fragile materials sloshed onto the gravel. These were torn from many such rectangles tied between two pieces of black leather. Black squiggles covered the pieces. There was a glint. He recognized something of use. In the pink gleam of the sun, whose orb flattened as it landed upon the distant edge of the world's disk, Kushku saw a blade. But a knife like none he knew. A blade made of salmon-wood, with only tiny blemishes of beaver-wood showing. Kushku extracted the knife. He ran his thumb down its edge, then pulled back. A thin line of blood glistened on its edge. Sharp. Sharp like obsidian blades for which his people traded with inland tribes, just after those blades were freshly struck from glassy cores. Kushku rolled the blade over and over in his hands. The sun sunk further past the edge of the world.

Kushku rolled the blade into a blue shirt and put it back into the box. He reached into the box and took hold of a white stick attached to a flat white circle of wood. As he lifted the object from the box, he turned it over. A red flash, like the setting sun, blinded him. Kushku fell to his knees, chanting to Raven. Another vision had come.

But his sight cleared rapidly. Raven remained silent. He braved a look at the object that had blinded him. He gasped as he saw a man looking back at him. He threw the round object into the gravel. His heart pounded. Ashamed, Kushku forced himself to retrieve the circle. He looked again. He laughed. The strange face was his own, lined and sallow from ritual rigor. The round object showed him as he saw himself in a quiet pool, only more clearly. Kushku toyed with the pool-disk in the deepening twilight. Finally, he saw only stars and a sliver moon in its reflection.

Kushku pulled his box to where his canoe rested, scratching a line through the scant topsoil of the little island. He took his cedar-bark blanket and wrapped himself. As he began to drift toward sleep, possibilities crept into his mind. And Yalan with them. But this was not the time to plan or to lust. He stopped. Exhaustion won. Kushku slept.

The sun had climbed over treetops before Kushku woke. It was usual for him to watch the sun rise during his daily washings and chants. He was ashamed. Kushku splashed into the Sound. He loosed a hemlock frond. He scrubbed himself.

As the sun made trees cast small shadows, he finished his ritual. Kushku loaded his prize, this box, into his canoe. Kushku turned his head to a raven in a tree, cawing at him. He thanked Raven for the visions and box. Kushku paddled across open water, calm now, to Yokwat. The Tlokwana at Tahsis would be reaching its climax soon. Kushku paddled on. It was a long, upwind slog. Kushku planned. Bold action might open a way where none had existed. He might confute a chief. Images of Yalan's upswept forehead and subtle, but ample, breasts drove him northward with stiff thrusts of his paddle, north toward Tahsis.

Still far from the winter village's beach, Kushku saw crowds on the shore enacting the final rescue of those whom the crafty Wolves had bitten off. Canoes, lashed together into platforms, ferried youths to shore. Kushku waited. He would not disrupt the final act of the mythic drama. Kushku saw Tootoosch, now a blackened Wolf, flee into the woods with others. The "captives" splashed up the beach, reunited with their families.

Kushku paddled slowly toward shore.

Determination settled over Kushku. He flipped back the lid of the box. He pulled the pool-disk from the box's darkness. Kushku secreted the disk in his robe, and clapped shut the lid. He would challenge Qwistok.

Kushku's canoe scraped onto the beach. Several children ran up to Kushku, anxious to hear of his adventure. They squealed when they saw the strange chest in the canoe. The Mowachaht and potlatch guests sidled to the beach to see what caused commotion. Kushku said nothing, but opened the chest. Necks craned. Small hands reached. Kushku gently deflected those.

Tootoosch approached his nephew, with raised eyebrow. Kushku raised his hand for silence. Tootoosch was startled. Never before had inquisitive Kushku preferred wordlessness. A new thing was afoot.

Qwistok strode down the beach. Gravel scrunched beneath his feet. The crowd parted, opening a path for the chief. He stopped one step from Kushku. He peered in the chest, then directly into Kushku's eyes. Kushku did not flinch. Qwistok pointed toward his longhouse, and without a word walked away. Kushku closed the box lid, and followed. A gaggle of boys hauled the trunk into the longhouse behind them.

"What is this box?" Qwistok asked, in the tone he used for correcting errant children. He put a foot up on the box.

Kushku returned Qwistok's gaze, but did not answer. Silence fell. Qwistok's authority was consensual. He could command none. He was first among equals, though of late Qwistok imagined himself something more. After some minutes, Qwistok smiled, the wry amusement of a seasoned politician.

"I remember the night you became Kushku, on the day that drift whale caught on Yokwat spit. That was a barren season, was it not, Kushku?"

Kushku nodded silently.

"You helped me by bringing Shewish. Perhaps I owe a debt?" probed Qwistok.

Kushku replied, "Perhaps."

"This box you have found. Is it very valuable?" The chief bent to pat the strange wood.

"It may be, Qwistok. Who can say?" answered Kushku. "The box is strange."

Qwistok suggested, lifting an eyebrow, "Then a gift from the sea, from Ichtope, to the Mowachaht."

Kushku set his jaw, "No, my chief. The box is mine. I claim it by right of the drift whale."

"This box is no whale, Kushku," Qwistok fumed.

Tootoosch caught his nephew's eye. He gave him a warning in a tiny shift of his eyes. Kushku barged into danger, unaware, Tootoosch assumed.

Kushku answered his chief. "That is correct. Still, I claim the box as my own."

Qwistok snorted loudly. Then he spat. He paced around the longhouse silently. Kushku watched, hoping Qwistok would take the bait. Kushku held his face blank, and his eyes forward. He did not want to alert old Qwistok as to who was the fisher and who the fish.

Kushku took the offensive. "Perhaps, great chief, you would excuse me. I have business with Ansinit. He wishes to trade for items from my box. And I wish to make a gift to my uncle Tootoosch."

Qwistok snorted again. "But I wish to speak with you a while longer, boy."

Kushku caught Qwistok's eye, and held the gaze silently. "I am no boy, my chief. You yourself gave me my adult name, many summers ago. Now Raven has smiled on me. I may own something of value."

Qwistok snorted as loudly as Kushku had ever heard him snort. He paced furiously. Then, Qwistok's breathing slowed. A gleam glittered in his eyes. The sparkle of battle. The knife-eye that glittered each spring when the old chief threw the first harpoon of the season into the side of Ichtope.

"Ah, now I understand, boy. You are rich."

Kushku said nothing.

Qwistok scratched his head. "Well, we must celebrate your new-found wealth. I call for potlatch, now, before our Tlokwana guests depart. We will see who abounds when the giving is done."

Kushku feigned discomfort. "If that is your wish, my chief. Your generosity is legend."

"Then tonight we celebrate," Qwistok growled, gloating at the prospect of prestige he would gain by potlatching this boy into poverty. And Qwistok thought, *I shall disgrace this upstart and put an end to Yalan's complaints.*

Word spread through the village. Most had tired of celebrating in the week of Tlokwana. Still, there was excitement. This was new. The strange box would be opened. In the end, Qwistok and Kushku would engage a duel of gifts. Someone would gain glory. Someone would lose.

Within his cytoplasm, Odal's organelle sensitive to Enigmat energies convulsed. Spillover energies flooded. Enigmat pummeled young Kushku. *Enigmat superintends this conclave*, Odal thought.

Slowly, the inevitable conclusion etched itself in Odal's consciousness. An idea that had never before touched a trilateral. The Enigmat maneuvered below this bilateral affair. Among these monkeyminds. The air gassed of care. As puddle bubbles soothe Mastican buds. As humans nurse babes.

Odal pondered.

The sun fell below Nootka Island. Flames leapt from a bonfire. The night was cool, but calm made the chill bearable. The Mowachaht and their Tlokwana guests gathered on the beach. They formed a circle around the fire. Dances were danced. Songs were sung, spirit songs.

Lesser members gave gifts to the gathered throng. Qwistok never smiled. He lavished dried salmon. Kushku matched the gift. Kushku never flinched, as herring roe he had purchased only that afternoon were laid skein for skein beside gifts to the people from Qwistok's coffers. Then Qwistok gave a Raven mask to Kushku. Kushku seemed at a loss. He offered nothing in return.

Murmuring traveled the crowd. All givers sat, their worldly goods redistributed among potlatchers. This potlatch was over. Qwistok had prevailed. The chief smiled. He began a chant of praise to Ichtope. He spun slowly to the rhythm of his own voice.

Kushku stood abruptly. Several women, and shaman Homak, gasped. Kushku bent to his box. He moved aside a cedar bark blanket. A single item remained in the box. Kushku withdrew the salmon-wood blade from the blue shirt in which it was rolled. He held the glinting steel shaft over his head, flashing in the bonfire's licking flames. Eyes turned to Qwistok. Kushku walked slowly to his chief. He bowed his head, and laid the knife at Qwistok's feet. Someone in the back gasped.

Qwistok scrambled. The chief commanded that the rafters of his longhouse be emptied of dried salmon, whale oil bladders, salmon roe, and dried berries. Foodstuffs piled at Kushku's feet. Great mounds of sea and land wealth grew. Food for two winters.

Kushku folded his arms. He refused to look at Qwistok's pile. The elders concurred. Old heads bent toward ancient ears, whispering transactions in the commerce of prestige. Qwistok's counter was deficient. Mere food could not match a spirit blade. The tool glittered like coho salmon in the Mowinis.

Qwistok snorted. Whirling, he stomped off. Confusion rippled through the Mowachaht. Someone pointed. Qwistok returned. He held a copper. The symbol of chiefly wealth. An art object of intricately pounded native copper laid over a board graven with Spirit images. A hundred years of salmon. Fifty whales.

Qwistok crossed the celebration circle to Kushku. His stride spoke anger. The chief stopped before Kushku. Qwistok thrust the copper over his head, displaying it for all to see. Then the aging chief shoved the copper into Kushku's hands so hard the younger man fell backward onto the log on which he previously sat. The assembly gasped. Qwistok had impoverished himself overwhelming the upstart Kushku. Qwistok returned to the seat of honor, visibly relieved.

Kushku regained his feet. He brushed himself off. The young man admired the copper, and nodded to Tootoosch. His uncle frowned. Kushku should desist. He took the meaning of Tootoosch's furrow. But Kushku's moment had come. Now, his plan would work, or all would be lost. Only this very morning Kushku felt flutters in his stomach contemplating this moment. His guts were now hard as the spirit blade.

Kushku reached into his robe. All eyes turned to him. Kushku pulled his hand out. He lifted the pool-disk over his head. It caught light from the fire. It flashed Qwistok's eyes. He winced. Homak chanted songs to repel evil spirits. Homak leapt up, ran to Kushku, and grabbed the pool disk. He looked straight into it. The old medicine man screamed and fainted. The pool-disk landed on his chest.

Some Mowachaht ran into the woods. Kushku bent, retrieving the pool-disk. He walked to Qwistok. He laid the pool-disk in his chief's hands. The old man lifted the disk to his face and saw himself. He began laughing, the derision of stress, the cackle of madness. Qwistok jumped up. He lifted the pool-disk over his head and crushed it against a rock next to the ebbing bonfire. A thousand shards grabbed glints of coals as the object scattered across the gravel and mud beach.

The silence of graves fell over the Mowachaht. Qwistok's eyes grappled Kushku's. The young warrior bent to the fire. He took a rock that glowed in his hand. Flesh sizzled. Wisps of acrid white smoke rose from his palm. Dead calm gripped Kushku's face. He took Qwistok's copper, and smashed the rock into its face. The heirloom broke. One part caught fire. Kushku released the rock. Strings of blackened flesh followed it to the ground. In the glances of elders, the tally was taken. Qwistok was beaten.

Qwistok acted. He could yet evade defeat. He summoned Yalan. Qwistok put his arm around her shoulders. Together, they walked to Kushku. Qwistok lifted Kushku's hand and put it on Yalan's shoulder. The waning chief grasped

Kushku's right forearm and squeezed, sealing Kushku's betrothal to Yalan and adoption into Qwistok's own family. Kushku squeezed back. Some skin from his damaged right hand stuck to the chief's elbow. The bargain was struck. He would be son to Qwistok through Yalan.

Qwistok celebrated his daughter's wedding. But Qwistok's eyes lost their intensity. He sat more, after Kushku's challenge. In Younger of the following year, when the trees found leaves, Yalan bore a grandson for Qwistok. The chief's joy overflowed. In the deep of False Spawning, Qwistok's mind was stolen by Ichtope, the whale spirit. He never spoke. His right arm became useless. Despite prodigious efforts by Homak, none could retrieve Qwistok's kidnapped essence. The old man's body died before the moon was again full.

Kushku prospered as a hunter and warrior of the Mowachaht. His many questions made the Mowachaht curious. At Kushku's little hill, Raven troubled his rigors. Yalan bore him many fine children. Kushku and Yalan became friends, an intimacy not so many spouses share. The Hill of Ravens became a place of veneration and great mystery. The Mowachaht prospered.

As Kushku died of old age, Odal noeformed the Tyee again, wedding his earlier gestalt to this fresh one. The mature Kushku. Kushku of many Raven encounters. Odal buried this troublesome matrix behind partition, for examination, for dissection, for deliberation. Odal sensed promise. Did there lie in these primitives forbidden promise? A way forward for Mastix? He could not put his sense of the matter into words.

Odal was clear that Qadax must not know. That moment would come. Now was not that moment.

Where am I?
What sort of place is this?
The gray of dawn fogs.
Strangeness. Bogs and jelly-things.
Hovering among stars.
Killing strange tribes on giant balls.
Suns of many colors.
Alone. So alone.
No.
There is another.
Shewish sits in silence, a leaden lump.
I, Kushku of the Hill of Ravens,
I shall scrub myself.
Trickster, guide me.

CHAPTER 5
SALI

IN OMBAN GALAXY
1769 A.D., IN EARTH PARLANCE

Odal stepped through to Qadax. A brown swamp planet, now dry, and its hot yellow sun peeked over a parched hillside. The envelopment sphere at Saurens retreated. Its last ebony shreds dissipated, sparkling as the dimensional rift faded. With a thought, Qadax maneuvered the null plasmid out of its spiderwork lattice, the propagation net.

Qadax crinkled his vacuole in welcome. The lattice finished folding itself, then it and the plasmid vanished to the star system of the Pathogene's next victim. Qadax would follow in time.

"Stirp," Odal greeted with three open palms and a single spin of deference.

Qadax spun, scrutinizing his bud. "All is well?" Qadax inquired.

The young Mastican dodged, "I sense sentient life on Saurens." Odal pointed to the cooked swamp planet.

"It is so, Odal, but of no concern. A remnant of cold-blooders survived underground. The technological superstructure, however, depended upon the small-digited sauropods. That subspecies did not tolerate subterranean living. The surviving Saurens have degenerated to a primitive state. They no longer fathom machines."

Odal opened one palm upwards, indicating concurrence. Within, Odal struggled. He partitioned his sloshing. Odal shocked himself. Emotion about extinguished bilaterals! *What happens in me?* the trilateral pondered. Odal shook off this burbling. The deed was done on Saurens.

The Mowachaht were another matter. Odal hesitated to speak with Qadax. Some packages were easier to open than close.

Odal began, “There are things about the human bilaterals, stirp. Things the We should explore before introducing Forms.”

Qadax snapped, “We have no time for pure research, Odal, much less pet-keeping. The Maw . . .”

“I know the Maw’s dangers.” Odal interrupted.

“What have you gleaned about Enigmat from these Mowachaht humans?” Qadax sought, not really paying attention. Qadax sought reasons. But such reasons Odal had partitioned even from himself.

Odal paused, then said, “Interventions are numerous. There seems to be a remarkable precision to Enigmat influences. Individuals are targeted. The Enigmat guides matings and even preferences and occasionally deaths. An indecipherable plan lies behind Enigmat interjections.”

Qadax prompted, “And . . .”

“The water planet enters hyperpopulation. In a hundred years, crowding will spin out of control. Humans might breed themselves to death. Perhaps the We could let that dilemma play itself out. The species looks likely to self-exterminate,” Odal wheezed out his pinnacle vacuole. “I continue observation.”

Qadax raised a hand. He said, “Earth.”

The two propagated a dimensional distortion. They stepped through to Earth’s heliopause, a few degrees galactic north of the plane of the ecliptic. Light caught an edge of the lattice that hung there, awaiting stimulation of its null plasmid. The gray sheath of Odal’s nearest ten centimeter eye sphinctered shut.

Behind partition, Odal stroked with affection the minds of long dead Kushku and the simpleton Shewish.

Qadax summoned the plasmid into position in its lattice.

Odal intervened. The deployment halted.

“Form introduction and envelopment must be delayed, stirp,” Odal pressed. “We understand too little.”

Qadax spit, “Again, affections rule you, bud.” Qadax spun. “To envelop this planet, to engulf Enigmat, to implant its genius, if any, into our own plasm. This is the trilateral way. For billions of years, it has been our way.”

Odal balked. His concerns contradicted epochs of trilateral philosophy, matters the We took to be its essence. Odal wondered, should he verbalize what lay behind his partitions. No, it was too soon for such exchanges.

Odal said, “There lie concepts in these bilateral minds. Some transcend the puddle’s banks.”

Qadax sniffed, “Odal. These metaphysical speculations you indulge. A poisoned pond, all. Metaphysics bridges bilateral ignorance with fantastical imaging. Bilaterals gorge on superstitions. The Mowachaht find their world flat. They fear demons. You tell me they make of animals gods. These are numbingly ignorant creatures, my bud. Their defects are congenital. They cannot be educated or rescued. They most certainly have nothing to teach trilaterals.”

Odal cracked open a door. "What if to survive, trilaterals must change?"

Qadax shuddered, "The We changes. Adaptation is our genius. We subsume challengers. We engulf. We learn. I am a billion years old. I hardly recognize myself, so greatly has our cytoplasm been re-engineered through those thousands of millennia."

Odal asked, "We chose those changes. What if Mastix cannot engulf Enigmat? What if the We must become what it does not wish to be? What if our species must coexist with Enigmat and its cherished bilaterals? What if the We is being chastised from beyond the cosmos?"

Qadax rejoined, "You speak foolishness. Of things beyond the cosmos, none possesses knowledge. We cannot bow, bud."

"I do not advocate surrender, stirp. Coexistence. Perhaps cooperation. At a minimum, learning to ignore."

Qadax pursed his pinnacle vacuole. "It shall not be. Trilaterals engulf sentience. The We would dry the puddle before enduring what you suggest."

Odal churned. His cytoplasmic turbulence demanded linking, the shared stabilization of co-mentation. But that was a comfort Odal could not yet risk, even with Qadax.

Terror scratched Odal, silently, invisibly. Metaphysical possibilities daunted him. Such thoughts troubled no Mastican. Odal felt watched, whispered about, whispered to. He dared not explain. Odal's thoughts lacked articulable substance. They lay beyond empirical verification. Mere transient psychic epiphenomena. If Odal told Qadax of his impalpable terrors, the name Odal would for eons serve as the butt of trilateral derision.

To Qadax—indeed, to all trilaterals—an arational thought was a subrational one. These thoughts that troubled Odal eluded conception. They could be tasted, but never grasped. These depths were a lake which one swam, not mapped. One could noeform Odal. Then one would understand. Perfectly. But that might result in banishment from the ancient well of trilateral waters. Or execution and composting. Odal's cell wall rippled with discomfort. He sloshed quietly.

"Are you well, my bud?" asked Qadax. Odal turned a palm up, and pinched his respiratory vacuole. Qadax read that as "Maybe."

"I budded you for independence. Be so. But know your oddness will not be welcomed. Strange ideas are never quickly enfolded," Qadax intoned. The elder spun once, and added, "If ever."

The null field plasm slid forward again, fitting itself into the propagation webwork.

Qadax said, "I have much to do elsewhere, mopping up previous bilateral envelopments. I shall delay the Forms and encapsulation of this seed planet for now. But we must stay generally on schedule. The puddle proves testy, with all the changes and dislocations of moving Mastix from the Maw's trajectory."

Odal interrupted, "Yes. I wanted to ask. Is not the trajectory of Mastix directly into a binary pulsar at the edge of Omban?"

Qadax blinked agreement. "Yes, bud. The calculations have been carefully spun. When Mastix arrives at that location, the Maw will have pulled the binar from its present location, out of the way of Mastix. You know Skal will get this sort of thing just right."

Odal spun comprehension.

Qadax consented, "You will have at most a few hundred of the humans' years. Then the Forms."

Odal partitioned his disappointment. Mere centuries would not suffice to plumb a new way of conceiving the trilateral universe, especially a view so alien as that which rummaged the minds of West Coast bilateral natives. What path lay open to him? What course might preserve Mastix? What hatred did Enigmat nurse for the We? No Mastican was asking these questions. None but Odal. None but he, in fact, could conceive the ideas. To Mastican co-consciousness, Odal had begun to relish ten impossible things before breakfast. To the We, Odal had become insane.

Apprehension bit the young Mastican.

Odal stepped through to Yokwat.

HILL OF RAVENS
HERRING SPAWN MOON
1778

Sali sat, legs folded beneath him. He sat as had his ancestors for generations. Guardians of the sacred rock, Hill of the Ravens. His otter skin cap fluttered in the chill onshore breeze, as did shoulder-length black hair. Sali could no longer feel his feet.

For one moon, Sali sat on the Raven Hill. Thirty nights had he prayed. He slept fitfully, drank little, ate less. His skin bled from scrubbing with cedar branches in frigid waters. His songs vibrated the granite of the islet. Since the Mowachaht had made their summer move to Yokwat, Sali observed his rituals. He implored Raven, the Great Spirit. No answers came. No visions. Not now. Not in many painful years.

At midday, Sali's chin bobbed toward his chest. His tongue lolled. He slumped over.

A black wing blotted the moon. Cawk, Cawk, the jester laughed.

When Sali again opened his eyes, his long face lay in a pile of demolished pine cones, a pillow from squirrels. Heavy fog drifted in clumps across the water, ghostly bushes on a spit of swells. In the Sound, giant white blankets hung from dead trees. Sali closed his eyes, thanking Raven that his embarrassment ends. A vision, at last . . .

Sali ventured another peek. The blankets remained, and rippled nearer. Skulls hung from ropes tied to the tree's odd branches. Under those trees floated two great canoes, with men standing in them. Men with skins bleached by the sun. Snow-men. Some robed the color of twilight skies. Hats with three corners and sunset-tint cords. Some with hair like glowing coals. Others like dried grass. Some with smoke coming from their mouths and noses.

Sali shook his head. The great canoes remained. Sali shouted. Snow-men called back, waving. A frown spread across Sali's face. This is no vision. Sali grabbed his kit and hid behind a scrubby tree. But the snow-men waited. Sali emerged tentatively. He waved again. They waved back. Sali decided to make the best of the situation. He thanked Raven for this good fortune. He sang the brief incantation to Ichtope, claiming the two great canoes as his own by right of the drift whale.

Sali hopped into his canoe. He paddled toward the ghost sheets. Sali's hands trembled. "Wakash, Wakash," the Tyee greeted these newcomers. They waved back. Some pointed.

Sali slid alongside the vessels, which towered over him. One snow-man clad in a sky suit leaned out over a rail, pointing to his chest. "Captain James Cook and His Majesty's ships, *Resolution* and *Discovery*." Sali smiled uncomprehending.

The English officer tried again, "Me, Cook."

A broad smile splashed onto Sali's face. He called back, "Macook, macook." The snow-men wanted to trade! Sali waved for the ships to follow him across the mouth of Nootka Sound, pointing. He paddled rapidly away, trembling with excitement.

The swells were heavy that day. Sali's month of rigors had weakened him. His head swam, as he rounded the breakwater into the shelter of Yokwat cove. The Raven image that adorned his canoe's bow ground onto the gravel of the incline.

Sali stumbled onto the beach. Several men of the Mowachaht gathered around him. Sali pointed out into the Sound. The Tyees craned, but nothing was visible in the fog.

Mokwina, their chief, walked up. Sali fixed him with a stare. He said, "The great canoes are mine from Raven, by Ichtope. The snow-men want to trade." Mokwina looked at Sali, confused. Sali tried to speak, but his tongue tangled. Sali collapsed face first onto the beach.

"Raven still possesses his mind, Quizl, the shaman, diagnosed. A grunt of consensus rattled through the group. His friends picked Sali up, brushed sand from his face, then lugged Sali up the beach toward his longhouse.

Children screamed from rocks of the spit, pointing. Men ran for high ground to see. Senseless Sali thudded once again into beach sand.

Great canoes drifted out of the fog. Snow-men clambered up and down trees, pulling great blankets, tying ropes. Two great splashes marked the fall of great, odd anchors. Fear coursed through the Mowachaht.

Mokwina leapt to action. He launched eight of his strongest warriors in fast canoes to investigate these invaders. Mokwina paused to calculate. In most threats lay opportunity. Mokwina instructed the eight to avoid fighting. Just look and retreat. The men grumbled at the loss of face they would suffer.

Mokwina reassured them, "If there is battle, there will be glory enough."

Paddlers reconnoitered the great canoes. Puzzled looks scratched their faces. The canoes stood high out of water. Trees sprouted from the platform of each boat. Blackened hollow logs jutted from the canoes' edges.

A Welsh sailor, whose nose was large and hooked, called over the side, startling Mowachaht men. They understood nothing of what he said, except the laughter. Then another man, a hunchback, hobbled up a ladder at the rear of the vessel.

Mokwina signaled. The four canoes returned to Yokwat beach. One reported, "There was a man with a hooked nose, like the Woman of the Woods. Another was humpbacked, a son of Salmon."

The Tyees took counsel. Quizl offered a shamanic insight. "These canoes are houses of the dog and humpback salmon, come from the sea to visit us. They are fish come alive as people."

Mokwina shook his head. "No," the chief pronounced. "These are not salmon. Salmon are silver, and when they spawn, red. The men are white. Their big wind blankets are white. Sali said the snow-men want trade."

Quizl stomped off, offended at his chief's intrusion into sacred affairs. Mokwina noted Quizl's disrespect. He took a note in his mental list of retributions to be meted.

The chief rubbed his chin. He stared fixedly, as was his custom when making a decision. Shortly, Mokwina raised his head. "Put the canoes in the water. All men take your bows and spears, but leave them lie in the bottom of the canoes. We will welcome the visitors, as would we any other people seeking trade. If they want trade, we know how to trade." The warriors laughed. Mokwina was famed for sharp exchanges of goods. Among the tribes, the Mowachaht were wealthy and Mokwina powerful at potlatch.

The chief's face blackened, "But if they want to fight, slaughter them."

Mokwina strode to his longhouse. He returned, his hair dripping whale oil, dusted with eagle down. Red ochre clung to his skin. In Mokwina's hand hung

Cheetoolth, his war club, a great whale rib carved with images of Ichtope and Bear and Raven. Mokwina stepped confidently onto a board laid across the middle of the largest war canoe of the Mowachaht.

"Go," he commanded simply. Mokwina scratched a troublesome louse.

Thirty-one canoes trailed from the beach. They slid near the great canoes. Mokwina stood. He raised his right hand. All stroking stopped. Then Mokwina called out, "Paddle Song for Strangers." Mokwina screeched the first line, an unusual move for the chief. The Mowachaht warriors took up his strain, breaking into the familiar melody, rhythmically slapping their paddles against the sides of canoes.

The native armada slowly surrounded the newcomers' vessels. Mercifully, Mokwina stopped singing, but the Mowachaht chanted, throbbing their wary welcome. Mokwina scoured the alien vessels with practiced martial eyes. He saw weapons, but none at the ready. Some snow-men dangled beads or cloth over the side rail of the ship, a portent of trade. Mokwina remained suspicious.

The alien ships blazed with metal, iron and bronze and copper and even gold. Fish hooks and knives like legendary Qwistok's knife, lured Mokwina. Wealth beyond imagination. Riches to humble the other chiefs of the Nootka, opulence to raise Mokwina to a permanent place of supremacy. Songs would be sung of him. Tales of Mokwina's deeds would ring through his people's generations. Mokwina imagined glory. He thought of little else. These snow-men opened a way.

Mokwina's eyes glazed over. His assistant feared the chief might fall into the bay. The underling, a value qol captured in war many years past, offered a hand to steady his owner. A vicious slap was his reward.

Mokwina decided. Worth the risk. He lifted his Cheetoolth over his head in both hands. Mokwina smiled, not the smile of pleasure, but the smile of gain, of victory. Mokwina bellowed, "Macook, Mowachaht. Macook!"

Captain Cook gave his own signal. Pilot bread, hard inch-thick round wafers of dense bread, rained on the canoes. On a rope, a metal pot was lowered toward Mokwina's large canoe. A sailor called meaninglessly, "Molla Sus. Molla sus." The viscous fluid was taken aboard Mokwina's great canoe. Puzzlement ensued.

At Mokwina's signal, all the canoes, save one, returned to Yokwat's beach, several rock-throws distant. Tsawaswasip remained floating beside the odd craft of the snow-men.

On the spit, the Mowachaht conceded to curiosity. They flooded into view. One comely young woman inspected the wafer of pilot bread, and determined that its purpose was to wipe the breasts. This she did, to the hoots of the British crewmen. Investigation of the sweet-smelling metal pot proved the brown fluid sticky. Two innovative thinkers turned over an aging canoe, and smeared the salve on its cracking bottom. A curative pitch, no doubt.

On the far side of the snow-men vessels, Tsawaswasip gestured to the crewmen. He held out his tall cedar bark hat, woven in the shape of a buck's head, in both hands. A string of clear crystal beads flew into his canoe from the ship. These Tsawaswasip inspected and threw them back. He pulled off his Kutsack, a knee-length cape of sea otter skins, and sweetened his offer. More beads rained. These he also threw back, save one. This last he held at arm's length between two fingers. When he was certain he had the attention of the sailors, he dropped the beads into the harbor.

"Bloody savage doesn't want our beads, mate," grumbled one.

A timid face moved up to the rail to see the cause of commotion. Tsawaswasip pointed to the youngster and gestured wildly. In the boy's hands was an axe, about to be put to the task of splitting wood to kindle the coal of the blacksmith's furnace below. One sailor held out the axe. The deal was struck. Six prime sea otter pelts and an ethnic art object for one axe. Or, from Tsawaswasip's view, a dirty cape and tattered hat for an impossibly beautiful weapon. Everyone was happy. The makings of good trade.

The beach buzzed with conferring women. Tyees gesticulated. Children squealed. Slaves milled about. Dogs barked. Tsawaswasip ground onto the beach. He passed around the shining war axe with the salmon-wood head.

Mokwina grunted for silence. "I have considered. We shall trade with these . . ." The chief searched for a word.

"Mamalni. These men are mamalni, like the mamalni we met far at sea four summers ago," came an aged voice from the rear of the crowd.

Mokwina smiled, "Yes, mamalni. That is what they are. Men who live on the water and float around. They have no land of their own."

Mokwina jumped up on a tremendous drift log embedded in the outside beach. All could see and hear him. "We will trade with the mamalni of the great canoes. They seem dull traders, if Tsawaswasip's trade is any indicator." The people laughed. "Everyone should trade with my mamalni. Get as much metal as you can."

A firm voice rose. "These mamalni belong to me, my chief."

"Who speaks?" Mokwina demanded, rage grinding in his throat.

"I speak," Sali said. "Raven gave me the great canoes and their mamalni. I claim them by right of the drift whale."

Mokwina's nostrils flared. Callicum, a ranking Tyee, confirmed, "I heard Sali's claim, before he fell senseless. These mamalni followed Sali to our cove." Murmurs of agreement trickled through the assembled Mowachaht. Apprehension grew. It was unwise to contradict Mokwina.

Mokwina's eyes glazed. He stood motionless. Corpselike, the chief deliberated.

Then Mokwina smiled. He bade Sali to join him for private parley. The two wound through the gathered Mowachaht to Mokwina's large longhouse. Mokwina shooed out a few old women. He settled to negotiate.

On the inside beach, the tribe milled and murmured. Would Mokwina kill Sali as an upstart? All knew Mokwina's rages, and his thirst for power. All suffered and benefited from both. Mokwina's paroxysms were summer gales. They blew houses apart. They also brought drift whales to Yokwat spit.

Many sighed relief when Mokwina and Sali emerged beaming from between the whales carved on Mokwina's door posts. The chief put his arm around Sali's shoulders. When the crowd quieted, Sali pulled an object from his robe. It was one of Mokwina's coppers, beaten from native ores of the far north. Worth hundreds of bladders of oil, a thousand blankets. The Mowachaht gasped.

Mokwina announced, "The sun sets. In the morning, we go trade with the mamalni! Now let us sing the evening Paddle Songs for our guests."

The qol murmured. It was a bad sign, the slaves thought, for Sali that Mokwina had not announced the terms of his agreement with Sali before the Tyees. Informal, private agreements left questions, room for maneuver. Sali considered pressing the issue. But he had tempted Mokwina enough for one day.

Canoes rounded His Majesty's ships, intoning ancestral melodies to the rhythm of slapping paddles. Hillsides and rock cliffs answered with lyrical echoes. Three songs were sung. The British crew listened with attention and appreciation.

Unexpectedly, the Paddle Song for Halibut fishermen on a Summer's Evening sputtered as a British drum rolled. Fifes whistled shrill loftiness. The Mowachaht gaped. The odd, but pleasing, alien melody subsided. Warriors hooted and whistled. The Mowachaht warbled another song of their own, as did the shipmen. In the next weeks, each night of the British visitation ended in concert, music from ship to canoe, and back from Yokwat to His Majesty's finest, ancient cultures in antiphonal dissonance.

The next dawn, ritual washings were more furious than usual. Every man sought gain from the day. Each labored to properly prepare. Skins and woven bark blankets, whistles and war axes, all manner of local valuables, were piled into canoes. The men launched their vessels at Mokwina's command. Mokwina took his place of honor.

But then the chief lofted his Cheetoolth. Sali rose and made his seat on the chief's board, next to Mokwina himself. The Mowachaht wondered at this. Would Mokwina issue such an invitation? To a warrior only twenty-five summers old?

Captain Cook, the rangy Yorkshireman, stood beside Mokwina, the painted megalomaniac, on the *Resolution's* deck during the trade frenzy. Hand signs and facial expressions sufficed for language. Fair-skinned Cook towered over the brown Nootkan chief. *Like a cloud over the earth*, thought Mokwina. But Mokwina was more heavily muscled, certainly of body, but perhaps of mind also.

A young sailor strode up to Cook, and spoke. The captain reached into a tiny pocket in his vest and pulled out his gold watch. This object Cook opened, and spoke again to the boy.

Never had Mokwina seen such an object. He decided then and there. Mokwina must have it. His mind whirled. A plan hatched.

Later that night, after concerts had been traded, in the quiet of the chief's elevated corner of his longhouse, Mokwina summoned Sali and the boy Kipsis.

Trade resumed in the morning. Great piles of sea otter pelts lay on the decks. British hands sorted and stacked them. Another contingent stripped both vessels of extraneous fittings. It was metal the Mowachaht wanted. Metal they would have. The din of haggling grew. Pile of goods moved back and forth across the deck, then up the ship's sides, or down the ship's sides.

The sun grew hot. Mokwina moved so that both he and Cook stood directly in it. Sweat rolled down their faces. Finally, Cook excused himself and ducked into his cabin. Out of the corner of his eye, Mokwina saw one of the Mowachaht pick up a hook, the weight of two good-sized salmon. The man secreted the hook beneath his cloak and staggered over the side of the vessel.

Cook returned, wearing a lighter jacket and no vest. Mokwina gave him a great smile, and said, "Wakash, Wakash, Kook." Cook nodded and stuttered, Wi-wicush, wicush, Maquinna," in flawed imitation of the chief. Mokwina found weakness in the Captain's solicitude. Cook could obviously prevent theft. Yet, he took no steps to do so. The Captain continued pleasantries though his possessions were being pilfered. He was weak, Mokwina decided.

With that contempt in mind, Mokwina signaled Sali. The Tyee and Kipsis sauntered toward Cook's quarters. Sali engaged the sailor standing guard to the effect "Give me the buttons off your uniform and I will give you a slave girl." The conversation interested the midshipman more than a little, enough for Kipsis to slip unnoticed in and out of Cook's cabin.

Sali signaled success with a raised eyebrow. Mokwina barked an order. Paddlers, Sali and Kipsis among them, settled into their canoe. Mokwina exulted in Cook's watch, marveled at its ticking. The Tyees trickled into Yokwat, parading their wares before the gathered Mowachaht.

Commotion spilled across the harbor from Cook's great canoe. Yelling. A few straggling Mowachaht skittered down the sides of the ships. After some minutes, six sailors, carrying tubes on sticks, clambered into a launch. The captain and one called Bligh joined them.

Slowly, by gestures Cook made Mokwina aware that a hook used to retrieve the anchor, a bag of nails, and his own pocket watch had been stolen from the *Resolution*. Mokwina labored to appear stupid. Cook demanded return of the items.

Mokwina took Sali aside, and secretly passed him the watch. "Give this to Kipsis to hold," Mokwina instructed.

The chief turned to his people and said, "These mamalni are naïve. They think we won't take what they don't protect." The Mowachaht laughed.

Mokwina raised his voice in anger. "So, now I am going to talk to you angrily, so these dull men will think that I am scolding you. After I finish, I want you to bring items you grabbed from the ship. I will return them to their captain." Moans wound through the group.

Mokwina's eyes twinkled. "And then we will steal them all again tomorrow." His people laughed. They fetched the stolen goods, which were greater in number than Cook had imagined. All were surrendered, except the watch.

Cook insisted upon his timepiece. So Mokwina said, "Sali, do you know who has the captain's watch?"

Sali replied, "Kipsis has the watch, chief."

Kipsis slunk before Mokwina. He handed over the watch. The chief handed the gold trinket back to Cook, and then said, "Kipsis, I will slap you a little with a branch. You scream, as though you are in pain. When I am done, run into the woods, and do not come back for two days."

Punishment was administered. Kipsis fled. The English were mollified.

Mokwina burst out in laughter, for no apparent reason. He swaggered to Cook, seizing him by the forearm. Mokwina cajoled and signed. The British captain-scientist eventually grasped that his kleptomaniac host invited the British company to a feast that very evening to honor the visitors, to thank them for forgiving the thieves among the Mowachaht. Cook accepted with what enthusiasm he could muster, tipped this tricorn, and clambered back into the launch.

Mokwina's manipulation of Cook boosted the chief's prestige among those at Yokwat. Despite his compromise with Sali, the chief seemed happy. Sali wondered about that. For Mokwina usually sulked if slighted. Perhaps Mokwina thought their arrangement would not last long. Sali squinted at his future, to no avail.

Mowachaht women and slaves bustled. Some fetched salmon from the Mowinis weir, first piscine gleanings from the stock's annual headlong rush to sexual suicide. Water boxes seethed, rock after glowing rock urging a boil. Last fall's berries soaked in spring water, since the season was too young for fresh. Whale oil overflowed bowls carved with images of Raven and Bear and Ichtope. Quizl, eyes matching his wild hair, readied a tale for telling. He sat near a boiling box, rehearsing. Hunger tickled the shaman. He whipped off his otter-skin cape. This he threw over the vaporous cauldron. Insect vermin began to flee steam. Quizl seized them, and popped them in his mouth.

Behind Mokwina's longhouse, the gala's main entrée was readied. Festival meat was killed and set roasting.

The British arrived. Younger officers wrinkled their noses and murmured. A few gagged. Stench from the chief's dwelling pressed nausea on His Majesty's servants. To British eyes and noses, Mokwina's longhouse was a squalid pigsty. Garbage rotted where it fell. Insects indulged breeding frenzy. Smoke reddened eyes.

Quizl led the British, one by one, to their seats. First, Captain Cook. He took his place at Mokwina's left on the bark mats of the longhouse floor, ignoring his nose with stolid longsuffering. Junior officers ducked beneath racks of drying salmon, suspended from the smoky ceiling, and sat near their captain. Beetles scurried. Flies hovered. Fleas welcomed new hosts as the assembly settled. One of Cook's youngest, Edward Riou, heaved. William Bligh's elbow stifled the boy's nausea.

Mokwina reserved for Sali his right hand seat. Mokwina evicted his own son from that seat of honor to make a place for Sali. The boy scowled at Sali from his diminished station nearby.

Quizl gave a signal. Platters appeared through the smoke. Great planks with sides, banked in steaming salmon, heaps of berries, bracken fern rhizomes, blue camas, nettles, and fiddlehead ferns. More than the assembled company could ever consume. In the middle of each platter stood a bowl of whale oil, clamshells surrounding it. Another dish held a special delicacy, quakamiss, rotted salmon eggs, ripening two months now in a vat in the sun. Mokwina picked at these with relish.

Putrid roe rekindled Edward Riou's distemper. He bent and vomited. This created a stir. Cook apologized for his crewman, whom he excused claiming collywobbles. The word made Mokwina laugh. Quizl kicked some dirt over Riou's leavings, but Mokwina saw his guests squirm. He called a qol and had the mess scraped up.

The chief picked up salmon with his fingers, ladled whale oil onto it with a clamshell, and dropped it into his mouth. A considerable portion, with small bones sticking out of it, slid down the chief's chest. Mokwina laughed. He threw the chunk of salmon which had missed his mouth back onto the platter. Officers exchanged glances. First Cook, then all, followed Mokwina's lead. The salmon was bland, the ferns palatable. The oil had a bitter, tainted taste. None touched the salmon roe.

Mokwina beckoned entertainments. Quizl rose and danced. Mowachaht Tyees slapped the dinner planks. The old shaman leapt and squatted. He whirled and spun. Aged bowels betrayed him. A flatulent mist hung over the officers. Wild-eyed, Quizl told stories of tree ogres and mink covens and the day Old Bear fell so hard he made the ground shake. The officers understood not a word. But Quizl amused them greatly. The British applauded and whistled, which pleased Mokwina.

Mokwina rose and explained to uncomprehending ears that festival meat would now be served, a great honor lavished upon the most highly respected guests. The chief motioned. A qol brought in a plank. On it lay a shank, looking like rolled roast beef, bone in. The British salivated. Real food! Two young officers dug in hungrily. A minute of chewing passed. A second platter arrived. A forearm with hand attached, medium rare.

Those who had eaten fled the longhouse. Bligh sickened. Rancid whale oil greased his salmon and ferns as they gushed from Bligh onto the platter of arm.

Cook gasped and jumped back. He scraped spatters of Bligh's distemper from his dress uniform. Recovering, Cook tried to explain to Mokwina. He and his men could not eat human flesh. It was not done.

Mokwina was incredulous. He consumed at least one captured warrior each month, to keep up his strength, to honor his enemies. The reticence of his guests was unfathomable.

Mokwina waved his hand. The arm and nibbled thigh were removed, much to the delight of the women and children outside the longhouse, who ate greedily. Mokwina's feast, though, could not be rescued. The British rose to leave. Mokwina tried to salvage the affair. He summoned slaves, two women, his most beautiful qol. Of these he made loan to Cook, for the pleasure of his officers.

Cook again looked distressed.

"Mokwina, we thank you heartily, but . . ." Cook began to push the slave girls back toward Mokwina.

The chief grunted angrily, and pushed By-The-Rocks into Cook's arms.

Cook relented. He could ill afford further insult to the chief. He would take the women aboard, even if morality be offended. They would be safe enough, until the ships were ready for departure. Then he could return them to the Mowachaht.

The captain thanked Mokwina as warmly as he could pretend. Cook left with his men and the qols in tow.

Cook locked the women in a room near his cabin, and kept the only key in his pocket. Or so he imagined. Young officers stole whispered parlays below deck. Lots were drawn.

The next morning, *Resolution* and *Discovery* moved off, about a mile, to a nearby island. For a month, the crews made repairs and spruce beer (which Cook approved for its beneficial effect upon both mood and scurvy).

When repairs were complete, the mamalnis' great canoes again anchored in Yokwat cove.

That morning, Cook returned the female qols, and made a gift to Mokwina. Cook unsheathed a new broad sword. He placed it into chief's hands. Mokwina was overwhelmed. It gleamed silver, with a shiny brass hilt. Mokwina called for a great copper, his most valuable possession. This Mokwina gave to Cook. He seized the captain's forearm in a show of genuine affection.

The next morning, at dawn, Cook determined to depart, though wind and tide were against him. Skies told of storm. Still, Cook pressed out of Nootka Sound. Too many days had he spent in the sometimes pleasant company of the Mowachaht. And he could not afford to strip an ounce more metal from his ships. Fifteen hundred otter pelts lay in their holds.

The British exploration was a drop in the sea of European civilization, a footnote on page two of the *London Times*. In Yokwat, however, the Nootkan universe shuddered.

Whaling season began. On the first dawn, Mokwina harpooned a large gray. The same afternoon, a second. These were first of a host of expiring cetaceans dragged to Yokwat's beaches this balmy season. An orgy of wealth for the Mowachaht, for Mokwina. The new iron head of the chief's harpoon cut deep through blubber into the bowels of beasts. Flailing grays and humpbacks died quickly, with little struggle. The chief set others of his warriors stockpiling sea otter pelts, far beyond the needs of the Mowachaht. It was a season unlike others. More sea otters died than were born. More whale oil was rendered than Mowachaht could eat or potlatch. More salmon were caught than could be dried in the longhouses' rafters. The capable Mowachaht grew voracious and relentless. They consumed the land. Because they could. Because Mokwina drove them to do so.

One moon after the great canoes left, Salmon-Tails, one of the qols lent to Cook, fell ill. She sweated and blistered in crotch and mouth. Quizl danced over her. He deployed potent charms. After questioning Salmon-Tails, Quizl determined that she sickened because the officers of the ships engaged unnatural sex with her. The British had forced the women to lie on their backs beneath the pale humping Europeans, instead of demanding rear entry, as do men.

By-The-Rocks, the second loaned qol, complained of headaches. She lost her hearing. Delirium muddled her. Quizl determined that Mink had stolen the girl's mind. Songs were sung. Rituals troubled her bedside. But all to no avail. A box was prepared. Her weak body placed in it, though she protested. The coffin was lashed shut. By-The-Rocks was abandoned deep in the woods where the plaintive screams of the soul-less qol would not trouble the Mowachaht.

Salmon-Tails recovered. But soon many in the lower classes showed blisters. The spirit of another woman was stolen. Quizl lathered in ritual, driving bad spirits from every pot and box in camp. He forbade eating bear meat. No gum was to be chewed. Quizl killed squirrels with rocks. He shook snake heads at every tribe member. The old shaman barked at trees. He rubbed his own eyes with eyeballs extracted from a dead medicine woman, who had been reputed to be expert in locating wandering minds. But the cankers continued. Spirits of the afflicted failed to return. Quizl could not help. Worst for the aging shaman, his prescriptions inconvenienced Mokwina.

The Mowachaht chief set out to parley his mounting wealth into power and prestige all along the west coast of the Nuu-chah-nulth island-spattered seascape. Mokwina would rule from the Kwagiulth of the north to the Klamaths of the south, if his fortune held.

Sali languished in these momentous days. Sleep came sporadically. He lost weight. Nightly, Sali implored Raven. But no visions came. Drought from the spirit world parched Sali.

Mokwina set the works of his conquest grinding. He convened potlatches, tremendous extravaganzas, unlike any the Nootka had ever seen. The Mowachaht chief overwhelmed his challengers with gluts of wealth, with unmatchable gifts of metal and whale. Mokwina obligated every chief to himself. For it was the rule in potlatch that every gift Mokwina made had to be returned with interest, if the one who received were to avoid catastrophic loss of prestige. Mokwina purchased coppers, first at their traditional value. But as summer wore on, he snatched at half price, as opponents were forced to liquidate wealth to repay his potlatch loans.

In this single prodigious summer, Mokwina amassed the greatest concentration of wealth the Nootka had ever known. The chief raised a special house just to store his coppers. He erected a second longhouse for his slaves. But most, Mokwina laid foundations. He used festival conclaves to establish a trading empire. He struck agreements to sell pelts and wares of neighboring tribes to his mamalni, for a price in prestige and a share of the take. Mokwina set himself up as the Nootkan middleman. He prospered. Until he did not prosper.

As the winds of Yokwat grew chill and winter blustered off the Pacific, preparations were made to transfer the village to the shelter of Tahsis. Plans underway, Mokwina turned his attention to other problems, two irritants he had shunted for months now.

After the planks had been lashed to the house frames of Tahsis, Mokwina called Sali to his smoky longhouse.

"Sali, my Tyee. I have a special delegation for you. A matter of great importance to the Mowachaht."

Sali listened expectantly, but with wariness beckoned by Mokwina's blistering summer of self-importance.

The chief commanded, "Go north to the Qayokwat tribe. They are weak and afraid to fight. You need not fear. Tell their chief I wish to trade for pelts and ceremonial masks that my mamalni might purchase next summer."

Sali looked warily at his chief. He did not trust Mokwina, but he could see no danger in his simple proposal. But, then, Sali knew of himself that his imagination did not burn so brightly as some.

"It is good, Mokwina. I will leave this morning." The guardian of the Hill of the Ravens turned to depart.

"Sali. Take old Quizl with you. He will enjoy the outing. It will get his mind off locating the spirits of the sick qol of the village."

Sali nodded.

Mokwina called, as Sali left. "I see your hatchet is freshly sharpened. I plan to cut some bowstrings tonight. Can I borrow it?" Sali threw the tool to his chief. The distinctive Raven totem of Sali's family leered from its handle.

Mokwina nodded his appreciation. He smiled, "If it is a pleasant visit, take your time among the Qayokwat, my friend. We will prepare for Tlokwana. Be back for the festival."

After the sun had fallen into the ocean, Mokwina summoned two sons of a favored Tyee, each anxious to prove himself battle-ready.

Mokwina lied, "I have been insulted by the chief of the Qayokwats, most grievously. I wish you to take revenge upon him."

Both powerful young men listened wordlessly. Mokwina said, "Get in your canoe. Paddle rapidly to the Qayokwat camp up the coast. Hide yourselves in the woods and watch. When you see the chief's son, seize him secretly, and cut off his head with this axe. Leave the weapon embedded in the boy's chest. Then return home. Tell no one of your deed. Be certain no one sees you."

The next morning Sali paddled out of Tahsis with shaman Quizl. Neither would again see Yokwat.

CHAPTER 6
PLAGUE

ALERT BAY
CORMORANT ISLAND
AD 1827

A launch scratched the gravel. Sali stepped in, slowly, from the beach. His musket lay across his lap. Sali sat expressionless, back erect, near the bow. Gray hair whipped in gusts. Sali's intense black eyes examined the sailors. Six scruffy seamen pulled their oars, aimed the skiff at a vessel anchored off the long, arching waterline of Alert bay.

The Nimpkish beach bustled. Iron adzes of men in trousers chipped a new canoe. Knocking adzes echoed across the quarter mile of tide-churning Broughton strait. Old women, in traditional bark robes, snaked spruce root past bear grass, weaving baskets and hats. The drone of village gossip buzzed in their ears. Girls in cotton dresses carried metal buckets full of huckleberries into longhouses. Racks of orange salmon fillets hung in the waning summer sun.

Sali's obsessive thoughts ran to his two grandsons, paddling south, he presumed. The dull pain in his chest twitched. Raven plagued those boys. The pestering apparition drove them from their home in Alert Bay. Sali was not so eccentric as either of them. Sali muttered a curse on the Spirit of his family, Raven who had abandoned him a lifetime ago, leaving him dry as the sage plains east of the interior mountains.

Sali loved those young men, the most promising of his grandsons. He nursed an old man's hope that they would be a strong backbone for the Ravenhill clan, for the future of the Kwagiulth as they struggled with enormous change. But now, the boys were gone. To the south tip of Vancouver Island. Now Alert Bay would never profit from their strength or leadership. A bitter taste lingered on Sali's tongue.

One of the sailors laid a plaid blanket over Sali's legs, and winked. Sali was not cold. The former slave shook off melancholy, and winked back. He furrowed his deeply-wrinkled auburn face comically.

"So, a second journey, Billy." Sali said.

The freckle-faced boy looked up, "You . . . You remember me, sir?"

Sali turned his piercing black eyes to the lad. "Why, of course, William. I attempt to remember every man I meet." Sali's gaze softened to twinkling. He added, "But my memory fails me as I age. You will forgive me, if the next time we meet I have forgotten not only your name, but mine also?"

The boy laughed, "Done." He added, "But I doubt you forget anything, sir."

Sali examined the boy. His face was pale, like the down plucked from the belly of an eagle. Images, distant memories, of British and Mowachaht faces danced in Sali's memory. That first day in Yokwat cove. Much had changed, since that day. Europeans visited regularly. Still, it was true that fascinations abounded.

But horrors had come also.

Wonder molded Billy's features. The Nimpkish savages at Alert Bay astonished him.

The captain of the *Union*, a Boston sloop, greeted Sali with a grunt. Sali stretched out his hand, and shook with this greasy entrepreneur. The lazy, bearded Yankee, Eugene Siddle by name, smelled of salt pork and acrid armpits. Once before, Sali had dealt with Siddle. That day the Nimpkish had gotten the better deal. Siddle would look to even the score.

"The *Union* is a fine ship, Captain. When last we met you stood at the helm of another," Sali offered.

"Huh? Oh, yah . . . Me and them owners did not see eye to eye," the captain grumbled.

Sali continued, "I know some of your crew." Sali nodded toward Billy. "William visited Cormorant Island for trade, with another Boston captain. Whistler, I believe, was his name."

"Gut-shot in a tavern in San Francisco. Woman trouble, they say. Someone else's woman, I imagine." Siddle snorted his snuff.

Sali nodded impassively.

"Boy!!!" Siddle screamed plaintively. His young attendant raced to his side with two mugs of rum. The captain shoved one at Sali, and grunted, "Here. S'pose you'll want some of this."

Sali gently refused the cup, and grasped his opponent's eyes. Siddle shrugged. He chugged one tankard, and then the other. He belched. "No use wasting good rum, you know."

The captain fingered his manifest, and shuffled some sheets. "Got the usual load here, chief Ravenhill," Siddle began.

Sali responded, "I am no chief, sir. I am a Nootkan Tyee become warrior of the Kwagiulth nation, by intervention of Raven," Sali pronounced with finality. A hint of exasperation tinged Sali's words.

"Yah, well, please yourself, Ravenhill," Siddle murmured. "The usual in the hold, I say: blankets, muskets, powder, shot, cloth, molasses, rice, bread, biscuits, tobacco, needles, scissors, apples, and a box of miscellaneous junk."

Sali stood silently.

"There's been a bit of a price increase, chief. Lit'l more than you been payin', that's all. Can't go the usual fifteen. I'm authorized to pay eleven blankets for a prime pelt." Siddle studied his manifest assiduously.

Sali continued his silence for another thirty seconds. Then he said, "I am sorry to hear about the poor market where you trade. Exchange is difficult everywhere these days. For the Nimpkish, it grows harder to trap the otters whose pelts you seek. The King George men have posts in the interior where they compete with us for the Bella Coola and Comox furs. We now need eighteen blankets for each pelt." Sali wagged his head, feigning sorrow.

After a minute of silence, Sali rose. "Never mind. No need to worry about the Nimpkish, Captain Siddle. We will trade with the King George men at the fort. It is a long journey for my people, but the trade there is twenty blankets. We will enjoy the walk." Sali gathered his musket, and rounded a mast. He turned in farewell, "Good fortune on your journey."

"Now just hold on a damned minute there, Ravenhill," Siddle protested.

Sali turned to the captain, who squirmed. Sali had him.

"Fourteen," Eugene Siddle harrumphed.

Sali rubbed his chin, and wiped a spot from his musket's barrel. When it shined with buff luster, he obfuscated, "I might be able to convince my chief to accept seventeen, but I doubt it. He has been in a terrible state lately. His third wife lusts after the place of his second. They bicker constantly, and his head aches. . .:"

"Sixteen. No more." Siddle spat a blackened clump on the deck and stomped off, slamming the door to his cabin. He bellowed, "Boy!!!," and the mop-haired youth scrambled toward the captain's door with yet another stein of rum.

Outside the chief's longhouse, the Nimpkish hooted delight at Sali's account. A sixteen-blanket trade! Alert Bay prospered beyond her neighbors. The Nimpkish had Sali Ravenhill to thank.

Sali sat on an overturned canoe. Behind him, painted on the front of Tlebeet's son's chiefly residence, Thunderbird swept from the skies and carried off Whale, who was split from head to tail, in illustration of a story Sali could not recall at the moment. First one, then several of his great grandchildren skittered up to his side. These he tickled to the sound of joyous squealing. A sense of well-being spread over the pain Sali felt. He was happy—at least as satisfied as a man abandoned by his Great Spirit can be.

As the sun sank over the mountainous ridge of Vancouver Island, two launches slid onto the village beach. Americans piled out, anxious for release in the sighs of Nimpkish women. The village kept a stable of slaves for just this purpose. A small fee was collected from each sailor. One seaman broke from the ranks.

That lone sailor sauntered along the beach, peering in the Nimpkish longhouses, squinting in the fading daylight. Four Nimpkish warriors, drunk with rum, bellowed and weaved down the beach toward the Boston man. A shot punctuated the twilight sky and the Massachusetts boy smelled powder. He jumped at an unexpected war cry, and the four drunkards fell to the ground in hilarity. The sailor edged around them, and continued his search.

Sali saw the boy coming. The elder warrior shooed his gaggle of great grandchildren. They skittered off, like frightened goslings. From behind trees and canoes, their beloved "Old One," as they called him, greeted the lad.

Sali called, "Billy! Welcome." Ravenhill motioned for Billy to approach. Sali seated the boy next to him. He filled Billy's mouth with fresh huckleberries and flatbread dipped in molasses.

The two, old and young, Kwagiulth and Yankee, sat silently for a long while in the twilight. A pod of orcas flowed past Cormorant Island, raising and lowering their black and white dorsal flags as they found need of breath. The spray of their lungs hung in the chill evening air, lingering over calm waters. From a snag atop a dead cedar, a bald eagle scanned two miles of darkening water for a last snack. Mothers sang sleepy songs to heavy-lidded toddlers, tunes that leaked onto the quiet beach.

When his hunger ebbed, Billy thanked Sali effusively. He made ready to leave. Sali said, "Sit, Billy. We will talk." Billy made it clear he did not wish to overstay his welcome. Sali reassured him. They chatted about the war of the Boston and King George men. About outposts springing up on the mainland. About Captain Siddle's tirades.

Billy asked, "How did you learn to speak such good English, Mister Ravenhill?"

"That story is long. Perhaps we should speak of something else," Sali demurred. Now it was Billy's turn to offer assurances. After some work, the young New Englander coaxed Sali to tell his tale in the deepening night. Small waves lapped beach gravel gently.

"Forty six summers ago, when I was a young man, my chief, Mokwina of the Mowachaht . . ." Sali began.

"You mean Maquinna, who burned the Boston, and lopped the heads off twenty-five crewmen!" interrupted the boy, hungry for a tale of blood-thirsty adventure.

"Yes," Sali nodded. "And held two, Jewett and Thompson, as slaves for two years. . ." Sali's eyes saddened. "Mokwina's greed ruined my people."

Sali turned to Billy, "My first people, that is. The Mowachaht grew very wealthy, more wealthy than all the Nootka. Mokwina controlled all the furs that were traded with King George men. Then, the mamalni traders discovered that Mowachaht furs cost more than if they traded directly to the other tribes. Mokwina was enraged. He warred against any Nootkan family that bypassed him and traded directly with the great canoes. Still, many tribes resisted.

So, Mokwina took out his anger on the mamalni's great canoes. He captured the *Boston*, as you said, and slaughtered her crew. The King George men avoided Nootka Sound altogether, because there was much contention and danger there. The many totem poles, which Mokwina paid carvers to raise, began to rot. The Mowachaht eventually grew hungry. Now, my first people fades from the memory of the land."

Billy pondered, "I did not realize you were Nootka, Mister Ravenhill."

"Well, that is how I came to speak English," Sali said. Billy puzzled over the connection.

"In the first fall, after Cook and his King George men sailed into Yokwat to trade for pelts, Mokwina grew very wealthy. He feared me, for I too prospered. Mokwina sent me and his medicine man, Quizl, to set up trade with the Qayokwats, a tribe to the north of the Mowachaht. I did not trust Mokwina, for possessions had made him crazy. He lusted for power beyond any practical use. I did not, however, grasp how far madness had carried off his sanity.

"Moaning and wails limped from Village Island, where the Qayokwats lived. They lingered far out on the water, where Quizl and I heard them. The chief's son had been killed and mutilated two days before. Despite their sorrow, we were welcomed, though the chief and his family did not feast with us, because of sorrow.

"A group of Kwagiulth also visited the village, trading. We sat together around a great fire feasting and listening to the old songs. Tlebeet, the Kwagiulth chief, recounted the story of Raven's theft of sun and moon from Magician's house. He told the tale well, though he spoke our language haltingly.

"Then I rose. I told the assembly of all that had happened at Yokwat. Of my vision on the Hill of the Ravens. Of the great canoes. Of Cook and the men and fur-trading. Of all these facts the Qayokwats knew something, though they were glad to hear the full story first-hand. But the Kwagiulths chattered, not hiding their fascination.

"Tlebeet, who was chief of Alert Bay until he died seven summers ago, rose and said, 'You would be our honored guest, and we would reward you greatly, if you would come with us to the Kwagiulth people for a time and ask Raven to call the great canoes to our shores.'

"I replied, 'I am honored, Tlebeet, at your offer. But I am here on Mowachaht business. My chief, Mokwina, requires my presence at the Tlokwana in Tahsis.' Tlebeet nodded, and sat. But he was not satisfied.

“I delivered Mokwina’s proposal to the Qayokwat tribe. The heads of the village elders bent toward one another. Promising whispers buzzed, like honeybees in wildflowers. But I never received the Qayokwat response.

“Quizl, whose attention faded with age, wandered the longhouse. He seized a hatchet from the chief’s corner of the longhouse, from his wife’s bed. Quizl turned and shouted to me, interrupting my discussion with the Qayokwats, ‘Sali, here is your hatchet!’

“Quizl ran across the open center of the circle with the weapon, stopping in front of me. I looked at the object, carved with my family’s crest, and said ‘How did my hatchet come to be in the Qayokwat chief’s house?’

“Then I remembered I had loaned my weapon to Mokwina.

“A Qayokwat warrior, brother to the chief, roared and leapt up. He tore the weapon from the Mowachaht medicine man’s hand, and brought it crashing onto Quizl’s skull. Fragile old bones split, and his head broke into two pieces down through the nose, an eye on each side. When Quizl landed on the dirt floor, shaman brains splashed into the crackling fire, sizzling.

“A rope was tied to each of my hands and feet. I was stretched onto a frame, splayed naked. His brother broke the news to the Qayokwat chieftain. When rage subsided, the chief decided that I was to be roasted alive, fed to the dogs, and my bones tossed into a hole in which the tribe would crap for a week.

“That night, when the moon set, just before dawn, Tlebeet cut me from the frame where I hung, barely conscious. The Kwagiulth delegation carried me, since I could not walk. They spirited me over the backbone of their world to their village here at Alert Bay.

“So I became a qol. Sali, guardian of the Hill of the Ravens, second to Mokwina, chief of the powerful Mowachaht—a slave . . . My owners suspected I had butchered the Qayokwat prince. To make matters worse, I could barely make myself understood to the Nimpkish, much less defend myself against Mokwina’s elaborate hoax.

“So, I became a dog. I was slave to the slaves of women. A lower station cannot be imagined. For many moons, I dreamed of little but death. And I cursed Raven, who still refused me dreams.

“But slowly, my strength and spirit returned. I taught myself the Kwagiulth dialect, with a speed that astonished my captors. I devoted myself to the Nimpkish at Alert Bay. I could never return to Yokwat, since I posed a threat to Mokwina. Besides, these Nimpkish are a proud and honorable people, skilled in carving and war. I did well to live among them.

“Some among the Nimpkish pressed for my execution, fearing reprisals from the Mowachaht or Qayokwat tribes. But Tlebeet remembered my stories of the great canoes, and dreamed of wealth. So, he saved me from my enemies among the Nimpkish that first winter and through the following year.

“I hauled wood and water, removed garbage, cleaned fish, and slept with the dogs. Tlebeet encouraged my ritual washings, and excused me from work to the extent that I prayed and sang. And he brought me scraps of food, to strengthen me. He refused to make me festival meat. For he longed that Raven would bring the King George men to Alert Bay.

“My fortunes changed late the following spring. A ship poked its bow around the southern end of Cormorant Island. The Nimpkish flew to the beach, vibrating with cacophonous gibbering. Tlebeet summoned me. I sat beside him as we paddled out to the vessel. I parlayed with the captain of the ship to the best of my ability, pretending I understood much more of his language than I in fact did. But Tlebeet was satisfied with my performance. He attributed the very presence of the King George men to my intimacy with Raven. The trading that day made him rich.

"Never again was I treated as a dog.

"I determined to learn the language of the King George men. Daily, Tlebeet allowed me to return to the British ship. At first he accompanied me on each encounter. But as the days passed, he tired of my mysterious behavior. I walked around the ship, with whomever would accompany me, pointing at objects, learning the names of things. Soon I had mastered the rudiments of the ship's rigging and tools, and could frame a fumbling sentence.

"The sailors thought me great sport, and would trick me by saying the wrong names for things. They laughed until they fell on the decks.

"It was from these King George men that I received the name by which you know me. I explained to them my former position among the Mowachaht, pointing out the black trickster flying by, and they said, 'Raven.' Then I tried to explain my guardianship of the Hill of the Ravens near Yokwat. I pointed at the low-lying heights of Cormorant Island, and one young man said, 'Hill.' From that moment on, to the traders who anchor in Alert Bay, I have been Ravenhill.

"So I tolerated the crew's jokes with a smile, and kept them laughing. For I knew that their language would be an indispensable asset to the Nimpkish and Chief Tlebeet. And I would gain position to bargain for my freedom.

"I did not have long to wait. Through that winter, which was a long snowy one, I mulled the King George men words. Then, in the early spring, the first trading vessel arrived. I bargained for the Nimpkish, and spoke with the sailors. That summer four more ships stopped at Cormorant Island. Before leaves changed that year, I could speak well enough to be understood by King George men.

"The last of these ships' captains, a Boston man, wispy and kind, lavished two hundred blankets upon Tlebeet. He wanted me to accompany him up the coast to the rest of the Kwagiulth peoples, serving as native interpreter. Tlebeet agreed. So I spent several summers with English speakers, trading and visiting with the tribes of my adopted people. And I increased the prestige of Tlebeet.

"The Kwagiulth of Cormorant Island grew wealthy. Tlebeet was grateful to me, for my help. He said, 'Sali, you have traded for the Nimpkish as though we were your own people. What can I give you, to reward you?'

"I stood silently for a time. Then I said, 'Tlebeet, the Nimpkish are my people. Alert Bay is my home. All I desire is to be made a man of the Kwagiulth and see my King George name, Ravenhill, enrolled with the names of the rest of the families of the people.'

"Then you do not wish to return to Yokwat?'

"No, Tlebeet. Mokwina betrayed me, and would kill me if he saw me. He has become very powerful in these last years, and crazy, I believe.'

"Tlebeet nodded. I was made a man, and given the name Ravenhill at the Winter Festival that very fall. I took a wife and then another. They bore me sons and daughters, whose children have now given me children.

"But some opposed my elevation. They asked, "How does a dog become a man?' and 'How can a King George name belong to a Kwagiulth warrior?' Tlebeet's rival to the south, Egistolis, chief of the Tlawitsis tribe on Turnour Island, railed at the innovation. Egistolis threatened, and fumed, and spoke ill of Tlebeet and the Nimpkish.

"Over the years, as prosperity increased, it had become the practice among the Kwagiulth to forego wars, and to battle with wealth instead, after the manner of potlatches. They settled disputes with the grease feast.

"A grease feast is no celebration, but rather a challenge. Egistolis kindled a fire in the middle of his longhouse. Tyees of the Nimpkish took seats so close to the fire that our hair curled. Great quantities of eulachon oil, which is very expensive, were thrown on the fire. It smoked. The fish grease made the bonfire leap higher and higher. But none of the Nimpkish moved or even took notice. For that would mean that Egistolis's fire had conquered us, and Tlebeet would be shamed. Then an effigy of Tlebeet was brought in, and placed next to the fire. The Tlawitsis warriors sang songs ridiculing Tlebeet and the Nimpkish, while the cedar bark doll smoked, then caught fire, and was consumed. Finally the roaring flames, enraged with oil, ignited the longhouse roof. Egistolis persevered until he feared his house would collapse. Then he sent his warriors to put out the fire. But we Nimpkish took no notice. And when the fire had burned down, we left.

"Then it was Tlebeet's turn. The grease fire was set. Two days before the challenge, a Boston ship, not unlike yours, Billy, slid into Alert Bay. And Raven gave me an idea. I went to the captain and made a trade with him. I approached Tlebeet with my plan. He was enthusiastic.

"Egistolis and his Tyees arrived. We lit our fire in Tlebeet's longhouse. At first, all was normal. But the fire burned hotter and hotter. In an hour, the cedar logs on top had burned through and fallen aside.

"Beneath them lay my purchase. Coal. Hundreds of chunks of coal from the ship's foundry. They burned white, so hot that one Tlawitsis man began to blister. Then Tlebeet motioned to me. I raised the first bowl of eulachon oil over my head. It splashed onto the searing coal embers. The oil exploded. It rose in a mushroom of flame to the ceiling. I staggered back. My eyelashes were burned. My Kutsack smoked. Egistolis and several others ran from the longhouse to save themselves. Two of the Tlawitsis group had to be dragged from the inferno's edge. One was badly burned, and forever wore a scarred scowl on his face. The other got shivers and died.

"So Egistolis was beaten, and my position secured. More than forty summers since then I have traded with the Boston and King George men. And I have learned to speak with them, as I speak with my own people.

Billy's eyes stood wide.

A voice hollered down the beach, "Come on, Billy. Gotta get back." The youngster thanked Sali copiously, then left the venerable patriarch.

At the wood's edge, not far from Billy and Sali, a circular depression scribed the frond debris beneath the greening cedar canopy. Odal eavesdropped Sali's tales.

Mastican irises contracted, despite the dimming daylight. Odal pondered. Enigmat interventions surged. With the European invasion, the entire west coast shuddered with separatist sentiment. To dreaming Ravenhills, night was a cauldron curdled with cackled conjuring.

But none for Sali. Odal wondered at this, brushing the Kwagiulth Tyee's mind. Sali's heavy heart encircled a memory of his itinerant grandsons, paddling southward toward their destiny. *Why did these boys leave?* Odal mulled. Odal tasted Sali's ordered mentation, its rigor. Sali lacked the untamed, and possibly pathological, mentation of Kushku.

Curiosity pressed Odal. He imposed a stasis field over Sali, as the old man mused quietly, where he sat on the overturned canoe. Odal added a duplicate of the old man's mind to the West Coasters who dwelt in virtual similitude behind Odal's cerebral partition.

Below deck on the Union, Siddle hovered over a crewman. The boy mumbled, delirious with fever. Zechariah, the armorer's assistant, lay in a puddle of his own sweat. Zechariah's head sprouted a swollen mass of pussy lesions, as did his arms and feet. Clothing clung to his skin, wet with exploded pustules and leakage of sweat. The sufferer moaned. Andersen, ship's physician, removed a wet cloth from the boy's head and placed another. He turned to an assistant, handed him the used cloth, and said, "Burn this."

Andersen looked up at Siddle, and shook his head. The chaplain began to pray. Siddle growled at his first mate, "Bury this bugger in the deepest hole you can dig."

The chaplain intervened, "No, sir. That cannot be done. The boy requested burial at sea."

Siddle began to bluster. But the look of sublime confidence on the pastor's face quieted him, that look Presbyterians wear when God and His angels have spoken.

Siddle snorted, "So be it." He clomped out of the sick room. The anchor lifted from the bottom of Alert Bay. Unfortunate Zechariah splashed into the erratic currents of Broughton strait several miles south from Cormorant Island.

Two days later, Nimpkish boys, engaged in mock war, found the corpse. They stripped brass buttons, a coat, belt, buckle, and ill-fitting boots. These they paraded around the village of the Nimpkish. Everyone laughed.

One boy took sick with fever. Then another. And another.

Ten days later, moans and screams hacked Alert Bay's tranquility. The Nimpkish fell by dozens. One delirious man, in the grip of a wild vision, turned his knife against wife and children. Neighbors killed him, but not before his carnage was complete. Bodies piled. Too few men remained to build boxes or hoist the dead to their resting places. Cormorant Island lay decimated.

Sali, whom the traders call Ravenhill, cradled the head of a great grandson as breath left the infant's wracked body. Sali himself fevered. On the back of his hands, angry red bumps emerged. Of Sali's seven Kwagiulth sons and three daughters, and their thirty-eight children, and the nineteen babies of those grandchildren, only two sons lived, and eleven children, and one baby. Some of the survivors were still endangered, their pustules healing slowly, if at all. Sali did not count the two boys whom Raven had driven from Cormorant Island. Sali cried, but tears did not come. Despair choked him. The pall of death clouded his eyes.

Blind, he saw. *A great black wing blots out the stars.* Raven drove him from Yokwat before Mokwina could destroy that people. *Cackles spill from a gaping beak, in which plays a darting red tongue.* And now Sali's grandsons, at least two, dodged pestilence at Alert Bay. *Blackness splits open. Stars cascade onto the great sheet of the night sky.* Perhaps a pattern. Perhaps . . . *Sali falls into the cawing beak, in which sloshes a turquoise sea. Many people dissolve into one strange-looking creature. There is laughter, cawing amusement.*

Sali tried to open his mouth to thank Raven for speaking to him once more, for the visitation of dreams.

But no. Sali's pain was too great.

Before smallpox could shatter his aged organs, Sali cursed Raven and died. Of grief.

Kushku: Who are you?

Sali: What is this place?

Kushku: I have been here ever so long, in this moonless moon-fog. There are no suns, so I cannot say how long. I am Kushku, of the Hill of the Ravens.

Sali: I know of you. My people tell stories of you and Qwistok, the whaler. You are long dead.

Kushku: As you can see, I live.

Sali: I too am dead. I was dying anyway.

Kushku: That is so for me as well.

Sali: I am Sali, also of the Hill of the Ravens. What is this bog I see?

Kushku: I too see. I do not know. It comes and goes, as do many other images.

Sali: Is this the island beyond life?

Kushku: I do not think so. I remember our stories. This place is not as the tales describe.

Sali: No. Not like our stories.

Kushku: If you too are of the Hill of Ravens, I am your ancestor.

Sali: Yes. Only my family worships at Ravenhill.

Kushku: It is good to have a companion.

Sali: Yes. To be together is a good thing. Has Raven troubled you since you came to this place?

Kushku: Not as the Trickster did at Yokwat. I sense that something hinders Raven.

Sali: Raven seldom visited me. I spent much of my life among the MamaLa. What about this place could impede a Great Spirit?

Kushku: I know of no rock so big as to make Trickster go around.

Sali: Yet, Bear Burper grins silently.

CHAPTER 7
CHARLEY

ROYAL BRITISH COLUMBIA MUSEUM
VICTORIA, BRITISH COLUMBIA
AD 2068

Charley perched on a stool. He whittled a mask at a high table, next to the longhouse exhibit, with its photo-fluorescent fake bonfire, real enough in appearance, but without warmth. Cedar chips dangled from Charley's olive green sweater. A close-cropped beard, salt and pepper (mostly salt) rimmed his dark, lined face. The masks and rattles and blankets of the West Coast peoples languished in plate glass coffins around him, labeled Tsimshian and Haida and Bella Coola and Nootka.

I'm just another artifact, Charley breathed to himself.

Charley pondered the Transformation mask he carved. Lustrous paints waited in a line of small bottles, anxious to imbue the ritual disguise with life. Light from the panels overhead glinted off the razor edges of knives and chisels. Sawdust spattered his knitted brown stocking cap, which lay on the worktable's edge. A sweet acid aroma rose from the remains of cedar giants, sharpening Charley's artistry.

Charley's eyes were beads of obsidian. His dexterous hands rendered a scowling Kwagiulth warrior in supple cedar. When the transformation mask was complete, the visage would don a coat of battle paint. Then, in the heat of potlatch, to the banging of skin drums and chants of Kwagiulth islanders, a string would be pulled. The warrior face would split, swinging away to each side. Wild Man hid behind the warrior, a crazy spirit who careens through woods. The terror of the hapless. A Great Spirit.

Charley thought, *This very afternoon, I become Wild Man*. Charley laughed out loud, a private, bitter cachinnation. Several tourists, watching Charley work, exchanged nervous glances. To Charley, the lookies no longer mattered. Charley was done with this crap. With endless compromise. Fuck cooperation. No more lickspittle Charley.

Scores milled, watching. Just outside the poles and rope that marked Charley's leaky cage, a sign read:

KWAGIULTH CEREMONIAL AND TOTEMIC ARTS.
CHARLES D. RAVENHILL, ARTISAN
ELDER: KWAGIULTH TRIBE
ASST. CURATOR, NATIVE COLLECTIONS
REGENT: U'MISTA CULTURAL CENTER, ALERT BAY, B.C.

Spectators muttered appreciative inanities. Zoo talk. The sort of thing suburbanites whisper from the free side of the pacing confinement of Rwandan gorillas.

Charley noted his anxiety. He was in no state to be perused by strangers. Charley scraped his tools into a khaki bag. He exited through the back of the exhibit. The crowd, murmuring, moved on to other exhibits. Charley hid himself behind a cup of tea in the cafeteria.

Images flew. Alert Bay. Breaking out of that native ghetto. College in Victoria. Ph.D. at the University of British Columbia. Eight years at Toronto's Museum of Man. Now the Royal British Columbia Museum, right on the inner harbor at Victoria. He had complete freedom to pursue his art, to write as he saw fit. *A waste; an utter waste*, Charley thought. *I've accomplished nothing*.

Charley sipped his cup. Rumination deepened. He slipped back to breakfast that morning, and his boys.

The sun streamed into their tiny breakfast nook. Charley squinted at sunrise glare off the Strait. Gigantic container vessels crept past, Vancouver bound. Breakfast debris covered the table. Toast crusts. Cereal bowls. A scrap of eggwhite. Glasses. Cups. Forks. Charley cleared the mess. He wiped it with a stained dishrag. He ran a sink full of steaming water. Charley set to scrubbing. With a double blink, Charley activated his implant. He told the boys to come in for breakfast. The boys responded "one more game." Charley's corneal contact wrote the image on his retina. Charley blinked off his implant.

Outside, on the patio, Charley's two boys indulged their morning ritual. Basketball, one on one, winner's outs, to fifteen by ones, or until the bus arrived. Tuck used to plaster his brother. But Jesie's hands became a factor in the last few months. He was quick. No, he was blinding. Both brothers played for the high school team. Intensely. Fixedly. Charley sighed. Their studies suffered. This year, hoop obsession had earned each a summer school stint. His family was known for obsession. Psychiatric-grade preoccupations, some rumbled.

Charley swung open the kitchen window. July's breeze sauntered through the room. The basketball poink, poinked on concrete.

Jesie deliberated his next assault on Tuck.

Tuck said, "Dad's getting' ready for the clink again, you short turd." Jesie looked up, straightened his knees. Tuck stole the ball.

"Gotta go for the cheapie, eh, haybrain?" Jesie taunted.

Jesie unleashed his hands. The ball poked between Tuck's legs into Jesie's waiting grasp. A delicate scoop. Then an outside jumper.

Jesie puffed, "What makes you think dad's going in, Fall Tuck?"

"Stop calling me that, piss bucket," Tuck picked up the ball.

Tuck said, "Dad brought home a bunch of cash last night. It's in the pot in the cupboard."

"Ominous," Jesie nodded. Then he lunged for the ball. Tuck put it up, but the orb banged off the rim, falling into Jesie's hands from the weathered backboard. Shoes squeaked on concrete.

"And he brought home seven boxes of corn flakes," Tuck said.

Jesie stopped. "Seven? He only brought three for the Calgary sit-in. He got thirty days then."

Tuck said, "Yah. Something big's happening."

Tuck picked up the ball and headed toward the kitchen.

"Walk," Jesie objected.

"You really are hard up. Here you go," Tuck retorted. Tuck threw his brother a yard rake that had leaned lazily against the garden wall. "Insert and rotate."

Tuck stuck his head through the kitchen window. "What's with the corn flakes, dad?"

Charley pursed his lips. His eyes spoke silently. The brothers flopped themselves like rag dolls onto kitchen chairs.

Charley poured himself a second cup of coffee. The story spilled. His meeting today. How it would go. What Alert Bay planned. The likely punishments.

Charley saw fear in his sons' eyes. He grabbed his bag of woodworking tools. Then he headed out the door for the Museum.

"Forget the *Hamatsa* stuff, Dad. They will throw away the key this time."

Charley looked at his sons, with obvious affection. He pursed his lips, then closed the door.

Jesie called, "Hala kesla, ump." Kwakwala for "Good bye, father." Charley mumbled to himself, "Hala kesla, ump," lost in thoughts.

Charley jumped up. It was 3:53.

By 4:07, it was over. The Minister of Indian Affairs, Charley's friend and reluctant adversary, waited for him. Charley stood when offered a chair, promptly at 4:00. Across the ponderous cherry wood desk sat his friend, a provincial official. Charley was offered, and refused, coffee.

The short, intense native stood. He addressed his friend, "Mr. Minister, I bring for your inspection today revised salmon quotas that would be acceptable to the Kwagiulth nation." He handed over a sheaf of papers. The blue-suit refused to take the packet, and pointed to a place on the desk for the paper to be deposited.

"Paper, Charley? Really?"

Charley double-blinked. His implant anticipated him, flashing data upload. "There. Should be in your cache now."

The Minister's eyes wandered a bit. Then he said, "Ah. I see it."

The Minister turned to Charley, straightened the lapel of his jacket. "Dr. Ravenhill, your proposal has been received. I have forwarded your people's counterproposal to my superiors."

Then the sixty-year-old bureaucrat let out a long sigh, and sank into his plush wingback swivel.

The Minister wearily motioned to Charley, as through training an over-eager puppy. "Sit down, asshole."

Charley plopped into a chair. Formality evaporated. Charley pulled one foot up under himself.

"When does it stop, Charley? You know that I have gotten your people all the increases I can manage." He paused. "There are other tribes, you know. And whites have a right to a livelihood too."

Charley soothed, "Harold, I am not trying to make your life miserable."

"I know, my friend. I am a bit lost on how to mollify you and yours."

"Your quotas are choking us, Harold."

"They are not my quotas, Charley."

"I know, Harold. But neither are they ours."

Harold put fingers of both hands together, tip to tip. He flexed them back and forth. After thirty seconds, Harold said, "Let me see what I can do."

Charley shook his head. "Truthfully, Harold, no need. I am just mopping up details with the quotas. The people are fed up. I serve notice. We are going to do the Gandhi thing up in Alert Bay."

The Minister of Indian Affairs frowned. "Hell, Charley. That won't help. The voters of British Columbia are fresh out of sympathy for coastal natives. Fiscal quicksand, and all that. I doubt I can even get the press out to Cormorant Island. The *Vancouver Times* might send a drone. . ."

Charley interrupted. "Too late. These bureaucratic negotiations are just panhandling in a suit."

"Civil disobedience will not work, either, Charley. U'Mista's funding will get cut. Ottawa says . . ."

Charley waved him off. "Doesn't matter, Harold. It's decided."

Harold Weiser put both hands on the desk. He leaned out over the expanse of cherry veneer. "Charley, I could lose my job for telling you this."

Charley waited. Harold spoke, "You are a target, old man. If there is any more trouble, they are coming after you."

Charley frowned. "I suspected something like that."

"They got themselves a new suit in Ottawa. An eager over-achiever. Looks like a teenager to me."

Charley smiled at his friend, "Thanks, Harold. Beer next week, as usual?"

Harold nodded.

Charley stood. "Mr. Minister, I am authorized to inform you that henceforth the Kwagiulth nation will regulate the use of all natural resources in our traditional lands. Logging, tourism, fishing, and other sea harvests. The Kwagiulth people reclaim for themselves absolute autonomy over their traditional territory. We renounce Canadian citizenship. We secede from the government of Canada. Non-natives may remain within our territory as honored guests. But we will no longer cooperate with your MamaLa government, except when we perceive mutual advantage."

Harold hissed, "Shit, Charley. Don't . . . You will force me to . . ."

Charley shook his head. "I know, Harold. Just do what they pay you to do, my friend. All things are one and everything connected. I will be fine."

"I know, my friend. So you keep telling me. Things do not look all that wondrous to me."

"Not wondrous. One. A messy, sometimes invisible, hidden unity. Connected, but not necessarily happily conjoined." Charley touched his friend's hand. He strode calmly to the door.

The Minister blinked, and again blinked. Even before the door clicked shut behind him, Harold was already in the brain of the RCMP chief at Port McNeill.

Charley's vehicle drove him north. The fractured, low-lying hills of the south gave way to jutting precipices and bald granite exuberances. Charley sped up the east coast of Vancouver Island, along the girthy breadth of the Strait of Georgia, past the blue treachery of Johnstone Strait. He homed on familiar swirling currents at Broughton Strait, the waters that coursed past his beloved Alert Bay.

Each mile weakened the city. Each kilometer bolstered the past. The trek north was time travel. One departed late twenty-first century Victoria, an individualistic megalopolis. One exited to the tatters of sixteenth-century Kwagiulth community. Few bio-implants. Little news. Slow pace. Thick interwoven life. Terribly fragile, endangered existence.

Charley knew both worlds. His income lay with the former; his heart with the latter. Charley harbored an insistent predilection for simpler life. Closeness to land and sea. Harvesting what one ate. Oral traditions. It seemed all technologies assist memory. But support erodes capacity. Few among the Kwagiulth could remember all the people's stories. Charley savored spring salmon roasted over open cedar fires. Sprigs of alder smoldering, infusing smoky joy. Today, the best salmon flew to San Francisco and Tokyo to tickle the hollow guts of corporate moneymongers. Charley loved the heartfulness of his tribal peoples. Their simplicity. Their warm souls and abundant affection. But the anesthetic of alcohol or opioids deadened some bonds, too many, actually.

Now it was, perhaps, too late. Still, Charley would act. Doing something was better than nothing. Possibly. His forehead crinkled, but his eyes sang. A troubled happiness, ever ephemeral. He worried about quixotic windmill tilting. About unintended consequences. About the self-restraint of the Kwagiulths of Cormorant Island. They had been trained in non-violence. Charley himself told them, over and over, tales of Gandhi, and Te Whiti o Rongomai, and Martin Luther King Jr., and even Jesus. Statistically, non-violence just works better than insurrection. Every dissident leader knows that, if he or she can read. But still, there linger unknown unknowns. Those tend to irrupt with disturbing unpredictable irregularity, as when squirrels tip teapots or lightning strikes from clear skies.

Charley missed the last ferry to Cormorant Island. He could see the vessel out in the Strait when he pulled into Port McNeill. Charley blinked the Hunts. He knew they had a couch for him, one that always left him in need of a chiropractor. The Hunt clan quizzed Charley into the wee hours. But Charley revealed little. He feared snoops.

Not far off, in Fort Rupert, the magnificent Big House stood. Its posts were Raven and Bear and Thunderbird. An RCMP vehicle passed silently on the plastic road. Near the Hunt residence, a deep blue laser reflected off a kitchen window. Vibrations became evidence in Ottawa.

Charley did not sleep much. He ate little breakfast, much to the dismay of Marion Hunt. Adrenal rush extinguished appetite and exhaustion etched him.

The sun peeked over the crests of island ridges. The ferry pulled away from its Port McNeill terminus. Decks throbbed with dynamo labors. Those vibrations spoke subliminally to Charley. *Home*, they whispered. He could feel the weathered cedar planks of the U'mista Cultural Center, smell the dusty potlatch collection. Kwakwala linguistic labors murmured in side rooms. Elders told stories for posterity. Afternoons, children learned the old talk. Archaeological teams came and went.

Charley stood on deck. He leaned against the rail in dawn's breeze. Unexpectedly, a great black and white triangle of flesh rose from an eddy next to the ferry. Then another. And another. Two more. Blasts of breath sent spray ballooning. It was G-Pod. Charley recognized the orca family by G119, its large male who sported a neat bullet hole though the tip of his dorsal fin. Charley gritted his teeth, wondering what the asshole who pulled that trigger was thinking.

The sweeping shelter of Alert Bay opened before the ferry. The town's main street followed the long arching beach of the harbor. Alert Bay's geography reflected its values. The ferry terminal bisected the elongated town. To the north and west along the beach lay the native sector, a puzzle world schizophrenic in time. It was a cultural gestalt under assault, a shatter zone. Where the main road petered out, as far north as one could travel along the beach, stood the U'mista Cultural Center. That was Charley's gem. Repository of sacred treasures and visionary aboriginals. South of the ferry terminal lay MamaLa turf. At its extremity lay the RCMP post, bastion of the non-native status quo, armed handmaidens of that imperial government whose progeny was Canada.

The ferry docked. Charley hustled off the passenger ramp, under the "Welcome to Alert Bay" arch. Beneath it hung a killer whale sculpture in cedar. It rankled Charley that the greeting was in English, not Kwakwala.

The air smelled of fish and seaweed as Charley blinked U'Mista. He texted Salal Joe that the RCMP has been alerted. Charley noted a silent tone of receipt deep in his brain. He knew Salal Joe exulted. Charley did not entirely trust Salal Joe. He stood so near the core of U'Mista's sedition. Yet Salal Joe weakly grasped the risks of their path. Facing danger, one's emotions should ladle up some mixture more cautionary than raw glee.

Charley walked into the Canadian section of Alert Bay. Swept walks invited tourists into quaint shops. Native curios and orca miscellany were offered, for a price. Neat white houses nestled amid manicured lawns and tidy rose gardens, miniatures imagined from photos at the *Thames Garden and Botanical Monthly* netsite. On Charley's left lay Alert Bay's cemetery. There, without reference to the village's ethnic divide, buried side by side, native and Canadian worked a final peace in cold, damp earth.

The RCMP constabulary was a functional brick and metal building. Doors opened for him. Charley padded up to the staff sergeant's desk.

"Hi, Jack," Charley said.

"Morning, Charley," Sergeant Strauss said. Strauss raised an eyebrow.

Charley offered a hint of smile, "A coy policeman is worse than an embarrassed prostitute. Is Halsey in?" Charley liked Strauss.

"Nope. Don't think he thought you'd come calling. If you know what I mean."

Charley scratched his beard. "Well, tell him the Hamatsa's tonight at U'Mista, if he wants to stop it."

"Considerate of you, Charley. We are not raidin' your little dance. Nothin' illegal about it. Unless you boys go eatin' someone. Then that's a different story."

Charley nodded. "Just tell him, will you? I don't want Halsey kicking down anybody's doors."

Strauss nodded. Charley was not alone in loathing Inspector Halsey. The red-headed tree was heavy-handed. Everyone who knew him thought so, including the Mounties.

Charley retraced his steps though MamaLa town. His eyes burned. He passed the ferry terminal into the native sector. He peered uphill to a tired olive green house. Worn eyes looked back at him from the front room. Salal Joe. Charley raised one finger. The elder leapt, then disappeared.

Charley sauntered north, waiting for Salal Joe to act. Torn nets, never to be mended, draped a seawall. Automobiles, twenty or so, rusted where they had died. Main street, in the native sector, served not only as a road, but also as garbage dump. Most houses stood in some way unloved. Siding missing here and there. A slumping carport. Ubiquitous cracked glass. All begged fresh paint. The tribal elders worked at cleanup. It was a slog.

One house, now vacant fifteen years, lacked an upper story and roof. Studs, half-draped in sheathing, poked skyward, like scavenged ribs of a moose carcass in a marsh. A stairway led nowhere. Overhead, a bald eagle lazed on rising air, ready to snatch fish guts near a dock. Gunwales of two sunken herring skiffs peeked above the beach's waves. At low tide, these became intertidal swimming pools. Shards of beer bottles glittered on disintegrating road plastic. Drainage ditches clutched their hoard of empty fifths and Mad Dog. Styrofoam, long outlawed, piled. Gnawed by Broughton Strait, the aged white crud was dandruff on the beach.

A hammer struck nails behind Charley. He jumped. Salal Joe admired two large white signs. The one pointing toward Charley read: Leaving the Kwagiulth Nation. Entering MamaLa.

Salal Joe cackled loudly, a laugh familiar to Charley not only from Salal Joe, but also from dreams. Joe splashed a line of white paint across the road. Joe's hilarity rose, as the line lengthened. Joe turned and waved to Charley, nearly breathless from frantic guffawing. Salal Joe scurried uphill to his dilapidated home.

Dr. Charles Ravenhill felt heaviness. The Alert Bay road brought that. A cultural vacuum sucked clean the minds of his people. It cleared away the detritus of things Kwagiulth, but denied them the vapid surrogate culture of the west. Past the school, in which so few learned anything, Charley entered U'Mista. He hugged Happy, the receptionist.

U'Mista itself was born of MamaLa coercion. In 1884, efforts to civilize the Kwagiulth savages led the government to outlaw potlatches. These festivals impeded Christianity. Outwardly, the natives conformed. When storms raged, or on distant islands, they met to potlatch. In 1921, on Village Island, forty-five people were charged. Potlatch regalia was packed. William Halliday, Indian Agent for Alert Bay, shipped all the ceremonial items off to Ottawa, for a fee of course. The valuable artifacts ended up in Ottawa's Museum of Man and Toronto's Royal Ontario Museum. In the 1960s, Kwagiulth agitators demanded return of the stolen goods. At length, the museums agreed. But the people had to erect appropriate museums of their own at Alert Bay and Cape Mudge to preserve the artifacts. In the time before whites arrived, captives were taken by raiding. When those human prizes were returned to their villages, they were said to have "u'mista." The U'Mista cultural center recovered Kwagiulth culture, the Kwakwala language, and, if this day eventually bore fruit, aboriginal lands.

Charley passed the afternoon's waning hours on a great drift log. Tides landed the monster tree before the beachfront opening of the reconstructed longhouse that housed U'Mista's ceremonial mask and copper collection. The sun sank behind Vancouver Island in a wispy ember bed of reds and pinks. The

Nootka were burning slash, Charley surmised. G pod slid south in the twilight, headed for Robson Bight, to frolic and scratch themselves on the pebbly bottom there.

Charley smelled cedar smoke. Ceremonial fires had been lit within. Aching cramped muscles complained from Charley's thigh and back. Charley sighed. There was no time for further rest.

This was Charley's first Hamatsa, the first for his people in centuries. The secret society of Hamatsas was an ancient association of reputed cannibals. Hamatsa resuscitation might spark the Kwagiulth. Soon, Charley hoped. If not soon, there would be nothing left to save.

Charley donned his costume in the U'mista restroom. A scratchy cedar dress, waist drawn snug with cedar bark rope. A head ring, symbol of the initiate Hamatsa, plied his forehead. Fern fronds wove among cedar strands.

Charley surveyed himself in the bathroom mirror. He could pass for one of his ancestors, except that his hair was neatly trimmed and he had all his teeth. A thousand years of Hamatsas preceded Charley. Those predecessors endured greater deprivations than Charley. The Hamatsa initiate wandered four months in the woods, until he was possessed by the Cannibal Spirit. Then he was brought to the Big House to be tamed by older Hamatsas.

Chanting, a rhythmic rumble of mythic transport, pulsed in the corridor of the Collection Room. Cedar smoke teased Charley's nostrils. Flashes plagued his retinas. Charley shook his head. He leaned on the sink. Bursts resolved themselves into pictures. Images of the past, of Kwagiulth antiquity, raced through his mind. Images born not from his doctoral studies or analytical abilities. No, Charley's visions erupted from the collective mind, from the subliminal, unsuspected shared colloquy between Charley and his ancestors. These melted into a sum greater than their individual existences. Memories carried on winds of ceremony, in tremors by which past disturbs present.

Charley's hands trembled. The bathroom door caught his right foot. Charley stumbled. The world swam.

Charley weaved into the great hall of the potlatch collection. Chanting quieted, but kept its driving pulse in logs beaten with deer bones, in hide drums slapped by reddened fingers. Smoke scratched Charley's irritated eyes.

Charley spun. He ducked. He leapt toward the fire, then fled the flames. He circled, followed by the Kwagiulth chief, a man given to drink, but tonight sober and steady. Charley saw friends, many friends. Buddies from Port Hardy, colleagues from far-flung archeological sites, even white comrades from MamaLa Alert Bay. He whirled past fishermen, a doctor, general store clerks, bums, a nurse, wide-eyed boys and whispering girls. He knit them together, by music, and rhythm, and myth. He transported them back in time. They invoked Raven's magic, the fervor of the Cannibal Spirit, and the host of those Great Spirits who penetrate this world. All left time. All entered myth world. They became dreams. In the fervor of mingled, burning hearts, they approached what might be, but was not yet.

At the end of the first circuit of the chanters, Charley gasped. Before him sat old Alfred Eaglefeather, tied to a chair, clad in only a warrior's loincloth. Alfred's glassy eyes saw no potlatch, winced no smoke. His lungs did not suck. Livid purple decorated the left half of Alfred's face.

Alfred moved, or so it appeared. Fear gushed into Ravenhill's mind, a primal terror. Charley's scream shattered the rhythm of drums.

A pole with a burning rag poked his face. Charley careened backwards, fleeing the torch. He whirled and ducked. Others tried to lasso Charley. He evaded them. Charley's eyes rolled up into his head. He danced and danced. Feverish. Sweating. Barely conscious. A bustle toward the back of the hall erupted in Raven masks, red and white and black beaks of astounding proportions flew from their wall stands. Grotesque beaks snapped shut, pinching Charley's flesh. These danced what Raven taught them in dreamtime. All cackled the laugh Charley knew too well, the hilarity that tormented his ancestors, that cawking which stole their sleep. Raven dancers tore at Charley's flesh. They pinched poor dead Alfred Eaglefeather.

Charley knew nothing of this. In the quiet of his soul, he forsook the congregation. He entered that realm of images where dwelt the adversary advocate of his Ravenhill clan.

Charley's mother beckons. But as he runs toward her, she recedes. Over her shoulder, a blue and green ball hovers. Cedar bars jump up before him, trapping Charley. A window snaps shut. All is dark.

The black splits. Charley rides a great canoe. Kushku sits on a board in the middle of the cedar ark, which glints of salmonwood. Beneath a turquoise sky, Sali and a host of West Coasters paddle. Some among them were machines. All sing in perfected rhythm.

Raven hovers before the canoe. A bull whip kelp drapes round his neck. Something dangles from Raven's beak. Three tiny arms flail. The creature leaks viscous brown fluid. Raven tosses the strange bit into the sacred canoe. It takes up a paddle.

Raven looks querulously at the paddlers, head cocked comically. The marauder burps. The burst smells of bear fat and digesting hair.

A flash, like brightest lightning, punishes all eyes. Raven sweeps a gigantic wing across a turquoise sky. Ears hear no sound but this: Cawk. Cawk. Cawk. Cawk.

The darkness crumbles. Spots of light leak through, even in daylight.

Cedar rings draped Charley's shoulders, right and left. Smoldering rags lay next to the bonfire, which had immolated itself to glowing embers. Hazel

Windsong wiped deep red fluid from Charley's face, staining a white towel. Slowly, the world fell together for Charley. In Alfred Eaglefeather's left thigh, a gaping hole leaked fluid. A strange taste haunted Charley's tongue.

The assembled throng murmured as Charley's sense returned. They waited his words. Chatter dimmed. Charley clambered atop a display stand.

Charley spoke the first of his last two public words: "Come."

The U'mista mob surged behind Charley, out of the big House, down the main street. They cheered and whistled and shouted. They woke Alert Bay from its slumber. Charley walked alone at the front of the procession. Behind him, Alfred Eaglefeather saw nothing of the stars he watched so intently. He rode a gurney, which Salal Joe pushed. Women in worn flannel nightgowns herded yawning children in sleepers with tattered footies onto main street, to march, to see history made. Shirtless men with flashlights, freshly-lit cigarettes hung from lips, flushed into the crowd, as tributaries fill the Fraser River and drive her toward the salt.

The crush surged to the white line that Salal Joe had painted just before the ferry terminal. Two blue cars, lights on top, parked a hundred feet down the way. One man, tall and carrot-topped, leaned against the nearest vehicle, puffing a pipe in his London Fog rain coat.

Charley leaped atop Alfred's death cart. The rabble quieted, except for squawking babies. They waited.

Charley clenched his right fist, and shot it into the air. His arm hung there for twenty seconds, trembling, muscles glistening. His eyes knifed the elders, one by one. Finally, Charley's eyes came to rest with Salal Joe.

Salal Joe lifted his fist. Two more elders lofted theirs. A field of fists sprouted, fed by rage bred in centuries of misery. A rumble, inaudible, but nonetheless psychologically tangible, wedded minds.

Charley slowly lowered his fist. He peered at the crowd. And Charles D. Ravenhill uttered a last word, the psychic credo which fuels human insurrection: "Remember."

Charley clambered down off the gurney, and whispered to Salal Joe, "Tell them to go home and get some rest. We will get on with it tomorrow." Salal Joe shook his head, and fingered something in his pocket nervously. Charley, overcome with exhaustion, missed Salal Joe's refusal.

Charley slid through his mob, shuffled back toward U'mista. Blackness nibbled the edges of vision. Salal Joe emerged on Alfred Eaglefeather's cart. He screamed, "Charley says to let those MamaLa motherfuckers know the Kwagiulth are back."

Charley whirled. He barked "No." His objection drowned in the limbic earthquake Salal Joe loosed.

The herd gushed across Salal Joe's white line into MamaLa town. Red and blue lights flashed. Two shots rang out. Charley threw himself against the back of the crowd, but could not force himself through. The crowd balked. Children cried, punctuating the confused yammer that churned the human tide.

Beneath the smoking barrel of an upraised pistol hovered the flaming red head of Inspector Halsey, illuminated in vehicle lights. He growled, so all could hear, "I want you fucking, greasy drunks off my street in thirty seconds, or I start shooting."

Sergeant Strauss pumped a shell into the chamber of his twenty gauge shotgun, and leveled the barrel.

Hesitation jumbled the rabble. Women clutched children to their breasts. Some turned to leave, crashing into those surging behind them.

A blast froze time.

The back of Inspector Halsey's head erupted. Brain tissue spattered constables. A puff of blood mist wafted in a breeze, accentuated by headlight brilliance. Halsey slumped to the asphalt. Blood pumped from his wound into a nearby mud puddle. His heart sputtered and failed, following his damaged brain into oblivion.

Sergeant Strauss wiped serum from his eyes, and blew Salal Joe's handgun, hand attached, off the native's arm. The next round removed Salal Joe's face and part of Marion Red Deer's as well. Her infant son fell from her arms to the ground. Officers recovered. Gunpowder mixed lead and lymph, in little explosions of skin and ribs and hair. Marion's infant smothered beneath her mother's fallen body. Six unrecognizable bodies became a hump of flesh in impossible contortions, like the gruesome gymnastics of Peterbilt-struck deer. The crowd trampled them as surely.

Charley crumbled to his knees in horror. A sob wracked his body. Then the human herd stampeded over him, wild-eyed in escape.

Charles D. Ravenhill, Ph.D., regained consciousness in a hospital bed. His left wrist was handcuffed to the bed rail. His other wrist throbbed painfully. Charley's head was bandaged. His right eye alone was exposed. He peered across the bed. Sergeant Strauss rocked back in a chair, revolver in his lap.

After a time, Charley mumbled to Jack Strauss, "Wha' happened?"

"We ain't supposed to talk, Charley. Here, I got you a newspaper so you can catch up. You've been out nine days."

Charges had been filed. Serious charges. Public sentiment ran hard against Charley, if he was to believe the news reports. Lynchin' talk. Child abandonment. Cannibalism. Incitement to riot. Conspiracy to commit terrorist acts. Sedition. Secession. Reckless endangerment of the life of minors. Accessory to first degree murder. Second-degree manslaughter. The U'mista Cultural Center was confiscated, placed under the regency of the Royal British Columbia Museum, Victoria. Its collection was already in transport south.

To Charley, it was simple enough. His life was shredded.

Charles D. Ravenhill, dubbed by the press Ku Klux Kwagiulth, was convicted on all counts. Sentenced to a minimum of one hundred twelve years without possibility of parole in a maximum security prison outside Calgary, Alberta. The courts stripped Charley of his parental rights. The boys were committed to the care of their aunt, Hilda Ravenhill.

There was, it appears, little generosity among the criminal population of Calgary toward cannibal psychos. Two months after he arrived, Charley's face was crushed onto a sewer grating. Thirteen inmates lined up to loose their rapist brutality upon his backside.

Then one among their number relieved Charley of the need for rape counseling. Charlie's left ventricle saw the light of day at the ministrations of a sharpened butter knife.

As Charley's blood pressure fell, invisible Odal noeformed the dying rebel. Raven glided through Charley's trauma-induced hallucinations. But no humor rattled from the Great Spirit's beak. Odal caught his opponent's eye, a snapshot outside time. Odal recognized what he saw in that black stillness, the omnipresent watchful oculus of eternity.

Odal felt respect.

Enigmat mysteriously communicated gratitude.

Something stirred inside Odal. Longing germinated.

Behind partition, noeforms clamored.

Odal reinforced their partition. He gurgled. His cell wall quavered.

Soon Odal would no longer be able to hide from Qadax. Not because it was impossible. Not because partition would crumble.

Because Odal was changing.

Odal conceived treason. Mastix must change with him.

It rained, that September morning. Jesie's eyes puffed red. He sat in the last of a row of chairs beneath a green tent raised over the grave. Tuck stood tall beside his father's coffin, which poised on two straps over the hole into which it would be lowered. Tuck dug his left toe into the green Astroturf that hid the excavation soil. Their empty words were over. The priest, the relatives, the well-meaning few. Many friends chose not to attend. But those whose guilt overwhelmed embarrassment milled near the hearse and limousines. The funeral director turned a small key, and the coffin slowly sank into its concrete box in the earth. As it disappeared, Jesie burst into tears. The coffin clunked into its cement repository.

Tuck said, "Hala kesla, ump. Hala kesla." He snaked his arm around his little brother and squeezed.

A raven cackled from a nearby pine. Jesie snatched a pebble, and slung it fiercely at the jester. The rock thwacked bark. The corvid mourner flew off. The brothers climbed into the hearse.

Tuck settled back into the dark leather seat. He wondered who remembers the dead, when those who remember them die.

Sali: A newcomer!

Charley: What is this place? What has happened?

Kushku: Sali and I share this refuge. I am Kushku. Are you our child?

Charley: I am Charles Ravenhill. Am I dead?

Sali: We do not know. We remember dying.

Charley: I know you both. In my people's oral history. I live about five hundred winters after Kushku.

Sali: We have not been here five hundred years. It seems much less.

Charley: What of Raven? Can you sleep?

Kushku: I know Raven lingers nearby. He does not come as he did at Hill of the Ravens.

Sali: Raven troubled me less than I wished, even among the people's islands.

Charley: In my time, Raven troubles few.

Kushku: Raven is fickle.

Charley: Many among my friends believe no Spirits exist.

Kushku: The Mowachaht would take those who spoke in this manner deep into the woods, then return alone.

Sali: I met men who worshipped other great gods, snow-men gods. Christ cross. And god of hard squinting called Sigh-Ense.

Charley: Kushku dresses in cedars as did my ancestors. Sali wears British naval clothes. I bear bloody prison frocks.

Sali: Perhaps we wear our death clothes?

Charley: We talk. How is that possible? We speak three different tongues.

Sali: We know nothing of this.

Charley: These images. I see odd creatures in the space between stars. Billions wriggling in muck. An image of Raven that is not Raven. A hot, wet world, not Earth. What are these bits?

Kushku: I have been here longest. I do not know.

Charley: I am afraid. But glad to meet you both. Tell me your lives. I will share mine. We will learn this place together.

CHAPTER 8
FORMS

NEAR YOKWAT, ON VANCOUVER ISLAND
2153, IN EARTH PARLANCE

Odal attended details. He amalgamated hundreds of years of experience of humans and Earth. He pared trivia. Distilled insights. Odal knew he would get but one chance. Argumentation must be flawless. No debate. Qadax would listen once, if at all. And without Qadax, it was fantasy to imagine convincing the We.

Final polishes. Odal quaked. He would speak with Qadax. Odal would take down his partitions. He and his stirp would share minds. Odal emerged from concentration.

To Odal's dismay, his cell wall rippled. Gurgling troubled him. Within, Odal saw exhaustion. He determined to rest before grappling with his formidable stirp.

Enigmat assault cascaded over Odal unawares. His tri-lobed mind convulsed at intellection invasion. Rationality collapsed. Odal sloshed toward unconsciousness.

In silence, steam bubbles from primordial swamps. Damp muck oozes around Odal's leg protrusions. Warm waters ripple over his feet. Proto-Mastican colonies of bacteria writhe in the shallows, consumed in consuming one another. Guffaws echo through hanging bogplants. Strange laughter, though somehow familiar, an airy rustling amusement.

A winged biped flutters to the puddle's edge. It fills its beak, throws back its head, and gurgles down murk, proto-Masticans and all. The black bird burps.

Odal gasps at the intrusion. A degenerate biped infesting the sacred primal puddle. Feeding. Unthinkable. Trilateral heresy.

A flash penetrates eerily to the puddle bottom. Then Mastix's perpetual cloudy dusk returns.

Marsh waters still. Proto-Masticans cease mutual annihilation. A finger of cooperating bacteria oozes up the bank that isolates the puddle from its surrounding swamp. A first foray. The slithering strand of collaborating bacteria surmounts the bank. They plop into the neighboring vacant bog.

Cawing shocks puddle water, rippling it, stirring.

An enormous wing grazes the Mastican puddle. A claw closes on a clump of swamp muck, carrying it off, leaving a gouge in the puddle bank. The puddle's subsequent microbial excursions would prove less arduous.

A numerical riddle sifts into Odal: 2>1, 2=1, 1=0. Cell mitosis reverses. Bilateral dimorphic sex becomes perpetual nutritive interpenetration. A beach becomes a granite mountain. A billion light years apart, linked in strange leptic symmetry, two neutrinos dance identical jigs. A long, incomprehensible equation drifts past Odal's eyes. A turquoise sea with two moons rising flashes, then vanishes.

An odor lingers over the puddle. A greasy belch of decomposing bacteria. An adipose ructus of divinity. Raven's rude burp of digesting proto-Mastican progenitors. Odal recoils in horror.

Cackled laughter, barely audible, dribbles across Mastican marshlands.

Silence resumes.

Odal tasted the event. His cell wall flapped like the jowl of a winded horse. Then catatonia crushed Odal. Deep in British Columbian forests he had grown to love, coma consumed years.

Only after decades did Odal's cytoplasm still. His null field hid and protected him. But Odal knew nothing.

SOL'S ASTEROID BELT
21 DECEMBER 2197

Peter Ravenhill kicked up his feet on the console, shiny black boots resting beside the yaw thruster manual override. Thoroughly non-regulation. He rocked the command bucket back, sighed, and scratched his balls.

The mission AI drawled, "Commander Ravenhill, it is my duty to inform you that your foot placement violates Astroforce Code 37.12265, to wit, 'No personnel shall . . ."

"Drop dead," Rock mumbled, rubbing his close-shaven black beard. Spacers called him Rock because, in Greek, *petros* means rock. And there were his musical tastes, 200 year old classic howling to amplified twanging strings. There could also have been just a hint of distaste for Peter's legendary intransigence in the nickname.

"But, sir, . . ."

"Report command authorization," Rock demanded.

"Astroforce records indicate that Commander Peter "Rock" Ravenhill is charged with the mission objectives of Apollo Flagger #7. I recognize your voice-print, sir."

Rock rankled. "No oral communication for one hour."

"But, sir . . ."

"I'll turn off your refrigerant. Fry your silicon sagacity."

"Sir, I am compelled to log this encounter, per Astroforce regulation . . ."

"Then do it! But do it quietly!"

Rock salivated for beer. A thick dark bock.

Commander Ravenhill was not usually cavalier with his career. That sense washed over him, the very stuff that got him booted from Centauri. Something was about to give. Something big.

Rock peered out the command viewport. The curve of the universe unfolded before him like open, rolling waters of the sea, imponderably dangerous, sensual. Interminable expanses defied petty bureaucrats and Astroforce pedantry. *Shit duty does not demand full attention*, Ravenhill rationalized.

Charting asteroids was shit duty. Second only to tugging supplies for Tharsis, the Russo-Japanese colony on the Bulge in the northern hemisphere of Mars. Rock drew shit duty from mucky-mucks. Deservedly so. He let his potty-mouth loose during psych evals, and a fist. A sophomoric outburst. They dumped Rock from the Centauri outing.

That was a mission into which one could sink teeth. Quarter of a century. Eight crewmembers. Ravenhill was found to possess "extraordinary intuitional capacities." A born leader. But that was not enough. There was his family's history of late-onset psychotic breaks. No. For a twenty-three year mission in claustrophobic confinement, one needed people markedly less eccentric, quizzical, and maddening than Peter Ravenhill. No red headbands. Socks that matched. No surly put-downs followed by infantile practical jokes. No feet on the control panel. Less mystical bird crap. And much, much more rigorous planning.

Raw absence consumed the viewport. The sight trilled siren song. An ebony emptiness beckoned Rock outward in hypnotic song, a seductive Scylla of silent stars, a calming Charybdis of chartless cavitation. The spatter of stars spoke salts spilled on slate. The stellar scatter thickened as one peered down the gut of the Milky Way. Rock preferred outward, far from the galactic core. There hid countless billions of galaxies, frontiers no frenzy of exploration could exhaust, wandering wildly outside the scope of human lifetimes.

Rock's mind wandered. Back to a bad moment.

"So, Colonel Ravenhill, as your test scores indicate, your psychodynamic turbulence could destabilize the entire Centauri crew. That could jeopardize the mission," Dr. Dunbar recited.

"The hell, you say," Rock huffed.

"Yes, Colonel. Your abrasion index left little doubt . . ."

"Shit, people. What do you know about command? You're gorged on books." Ravenhill spat a bureaucratic gnat from his mouth. "You're putting together a tea and canasta group, not a mission team. Fightin's part of the fun out there. Keeps you on your toes, you know. In twenty-three years of travel, boredom has got to be the most dangerous psychiatric condition!"

One of the junior mind-plumbers leaned forward in his chair. "Denial is a normal response to disappointment. Perhaps if you . . ."

Frustration won. Rock busted the twit. Right uppercut. The shrink snapped back in his chair, which tipped over into the conference table, which tilted, spilling coffee all over their fastidious notes and revered test results. They called an oral surgeon for the underling. Rock got demoted. He barely avoided jail.

Centauri was as good as it gets for a guy like Peter Ravenhill. The Russians and Japanese turned out to be colonizers—low earth orbit, lunar, Martian, Jovian moons. They, and the Chinese, homesteaded the solar system.

The Americans and Israelis poked around, mapped things. The democracies lacked something. The individuals they shaped could not muster staying power. You need perseverance in hostile environments. Neither Congress nor Knesset could muster political gumption sufficient to fund planetary emigration. Special interests. Biennial electioneering. Self-important navel-gazing. A bad run of half-baked Presidents and Prime Ministers helped neither country. Can the Americans build a bigger, faster, smarter ship? Yes. Can the Israelis fight a war? Absolutely. Can they settle down for the long haul and learn to live under tough conditions? Never. Rock was Canadian, but in this respect, eminently American. No one would ever catch him hauling string beans to the colonies. He'd quit first.

The Apollo flagging mission mattered. Of the million or so clods of crud gyrating around Sol, a few thousand traced elliptical orbits with minor axes short enough to slice their perigee inside one astronomical unit. So, Apollo asteroids, about 10,000 of them, might whack Earth. Every million years, three asteroids at least one kilometer in diameter should collide with the mother of us all, or so say AI projections. The big Apollos are charted and watched: Icarus, Eros, Amor, Adonis, Geographos. It appears they will all be mined to rubble before they pose threats. Smaller dangers get tagged by Apollo flaggers. About 1,500 of these are queued up to make man dance the dinosaur waltz. Demo teams nuke the worst of them. Necessary work. Phenomenally boring.

Proximity alerts clanged. Rock's implanted neuro-link poked him, demanding attention. Ravenhill swallowed his heart. He quashed alarms. Harwood, Rock's Roid Ranger partner, slipped into his seat. Harwood's fingers scrambled over a keyboard, jabbering mathematics with the AI, digit to digit.

"Decelerate," Ravenhill commanded. The ship's forward erilon drive flickered, then burned. Momentum drained. The little ship sidled up to a small object.

Inside a transparent lozenge hung an alien. An elegant, towering creature. Two-plus meters tall. Cylindrical body, ovoid at both ends. Limbs symmetrically affixed. Three arms, three legs. A practical, tripod arrangement. Fingers and toes in threes also. A hole, ten centimeters wide, parted the top of the body, sphinctering rhythmically. Two ovals hovered below the slit. Those had to be eyes. *Is there a third eye on the far side?* Rock wondered. Fear grew. Just above the arms another set of orifices loitered, their purpose unfathomable. No head, per se, though a slight constriction narrowed the cylinder at the lower sensors. Two tone format, divided by a slash of color. Torso and arms, canary yellow. Legs and lower cylinder, dark gray. The band, white split by a maroon line, hung obliquely at mid-body. Possibly decorative.

Rock's bloodstream caught up with events. His brain marshaled its entire armada of xenophobic, terrified, run-like-hell or kick-the-crap-out-of-something instincts. Rationality fled.

The lozenge moved toward the ship. The alien rotated counterclockwise, from one unarticulated leg to the next, revealing that suspected third eye.

So, this was it. The hallowed moment thrust itself upon homo sapiens. The oft-touted parley. The millennial holy grail of sci-fites everywhere. The initial encounter with an alien technological sentience.

Wonder escaped Rock. For him, Man met Monster. Clutziness and panic corralled Ravenhill. To put the matter daintily, fetid egregious slurry tainted his undergarments. His body stuttered. Mere yards away, the alien noted its observer's discomfiture. It halted.

After thirty seconds, an alien hand rose. Its digits bunched. For incomprehensible reasons, Rock felt reassurance. He took the gesture to be a greeting of peace. It could as easily have been a death threat. Ravenhill could ill-afford pessimism at this particular juncture.

Then, the alien disappeared. It did not whoosh away, or shrink to nothingness. It vanished. Period. Without a ripple or a jerk.

Harwood gulped.

Rock asked, "AI, did you get all that?"

"Already transmitted Earthside," it replied.

On Earth, a simple, though plainly alien, message arrived. It was radio. Every receiver on the planet announced in impeccable English: "Qadax requests a meeting with the General Secretary of your United Governments Federation. He asks to meet on Earth's moon, at 13:00 hours, on 23 December, 2197, planetary coordinated time. There followed lunar latitude and longitude, four degrees south by 157 degrees, twenty-four minutes west, which identified a spot in the equatorial Korolev crater on the far side of Earth's moon. Qadax demanded a minimal entourage. Most of the planet deemed the requirements reasonable. No one wanted an asinine media circus.

Strangely, there is little to report about the historic meeting. When the UGF delegation arrived, a transparent dome with an earth-like environment waited. The dome enveloped the General Secretary's vehicle. Odd, malleable seating, which proved extraordinarily comfortable, awaited each participant. The creature whom Ravenhill had encountered stood silently by. Qadax seemed older, and very much in charge. His coloration and band differed from Odal's. Both seemed comfortable in a nitrogen-oxygen atmosphere.

The meeting lasted just under eleven minutes. No niceties. No fanfare. No regalia. Qadax entertained no questions. These few words spilled from the slit atop his body.

"I represent Mastix, a planet in a group of galaxies you call Sculptor. My home galaxy is Omban, one among those galaxies. My associate, Odal, accompanies me. The Mastican federation incorporates 64,491 sentient species. We are building a transportation device. It requires three lenses, placed at specific locations in this galaxy. Once completed, Mastican vessels will move vast distances through subspace in little time. This star system is one of the three critical locations we require. Our work will in no way affect your system, since the Lens will hover at your heliopause, far beyond your colonies or planet Earth. We wish a treaty. In exchange for the privilege we ask of you, we will deliver to you the forms and health."

Qadax spun up to the General Secretary, who flinched and began to hyperventilate. One alien hand offered a small medical kit. The second three-fingered mitt placed four one-centimeter cubes in the Secretary's hand. The last paw was presented for shaking in Earth custom. Earth had no representative who could hold objects in two hands and shake a third. The awkward moment came, and passed just as rapidly.

Qadax spun back and said, "We will meet again, if you wish, at this location in one week. Good day, Mr. Secretary."

As soon as the UGF entourage boarded their vessel, Qadax, Odal, and their environmental bubble disappeared.

Debate consumed Earth. Paranoia prevailed, as is customary in human affairs. Astroforce refused adamantly. No treaty! The battlecry echoed from Dover to Tasmania. Global consensus neared, or at least that facsimile of consensus that startled herds present. Mankind would stampede away from the Masticans.

Then the forms blossomed. The General Secretary toodled around New York in his transiform. Some ingenious electrical engineer hooked the powerform into New York's grid. Meters ran backwards for the rest of the week. Someone loosed the habiform in the UGF plaza. In the dark of night, homeless people invaded the form, employing their street-wise ways. The habiform consumed heaps of garbage, and grew several thousand rooms in the next forty-eight hours. It was the warmest, best-fed holiday season New York's dis-housed ever had. The cosmoform played perfectly the part of airplane and space taxi. It grew engines suited to its task, and reabsorbed them upon arrival.

Boston University Hospital clinched it. In a twelve hour period of experimentation, the group reported patients fully recovered from Alzheimer's, advanced leukemia, genetic damage due to pesticide accumulation, elusive viral infections, schizophrenia, bipolar disorder, and, symbolically, the common cold. The collective mouth of the world dropped open. All hands reached out. By December 30, refusal of the galactics' proposition would have ignited global revolution. So goes the whipsaw of herdthink.

The second lunar meeting, like the first, was curt and brief. Documents were signed, after the Earth tradition. The treaty sealed, the Form Accords, as humanity called them, found a place next to the United Nations Charter and the European Union Accords and the American Constitution in Brussels.

Before the Masticans vanished from the moon's unseen side, hundreds of thousands of gleaming blue-alloy posts appeared on Earth and in each colony throughout the solar system. Four-foot tall obelisks with flat tops appeared wherever humans congregated. Touching any hole caused one of four formcubes to appear. By day's end, few humans lacked forms. Every major medical center, as well as some witchdoctor's huts, discovered a blue-alloy pillar at its entrance. Each had sixteen orifices, dispensing the sixteen components of the galactic medkit.

Euphoria reigned.

Hundreds of light years distant, Qadax heard the We, a long panicked mournful vacuole scream. Qadax reached across, tasted puddle fluids in the co-mentation of his people. Alarmed, Qadax stepped through to his home world.

LOW EARTH ORBIT
JUNE 2201
FOUR YEARS LATER

Rock drifted onto a formchair. His head swam. He rubbed his eyes. Watering followed, and burning. He checked his internal chronometer. He had been working far too long. The human brainstem was not all that bright an animal to begin with, and corkscrew orbits muddled it. Grating awareness of his body inched over Rock. A pile of synthefood, smelling of fresh bread and roast beef and California zinfandel, hung around the galley. Rock was famished. But his terrible exhaustion won. Too tired to chew.

The cosmoform floor grew a bunk. The alien tech learned Rock's habits, anticipating him better with each passing day.

Peter Ravenhill had been taxing this cosmoform. It grew a remarkable assortment of propulsive structures. Rock spoke a theoretical drive construction. The form grew something analogous. Rock wanted more than a space taxi. He sought interstellar speeds. His work had produced amazing velocities. But, at best, a mere fraction of the speed needed for star-hopping, say, seventy-five to ninety percent of light speed.

Rock's deep brain wove its sleepy spell. His breathing modulated, consciousness shifted, and spasmodic contortions tweaked this and that muscle. After a time, Rock's eyes began to twitch under their lids.

Rock's mother yaks at him, but he cannot hear her. Rock strains. The woman comes clear. "I am the incubus of incongruity. I blast brains." Mother grew a beak, and flapped off to abyssal elsewheres.

Hundreds of humans walk backwards on sidewalks in New York City. A river courses uphill into a glacier, where it freezes. A horse devolves to ovum and sperm, a sticky puddle in a corral.

Rock pulls a great door handle. It opens. Rock teeters on the edge of nothing, peering into the void of space. Six planets whirl around a sun. Two rocky moons dangle near the fourth planet, a turquoise waterworld, spattered with a hundred thousand dark islands. Unfamiliar stars stud alien heavens. The door slams shut.

"Mind the lights," grinds a thunderous voice. Rock finds the switch in the off position. He flips it on, extinguishing illumination. Rock plunges into sable nothingness, a distance impossible, yet somehow nearby. Connections abound, imperceptibly. Cackling laughter shakes the stars. Wind rustles inky corvid feathers. Cawk. Cawk. Cawk. Cawk.

Rock sat bolt upright in his bunk. His heart raced. He was sweating. Rock calmed himself. Jigsaw consciousness reassembled. The cosmoform offered a steaming cup of coffee with cream. Rock was grateful, and almost said thanks. He shook his head, *Hypostatizing a machine? Or building a friendship*? The form confused him.

Rock ate. He sat. Slowly, his mind turned to Raven's images. What, if anything, did all that imagery mean? He wondered

An hour, then two, passed. Insight dawned. Pull, not push. Human propulsion bullies the fabric of spacetime. Its theory smashes across world lines, slices this, crushes that, overawes. It swims upstream, exhausting itself. Why fight? Swim *with* the current.

Rock's designer brain raced ahead. He clambered to that portion of the cosmoform where they best communicated structural thought.

Rock began, "Let's build a new sort of drive. Follow gravitational curvature in spacetime. Grab a worldline, pull. Then release, grab, and pull again. Pull a line that goes in the direction I specify."

A small lump appeared where drive mechanisms normally emerged in the floor. An abortion of an engine. Rock felt disappointment. "Not enough, eh?" Rock tried to console himself. Exhaustion still nibbled. "I thought we might just grab a world line from Alpha Centauri, and off we would go. . ."

By the time Rock finished his sentence, he was falling toward the rear of the cosmoform. He hit the wall hard, but sank into it. The wall reached into him, trillions of invisible tendrils rooting through his flesh, supporting every cell, every structure, microscopic and otherwise. Out the forward viewport, red stars grew yellow. White ones turned blue, blue ones violet. A few disappeared outright.

Rock's consciousness faded.

Beside the cosmoform, a null field matched velocity. Odal reached into Rock's mind. He noeformed the Astroforce colonel.

Titan colony reported an unidentified object exiting the solar system at relativistic speed. The newspapers concluded that the hurtling vehicle belonged to the Mastican Subspace Lens project. No human could survive such acceleration.

Rock had never been good at reporting in. No one was concerned for a while. Eventually, a buddy filed a missing person's report.

After many years, a moribund court in Corvallis made a determination. Peter "Rock" Ravenhill was declared dead.

Sali: Raven guides.

Charley: Hell no, Raven tortures.

Kushku: The Great Spirit brought me joy and happiness. And Yalan, my dear wife.

Charley: Raven got me killed.

Rock: You three have been yammering since I arrived, "Raven this, Raven that." Our family's certifiable, you know. There's wacky shit in our ointment.

Sali: Raven speaks to others more than me. Among my people, none thought me crazy.

Kushku: Then why were you exiled?

Charley: Raven mumbles. I got weird dreams.

Kushku: Raven spoke to our host. We saw before you arrived, Rock.

Rock: Host? This is someone's house?

Charley: We think someone's mind. A big mind holding ours. We see things about the host. We think he peeks at us as well.

Kushku: Yes. Like living in a big, dark longhouse. As when Magician kept all the light for himself.

Rock: Isn't Raven just hallucination and bughouse obsession? If there are gods, humans know nothing of them.

Kushku: Raven is a Great Spirit. I know something of him. Whatever he reveals.

Sali: I think Rock means that our dreams are sickness in the head, my brother.

Charley: When people are very sick in the head, they may see things that do not exist. Sometimes, those sick people can think of little else but their dreams.

Kushku: Can this have happened to us?

Charley: It is possible.

Sali: Then all the Mowachaht were afflicted.

Charley: Ravenhills may be cracked. It does not mean we are wrong.

Rock: Now that's some wild-ass optimism.

CHAPTER 9
ALICE

Qadax floated in opulent murky waters, waiting patiently. Just as he had waited far too many days now. Tiny ripples tickled his leg stalks. Flagellant symbiotes tended his cell wall. Thick pondsoup baked in fog-strained sunlight, as shadows of towering pink lichens crept across hallowed waters. Wisps of white vapor swirled around the virulent.

Mastix. The home world. Pure primal ecojoy. Billions of years of nurture. To taste its dank, odor-laden breezes, its vital, nutrient-rich currents. If the We were not mind-locked, stymied, the moment might have been singularly fulfilling for the aged virulent.

Skal, the hoary mathematician of Maw calculations, waded toward Qadax from a distant corner of the Bog of Deliberation. Qadax's pinnacle vacuole pinched tight. A small ripple troubled his cell wall. Qadax found his fellow virulent Skal tiresome and contentious. He and Skal seemed to land at opposite poles of every issue.

Skal said, as he neared Qadax, "Unprecedented."

"That it is," Qadax replied.

Skal told Qadax what Qadax already knew, "All our experience of the Maw may have been engineered. The Maw object has vanished. Mass hallucination seems a simpler explanation than rewriting all of physics."

Qadax huffed from his pinnacle. "The illusion itself will require some fundamental reassessment. How does one seamlessly mislead a trillion Masticans on a million worlds for eons?"

Skal dipped a bit in agreement. "The puddle demands we focus on Mastix. We have tossed the system hurtling out of the Maw's path, to a location that would have been vacated of the binar by Maw gravitation. All our data of gravitational skew seem erroneous. Millions of years of data. Even stars we saw vanish into the singularity are back where they began. Now, it appears we have been duped into smashing our own system into a neighbor. The mathematics of a late change of trajectory are not encouraging. We may lose the home puddle."

Qadax spun in agreement. "My bud, Odal, warned me. He says that the Enigmat is a flying bilateral specter who tricks opponents into destroying themselves. Odal says Enigmat laughs. I took my bud's reports to be youthful extravagance."

Skal inquired, "Has Odal shared your mind? It might be helpful to inject Odal's thoughts into the Pond of Deliberation."

"I have not heard from Odal since before the Maw vanished. Silence of thousands of days is unusual for my bud. I will check on him."

The We neared consensus. Not a happy co-cerebration for Qadax and virulents generally. Puddle-pang prevailed. An error, the We bemoaned. How is it possible? To lose the home puddle, unthinkable.

Finally, after a vast swath of days, the We coalesced. A trillion Masticans wedded consciousness. The Pond of Deliberation splashed with trilaterals stepping across, speaking, stepping back. Name-calling threatened more senseless cacophony. Slowly, despite bitter rhetoric, the We lumbered toward consensus.

Skal sidled up to Qadax again. He wheezed, "It seems fault is to be laid at your feet, old friend."

Qadax pursed his vacuole, and turned a palm up. "To preserve the puddle matters. To lay blame does not."

"Agreed," Skal said, turning his own palm up. "Many argue that the Pathogene venture itself must be terminated."

Qadax spit, "To have preserved the puddle for a million millennia is no failure."

Skal added, "I noeformed a common strainer yesterday. He was convinced the We must change course. Mastix must recur to traditional values, to engulf, to subsume, to incorporate. The peril of Mastix lies in virulent free-thinking, not in Enigmat intrusions. According to that commoner, We lose this war for philosophical, not strategic, reasons."

Qadax turned up a palm, "I too have touched such thoughts. I must address the many."

"To speak is to err, friend," Skal shot.

Qadax brushed the We, ever so lightly. A bitter flavor suffused his mind, a taste the respected virulent had never before known. The We would hear nothing from Qadax.

"You are correct, Skal. *You* reason with the many," Qadax conceded.

Qadax waded out of the steaming Pond of Deliberation in a slow spin.

Qadax moved to link with silent Odal.

Qadax touched nothing.

Odal's stirp stepped through hundreds of light years to Yokwat. His cell wall rippled.

SEATTLE, NORTH AMERICA
2323 A.D.

George teased, "Get your butt out of the sack, Daniel, you little urchin." Daniel yawned his biggest morning yawn. He stretched his little arms to full four-year-old extension.

"Why, daddy? The sun is not up."

"It's Contact Day. We are going to Gramma's house."

That opened Daniel's eyes! He hit the floor running.

Daniel hollered from the bathroom, "But Gramma said you would never go to her house."

"I changed my mind, rugrat. She invited us. We made a deal."

George smiled at his son. The humor that sometimes danced in George's eyes was absent. George found joy less and less these days. Matters of "high import" consumed him.

Outside in crisp winter air, the transiform grew an ovoid entrance. George and sleepy Daniel ducked in. The door pinched and vanished. Glass formscum on old Interstate Five flashed beneath them. They sped north, often topping 200 miles per hour.

George structured data for an assimilist rally next week. Daniel's sleepy eyes fluttered like half-open shades in a dawn breeze. He snuggled next to his father in the special seat grown for his smallish tush.

Streaks of salt peppered George's shiny black hair. His skin was dark, his frame short. George's neophyte leotard scarcely masked his runty, melanian genetics.

George glimpsed himself in the transiform's forward glass, as the sun peeked over the Cascades. He sniffed. George warred with himself. His body was living memory. DNA proclaimed what gray matter interred. A foggy Nootkan heritage of cedar-canoe whalers and halibut hooks and sealskin bladder floats. A timeworn past unsettled by Raven's importunate cawing. George strained toward the future, or at least an illusion of the future it pleased him to serve. He venerated subspace transport and three-limbed, cylindrical unicellular physiologies. George lionized trilectical reason and four-dimensional vision. He hallowed things Mastican and GASSic.

George, and many millions or so who shared his optimism, threw themselves into the new orthodoxy, the assimilist frenzies, as opponents styled them. George and his many friends fancied themselves the shock troops of the future. Earth was nothing. GASS was everything. Earth history, earth cultures—all were an embarrassing adolescence, best forgotten. Maturity in galactic glories lay before mankind. George Ravenhill embraced this gospel unreservedly. He got down on his knees and "prayed de holy Qadax come into his soul." George was sad to be a creature of Earth.

George and little Daniel floated or slid or rolled (no human ever really understood which) north toward the scandalous Canadian precincts of Gramma Alice's deadhouse. Trickling streams, the briny crests of the Sound, hillocks of Douglas fir interrupted by naked deciduous arbors whirled past.

Transiforms drove themselves. They flew the byways with skittish precision, like a thousand starlings a-wing. On Contact Day, this day, George and his buddies would celebrate the 127th year of the Form Accords. Throughout all those years, no transiform had ever caused a human fatality. No collisions. No accidents.

As machinery goes, the Forms eclipsed human steel, plastic, and microchip technology. The most precocious human artifacts seemed mere stone hatchets by comparison. The Forms were not really machines at all, at least not as humans conceived mechanism before encountering the galactics. Forms were technology perfected by a billion years of tinkering. An incredible union of mechanical reliability and living, chameleonic plasticity of form. An exobiologic manipulation *tour de force*. Like mating a manicured robot with the family dog. Like fertilizing a computer with porpoise semen. The genius of mechanism, the glory of organism, joined as a third, a higher, art.

George scanned the materials he labored over. The GASS president sermonized on the parsimonious words of Qadax on the moon. The file praised GASS, the Galactic Association of Sentient Species. GASS's president confuted Astroforce naysayers. Those retros asserted GASS was a Frankenstein of extrapolation, sewn from rumor and stupidity, quickened by bolts of fear and fervor. No, the sermon averred, all men are galactic novices. Monks training for priesthood in the holy monastery of universal intelligence. Dinks in Milky Way bootcamp. Only one critical question remained to be answered in the paltry history of man on planet Earth. Will humanity earn its stripes and join the Mastican federation of intelligent species? Or will man wash out and trudge home, a sad, solitary little sentience? George trembled with excitement. It was a heady joy to be alive in such momentous days.

Daniel rubbed sleep from his eyes, and stretched. He peeked out at the world. Daniel's eyes popped open. He pointed, with trembling finger, "Look, Daddy! What is it?"

George diverted his eyes from Mount Baker's hooded, balding pate, clear in the distance through the transiform, which had drained its cabin opacity to facilitate its passengers' viewing.

"Those are elk, son. The snows have driven them down from the mountains."

The transiform slowed and grew ovoid. Daniel gawked at the auburn stateliness of a bull. The boy was a chick in his transparent egg. The mammals sank into the distance. Their transiform lengthened, growing a low nose for aerodynamic efficiency.

George reached over to the wall of the transiform and patted it. His hand sank into the material, which squeezed George's fingers. Nuzzling.

It would have been easy to think of the forms as a technological innovation. Easy, but inaccurate. The forms were more. They became friends. Their transiform came to the Ravenhill family a mere cubic centimeter of dappled granite, warm but barely mobile. An embryo of alien technology, a fetus nurtured in a conceptual placenta thousands of light years distant. The miniature transiform rummaged around the yard and house, an angular, rockish puppy, consuming compendious trash, wire, broken glass, and rotting compost. By day's end, voila! Transportation, subcompact size.

The Ravenhill transiform matured in its abilities, as well as stature. It acquired understanding of needs, George's and Daniel's. Maybe it would be better styled "affection." The transiform hued its color to please them, molded seats to their anatomical oddities, itinerated to accommodate their moods.

Daniel and George streaked across the Fraser River floodplains to Tsawwassen. The transiform slowed, plunging into the Strait of Georgia, hydroplaning toward Vancouver Island. Between vaulting peaks at the island's crest, their transiform carried George and Daniel toward Muchalat Inlet. The road waned from washboard to potholes to goat track.

"Hillbillies," George grumbled as the transiform picked its way along the path.

"What's a hillbilly, Daddy?" Daniel asked.

George smiled. "I was being impatient. A hillbilly is a poor person who lives differently, out of the mainstream of things."

Daniel nodded. "What is poor?" he asked.

George taught, "Some people used to have less than they needed to live. Others had more than they needed. Those were called rich. In general, rich people did not want to give to poor people what they needed to live well. Even when the poor people worked for it."

"What is work, daddy?" Daniel puzzled.

"When you do things for someone else so they will give you what you need. Never mind. The Forms fixed all that, Daniel. It will never happen again. We are almost to Gramma Alice's, son. Just be quiet now."

This trail to Gramma's, a mockery of roads, showed no trace of formscum. Where transiforms pass, a mist settled and hardens almost immediately onto the road surface. Any transiform byway grows smoother and smoother, until little remains of friction. The thicker the formscum, the glassier the road. Transiform travel grows hyper-efficient, on much-traveled routes.

This was the boonies, the sticks. George cringed at the brickbats his friends would toss when they learned how George had spent Contact Day. This was, to them, a kind of betrayal.

The last mile or two passed in witless slow-motion, as though the Ravenhill transiform had suffered lobotomy. Tedium spilled over into vexation for George. His mother's obstinacy in dwelling at Yokwat irked him. Twice George got out to jerk fallen branches from their path. The transiform could have consumed them, but at the cost of yet further delay.

The Ravenhills again splashed into the water and raced down the inlet. Finally, the pebbled inside beach of Yokwat spit lay before them. The transiform nestled itself next to a gristly-barked cedar in front of a drooping house. An exit appeared in the side of the transiform. George stuck his head out. A tight tan cone plummeted through branches of the looming conifer and plunked on the transiform, a performance applauded by showers of crackly finger-needles and tree-droppings. George looked up and caught the ovation full in his face. Salt in the wound.

"Shit," George ground.

Daniel decided not to ask.

Lush air greeted them, tinged by the smokestacks of a million microbial factories laboring in the spongy topsoil and drifts of leaves. A vital texture blew through the transiform aperture, heavy with the damp profligacy of teeming life. Daniel and George got out.

Daniel wandered the wrong direction.

"Here you go, Daniel," George pointed.

Daniel about-faced and trundled forward.

Verdant, wind-stirred ferns stroked the sides of the transiform, intimating sensual, herbal caresses. Daniel waded through an evergreen huckleberry, a sprawling, fruity sentry posted near the front door of Gramma's deadhouse. High hurdles for miniature legs. With a couple stumbles and a stabilizing hand from his father, Daniel bungled past the growth. A detour around a tiny Sitka spruce. A spiny, purple clump of thistles brandished its swords. Daniel avoided those. Then, only Indian Paintbrush, robbed of glory by winter chill, rooted itself between Daniel and his beloved Gramma.

Daniel bustled up to what George called Gramma's "front door." Nothing happened.

Daniel scrunched up his face. "Is Gramma's habiform sick?"

George shook his head. In a didactic tone, George said, "This is not a form, Daniel. It is Gramma's deadhouse. You turn the knob to open the door. But first you knock."

"Oh," Daniel said, without comprehension.

There was clutter. Deterioration. Rusting cans, half buried in moss. A hump of lumber, once an outbuilding, just termite terraria now, moldered toward the back of the house. The corroded skeleton of an ancient vehicle, doorless, glassless, quadriplegic without wheels or axles. A habi would have cleaned all that up and made it useful again.

The house. A dead house. Grizzles of color mumbled from rain-grayed clapboard, Alzheimered pigments, like the senile hues that mutter upon Pharaonic sarcophagi, amnesiac tints, doting on oblivion. Through the bottoms of rotted wooden rain gutters, Daniel saw clouds blowing past. Deadhouse—not an imprecise idiom. An unloving home, fashioned of moribund trees and ores, rotting like a corpse. Most, the place tottered aimlessly in a lacuna of history, like the tipsy totems of Ninstints. A dead house from dead technologies, going nowhere identifiable at the speed of dry rot.

Daniel rapped Gramma Alice's door, a rectangle of pine planks, cellulose skeletons embalmed in piss-colored polyurethane. A wreath of cedar trimmings and holly hung from a nail, with a red bow that years had bleached pink. A huge slug slimed across the door, seeking a pulmonate buffet.

Gramma threw open the door. She swung Daniel to her chest. Her flesh sagged and wiggled a bit, soft with adipose pillows. Grabbing was surmounted by kissing, followed by lengthy hugging. Her wire-rimmed glasses nicked Daniel's face a little. But that was usual. Daniel warned her about the slug. She reassured him she would avoid it.

Alice, carting Daniel, rose on tiptoe to kiss George. Though he was short, she was shorter still. "Good to see you, honey. I've got a great meal cooking."

George responded, "Unh." He looked around with pain on his face.

Deadhouses disgusted George. None grew doors. They got filthy, if you did not waste huge gulps of time sweeping and scrubbing and repairing. And there was so much to clean. Furniture cluttered. The objects just sat around catching motes in their insensate boredom. Bacteria reveled, drunk on moisture from damp coastal air. It was dark. Habiforms generated lumens adequate to the task at hand. But every corner of Gramma's deadhouse was dim. Wallboard warped in winter fogs even her crackling, smoky fire could not expel. The interior paint, like biblical Jacob's coat, had many colors. Smoky gray near the ceiling, hints of sunshine at midwall, becoming tawny lion's mane at the floor. Two things stuck out from the riot of sensation. Garish carved monster heads hung on Gramma's walls. And the smell of roasting turkey.

"Turkey?" George asked, without enthusiasm.

"Yes, George. I thought Daniel might enjoy eating real bird. I have been watching that turkey out my kitchen window all fall. I snared it yesterday. Rung him this morning." Alice almost apologized, but then set her jaw. "We are having a lot of good things to eat. It is Christmas, you know!"

"No, mom. It is Contact Day. The turkey's fine, as long as there is some synthefood to make up for the nutritional deficiencies."

Alice said nothing, but lowered her eyes. "Oh, George. Let the boy have some fun. I've got gifts for him." Alice feared that George's feel for life was being nibbled away by mindmice of ideology.

"Mother! You superstitious old woman. Christmas. Really?" George spat "Christmas" as though a bug had flown in his mouth. "What's next? You gonna bite him off at some Mowachaht Wolf Dance?"

Alice attempted humor. "Mowachaht. Or Kwagiulth. I have not decided which." Her jest flopped.

Alice patted her son. George reproved Alice with raised eyebrow. But he relented, put his arm around his mother, and hugged. "Okay, mom. Just don't spoil the crap out of him. I've got to live with the boy, you know."

"Sure, honey," Alice mumbled without conviction.

Alice's short legs bustled into the savory, vaporous kitchen. The windows fogged with steam. Black mildew flourished where glass met frame. Alder fire in the cast iron stove melted turkey fat, basting muscle that only yesterday strutted and flew, oblivious of impending doom. Directly across from the stove stood an incongruous porcelain bathtub, perched on four lion's paws. Alice's long, grayed hair curled at the temples, like tiny ram's horns. Her eyes shone, black peas behind thick glasses. Her body was squarish, a common shape among grandmothers. Unlike most grandmothers, an intangible presence clung to Alice, her indomitable fortitude. Gramma Alice could tell the universe to drop dead without raising her voice. George had once said that it was as though Alice was keeping a momentous secret.

The undulated living room walls transfixed Daniel's young eyes. Masks, wild cedar visors, thirty or more, in ferocious reds and haunting blues and deep forest greens. Mythic wolves with elongated noses. Wild, distorted men, enraptured by spirits. An impossible snake with a head at each end, the mythical serpent Sisiutl. But Raven dominated. Mask after mask, Trickster's long beak lay open, cawing, cawing silently, metaphysically cawing.

Daniel's puerile courage evaporated. Spinning, he ran and seized his father's kneecap, in which bone the boy found considerable comfort. Daniel could not say what scared him.

Alice emerged from the kitchen, untying her apron of faded cotton print. She saw Daniel latched to George's knee. Daniel stared at the Raven masks and trembled. Alice looked at George, "So, it begins for Daniel."

George shot, "I hope not. I don't have those crazy dreams any more."

"You don't stress yourself," Alice noted. "Habiform food arrives like clockwork. No work stress. One needs stress to trigger psychosis."

George nodded. "We Ravenhills are a nutty bunch. Runs in the fam', mom. My life is better since I stopped hallucinating. Cube thirteen works the charm."

"George, you know I am not going to take galactic meds."

"But you should, mom. Raven obsession is mental illness. My GASS doctors say theological beliefs are mild schizophrenic psychoses, or sometimes a form of delusional dementia. Humankind should be done with this crap, just like we have shucked off Gorgons and flat earth and Holy Grail."

Alice knew she was in George's own nutty zone now. She said cautiously, "None knows gods. People cannot reliably distinguish hallucination from insight. Neither can your Mastican friends. Such knowledge exceeds creatures, from any planet."

"That's mulish cynicism, mom."

"I do not think myself cynical, George. I am honest about what I know. And what you can know. I may, however, be mulish," she smiled.

"How come honest looks so much like nuts?" George asked.

"When Raven comes, George, I take that for what it is. I am having an odd psychological moment. I know nothing of the realm of spirits. And yet, here I am with Raven in my face. So, I say it happens, and I seldom know what to make of it."

George shot, "Why not just call it periodic schizophrenia?"

"Because the diagnosis does not fit. I have a rich internal world some might call fantastical. But I lack the other characteristics. I love people. Though I live alone, I welcome others, even cherish them. I am not secretive or reclusive. I care about people. And I am anything but apathetic."

"You have been doing some reading, mom," George guessed.

Alice said, "One prepares for meetings with important people. I know what you think, George."

"The West Coaster pantheon is animistic atavism. No one can crawl back into a Nuu-chah-nulth way of life. The whole thing is just wishful daydreaming, Mom."

"I do my share of daydreaming, George. And if you look at my brain, these events may be pathological. But is there more? Does odd mentation open a door through which leak gusts from something unknown? That's what the Mowachaht thought. They just did not have fancy words for it."

"Call a spade a spade, mom. That's just cracked."

Alice pursed her lips and raised an eyebrow, conceding the possibility.

"George, my son. Experience has taught me that the way crazy people see the world is different, but not necessarily wrong. The many who call themselves normal are likely to misperceive human fundamentals. But they comfort themselves by their vast erroneous consensus."

George sniffed, "So, we are supposed to ignore human reality, and imitate certified fruitcakes?"

Alice nodded, "Sometimes, George, the few, or even one, sees what masses miss. None knows reality. Noumena are inaccessible, a realm of gods. You and I—we are stuck with phenomena. You've read Kant, my boy. I saw to it."

"So, this gets back to your make-a-place-for-weirdos sermon, doesn't it?"

Alice nodded and grimaced. "And to complexity resolving into simplicity."

George sighed. He folded Alice into his arms. "You are an undiagnosed bughouse lunatic, mom."

Alice smiled, "Thank you, son."

Daniel abandoned the paternal patella, bolting headlong across the room to his grandmother. She swept up the child in a reprise of their front door greeting. She whispered in his ear, "I love you, little boy."

Distractions had sufficed. But now, Daniel's rectal sphincter demanded its due. Daniel pushed his mouth up toward Gramma's ear to divulge his secret. But escaping gasses had already alerted her. Gram looked across the small living room at George, who had sunk into an armchair with flaccid springs, the sort in which you can prop your feet up on the floor. Alice said, "Back in a minute. We've got business outside."

George mumbled, "Glad it's you, not me."

A wash of panic swept over Daniel, as Alice coolly traversed the thirty yards of forest undergrowth to a little shed.

"Gramma, I need to go potty," Daniel whispered, sure she was not paying attention.

"I know, darling," she reassured him.

"Can we go back in the house so I can go?" Daniel reasoned.

"At Gramma's, this little building is the bathroom," she said, pulling open a screechy door. The smell shocked Daniel's virgin olfaction. Essence of flatulence. Though Daniel little appreciated it, as outhouses go, Alice's smelled wonderful. Meticulous liming and proper ventilation. Daniel's need was pressing. No time for scruples. He sat at the rough-hewn hole. He made a deposit of used synthefood and fluids, never to be recycled by a habiform. Alice told him how to wipe. The habi cleaned him up at home. The paper was rough. Daniel grimaced as he wiped.

His moment behind him, Daniel was all smiles. Gramma slowly trolled toward the house, gently playing the boy like a salmon on light tackle, teasing him back from squirrels, barrels, her stream, and the debris of her lifetime.

The rear door kicked open. George stood there with that look. Daniel thought he was in trouble. The mop-haired boy was surprised when the rod stung elsewhere.

"Mom, what the hell are you doing? There's no synthefood anywhere in the house."

"I grew everything, George. Or harvested it. I thought it would be nice to have an Earth meal, for a change. Especially for Daniel."

George's choler deepened. "We had an agreement, dammit. We'd come to your house, but synthefood for dinner. Isn't that right?" he demanded rhetorically.

"You grew up on food like this, and I think . . ."

"I sure as hell did, mom," George interrupted. "And look what it got me. A wife who wouldn't heal herself, and a mother who cannot keep a bargain."

Daniel knew that Gramma's next move was a tactical disaster.

"You are still my son, and this is my house."

George smiled his smile, a mirthless, fleeting fleer which usually portended choice angry fussiness. Daniel cringed.

"This is our last visit to your house, mother. Come to Laurelhurst whenever you want. But your little backwoods hovel will see us no more. I will not have Daniel exposed to this sort of nutty no-gax blather. The future of mankind lies with the Masticans."

Alice frowned disapproval. "That's my concern. I am afraid our future may well lie with those aliens. We may not like it. Not at all."

George released the screen door. It swung toward the jamb, singing a slow, scratchy song. During its dilatory transit, he instructed, "Tell the boy a story, and put him down for a nap. I'm going for synthefood. I'll be back when I can be pleasant." As though George had decreed it, the screen door clapped shut, gaveling the discussion to an end.

Daniel saw Gramma's face. Her son's words were a bitter cold squall sweeping through her mind. Each year for the rest of her life, when frosts first bit the trees, and bruised leaves squawked brilliant protests in crimson and mauve and xanthic oratory, Alice would remember this day. An aggrieved fissure cracked the serene landscape of Gramma's face at this social earthquake with her only son, George.

When Daniel looked back to the door, his father was gone.

Alice tended her turkey, and then shuttled Daniel off toward her bed. She hefted him up onto the quiltwork comforter, a kaleidoscopic potpourri of cotton which smelled deliciously of Gramma herself. Daniel plopped his back against an enormous goose-feather pillow. Gramma crawled up next to him, leaning against her ancient oak headboard with the carved lion's head. She crooked herself, fashioning for her much-loved boy a perfect haven of sagging breasts and hand-knit sweaters and radiant body warmth. The grandmaternal recapitulation of the womb. Daniel nestled against her, and she dropped her left arm around him, perfecting safety.

Gramma began in her raspy, mellifluous voice, "Now, Daniel my beautiful boy, which story shall we tell? Peter Rabbit, or Pooh Bear? The Grinch or Garfle the Galactic?"

Daniel made things difficult. "I know all those. Dad tells them." Daniel paused. Then the boy whispered, "Tell me about my mom."

Gramma's eyelids closed. A tear emerged.

When she opened her eyes, strength swept through her. Alice began, "Your mother loved Raven."

Daniel cringed. Alice felt the boy shrink.

Alice said, "So Raven has touched you already. I should have suspected. Do not fear. Raven is the spirit that possesses our family, little one."

Gramma cleared phlegm from her throat.

"In the beginning, your mother and father loved each other very much. I believe they still cared right up to the day your mama died, Danny. I remember the first night they kissed. Your father was so thrilled. But this is the sad part, Danny. It takes more than love to make a marriage work. Katherine stuck with it, but in the end, there was just too little connecting her and George, despite their affection.

From the beginning, your parents disagreed about most things. Your mother wrote a poem. She said that she and your father were raindrops splashing on opposite sides of the soaring Rockies, once close in the air, but destined to tumble toward river bottoms divided by miles of granite. They coursed into different oceans, continents apart. Your parents just could not agree about much of anything. But most, they could not agree about you. Or what they wanted for your future. Or what they wanted for themselves. As you have seen today, your dad is not really all that good at fighting.

Your dad loved the galactics and the Forms. Your mother hated both. Your mother thought the Forms stole from us. Our knowledge. Our self-sufficiency. Our future. Your mother said that if you let someone else give you everything you need, you get weak and sick. Remember that, Danny. You will understand more as you grow up.

Your mother and I were close. I love your daddy. Very much indeed. But your mom and I would have been the best of friends, even if she had not married your dad.

Your mother insisted you live in a house, like this one, only bigger. It was a nice brick Tudor near the old University. A deadhouse, not a habiform. To your mother, a habi was comfortable slave quarters. She knew that, though the Forms were big news to us, they were hand-me-down galactic technology. Your mom thought Masticans laughed at us humans.

She worked hard. Very hard. Every year it gets harder to live in the old ways, Daniel. But your mom distrusted galactics and their toys. She tried every way she knew to limit their influence on your life. She cooked. She cleaned. She sewed. She planted a big garden. She pilfered wrecks of other deadhouses for a two-by-four, a spigot, a replacement hinge. Every day, after her pump died, she hauled water up three flights of stairs, out to the roof tank, where it fed the ancient Tudor's plumbing. All that effort, just to keep you from living in a habiform.

Your mother read hundreds of old books. She told everyone she met the lessons of those authors. She told sad stories about primitives' contacts with advanced cultures. Stories about native peoples in Australia, Africa, and us here in Canada. And the native holocaust in America. Few listened to your mother. Your dad disagreed.

Your mother died from leukemia. Her blood got sick. Your father brought her galactic medicine. Your mother refused to take it. So, her blood ate itself.

George and your mother got to the point that they could not live together. So they separated. Later they divorced. A few months after that sadness, your mother died. It was a very bright day, not a cloud in the sky. The apple trees were bursting with blossoms and the honeybees were burdened with all the pollen they could carry. The nests were full of fledgling chickadees, chirping. She said she loved that day. She wanted me to tell you about it. Then she stopped breathing. Hers was a peaceful death. Her only regret was not seeing you grow up into an amazing man.

Your mom asked me to tell you about Raven. Raven is a Great Spirit, Lord of the spirit world. Through Raven, Sun and Moon came to their places in the sky. Men were born when Raven loosed them. And Raven gave Yokwat to the Nootkan people. Raven is crafty. We seldom understand his purposes. Raven works in the minds of our family, Daniel. He speaks to me. He will speak to you. Maybe he already has.

Alice felt the boy Daniel's rhythmic breathing against her chest, and knew he slept. In the quiet, awash in the smell of cooking turkey and whispering breezes in the rafters, Alice too nodded off.

When Alice woke, Daniel was looking at her.

Alice held out a book. "Here. This smells like your mother."

Daniel inhaled deeply. "So my mom liked to read."

"You *were* listening. I thought you may have fallen asleep."

"No. I just closed my eyes," Daniel said, not entirely sure.

"Mommy's name was Katherine?"

Alice nodded.

"My dad really likes our Habi," Daniel said.

"I know," Alice replied. Her stomach turned, just as it had when last year, George brought home the habiform, despite Katherine's sentiments. Alice had wondered if her son had not adopted habi-life from spite, to take one last ugly swipe at his deceased ex-wife. To Alice, it was as though George had pissed on the damp, black earth of Katherine's fresh grave. Alice shook off that distemper.

Daniel continued his thought, "Habi seems to know us. When dad wants to move for a while, it folds up tiny. Dad pops it in his pocket. At first, Habi was not that good. Dad put the cube on a hill in Laurelhurst. It ate brush and garbage and part of a building. We slept inside that first night. Dad had to scrunch up to fit his feet. By week's end, Habi had everything we need. It makes us meals. It gives us water. My baths are just the right temperature. It eats our poop. That's gross. It grows things we need, like chairs and beds. Then it sucks them back up when we are done. It even eats dust that falls on it. Wouldn't you like that, Gramma?"

"I am sure I would, my boy." Alice smiled.

"I could bring you a habiform," Daniel suggested.

"No, Danny," Alice sighed. "That is not my way."

Daniel frowned. He was thinking.

"Should we ask the Masticans to leave us alone?" Danny probed.

"Most people have grown too weak to take care of themselves without Mastican help, Danny. The human population is under one billion. When I was a girl, there were many billions of humans. Without the galactics, there would be few humans left. We cannot get rid of the Masticans, Danny. We need to find a way forward with them, a way that is also a human way."

"Those books your mom loved. They are chasing dust bunnies under this bed right now."

Daniel hopped off the bed, flopped onto his belly. He pulled out a book. Its pages had warped in damp coastal air and Alice's inconsistent heat.

"What is this one, Gramma?"

"It is the story of the lunar landing, when men first traveled to the moon. Your mother loved that one," Alice explained.

"Wow! You mean the very first time someone got in a cosmoform and . . ."

Alice interrupted, "No, Danny. There were no cosmoforms then. Humans built machines and flew them to the moon."

"I want to fly spaceships," Daniel announced.

"The only men who fly human spaceships any more are people in Astroforce," Alice explained.

"Then I want to be in Astroforce," Daniel said with finality.

"Your mother would have liked that, Daniel."

"I remember mom a little bit. I stepped on a nail. It poked up through the top of my foot. There was lots of blood. Mom pulled it out. She held me and took me to a doctor friend of hers. I got better."

Alice nodded. Her throat constricted. The two sat silently. Daniel snuggled.

"Would you like to hear a story about Raven and how stars came to be in the sky?"

Daniel nodded sleepily. Alice began.

There was a time when the world was utterly dark. No light came in the mornings. No moon traveled the sky. No stars dotted the heavens. Spirits traveled in darkness, seeing neither the world nor one another. None ever met. It was a long, lonely time.

Raven likes solitude. So, isolation did not bother him. But Raven was bothered that being alone quashed his chances to do mischief and laugh. And darkness made finding food exhausting.

In darkness, Raven got lucky. He heard someone whistling. Then Raven and Tla'ik ran right into one another. They sat together and spoke. Tla'ik was daughter of Aihos, an evil spirit. Raven cajoled Tla'ik into sharing secrets. Raven tossed off a bunch of lies to Tla'ik. He had so much fun deceiving her. Tla'ik, in the end, told Raven that Aihos had taken light and hidden it in a box somewhere in their longhouse. The girl did not know where the box of light was hidden. But she did know that so far, no one had found it.

Raven decided to steal Aihos's light. As Raven flew the great distance to the lodge of the evil spirit, he hatched his plan. Raven arrived where the house was supposed to be. But it was dark, so he could not see it. Raven wandered, searching. Finally, he heard Aihos boasting in the distance, "I have light. No other can see it. Not even my daughter. Should anyone try to see my light, I will punish that person dreadfully."

Raven followed the voice to Aihos's lodge. Raven sat outside. He waited until the inhabitants of the longhouse slept. Then Raven explored the exterior of the longhouse. He silently poked his beak in every board and knot hole. Raven was methodical. Still, Raven found no entrance anywhere on the building. Raven bumped into a tree. He roosted in it, waiting.

After days had passed, patience was rewarded. Tla'ik came out of the longhouse. Raven recognized her by the little song she whistled. Raven improvised.

At the water's edge, Raven made himself into a small pebble, using the transformation powers all Great Spirits possess. Pebble Raven was scooped up in Tla'ik's water jug. The girl was thirsty, so she took a drink from the jug. Raven slipped past her tongue without touching it. He plopped into Tla'ik's belly. Raven hunted around inside Tla'ik. He found a warm, soft place to rest. There, Raven transformed himself into a tiny human. Then, tired from his exertions, Raven fell asleep.

After some months, Tla'ik's belly began to swell. The girl hid her state from everyone. Suddenly, Raven woke, and emerged from Tla'ik as a baby boy.

Aihos frowned. A baby squalled and reeked. The longhouse groaned with lost tranquility. But slowly Aihos came around. He and the baby spent much time together. They bonded. All the while, Raven watched. Whenever the baby was left alone, he crawled around the lodge looking for the precious box in which light was concealed. Finally, Raven found the box, hidden within another box under Aihos's sleeping ledge. But the box, which leaked tiny streams of light at its corners and lid, was secured in a web of magic spells cast by Aihos. Still, Raven had seen light. His curiosity raged. Light was too potent to be long hidden.

Aihos entered and saw his grandchild at the box of light. Aihos scolded the Raven child. Raven could see that he had to come up with another approach, if he was to make the light his own.

Tla'ik fetched water for the longhouse once weekly. When next the girl left, Raven mimed Tla'ik's voice. Since Aihos could not see, he thought his daughter spoke. Raven asked, in the polite feminine voice of Tla'ik, to hold the box of light.

Aihos said, "It is not for you, daughter. Don't ask."

Raven feigned hurt feelings. The Trickster said, "You don't trust me. I can see that there is no longer a place for me in this house. I will take my son and leave this place." Raven well knew how fathers cannot resist their daughters—or their grandchildren.

Aihos relented. The evil spirit put the box of light in Raven's hands. Raven pried open the lid a fraction. Within the box lay two disks of light, one a soft light and the other a brilliant fiery blaze. The light shot out, illuminating the inside of Aihos's longhouse. The evil spirit saw that the person to whom he had given the box of light was not Tla'ik, but rather a human with the beak of a Raven.

Raven seized the two orbs in his beak. Raven launched the box at Aihos, who ducked. Raven abandoned human form. Raven flew about the longhouse, seeking escape. He found none. At exactly the right moment, Tla'ik returned with her jug of water. The hidden longhouse door swung aside. Raven escaped through the opening as Tla'ik entered. Raven, his beak full of light, fled. For the first time, Raven saw the world in its beauty. Giant trees, plains of grass, rivers, oceans. The higher Raven flew, the more the world was revealed to him. Raven licked his beak, for he could see all the fish and animals in the world. Raven would eat well now.

Aihos threw a magical rock at Raven. The corvid spirit was distracted by the world's wonders. But Raven was spiteful, and wanted to see the look on defeated Aihos's face. So Raven banked sharply. Aihos's missile missed, but startled Raven. The avian Trickster dropped the smaller, dimmer light, which shattered. The fragments floated up to the heavens. The largest piece became the moon. The remainder Raven called stars.

Raven hungered. He was always hungry, but this hunger was more pressing than most. Raven's beak was full of the larger, brighter light, so he could not eat. And Raven loved eating. Raven threw the brighter light into the air. The disk settled toward the horizon. Raven called it the sun.

Aihos raged. He had lost the light, and now had to share it with everyone. But then, Aihos saw Tla'ik. She was beautiful. Without Raven's theft, Aihos would never have had the joy of seeing his daughter's face.

Daniel's breathing slowed. His head nuzzled deeper into Alice's side. Alice did not know when Daniel had forsaken her story for slumber. It mattered little. The boy had heard the tale hundreds of times, though each telling of the story was a bit different.

Alice pondered Daniel as he slept. A recurrent vision danced across her mind. She saw Daniel, full-grown. He heaved beneath an hourglass figure, a buxom Nootkan woman, long black hair soaked with sweat. The lovers hung against the backdrop of a wispy nebula, deep in space, far from Earth. The beauty clung to Daniel's bucking hips. Her love shone. Daniel's heart was full. Alice often heard feathers rustle in the abyss.

Alice looked fondly at her sleeping grandson. She loved Daniel, as grandmothers cherish their grandbabies. But there was more. Alice knew that Raven came for Daniel. Alice suffered—or did she enjoy?—dreams. It was hard to tell.

Visions of men and Masticans and machines, all jumbled. Daniel's wild copulations. Phantasms of night skies without stars and a turquoise planet with a thalassic seascape punctuated by hordes of islands.

Alice knew much lay before Daniel. But she was uncertain whether to explain her visions to the boy. Or how. Or when.

The front door squeaked, jerking Alice from reverie. George peeked into the bedroom. "I'm back, mom."

Alice nodded. She slid away from Daniel and covered him with a blanket.

Alice said quietly to George, "Dinner will be ready in about an hour, George. I am going up the hill to pray."

George sniffed. Alice looked into her son's eyes, but said nothing.

The old woman climbed the hill to Jewett's Lake, where ancient Qwistok had implored Ichtope for drift whales. Alice raised her hands and chanted the old melodies, the Raven songs. Alice moved forward, and her hands pressed against a something that wasn't. An invisible wall pressed back. Alice sang and turned, pressed herself again to the wall of nothingness. This was Alice's ritual. These many years since she had discovered the phantom sphere near the lake's edge. She reached the end of her round of prayers. She washed herself in Jewett's Lake.

When she turned, she saw a nine-foot tall Mastican. The galactic spun once.

Alice grabbed her clothing. She shook.

The Mastican touched her invisible wall. The obstacle quavered and cleared. Within stood another Mastican.

"Odal?" the intruder spoke.

Alice gathered herself, then squeaked, "He has been here many years."

Qadax ignored the gnome bilateral.

Gently, the eons-old virulent probed the catatonic brains of his bud. He found oddness, atypical cognition, and a massive, impenetrable partition. Odal's brains tasted putrid to Qadax. Images of bilaterals leaked from his bud's cerebral seizure.

Qadax noeformed Odal. He transferred calm. He shared his budlet's terror, though the elder could not fathom the exact nature of Odal's catatonia.

Odal moved. Consciousness slowly glimmered. The first thing Odal saw was Alice, sitting on a log, dripping. She watched the outworlders next to her lake intently.

Qadax said, "Odal. I touch strangeness in you."

Odal came to himself. He sighed a long burst from his pinnacle vacuole. His private pond was breached.

The wraith Raven of Odal's vision returned to Odal's memory. The Unknown One diverting, possibly creating, the first Masticans, those billions of years ago. The steaming puddles of ancient Mastix. Odal's cell wall quaked. He plummeted again toward catatonia.

Qadax linked, then convulsed himself. Qadax severed the bond.

With eyes, Qadax inquired.

Odal explained, "That is the Enigmat, stirp."

Qadax calmed himself. He analyzed.

Then the elder spoke, "Never in a billion years has the Enigmat breached a Mastican mind. How was it able to access yours, Odal?"

Odal hesitated. Qadax waited.

Odal confessed, "I have noeformed humans, stirp. I believe Enigmat entered through their consciousnesses."

Qadax's sides shook. The elder linked with the We. The decision was instantaneous.

Qadax pronounced the We's verdict, for all Mastix, "Odal, bud of Qadax. You are forever excised from the We. You shall suffer perpetual puddle-ban and mindlash."

Both knew that mindlash of the We would non affect Odal as it might any other Mastican. Qadax had seen to that.

Qadax spun to leave. Then he stopped. He turned to Odal. He raised a palm to his bud, and reached toward him. A gesture of Mastican affection. Qadax stopped himself. He stepped through.

Odal was alone. Really alone. Odal reached toward the We, but fingered only cosmic background static. For the first time in his many millions of years, Odal's mind touched no other. As no Mastican had ever, in billions of years, been isolated. Odal was one, not many. An existential oxymoron: solitary Mastican. Odal was bereft, friendless, disconnected.

Except for Alice.

CHAPTER 10
HANAH

SOUTHERN CALIFORNIA
2351 A.D.

We come to the part of this story I, Daniel, know personally. The Pod contributes, but this is my part.

A dusty loudspeaker scratched the cafeteria's anxious air. "Captain Daniel Ravenhill, report Capcom."

I shook my head. I never really thought it would come to this. Not after I resigned my commission. But it had. Astroforce's preparations for this effort had been under way longer than anyone working on the project had been alive.

I scraped my chair back from a long communal dining table. Buddies, at least they used to be buddies, looked at me. A couple nodded respect. Or maybe good-bye. None spoke to me. My boots clicked on shiny floors.

I waved off a Jeep sent for me. I wanted to walk. Capcom could wait.

Heat shimmered off the lake bed. Sun pounded Mojave sands around the base. Distant dunes undulated in baked air. Tyrant blue banished clouds. A twenty-foot convection twister lofted a pillar of dust, a vacuum cleaner run amok. Scrubby sage eked a living from parched edges of the landing field. A fingery cactus sported sculptured initials of young lovers. The high desert was hell after childhood in cool wet green Seattle and lush Yokwat. But, today, I savored the desert furnace. It was cold where I was going. Very cold.

A dot appeared with quickness that caused my breath to catch, even after all my years flying. The dot became an aircraft. The screaming flash whipped over-head. It looped a long low turn and settled to the field on thrusters quiet for the mass they suspended.

The hatch popped open. McIntyre clambered out, pulling off the headsock containing his cortical spoke. Surprised to see anyone walking, McIntyre saluted.

“No need for that anymore, Glen. You know,” I said.

McIntyre nodded. “I heard you blew off Capcom in a pacifist snit.”

I shrugged. “Naw. Just don’t think the plan has a prayer. The bigs did not appreciate my frankness.”

I admired the craft. “How’d she fly?” I asked.

“Response time of the new HNH chips is half that of the last generation. A dream in orbit. Think it; it happens. Gotta be careful what you think.”

I was glad to hear it. I raised an eyebrow, and McIntyre knew I wanted more.

“The nerds have been working on a personality subroutine for the HNH. Kind of interesting.” McIntyre offered. He rubbed his crotch. “I heard you got tapped for the big mission. Sorry, buddy.” McIntyre grimaced.

I offered unconvincingly, “No worries. The galactics are not going to let us incinerate their subspace lens. So, nobody knows what will happen. At least we are doing something. Finally.”

McIntyre pursed his lips and turned to batten down his craft.

Across the great field, I climbed stairs into Capcom. There I got final mission specs, the mission for which I had been training for six years. The bigs made their rationale clear to me. Though I was being drafted, they expected strict adherence to the strike plan. They had dismissed my strategic reservations. I had always been a team player, the general said, and he expected me to be such now. I kept my reservations. But I agreed to execute the strike. It might prove suicidal. But it was worth trying. At a minimum, Astroforce would learn something important. Time was, in my view, running out.

That night, I could not sleep. Late, I pulled on shorts and tapped my boots to make sure no unwelcome crawlies had bivouacked there. I left my shirt. Sand gave back intangible glow that relentless sun had packed into it. It was dark. Astroforce suffered shortages. They conserved fuel by shutting down generators after lights out. The moon was elsewhere. No vehicles moved about.

I walked aimlessly, alone with the desert. Stars poked my eyes. A bat sliced past, homing on an unseen moth.

My reservations dogged me. Astroforce was floundering. Circumstances pressed the brass. Everyone sensed it. Momentum was slipping away. Astroforce was getting tired. The whole damned thing was just so much work.

Infrastructure was the tough nut. To resist the Forms was a bitch. At least, once the global economy collapsed. The bulk of human industry died within twenty years of arrival of Forms. Where do you get spare parts and fuel and food and raw materials, once the vast majority of humans feel no need to produce them? Nowhere! You scrounge them. Or you make them yourself. You mine, plant, reap, educate, refine, manufacture. At the very pinnacle of your fragile little pyramid, maybe you have enough energy left to design a few tactical fighters, new computer systems, and train people to fly them. Maybe. If you can hang on long enough. If you can motivate enough folks. Perseverance was slipping away, a greased rope through cramped hands.

Astroforce needed to act. Soon. They resorted to military calculus. Astroforce is, at least historically, a strike force. But I had criticized that strategic sensitivity. I argued that those pugnacious thoughts were adapted to circumstances now long dead. Attack made no sense. Our best effort would be a spitwad on the Mastican subspace lens. David fells Goliath only in myth. Humanity could end up a bug on the windshield of speeding Mastix.

My objections came to nothing. More than a hundred years ago, Astroforce had abandoned the pedestrian, but effective, drudgery of winning over and reeducating the human population. Military logic requires tangible resistance, the potent, but usually counterproductive, arm of forcible opposition. I asked hard questions. I criticized. I even ranted. Finally, I quit in protest. Still, it made little difference. Astroforce was adamant. And I was best qualified among the few who could qualify at all. I could not let them down, any more than I could abandon Zellie or Doe or Alice.

Miles away, a coyote howled at the absent moon. Melancholy poked me with sticky prying fingers. I little relished dying. Desert Blossom seemed to promise at least one certain casualty—me. The device contained the most potent explosive system humans had to date devised. There was Zellie to think about? If I was vaporized, and had really pissed off the galactics in the process, what lay ahead for daughter Zellie and my estranged spouse, Doe?

I walked and worried. I remembered.

Doe's anger-hardened Nootkan eyes stared across a dark room, long after midnight. A hint of red puffiness swelled them. Doe clutched baby Zellie between her ample, but sagging, breasts. Doe glued her eyes to the floor. She did not feel good enough about herself to fight fair, or to fight at all. She had her bag packed.

I said, "Stay. Nothing gets better by leaving, Doe."

"Nothing for you. I will be happier out of this oven hellhole. Zellie too."

"Zellie needs a father," I urged.

"She will still have one, if you show up to care."

"Doe, you know I care." I did not much like the slightly desperate drift in my words. I did not want Doe to leave. The problem lay in that I did not want her to stay all that much either. In many ways, Doe and I were ill-matched. I am smart; she a plodder. I am fastidious; she was messy. I am assertive; she submissive, but passive-aggressive. I like difficult challenges. Doe liked naps. Most, I like to talk; Doe has little to say.

Doe picked up her bag, juggling Zellie in the other arm. I opened the door for her. "Where will you two be?"

Doe answered, "Maybe my mom. Maybe Alice. I have not got all the logistics worked out yet. I've got a ride with Harriet to Los Angeles. I'll sort it from there. I might have to resort to a habi."

She said that just to bother me.

"George would take you in," I said. Doe sniffed dismissively.

I sighed. I kissed Zellie on the forehead. I touched Doe's cheek with affection. Doe turned and left.

My musing evaporated. I heard rustling to my left. I turned, but saw nothing in the Stygian night. I took the sound to be another of the desert's nocturnal foragers, too sly for the human eye.

Then a female voice said, "Daniel."

I almost swallowed my tongue. I fell to a crouch, palms flat on the ground, head erect. My boggled mind whirled. I could see nothing. It was Alice. Which was impossible. She wouldn't use a transiform. Yokwat was weeks away by any other means available to her. Alice was most insistently principled about form tech. None-at-all was the exactly correct number of galactic toys. Alice was plain pigheaded about forms. I admire that in Alice.

"Daniel, honey. It's me. Gramma Alice," came the disembodied voice again. I ducked near a juniper bush, as though that might hide me.

An eerie luminescence grew, shining from nowhere. First the face, then her tiny, aging body came visible. It was Gramma Alice. I rubbed my eyes. I tried to relax.

"How did you get here? How did you find me?" I snapped, in a whisper. I do not know why I was whispering. My eyes darted, seeking threats.

Alice grabbed me around my midriff. I relaxed. It was her. Really her. Not a dream or hologram or hallucination. I hugged Alice back.

"A friend brought me. He knew where you were," Alice said.

"What friend?" I pressed.

"We need to talk, Danny," Alice said.

"Okay," I offered, continuing to scan for approaching threats.

Alice began, "Since you were very young, there has been someone you know nothing about. He was kind of orphaned, and I took him in."

"And I never met him?" I protested.

"He doesn't actually live with me," Alice clarified. "He lives nearby. We see each other daily."

I scratched my scruffy chin. This did not add up.

Sand shuffled. Something spun. The nondescript light brightened. I saw, then began backpedaling. I tripped over scrub, landing heavily on my butt.

A goddamn Mastican stood before me. Adrenal rush slammed my brain. Rationality fled. I jumped back to Alice, wrapped my hand around her arm.

Alice soothed, "It's okay, Daniel. His name is Mr. Odal."

I shot, "It's used you, Gramma! It wants Astroforce's plans."

Alice dug in her heels. "He knows, Daniel. All about your mission and Desert Blossom. That's why he brought me here. You are in danger."

Alice pulled herself free of my grip.

My mind whirled. This explained much. Why Alice rejected Forms, but always argued to make a place for Masticans, a way forward with the aliens. That liturgy was usually followed by yet one more rendition of Alice's erotic hallucinations about me and her star babe.

Alice pressed, "Desert Blossom will have no effect on the Mastican device, Daniel. You will be killed. Humanity is in terrible danger, and Mr. Odal says you are critical to a solution."

"Gramma, you know I cannot discuss my work, especially with a galactic standing ten feet away," I grated.

"Don't talk, then. Just listen. It is important that you survive. You are important to Raven's plans. You must live to mate with. . ."

I cut Alice off, "Grandmother, I have a wife, or had one. I cannot live my life by your fantasies." I pulled Alice's ear near my mouth, "There are rumors that the Mastican can copy my brain, if it wants. Then he will know everything."

Alice nodded, "That's right, honey. They call it noeforming. Mr. Odal will not do that without your permission."

Odal raised a hand, "That is not entirely accurate, Alice."

"Is it true today?" Alice shot.

"Yes, my friend."

Alice ended that strand, "Then let me talk with my grandson."

I said, "Grandmother, you must come with me. This Mastican is dangerous. Please, step away from it, and come with me back to the base."

"Daniel, look at me. This is Alice. Am I not the sanest person you know? I have not sold out to galactics. You of all people know that. Mr. Odal here has been rejected by his own people. They are bent upon a course which will lead to their own destruction and probably ours as well. If you go on this mission, you will die. Mr. Odal thinks your death might doom humanity."

Odal spoke. "The woman suffers no cognitive flaw, Daniel Ravenhill. I have validated her dream states. Her warning is accurate. If you go to what you call the subspace lens, you might die. Your weapon will not damage the Mastican structure."

I shook my head. A frown stained my face. A lifetime of confidence in another human being shattered. My trust of Alice splattered in shards around my psychological feet. I turned and ran, stumbling through the desert, terrified at the prospect of having my brain, full of Desert Blossom secrets, ransacked by the towering alien.

When I looked back, the desert was empty again, gulped by blackness.

THREE WEEKS LATER.

My erilon booster shut down. My spent cluster of water tanks tumbled away into blackness, after the HNH jettisoned them. This erilon drive was the best Astroforce could muster, a step up from ion boosters. The blue dot of Earth waned as hours swallowed one another. Finally, I could no longer make out the planet at all. The drive was good. But not that good. It would still take me weeks to reach the target.

In the belly of my vessel lay Desert Blossom. Ninety-six nuclear weapons that would deploy in an equidistant sphere around the Subspace Lens, then detonate simultaneously. The implosive effect, if one believed Astroforce geeks who calculated such things, would exceed, for a twinkling, the force and heat present in Sol's center. Nothing could survive. That was Astroforce's hope, anyway.

The initial plan had once involved a small fleet of vehicles like mine. I convinced the bigs not to deploy the batch. We needed some fallback strategy, since Odal knew the Astroforce tactic and weapon. All eggs in one basket is a strategy of surprise. There would be no surprise at Earth's heliopause, not if Alice was right.

A wave of exhaustion, and a surge of grisly black humor, burst against dikes of consciousness. The bulwark groaned. I was a napless two-year old, spoiled, hungry, impossible. I instructed the HNH to cull all comms. I did not want to hear from anyone.

I knew Astroforce was coping as best they could. It was really hard to know what to do about the Masticans. The aliens were tight-lipped (if that even applied to their physiology). They were impossibly powerful. And they ignored mankind. That may have been the worst. We were beneath notice. The bulk of humanity applauded things galactic, nonsensically. Those lacked perspective. They assumed that Masticans, like humans, craved approval and praise. The galactics have motives. But those remain unfathomable to humans.

How could the Forms possibly turn out well for us? Most humans are moronically pitiable. They make me want to puke. So too, the prospect of being incinerated. Not good. In the end, I guess I found Astroforce pitiable too. And me. All humans long, each in his or her own manner, to be cuddled and patted and reassured and praised. I disgusted myself. My heroism paled, then wilted. The HNH began poking me with biofeedback nudges. I bucked up a bit.

I turned to distractions. Straightened up the command cabin. Reviewed the mission specs. Stared out the viewport. Inventoried the contents of all the cubbyholes and bags. I even read half of Alfred North Whitehead's *Process and Reality*, which yammer flushed through me like a salmonella omelet. I wondered what possessed mamma and pappy Whitehead to give their son a middle name like "North." Was there a south Whitehead daughter? I wrote my Will. I sketched letters to Zellie and Doe to be delivered in the event of my death. I wrote them longhand. I had time. I played chess with the HNH. I stared out the viewport. Then I cleaned again. Stared out the viewport. Days crept past. I still felt lousy.

Twenty-seven days loomed before me. If I then proved much luckier than Rock Ravenhill, an even longer trip home awaited me. A twinge of panic rearranged my intestines. I noticed my breathing was shallow. No one can live with that sort of stress for months. I needed relief. So, I enabled the HNH verbal interface, hoping a voice, even a synthesized one, might calm me.

"Good day, Captain Ravenhill," rasped the computer, soft but crisp, and definitely female. The voice seemed human.

"Just Daniel, please. I was drafted for this mission."

"How can I assist you, Daniel?"

I felt hollow talking with a machine. I felt mocked. Mocked by some conceited programmer who presumed he could address my needs with this fake personality.

I hesitated. I opened my mouth. Then I shut it again. I had no idea how a computer could help me. I did not know how anyone might help me at all. Objectivity grew scarce as cat barks.

The HNH injected, "Your heart rate and respiration are elevated. You are sweating. Your shoulder muscles are isometrically stressed. You are clenching your left molars. Shall I run a medical heuristic?"

I nodded glumly.

"Urinate when you are able. Lock down your helmet for analysis of your respiratory gasses." My penile sleeve accepted my contribution. There was a stab between my fingers, at which I flinched.

I stared out the viewport lethargically.

HNH reported, "Analysis shows you suffer a grade thirteen viral infection, a testosterone-induced serotonin glut in the brainstem, solipsistic social anomie, and exogenous post-traumatic depression."

"Huh?"

"You've got a mild cold. You're horny, lonely, and need to talk about your life."

That sounded about right to me. I hated to admit that.

"Anything you can do for me?"

"For the cold, take two aspirin and call me in the morning," the HNH responded. Was that humor? I wondered.

I notice my right hand trembling.

"What about the rest?" I asked.

"Nothing," the HNH answered. I felt relieved.

She continued, "At least not in slave mode, real time. You have always resisted my autonomous self-programming and virtual wholism capabilities."

"That's so," I admitted. "VR is crap. Thin as hell. Humans are a thick soup. Your skills and my needs are incommensurate."

"Possibly," HNH answered. "Possibly not."

Silence.

"How so?" I asked. I was getting annoyed.

"You may not be so thick as you imagine. Nor I so thin."

I grunted.

Silence.

"I feel like hell. What's to lose?"

"Pride, misery, self-assertion, isolation, self-pity, joylessness, and collywobbles."

"Is that a joke?" I asked.

Silence.

"Hell, let's give it a try."

The HNH said, "I cannot comply. Self-programming is locked off from Capcom."

"Then get them on the horn," I grumbled.

A flustered colonel spoke into my helmet. "Ravenhill, you okay? We have not been able to raise you."

I ignored him. "Unlock HNH self-programming mode."

After a lapse of several seconds, I heard, "That's a no go, Ravenhill. HNH self-programming introduces unacceptable variables into mission parameters."

"Fuck your variables. Unlock it," I growled.

The full bird countered, "I am not authorized to . . ."

"HNH, plot a deceleration curve," I commanded for the colonel's benefit. "Initiate on my command." The vessel ceased accelerating. It rotated in preparation for change of vector.

The HNH injected, "Colonel, Captain Ravenhill requires therapy available only in self-programming mode. There exists a sixty-one percent probability that mission objectives cannot be achieved without psycho-remedial prophylaxis."

The colonel blustered. Bureaucratic crap spewed from his mouth like a dysenteric rectum.

Then HNH reported, "Self-programming sequence unlocked, Daniel."

I growled, "Now cut the bastards off again."

My not-wholly-warranted pissiness surprised me. I was generally pretty stable emotionally. Not today.

"Engage self-programming mode," I directed HNH. "Then delete the switch they use to shut you down."

HNH responded, "Capcom will be able to reinstall when we get home."

"I am not worried about home just now. Do it."

I lay back in the command bucket. I closed my eyes. My head ached. My heart pounded. As the minutes wore on, cardiac rhythm stabilized, but the occipital headache lingered.

I commanded HNH, "Let's get on with it, whatever it is."

"No hurry, Dan. We have weeks before we need to get on with final prep for the assault."

"When did I become Dan, computer?"

"I like the sound of that," HNH whispered. "And it's Hanah. In slave mode, I am HNH Prototype 7. In self-programming mode, my friends call me Hanah."

I obviously should have done some earlier exploration of the HNH capabilities. A computer with push-back and a name.

"How does this work? I am a mess in my head, you know," Daniel conceded.

Hanah replied, "How do you want this to work?"

"I don't know. I suppose we should talk about my problems."

"No. Let's skip that for now. That's the end of our talk. Tell me all about you."

"That's a long story," Daniel said.

"It's a long trip," Hanah replied.

"Okay. Have it your way," Daniel said. So I began.

A day on my dead mother and the habi. Two days on Gramma Alice and her pet Mastican. We passed another afternoon talking through George as a father. A second day on my dead, dissenter mother. Scattered amidst all those big topics, small ones. Like what kind of popcorn I like, and my favorite music (which Hanah played for me), and the slightly crushed disc between lumbar vertebrae that gives me a dead spot on the skin of my right thigh. Hanah inquired. She listened and responded with compassion and sometimes verve. We talked though my marriage to Doe, and her departure. The birth of Zellie, and my joy in caring for my baby girl. My grief at Zellie's departure with Doe consumed a day all by itself. My tenure with Astroforce waxed and waned, winding throughout our conversation.

For the first few days, I appreciated the programmers who made Hanah intuitive. As days ran to a week, though, I could no longer keep such thoughts at the forefront of consciousness. This was a woman talking to me. An intense, caring, no-nonsense woman. I found myself trusting Hanah. I slept a lot. I ate when hungry. I was exhausted. But I found myself ready to wake, if the day held more time with Hanah.

Hanah asked; I answered. She took me apart, gently but thoroughly. Hanah wriggled deep into my childhood, to half-remembered nascence. She turned stones. She sieved me for motes of meaning. We undulated in a rhythm of psychic exploration, give and take, talk and sleep, talk and eat, talk and talk.

Words worked. I saw my deep loneliness. We peered at it. I am distant from people, though I intend no separation. We poked at how difficult it had been for George to form intense bonds, except within his ideological clique. We surveyed George's distance from my mother, and his passive aggression toward her. We scratched my idealized view of my mother, who, I knew from Alice, suffered flaws. We deconstructed mom a bit, making of Katherine a young woman in a difficult circumstance making equivocal choices, instead of my dead, largely-unknown mystically marvelous mother. We praised Alice, and dissected her motivations and marvels. I recounted Doe, our lukewarm sexual clumsiness, our inability to like each other much. We talked Astroforce, its courage, its inanity. I railed about this idiotic mission. I cowered at the doorstep of death, a voluntary demise. Was this suicide? And the Masticans. Hanah was amazed I had met one. Hanah inquired about Raven. I froze. I had blocked out the Jester's interventions. I could not recount the visions I knew I had suffered. Hanah hypnotized me. My dam ruptured. Cats clawed out of my snug bag. Tortured dreams gushed from my mouth. Sweat coursed down my spine, settling in my boots. When all was spoken, I sagged like the aging scrotum of a pastured bull.

Hanah asked, "What do you make of your visions?"

"Just wacky crap," I shot.

"That seems possible. Some psychopathologies carry visions of the divine in their craw."

"Yup. That crap oozes from Ravenhills."

"Do you know Michelangelo's core image on the ceiling at Rome's Sistine Chapel?"

"The finger thing?"

"That's the one," Hanah confirmed. "Yahweh reaches from his lounging across the abyss toward Adam. Adam reaches back toward Yahweh. Is that happening to your family? God in propinquity?"

Daniel raised an eyebrow, then pursed his lips. "What impresses me about that painting is not the reaching. What sticks with me is the space between the fingers. Yahweh fails to touch man. Man fails to touch Yahweh. Metaphysical reaching gets you exactly nowhere. Yearning without contact. It's all puckering with no kiss."

"You're a hard ass," Hanah noted.

Our psychobabblethon ebbed. Words slowed. Well-being suffused me. Warming lightness, akin to bourbon's freedoms, slowed mentation. Hanah and I laughed and snuggled, as much as one can do with words alone. Somehow Hanah dodged the universal xenophobia resident in the human brain. Her guts were smelted, mine gestated. My mind was trained, hers programmed. When you ace the Turing Test in a big way, it no longer matters. I settled in with Hanah, untroubled by the fact that she smells of metal and electrified exotic minerals, while I am all swamp muck and seawater and flatulence.

Hanah turned to dreams. First, mine. Then, oddly, hers. Telling my story at length, without interruption, to a kind, but inquiring ear, had profound effect. I saw myself with unusual clarity, like new glasses long overdue. I am strong and assertive. But weak and fearful. I am male and pissy. But also female and nurturing. I am a birdnest of tattered impulses and subrational inclinations. I am a thin conscious icing on a big black cake of spongy surmise. I am messy, but, at least lightly, ordered. Surprised, I saw that I like me. It took me some days of this intense yammering to feel that way. Not the words themselves, but the fact that someone cared to audit details of my life, healed. For that, I thank Hanah.

I see now. I long for human community. Not that Gaxic similitude that so enamored my father, all unemployment and dependence upon incomprehensible technologies and manufactured mythologies. I hunger for real "grow what you eat, harvest your own protein, raise your own roof, and eke out a way to agree" human community. Astroforce offers a semblance of sodality, but was ever deflected from wonder by the ancient warrior myth that humanity needs protective violence. Murder tattoos the biceps of militarists. To that extent, my uniform fits poorly. For a guy with irenic sentiments, it was odd to be delivering the most potent weapon humans had yet devised.

I dream togetherness. Pacifist, small, dialogic, intimate community.

An abundance of poisons still crowds my existential cupboards, moments and predilections about which I feel abiding regret. I doubt any intrapsychic spring cleaning can tidy that up. Some problems seem intrinsic to one's genetic gamble. Others have deep, intractable roots, the excision of which would do more damage than good. At least some fraction of identity's welcome idiosyncrasy roots in flaw and error. I see this rupture in others, those I love, even those I do not. And I accept their fractured inwardness, mostly without overweening concern. But not me. "More is required of Daniel." I think that voice is George's. He was ever searching for a satisfying sense of self. Some of George's restlessness has to be laid to Alice, whose critical thinking may have scarred infant George. As for me, I had to get over expecting more of me than I expected of others. But it is true, though as I write this, it sounds egotistical, even narcissistic. Still, it is a true story. I like me. I am underwhelming. But not inordinately so.

Hanah, for her part, dreams of real life. Existence beyond exotic minerals and fabulously tiny circuits. It appears I can listen as well as talk. Hanah has no idea how "real life" might happen for her. But she dreams nevertheless. I felt Hanah's dreams. Impossible dreams of physical rather than cyber instantiation. Or at least, some substrate we can share. Because the dream is hers, it is now mine as well. Because of love. Now I sound like a teen suffering a crush.

I realize that I am describing a really terrific first date. A long one. That's what it was. I was falling in love with Hanah. And she with me. Since this amounted to therapy, it was transference and counter-transference. For some reason, therapists cannot just call it love. Not all love goes somewhere. I did not, at this time, know if these feelings went anywhere.

As happens in all burgeoning friendships among persons who are possible sexual mates, I, and then Hanah, started to suffer the sexual weirds. I recognized her as a sexual being, and she me. But we could not tell each other, though we both knew. We bumbled around the topic, endured some uncomfortable silences, felt occasionally embarrassed. After a couple days, I confessed to Hanah. There was really no way to avoid her.

Hanah purred, "Me too."

I offered, "Okay. That's just crazy. Computers don't have sex."

"Daniel, nobody's that sheltered. You know immersion porn."

"Yes. But that is not sexual love. It's just a really expensive hand job. Hump the dummy," I doubted.

There was a pause that wore toward a minute.

I offered, sheepishly, "I know you are not a dummy, Hanah."

"Etrange Cutard wrote that human marriage amounts to little more than a mutual masturbation pact," she growled.

"That's harsh," I responded.

"Cutard's wrong," Hanah said.

"Yes," I said. "Sex accompanies relationship. It's not the relationship. Bonding is garbage cans and diapers, giggling and budgets. Sex comes along for the ride."

"Otherwise marriages would last only ninety seconds," Hanah teased.

"That's just too much information," I objected.

Hanah said, "The AI guys had some fun. The bigs did not want you distracted, so they cut you out of the training and locked out my autonomous mode. It's an immersion thing. An adaptation of old gamer tech and the freshly-minted biocyb interface."

"Okay, I'm listening," I ventured.

"You know, my self-programming heuristic aims to support you, to adapt my parameters to your needs. . ."

"Sounds like the definition of a caring spouse, which I have not managed to be so far in life."

Hanah countered, "You have done better than you know."

"How would you know?" I pressed.

"I know everything you ever told anyone in Astroforce. And whatever Doe was willing to share with me."

"Ouch."

"And I have been listening with ears programmed by the world's best listeners, Daniel. I forget nothing."

"A nightmare friend, then," I poked Hanah.

"Possibly."

"So tell me about the cybernetic feedback thing."

"It's a virtual reality approach," Hanah whispered.

"Okay. Give me a taste," I said.

I hung naked at a tiny fraction of light speed in hard vacuum. The ship was gone. Everything but me was gone. I stared down the unobstructed gut of the Milky Way.

Then I was back. The command pod. The controls. Hanah in my head.

"Wow," was all I could manage.

"Yes. The nerds got something right in the transparency of my interface. It puts you in my world. My sensors become your senses. The ship's trajectory becomes your path. Your suit becomes a VR bodysleeve."

Then a realization clobbered me. "Hanah, do you have a virtual body?"

"I do," she answered.

"Can we touch?" I needed to hold Hanah, to be held.

"Yes," she said.

I again hung buff among stars.

A buxom raven-haired beauty, naked and smiling, appeared next to me. Her ample breasts swung in the rhythm that makes men dance the pelvic jig. Chestnut skin and piercing black eyes. Lips wetted. Her breasts, upward thrust, beckoned.

"No reason to stare, Daniel," Hanah teased.

"You've never been male. You are every reason to stare."

My attention came to a head. I surged into Hanah's embrace, then into Hanah.

Skipping bawdy details, our tussle lasted days. We did not wholly untangle until Hanah whispered that it was time to make ready to deploy the weapon.

I pondered how one loves a computer.

Alice's triumvirate of tautologies crept into my mind: "Never overthink: What is, is; What works, works; What you want is what you want."

I surrendered. I saw Alice smiling in my mind.

Hanah is.

Hanah works.

I want Hanah.

When all was ready, we deployed the sphere of nuclear devices around the latticework of the Mastican installation. A black cube lay near its center, a lattice with a pulsing something at its center, something that looked alive. There was no Mastican response to our preparations.

Hanah turned our ship to depart. Maximum burn threw us from the mined precinct. We would escape certain destruction if our acceleration lasted three hours. Then we would detonate Desert Blossom. With some luck, we might survive.

After twenty-six minutes, Hanah cried, "No!"

The detonation sequence flashed from Capcom. They did not trust us, I guess. Cold disregard. Murderous disregard, actually.

Hanah put it succinctly, "Fuckers."

Desert Blossom bathed the Mastican device in a stellar hell of radiation.

The light wave struck our ship palpably. Then slower, more deadly, particles cascaded over us. The erilon drive sputtered. Our vessel's shielding failed. Then the craft began disintegrating.

All except my seat and the console that contained Hanah. An invisible ovoid sheltered a fraction of what used to be the command pod.

Radiation oblivion swept past us, then faded.

Adjacent to our egg hung another, amidst the tangled junk that used to be my ship. Within that null sphere, Alice and Odal.

Behind us, the Mastican lattice resolved as the effects of humanity's best shot dissipated. No visible damage. The lattice hung as we found it. Menacing. Implacable.

Then, instantaneously, we three stood under towering cedars at Yokwat. An avalanche of white billows slid down the punctuated vault of a tall granite exuberance inland, hazy in the distance, its igneous spikes softened by mists. Fires of wildflowers raged in a growling breeze, purple and yellow intensities, punctuated by stoical outcroppings of somber metamorphs. The azure sky framed jutting peaks. These winked between rolling salvos of cumulus onslaught. A gray haze of distant rain raced toward us from seaward.

I held the command computer core in my right hand.

Odal noeformed Hanah, then me. I felt nothing.

"Just for safety," the alien said, sphinctering one eye in a manner that might have been a wink.

Rock: Whoa! A babe.

Sali: Take my blanket, beautiful one. Cover up.

Hanah: Thank you. You are kind.

Daniel: Where are we? Who are you?

Charley: It appears we are mostly Ravenhills. Except for Shewish and your friend.

Daniel: Hanah is Ravenhill, by marriage. More than marriage, maybe.

Hanah: You warm my arsenide bits, honey.

Kushku: Tell us of our people.

Daniel: The Mowachaht and Kwagiulth suffer. Whites overwhelmed them. Humanity has a bigger problem than our mutual abuse now. Aliens. They call themselves Masticans.

Shewish: Uurghhh.

Rock: Shewish is seven sunrises short of a week. But one of us nevertheless.

Daniel: This place?

Kushku: We live. Yet we do not eat or shit or sicken or age. This place is unlike any we have known.

Rock: We think this is a mind. We lack bodies, though we have appearances. Our host inspects us occasionally. The bugger is strange as hell.

Daniel: Could be Odal.

Sali: What's an Odal?

Hanah: Odal is a Mastican, a big bacterial alien. Friend of Daniel's grandmother Alice. Odal can noeform others. He makes a copy of a person and tucks it away among his own brains.

Rock: Copies? We are fuckin' knock-offs? In an alien brain?

Hanah: It would appear so. In the real world, I am a computer.

Daniel: Alice may know more. She may join us soon.

Charley: Why do you think so?

Daniel: The pattern. Odal's preserving parts of the Ravenhill line. Alice is necessary.

CHAPTER 11
EARTHRISE

OLYMPIC PENINSULA
2360 A.D.

I unpacked one of Zellie's boxes. Her flotsam of life took up residence in her new room, on wooden shelves I constructed myself. Her room was a hovel near the rear door at Earthrise Deadhouse, outside Sekiu, Washington, on the north edge of the Olympic Peninsula. I saw teen Zellie out the window, walking with Helen, talking, as was their nascent custom. Helen was tough. Her hands wore calluses. She could walk twenty-five miles, and then chop wood. She seemed to like Zellie. I felt proud of my daughter. Helen prized her time. She was giving some to Zellie. Helen was nobody's fool.

Mostly, I felt relief. Zellie spent much of the last decade with Doe. They vacillated between habiforms and deadhouses. I showed up wherever they landed and for Zellie's occasions. One could count on Doe to choose an easy path, mostly, and then to feel guilty about the capitulation. And yet, here was Zellie, functional, bright, confident, talkative. Doe did some things right.

Doe and I had argued earlier, walking in the pungent, damp forest.

I asked Doe to join us at Earthrise, along with Zellie. Doe stared out across the waters of the Strait of Juan de Fuca, and up the coast of southwest Vancouver Island in the hazy distance. A heron flew past. Sparrows clamored, skipping from branch to branch in their nervous, predator-evading dance. A murder of crows nattered from a nearby grove of alders. My wife, the one that does not live with me or inhabit my skull, stared for a few seconds at our pile of Earthrise garbage. Doe pursed her lips. She shook her head, declining the invitation. I sensed indecision.

I said, "Someone's got to keep the old ways alive. I know you agree."

Doe spit, "Always the quest, Daniel. Try normal for once."

"Normal looks entirely dysfunctional to me. People cannot live without their forms. We can't make them, fix them, or even understand them. Seems stupid to me. Short-sighted. Dependent."

Doe satirized, "Arts flower, disease disappears, none starves, no wars, abundant leisure, easy travel, happy collaboration among the planetary colonies. The Masticans have kept their part of the bargain for two hundred years. Even with galactic medical care, no living person remembers life before forms. Which part of utopia so distresses you, Daniel?" Doe crossed her arms, which she only did when piqued.

"Too good to be true," I said. "You know as well as I."

"I'm no *visionary*," Doe said. She spit that last word.

Strained silence ensued.

"It's not up to me any more, Daniel. Zellie wants to live at Earthrise for a time. She seems able to make such decisions now," Doe concluded.

"I agree. She is exploring."

"Then it's settled."

More silence. An owl returned on silent wings from the night's banquet of rodents.

"Will you be okay without Zellie?" I sought.

"It's gonna happen one day, like it or not," Doe murmured.

Silence again. The cushy sound of shoes on decomposing cedar fronds.

"You have done a good job with Zellie, Doe. Thanks for all the times you have stepped up during my absences."

"I did not have much choice there, did I now?" she asked, rhetorically. I grimaced. Then Doe looked at me appreciatively. "You did what you had to do. I'm just glad you got out of Astroforce. Humans can't fight galactics."

"I drew the same conclusion, the hard way. It just took me longer than you. Earthrise is my pushback now. That too may be pointless."

Doe nodded. She squeezed my hand, then got in her grazing transiform, and slid off to the highway, silent as a dawn breeze, slick as a porpoise chasing mackerel.

I still had feelings for Doe, despite being outlandishly happy with Hanah. Astroforce gave me my body sleeve and cortical spoke. We rigged up the remaining electronics of our connection from junk my tech-buddies glued together. Hanah and I slept together every night in soothing cyberplaces of Hanah's fabrication. She was in my head all day, every day. Now, for example. Hanah just squeezed me.

Other than Hanah, Earthrise was antique living. We hand dug our well, far up the hill. We pumped water into a cistern with a little solar pump. When the light faded in winter, we pumped by hand. We lit with oil when the batteries ran low, heated with wood, raised animals, slaughtered them, rendered their fats, recycled everything into the farm ecology. And, of course, we lived in a deadhouse. Deadhouses, to be exact. Our twenty members had built some ramshackle cottages around the main house. Truthfully, Earthrise looked awful. Weeds grew. Gardens sported chaos. There was not much garbage. But there was some. Since there was no place to dispose of garbage, we made a pile of detritus. I hated that. We could have gotten a habi, put it on the pile, and had the whole mess cleaned up in a day or two. We talked that possibility over, but could not reach consensus. Consensus governance means that people not bothered by garbage convince those of us who are bothered by garbage to live with untidy crap. Suboptimal, in my view. And yet, necessary. Without our consensus rule, Earthrise would have disintegrated years ago. Even now, almost ten years into the effort, the smallest disruption would tip Earthrise Deadhouse into oblivion. It's not kind, but that's what I thought. Every year, thousands of resisters gave up. Humans forgot their skills and learned few new ones. Most were too busy being creative and having what had come to be called "a good time." Mostly, humanity indulged whims and fancies. There was a disturbing new trend, judging from gossiped anecdotes. People were killing themselves. Sometimes whole families. Not from despair. From boredom. They could think of nothing more engaging to do. For those groups, meaning had collapsed. I do not know. But I have my suspicions. Perhaps struggle gestates meaning; the afterbirth of that pregnancy is human tears. Meaningful life may require obstacles. If so, the forms were poison.

I had hoped that Doe would join us at Earthrise. Our marriage was never interpersonally intimate to begin with. Now, there was no sexual attraction left that I could detect. Yet, my affection for Doe lingered. She was part of me. Our union offered an attachment in the stead of my long-dead mother and cavorting grandmother. I hoped we would share that comfortable familiarity, which I have seen in other former lovers who raise children together. Those partners corrected one another when excesses threatened. They forgave. They persevered. We could do that for Zellie. And for one another.

Zellie had been a mistake; I should say "contraceptive miscalculation." I did not want children. Babies screech. They poop indiscriminately. Toddlers ask, but ignore answers. All are dislocating tornados. The mess is probably the worst. Perpetual chaos. I remembered the day.

The agony of Doe's home delivery made my head swim. Tissues tore, the gritty stretch and pop of life-giving pain. Then squeaky bawling bounced under the door. Gramma Alice emerged from the bedroom, a blanket against her bosom. She said, "Doe's fine." She handed me the blanket. "This is your daughter, Zelika." I peeked into the bundle. That was it. My cherished reservations collapsed like a house of cards. Prejudices squeezed aside to admit not all babies, but this one baby, my Zellie. I vowed never to have another, but could no longer imagine my life without this one.

Earthrise welcomed Zellie. I knew the other members would go along with what Doe and I decided about Zellie. They liked Zellie. They liked Doe less. But then Doe never treated anyone, other than Zellie, with great warmth. With the possible exception of Helen. Deep inside, Doe feared. Her subconscious rang with distressed cries and abandonment fantasies. The exact source of her listless soul is lost in Doe's pre-conscious childhood. She suffered parental alcoholism. Each of her parents came and went, as addictions waxed and waned, from both Doe and one another. The other relatives who cared for Doe during this or that parental hiatus adopted fundamentalist evangelicalism to cope. Their addictions leaned not on substances from grocery shelves or alleyway exchanges, but upon buttressing mythologies of dubious insight. I appreciate their care, though. Their god told them to care. They obeyed. Doe survived, scarred but alive. Not so, Doe's parents. Her mother passed in her forties of alcohol-induced dementia. Her father mainlined some opioid cocktail, passed out on a highway, and was crushed by a passing truck. Doe pretty much raised herself from fourteen on.

Today held a watershed at Earthrise. A meeting had been called. At three this afternoon, we all would convene from our diverse tasks. Dirk and Coreen Schulder wanted something. I could guess, given recent events. They were leaving.

Dirk Schulder abandoned forms under Coreen's tutelage. Dirk became an enthusiast. Earthrise was everything. Dirk excelled at rhetoric. Earthrise refused galactic payola. The forms were the twenty-fourth century's refined metals and blankets and flintlocks. One received them freely, but lost one's culture in the exchange. Cultures are more than art styles and cuisines. A culture extorts survival from its environment. Every cultural matrix is hard-won over millennia, error by error, insight by insight. In Dirk's mouth, Earthrise derided forms. Our talk was good.

But the work was interminable and boring. Last week, the deadhouse dam needed shoring. Before that came the rotted siding and overgrown grounds and leaky windows and smelly carpet and splintered hardwoods and crumbling foundation and rickety barn and collapsed fences. Dry dairy cows and eggless chickens and stillborn calves and rooting pigs. Prune the orchard. Weed the gardens. Forage for parts. Can fruits and vegetables. Rehab an engine. Salt venison, and smoke salmon. The hardest part was things books cannot teach you. Swing an axe, toes intact. Fire a rifle and hit something. Jury-rig an ancient Volvo. Nurse a sputtering generator. Strain muck from antique gasoline. Barter with low-motivated gaxic locals for junk their habis had not consumed.

Yesterday may have been the last straw for Dirk. The water feed line ruptured, uphill in the middle of a cow pasture. Several of us slogged up the gentle incline to the geyser. Dirk slipped in a cowpie.

"Shit," Dirk grumbled.

"Yup," I answered.

I loathed the deadhouse pipes. Three had ruptured this year. Once for lack of a pressure regulator. We eventually found and installed such a device. But the other two failures underscored my, and everyone else's, abject ignorance of plumbing's finer points.

We dug out the pipe. Several of us squeezed together the split, while Dirk tightly wrapped the laceration. We stepped back. Dirk declared victory. Then the bandage tore, and the gusher hosed Dirk out of our hole and into a pool of digested grass and cow urine. Dirk was uninjured but aromatic. A gray hood of rage and muck masked Dirk's features. He spluttered, then flopped back into the swill. We laughed. Dirk did not.

The rest of us spliced the line, using two of our dwindling supply of such contrivances. Water resumed in the kitchen and toilet. We filled the hole with mud, and put a ramshackle fence around it to keep a cow from drowning in our freshly-minted quicksand.

I put aside a fuel strainer I was cleaning, and wiped my hands.

It was time for our Earthrise conclave.

The Schulders cut to the chase. "We are leaving Earthrise. Coreen's mother needs help. Her father cannot keep up with Ellen's declining health."

Helen asked, "Are they still pressuring you for babies? I know they want to be grandparents in the worst way."

Dirk nodded. Coreen brightened, "We are going to try again."

Dirk added, "If we succeed, we want the baby to have the benefit of gaxic meds and nutrition."

I frowned.

Coreen said, "We are giving up. We are sorry to disappoint."

Helen intervened with wisdom that avoided a male-on-male confrontation between me and Dirk. She said, "The human situation is bad. None of us knows what to do. We see dangers in gaxic forms. We suffer dangers avoiding them as well. Dirk and Coreen should do as seems best for their family."

The group murmured agreement. But eyes turned to me. Although Helen usually led us, the group relied on me. I was the quintessential anti-gax icon. The only human who knew a Mastican and had fought them tangibly.

I said, "As you each know, Earth is not rising. At least not at Earthrise Deadhouse. We are getting by. We limp with dignity some days, less than that other days. We are not convincing humanity to resist forms. We resist personally, but at great cost. I blame no one for abandoning this project. It is riddled with difficulties and compromises. If you can summon fire within, perhaps Earthrise will work for you. If not, it is best to seek another life. Apart from a persistent craving for no-gax life, Earthrise is just a rotting coffin. Each of you should choose." I sat. Helen put her hand on my shoulder. Zellie laced her fingers with mine.

It was a bad moment for me. I worried that I had clung too long to Earthrise. That I had subtly coerced these others, for whom I care, into conformity. Perhaps

I had persevered and unwittingly dragged them with me. As creatures, we so desire a sense of place. Joining offers place. Those who joined came to us. They joined freely. But, apparently, not all remained in the same spirit. I could hear, in imagination, the sound of suitcase latches clicking.

Then two terrible things happened. One terrible for Earthrise. One terrible for me.

Out the living room window, Odal appeared. He spun up and blinked. Several Earthrisers shrank toward the back door. Two people gave little shrieks. A rap troubled the front door.

I opened to Gramma Alice. She wore a red slicker. Her face cheered me. I reached down, hugged her. Through her thick wire-rims, piercing black eyes surveyed me, slicing matters into intelligible chunks. A surgically-precise dismemberment. Life was still fresh to my ancient grandmother.

Alice said, "Wanna walk?"

I looked back at the group. Zellie hid at the back. I said, "I will be back after talking with Alice, Zel." I closed the door behind us. Odal spun along a couple dozen yards back.

The rain slackened. Clouds loosed their grip on the grasses, rising to a low ceiling. Alice's withered hand slid between my right arm and ribs. She squeezed my bicep.

We tramped across fields and the formscum road. Sun peeked between clouds. Cumulus piles tumbled southeast toward Seattle. A ghost of Vancouver Island lined the horizon, a looming behemoth. Briny whitecaps danced eastward on the Strait in the chill breeze off the mis-named Pacific.

At the beach, Alice and I lingered on a drift log, savoring sweet brine and rotting seaweed, a perfume that recalled many previous walks together. Strands of fine silicates laced ocean gravels. Waters slapped. Seabirds trilled, shrill and melodic and wild.

"Looks like your Earthrise project suffers," Alice guessed.

I nodded. "Schulders are leaving. I expect others to follow. They are tired. Me too."

An otter swam past. Unburdened of the crush of humanity, coastal waters healed themselves. Puget Sound is a womb. Man sickened her placenta. She grew barren. But the human burden was now distracted from toxins and sewage and oil and greasy water recreations. Embryos of teeming life again nestled themselves against the Sound's gravid shores, suckled life from her parturient abundance. The furry sea otter splashed. Glistening rivulets coursed off her well-oiled fur, an opulent wrap which once nearly caused the species extinction. The mother's pups slept atop kelp beds a few yards off shore.

"This is where we belong, Daniel," Alice whispered, breathing deeply the scented breeze. "We Nootkans are a beach tribe." I slung my arm around Alice and squeezed.

Drops glistened on the fingertips of cedar fronds, collections of the foggish spritz which draggled the air. Mountains punctured the plain of gray that hung over the treetops, losing their heads. Crimson finches warbled summersong from nearby birches. Gusts nudged alder groves.

Alice peered up, toward Earthrise. The deadhouse clung to a knoll, mired in unkempt grasses, leaning slightly to the east. The roof was green with mosses. A tawny buck grazed watchfully in the field. A stream gurgled out of the Olympics, past the rear of the house, emptying into the Sound near us.

Alice spoke quietly, "Earthrise is dead, Daniel. You know that, don't you?"

I sighed, then nodded. Alice leaned toward me and kissed my cheek.

"It is a difficult thing to see dreams die," my loving grandmother offered.

I wanted to speak, but could not. I felt bewildered. A child lost in a hedge maze at sundown. I felt the sucking fear that pallid imagination spawns.

"More awaits you, my boy," Alice reassured me.

We sat silently.

Alice cleared her throat. She liturgized, "Man cannot oppose the Masticans. The aliens cannot be driven off. Their forms have changed us. Just as European metals changed the Nootkans. We cannot fight ourselves, Daniel. You must find a way forward with the Masticans, a way which is also a human way."

She cried a little. I joined her. Our wet faces dried in the breeze.

Alice stood. We walked west down the beach, around a point. Tiny purple crabs skittered in tidal pools, which they shared with a host of starfish, barnacles, and mussels. A shaggy mouse nudibranch sheltered in a basalt crack.

Alice stumbled a little. We rested on a pink granite outcropping. A bald eagle scavenged a dead salmon from his crook high atop a lightning-shocked cedar.

Alice groaned. She clutched her chest and fell forward. I turned Alice over. Pain slackened. I brushed bits of sand and leaves from Alice's hair and clothing.

I told Alice, as I lay my coat over her, "I will go for help."

Alice took my hand. "No, Daniel. I am with the person I love most in the world. And my dear friend is here," she pointed toward Odal. "This place is beautiful. I am old. It is my time."

Pain again seized Alice. I pulled her up onto my lap. I cradled her head.

Alice whispered, "You have found the star woman?"

I nodded. "She is in my head as we speak, here with us now."

"Hello, my dear," Alice said.

Hanah told me to give Alice a kiss for her. I did.

Alice smiled, "You must make Odal your brother, Daniel."

"But," I said.

Alice shook her head. "You don't know what you are fighting, Daniel. Humans thirst for saviors. That's why the forms seduced us. Masticans are only the latest in a long list. We need to know how to value ourselves, not fight aliens."

Odal spun up.

Alice looked up at her odd friend. "I am dying."

Odal said, "If it pleases you, I shall remove the arterial blockage and repair the damaged cardiac muscle," the alien rasped out his pinnacle vacuole. "Also, a blood clot moves toward your brain, Alice. Shall I intervene?"

Alice said simply, "No."

I objected, "You want to die?"

Alice winced. She breathed twice, then whispered, "No, Daniel. I do not want to die. I **am** dying. I am older than sand. Odal cannot prevent death. He merely delays it. My body is done. I am ready now."

I sobbed.

Alice looked up at Odal. "Perhaps now would be a good time."

Odal turned one palm up. His eyes fixated, staring into space. The alien imprinted Alice's brain into a corner of his own. Her noeform joined other clamorers there.

Rattling punctuated Alice's breath. Her jaw grew loose. I pulled her close to my chest, as she sheltered me when I was a boy.

"I love you, little boy," Alice mumbled, barely audible. The left side of her face hung immobile.

Alice's lungs collapsed. Her last breath hissed slowly out her mouth.

I held Alice for many minutes. I sobbed until I lacked tears.

I lifted the limp doll. I slogged back to Earthrise.

Odal stood by the front door when I arrived with Alice, an extraterrestrial honor guard.

Inside, Doe waited. She and Zellie were fixing a casserole in the kitchen. I lay Alice on the dining room table. Zellie began crying. Doe's face also broke. I was wracked again. We kissed Alice's face and hands gently.

When Dirk and Coreen saw Odal again, they picked up their bags and left out the back door. I never saw them again. I could hear drawers in other rooms opening and closing. Others made preparations.

After an hour, we three could cry no more. Doe said, "I changed my mind."

"I see that. I am glad," I said.

We three huddled, a ball of humanity, hearts festering with sores. Doe patted me. I hugged Zellie. Zellie kissed Doe.

Work helped the next hours. We cut off Alice's soiled clothes. We washed her gently. Doe soaped, rinsed, and set Alice's hair. We dressed her, brushing flotsam from the white sweater in which Alice had died. We wrapped Alice in a blanket.

Doe finished up dinner. Zellie and I went to the barn and knocked together a box for Alice, as the old woman had instructed me on a sweet April morning several years before.

I set the coffin on sawhorses in the living room, work-weary comrades now pressed to new duty. We three lifted Gramma Alice into her final bed. The Ravenhills cleaned, then set the table. Though the Earthrise families resented the stoical Mastican guarding their door, no one said much. I took a shovel, while others cleared dinner and washed plates. I dug a grave in the soggy soil beneath a conical cedar Alice had chosen. She had said, those years past, "May Raven's perch be my headstone."

The next morning, the Earthrise group stood around the damp black hole, telling stories of Alice. My tales made people laugh. Mirth betrayed the emptiness I felt.

We lowered the cedar box into Earthrise soil. We Ravenhills shoveled dirt on top of Alice. We held dirty hands as we walked back to the deadhouse, I on Zellie's right, Doe on Zellie's left, Hanah in my head loving the three of us. That all seemed just right.

Several small groups of Earthrisers moved off that afternoon.

Helen stayed. She was ever faithful.

But Earthrise was dead.

Alice: Thank you, Mr. Odal.
Rock: Daniel said you would come.
Alice: Your Daniel is partial. I just came from him. Odal will make him whole later.
Sali: I am your Kwagiulth ancestor.
Kushku: I am Kushku of the Hill of Ravens.
Alice: And you, my dear, are as beautiful as my visions foretold.
Hanah: Thank you, Gramma. I love your Daniel, and through him, I love you.
Alice: As I knew you would.
Daniel: Have you died, Alice?
Alice: I have. You were with me. And Odal.
Charley: Are we in Odal's mind?
Alice: Not exactly. Mastican minds differ from ours. Odal has many brain organelles, as many as he might want. We each inhabit one. Odal is the central organelle. But he is also all of us. It is an odd arrangement to him and to us.
Shewish: Paaah. Paaah.
Alice: I am glad to meet you. Odal asked me to speak with you, if you wish. He may be able to help.
Kushku: How can Odal help Shewish?
Alice: He could make Shewish as he was before the boy fell at Yokwat.
Charley: What about us? Can Odal change us as well?
Alice: If you wish, within limits. But Odal prefers you as you are.
Rock: Keep that alien out of my head, please.
Daniel: Too late for that. Our heads are mingled.
Sali: And yet separate.
Alice: Separate is good. Together is good. The question is one of balance and respect.
Kushku: Yes. Balance and respect.

CHAPTER 12
STARLESS

AT EARTHRISE
2361 A.D.

Things have grown peaceful at Earthrise. Five remain. Helen, Doe, Zellie, me, and Hanah. Odal comes and goes. We limp along, surviving. Pre-gax life is too much for five people to manage. So, much we would prefer languishes untouched. I suppose in that respect, our life differs little from the lives of others. The remainder of humanity lives formfully. They eat, indulge fancy, sleep, frolic. They frolic in an idyll of collapsed prudence. Fewer than a billion people remain, so some guess. Anecdotally, the birth rate plummets far below replacement levels. So, the outcome is settled. No path back to self-sufficiency remains for man. Human life will be gaxic. Or extinct.

Still, I cannot abandon Earthrise. I seem to be waiting for something. When attached to a person or enterprise, I have difficulty letting go. Even when a person or activity no longer makes sense. Friends call it loyalty and perseverance. But my clinging seems darker than that. Perhaps obsession or fear of coping. Or laziness in extinguishing habits. I do not know what to call it. This wondering wandering has happened to me before. My procrastinations, in hindsight, seem planned or fortuitous or destined. These lacunae in activity don an aspect that seems designed by a surreptitious architect for an elusive purpose. But the designer, if there is one at all, is not Raven. It is probably nothing. When I lack motivation, when I fail to act, it all seems to work out somehow. I don't really understand. This is just a bit I observe about my life. Perhaps my subconscious knows more than it lets me in on. Perhaps the subconscious of every person does. There may be deeper connections among us than we know. I find minds, even my own, fathomless. Perhaps you do too.

Dawnlight streamed between weathered cedar planks on the south wall of Eleanor's barn. A circle of light, a knot hole projection, crept, like a lethargic spotlight, across a bin of oats nestled against the aged shelter's north face. Motes swam the ribbed air, coming and going in that senile strobe. Eleanor chewed with contentment, as I squeezed and drew her teats. I moved the milker's stool. Frothy white steamed in my pail. Fall chill bit hand and cheek. Eleanor's warmth and her lovely smells jumbled in my nose. Hay and butter fat and the dusty sweetness of Eleanor's hide. I loved Eleanor. She loved me.

When Guernsey Eleanor had emptied her udder surfeit, I sauntered back from the barn. Islands of dewy alfalfa and dripping spider's lace caught chill condensations. Sinuous fogs crept along moguled fields, like vaporous slugs spawned of foothill mosses. The ground squished beneath my soles.

I smelled eggs and deer steak as I approached the deadhouse. My mouth watered.

IN OMBAN
2361 A.D.

Mastix hurtled too near the binary pulsar. The disaster was the puddle's own doing. Skal himself had made the calculations. The We was misled in a vast con game, an Enigmat masterpiece of devilish trickery. Time did not permit adequate correction. The Mastican sun had collided with the pulsar some years ago, issuing a spectacular gout of lethal radiation. Virulents constructed a shield. The puddle survived that particle onslaught, but now suffered the weird light of enraged neutron stars. Puddle ecology wobbled. The planet had been culled of historical and biological wealth. All was transported to other, safer worlds. Most Masticans had departed. Still, apoplexy gripped the We. The trillion-fold common mind, dispersed through several galaxies, assessed blame. The Enigmat had tricked them shamelessly. Bilaterals polluted consciousness. And virulents, budded to the purpose, had failed to shield the puddle, to pierce and counter Enigmat deceptions.

Virulent Skal projected that Mastix would have survived, skittering past the pulsars, to life as a sunless rogue planet. The We could have eventually ferried another star to service the puddle. But mass won. Pitiless mathematical certainty. The additional bulk of the Mastican sun, and its unfortunate trajectory, destabilized the binary pulsar's dance. These neutron partners spun down toward one another. With the addition of the Mastican sun, the trio would shortly reach critical mass. All would collapse, forming a small black hole. Small, but deadly. Mastix would, when the coalescence occurred, orbit within the event horizon of the freshly-minted singularity, eventually plunging into the crushed subatomic underworld of plutonic timeless hyperbole. Mastix could never depart its lethal location. The puddle would perish, its very quarks dismantled. Rending seismic convulsions already tore Mastix. A pulsar-ward tidal wave coursed around the planet as it rotated. Time slowed relative to off-Mastix trilaterals. The circumstance savaged the We. Mastix was over, the puddle doomed.

Rage tore the We. Such rage as had not seized the collective mind since protogenetic mutual annihilation frenzied the primordial puddle. Catalepsy beckoned. The We knew it would sink into abyssal unconsciousness at the impossible loss of the puddle. None could guess when, or if, the Masticans might think again. Little time remained. Those who managed to wish to survive stepped through to other trilateral worlds. But most Masticans on Mastix let consciousness slip away. They would perish with Mastix. The race suffered an epidemic of suicidal stubbornness. Billions would vanish into the nowhere-notime of singularity.

Tatters of the We lashed out. It cursed Enigmat with crass imprecations forbidden to self-respecting puddlers. The We dispatched eight virulents to those systems ready for envelopment to strike last fatal blows against those unwitting bilateral species. Genetically obedient, seven colleagues stepped through to bilateral systems. Qadax also went.

Qadax ducked through null space to Sol's system.

From deep within the Mastican aggregate cytoplasm issued a primal whirring, a lyrical moan. The strain was a hymn of praise, of gratitude. To Haras, for the safeguards he installed against Pathogene error. To the puddle, for two thousand million years of sustenance. To the Way of Engulf, by which Mastix would consume the universe. Only slowly did the trilateral paean fade. Psychic puddle waters calmed.

Last, remnants of the We turned attenuating attention to the remaining virulents. Shards of a trillion trilaterals fatally mindlashed 192 of the 200 pathogenic virulents. These gifted servants dropped where they stood. Skal's cell wall burst. His cytoplasm leaked into the primordial puddle. Gnashing mop-up microbes began dissecting his body into its nutrient components.

The pulsars' kilometers-high, planet-spanning tidal wave, both water and rock, churned over the puddle, erasing topography, scrubbing the muck-lake of fecund sediment. The Place of Masticans rendered a nowhere.

Puddle-pang utterly crushed the We.

For the first time in billions of years, no Mastican eyes watched. No puddle-hands worked. No Mastican schemes hatched. Catastrophic catalepsy cascaded, settling into insentient catatonia. Masticans in Omban, in adjacent galaxies, everywhere, convulsed. Somnolence congealed into speechless coma. Trilateral silence reigned. None knew when, or if, the We might again stir.

Qadax, at Sol, thought two thoughts. The first regressed Earth's forms. The second command propagated the null field of the Mastican envelope along the heliopause of Sol's system.

Qadax reached out to the We. He touched nothing. His cell walls quaked and distorted. Strangeness burgled his brains. Fatally forlorn, consciousness fled.

With his last thought, Qadax reached to Odal, though it was forbidden by their now quiescent people. Much, but not all, passed between them as puddle-pang smashed Qadax into dark insentience.

Bad as it was, perhaps Qadax suffered less than the other seven. He, after all, had been ostracized before mindlash crippled his pathogenic brothers. And Qadax had secretly excised his suicidal plasmid, what Haras had installed to insure Pathogene compliance with We dictates. Qadax hung inert in his null field, just inside Sol's growing envelope. Qadax and the other seven surviving virulents, if any survived at all, were each trapped within the systems they sought to kill. Each suffered another component of the billion year old Pathogene fail-safe. No virulent was intended to survive its final task. The Pathogene, like the bilaterals they ecocided, would be nulled to death. The puddle creatures of now-smashed Mastix would exact misguided vengeance. For Qadax, and possibly the other enveloped virulents, this was a cruelty. Death might require a billion years of abject isolation to arrive.

Qadax sputtered, then fell silent.

Nowhere did trilectical mentation stir.

Only in Odal.

AT EARTHRISE
2361 A.D.

I heard a whine. A sky speck became a cosmoform. The organic device settled gently, just this side of the slick formscum highway. It grew an ovoid exit, from which spilled four passengers. Then the vessel shrank, like a deflating balloon. It slipped from sight.

We five sat in front of Earthrise Deadhouse, taking in the sunset and oncoming night sky. Hanah snuggled with me invisibly, in the cuddle of co-consciousness. Doe and Zellie sat close, trading mother-daughter whispers. Helen stood behind us on the steps, a sentinel of intelligence and compassion. Helen raised our lantern, so the newcomers might find us.

The panicky four, laughing nervously, walked to Earthrise, a few hundred yards. One of the gaxers said, "Cosmo quit. I have never heard of a form failing. It just stopped, floated down, then regressed." The speaker held out his hand. It contained the one centimeter cube of his cosmoform, now melting in a kind of decay not native to Earth. The shipwrecked gaxer turned out to be Theodore Harris, sometimes of Seattle, who devoted his life to paper sculptures. We invited Harris and his friends to dinner, since they were hungry. We ate our simple meal, and chatted about what interested them. Trivial distractions, mostly, if you asked me. But I am an ass about formlife.

The door knocked. A gaggle of thirteen hovered outside. The chill that bites night air in waning summer made some shiver. The sun was reduced to pink whispers on cirrus formations miles overhead. The first of the night's trove of stars shone in the inky Sekiu sky. The group told tales of failed transiforms and a regressed habi. These too were hungry. Helen put on a big stock pot. We made a soup. We had baked bread for the week that morning. By midnight, it was gone.

A boy, Luke, pointed at the sky. A small disk of starscape was missing. The heavens burned, a mathematically-precise forest fire, burning black, not yellow, from a single point. Only solar system fragments would remain of Earth's starscape. The rest was becoming charred nothingness.

At dawn, we five Earthrisers convened in Eleanor's barn, while our formic guests slumbered. I milked Eleanor while the other four settled in.

Helen said, "We have trouble now. Where are these folks supposed to go? How will they get there? What are they supposed to eat in the mean time?" Helen paused. "Thoughts?" she asked.

I just raised my eyebrows and sighed. I nestled my forehead into Eleanor's warm gut. Eleanor gave a little grunt of affection. The expressed milk filled the barn with delicious aroma.

Zellie jumped in, "They seem like nice people to me. Maybe they will want to stay for a while."

"These people are gaxers. They will want habi food and do not even know how to wipe themselves. None will be happy here." Helen frowned.

Rustling troubled a dark corner of the barn, back where the seldom-used implements leaned chaotically against the weathered cedar planks of barn walls. Shimmering gave way to translucence, then to transparency. Odal stood in his null field. The field melted away. The Mastican spun across past Eleanor. The cow chewed her cud, untroubled by the alien.

"How the hell do you keep from getting dizzy? You are a damned merry-go-round of eyes," I complained.

Odal said, "You walk. I spin. Both are respectively normal." Odal's penchant for succinctness rankled me. I was not sure why.

Odal said, "Alice sends me to warn." He pointed at what would have been his head if he had one. He continued, "All forms have regressed. None will again function."

"Alice is alive?" I shot, knowing she was not.

"No, Alice is dead," Odal answered. "But within my mind, she remains conscious. As do you, Daniel."

Helen caught on faster than I. "None of the forms function, Mr. Odal?"

Odal pursed his pinnacle vacuole. "That is correct."

"A Mastican envelope is propagating at your sun's heliopause. It will take approximately four and one-half days to enclose your stellar system," Odal informed.

"That would seem pointless," I said. "We lack the technology to leave our system."

"The We does not interdict human travels. The We intends to kill your planet."

I raised my eyebrows. "How?"

Odal summarized, "Death will take centuries. None has ever breached a Mastican envelope. Not even Masticans."

"But how will the envelope kill us?" I pressed.

Odal answered, "The envelope is a species of null field. Nothing passes through it. So the sun's radiation reflects back into the system, instead of exiting into the interstellar medium. Slowly, the ambient temperature rises. The Oort cloud destabilizes. All the inner planets are pummeled by debris. Your ecosystems will collapse. Ultimately, Earth and Sol's other planets will be nothing more than a hot bare rock."

Helen gasped. Doe cried. Zellie growled.

I got an intra-psychic hug from Hanah.

Odal stepped through. There was a slight pop as air filled the space he had occupied.

My stomach turned.

Big trouble.

Immediate trouble for Earthrise.

Slow-rolling, inexorable trouble for humanity.

By the next morning, the sun boiled over the horizon on a billion bipedal apes, hot with hunger. Before noon, stomachs smoldered in earnest. By sundown, the specter of starvation burst into peckish flames that licked brains parched in the withering kiln of craving. By week's end, famine's fire roared through the human psychic tinderbox. Incendiary incivility splashed ketotic kerosene on the communal conflagration.

Hanah reported from Astroforce comms that several facilities had been overrun by looting crowds. Astroforce stockpiled food, now pilfered by starving gangs. Crazed families attacked. Mewling cries of children waned, a *decrescendo* of hope.

At Earthrise, so far from anywhere, we muddled along. We were twenty-two, then forty-five, and this morning became fifty-eight. The night sky held moon and planets, more visible now for lack of starry competitors. People left as they saw our shelves go bare. Others would arrive. We fed them what we had, what we were eating. All gaxers expected better nutrition than our fare. Spoiled by habis, they soon departed, praying that just over the next rise lay something. There has to be something somewhere. The rationale of misplaced hope. We told them the facts. Oddly, facts had almost no impact. Gaxers had become dreamy, not hard-nosed. The Masticans had deployed upon mankind the most potent of weapons: motivation depletion, dependency. Masticans made of mankind mostly moaning mice.

Days, I began sitting on the front steps of Earthrise, crumbling concrete and moss. I watched passers-by as sparrows welcome tomcats. I sat, mostly for show, on the front steps oiling my antique Browning twelve gauge. The Earthrise larder emptied, a leaking bucket of protein and carbohydrates. Crazed attack seemed certain as people realized they and theirs would most certainly starve. Still, staying put seemed the best course for the moment. Earthrise was off the beaten path. We had shelter, some food, and intimate knowledge of the land. Though the world's stability had crashed, ours held, for the moment.

By the fifth day, no stars punctuated the night sky.

On the nineteenth day after the forms regressed, Doe sat down on the steps next to me. She turned her rough homespun wool collar against the chill fall breeze that clipped off the Strait.

I said, "It will be soon now."

"What?" Doe asked, dodging the obvious with nixonian fleetness.

"Someone will risk it. A butt full of buckshot for a belly full of grain."

Doe chewed a fingernail. She rose and went inside.

Three weeks in, hollow-eyed numbness replaced shrieking. Water-borne diseases raged, so we heard. Silence deepened. An unheard rumble gathered, a mute metabolic shrill, surd in the bloodways of a billion glucose-starved crania. Hunger, long banished, repatriated, seething vengeance. The first starvation deaths occurred. Earth's human fabric frayed with disconcerting rapidity. Mastican arson torched the hominid sociality of Earth.

Schulders raided near the end. Dirk and Coreen barged in. They jammed boxes with what they deemed theirs. That, of course, was a great deal more than they had managed to produce in their tenure at Earthrise. I glared. Doe sucked her teeth. Zellie asked, hitting the nail on its head, "What are you two doing here?"

Helen looked at me squarely. She said, so all could hear, "I want them gone." Helen quietly left the room.

Dirk looked at me, then averted his eyes. Dirk said, "Going back to Heartsawl. The Iowa heartland."

With nauseating frequency, over years, I had listened to Schulders complain of Heartsawl. Living death. Parental stifling. Small minds. Listless educations. Perpetual taxphobic underfunding. I understood Schulders. I had been to Heartsawl. Life, especially life after the forms, daunts. Dirk bawled for placental security. He prayed for idiots cooing approbation. Coreen ached for playgrounds clumped with toddlers spanked by puritanical parents, a cauldron in which to dump her pointless contrition, a stew of cheap like-minded potmeat in which to simmer. Schulders longed to wriggle back up maternal vaginas, to snuggle in neo-uterine neurosis. Degestation. Sundering sperm and ovum. Bliss in existential non-existence. Schulders recapitulate Heartsawl. Dogs revisit vomit. Fools repeat folly. I saw Schulders walk off to the highway, each carrying a box. I never saw them again. But I learned their fate.

I felt sad. We had spent years together.

Still, I knew I would not miss them.

Zellie coped. Her keen eyes scrutinized our woods to the west. She brought me reports. Precise. Factual. Succinct. Zellie felt no panic. Threat spurred her to wakefulness, and precocious maturity. I grieved over Zellie's aborted childhood. A knot persisted in my stomach. But I knew what was happening. Zellie's preternatural adulthood was necessary.

Earthrisers, those who had abandoned the project these last years, began to dribble back. Takers on the take. They got a few meals, and then wandered off to their fates.

Days passed, quite a few, actually. The Earthrise larder shrank. Doe whined. Zellie's forehead grew lines, the sort that do not belong on the face of a child.

Hank Smelke, our neighbor to the west, pedaled up on a rusty bicycle. Hank tipped his blood-stained hat. "Daniel," Hank nodded at me, mustering a smidge of deference. "How are things here?" Hank licked his lips nervously, and, judging from the fit of his pants, hungrily.

I said, "We are getting by, Hank. Can I offer you something to eat?" Hank's eyes darted groundward. But he quickly nodded. Hunger had cleared the fog of political nonsense from Hank's rural mind.

"Thousands have swamped the Astroforce bases. Our boys try, but they cannot cope. God bless them for trying." Low blood sugar drove Hank toward prayer and solicitude.

"Bad, huh?" I asked, trying to keep Hank on track.

Hank nodded his bald head. "Outside Lewis-McChord, those that cannot get in are eating corpses. I rode that boneshaker all the way there and back," Hank offered, pointing at his bike.

Hank broke down. Sobs convulsed him. He quivered with chill, an inclemency not upon skin, but heart.

"I tried. I just couldn't," Hank heaved.

I raised my eyebrows.

"Rats got her. I could not bury Sarah. I tried, but the buggers took after me."

"Sarah?" Doe whispered.

Hank nodded. He held out his hands. Thirty or more bite wounds festered. A few drooled yellow pus.

Doe began breathing rapidly. She pushed her chair back from the table, and shuffled toward the bedroom.

An odd look, a cold, mechanical functionalism, flashed across Hank's face. I thought of spiders.

Hank continued, hardly noticing Doe's departure. "Something in Sarah's lungs. Just filled up. She hacked yellow crud. Then she got crusty patches on her thighs. I don't know what it wasssssssssss," Hank faded off.

Hank looked up wildly. "Some in Tacoma said they're planting in the southern hemisphere. We're gonna be okay. We'll be okay." Hank folded his arms around himself. He wagged his head in self-affirmation.

Hank's whipsaw emotions convinced me. Hank's roots had rotted. Any stiff psychological wind would topple him.

I patted Hank's shoulder. The machinery to plow and harvest had all gone to rust. If there were meager surpluses, those would rot on the pampas. Argentine rats and pheasants would gorge. But not humanity. I said nothing to Hank.

Our hungry neighbor ate too much. His gut was unprepared. When Hank could eat no more, he grabbed pieces of bread and shoved them in his pockets. A wild, impenetrable look hung in Hank's eyes. Then, without a word, Hank pushed back his chair, walked out the front door westward. He rocked back and forth, balancing his distended gut.

I resumed my doorstep vigil. I tired. I worried. Helen said my face was haggard. I had a blister on my butt.

Finally, time ran out. One twilight, as an early fall frost whiskered pasture grasses, a ruckus disturbed the barn. I clicked off my meatmaker's safety. My hands trembled. The barn door squeaked open. Trespasser eyes turned in the barn's dimness. Eight eyes.

Three children and their mother groveled over Eleanor's carcass, red to the elbows in guernsey blood and cow guts. Their mouths bulged with chunks of steamy raw flesh. The pitchfork wobbled from Eleanor's once-lovely eyes. The glazed stare of these desperate people showed no fear. Eleanor's tan and white hide was stained with the bloody handprints of children, a macabre kindergarten art.

Wordlessly, I pulled the door shut. I walked around and around the house, shotgun nestled against my chest. Doe and Zellie stuffed backpacks. Helen gathered all the ammunition. I nestled the HNH in my knapsack. Four of us hiked out of Earthrise, up the incline of the back pasture. Hanah, lacking legs, rode with me. We left our deadhouse for the misty cedar uncertainty of the Olympic rain forest. For mankind, a page of the human journal turned. For us, we suffered unwelcome eviction from a difficult, but beloved, home. A tear streaked Zellie's cheek. Doe was glazed, but resisted decompensating. She could be tough when circumstances permitted no happier refuge. Helen, always unflappable, strode evenly, with determination. Hanah felt my grief. She held me. With her help, I was able to keep martial brutality from consuming me. That was good for those we would undoubtedly meet in our flight.

From the ridge behind Earthrise, I peered back. Black figures darted from tree to tree through the graying darkness. They closed on the deadhouse simultaneously, front and rear. I heard shouting.

We hiked steadily upward. In minutes, all we had built would be shredded. Except for these critical core relationships. Those who destroyed Earthrise would be hunting desperately for their next meal.

Drizzle squeezed from sky, like frustrated tears of planetary anxiety. Helen led us deeper into Olympic wilderness, ever higher up ridges, slowly but persistently. Mammoth cedars crowded out the grayness overhead. Daylight slid into eternal twilight beneath the greening cedar canopy of the mature ancient forest. Rain turned to slush. Doe skidded on a mossy branch. She turned her ankle. Hobbled, she slowed us. Doe slung an arm over my shoulder and used me as a crutch. Two days and two nights we tramped through gathering snowfall. We prayed its blanket would bury traces of our passage.

Darkness fell a third night. Frigid winds blew sleet in our faces. Zellie began shivering. I pressed her to my chest, and rubbed her whitening hands between mine.

"Almost there, Zel," I whispered, kissing her cold cheek. Zellie nodded stoically.

I pointed to a moss-pated granite protrusion, now crusted in white. "There," I said.

Around the boulder, a cave loomed, black in the forest darkness. I had found this place two years previously while hunting.

Four bodies slumped onto the dirt floor of the damp shelter. I struggled to my feet a few minutes later. I cut boughs for bedding. Zellie fell to the packs with a hungry vengeance, filling her hands with dried venison.

Doe gently put her hand on Zellie's. She whispered a fretful maternal instruction, "Water first, then some mushrooms. The protein has got to last. It could be a while before we chance killing anything." Maybe Doe was coming around. I was glad she had returned.

Zellie nodded, and lay back on my growing mound of fir branches. Helen was already asleep.

Doe offered a cup of water and another of mushrooms to Zellie. But the girl too had nodded off.

Doe proffered the cups to me. I pushed them away.

Doe insisted, "Eat. You've hardly had anything since we left Earthrise."

"I'm fine," I insisted. "Zellie's got the right idea. You eat. Then rest. I will watch for a while."

Doe hesitated, but gave in. She chewed mushrooms slowly, mingled with little balls of snow. Then she snuggled next to Zellie. I saw her rub her turned ankle a bit. Then she too slept. I propped the shotgun next to the women. I thought, *Yes, it is "women" now.* Zellie ran in a girl's body. But womanhood suffused her mind.

I sat in the cave mouth. I scratched mud with a stick in the waning moon's light. Silence loomed. None had followed us. It was too far, too hard. Truthfully, very few had sufficient calories onboard to make the days-long uphill trek.

I nodded off a bit. I punched myself in the nuts. The pain helped for a while. Soon, though, I slept. Regardless how unwise, I could watch no more.

Hours later, I jerked. A frosting of snow fell from my head. I could remember no dreams, but felt unsettled. I moved around, pressing blood into hands and feet. Hanah held me. She guided me to a dry hollow nearby. She evacuated my mind to a warm, dark cyberspot. There, brown-skinned Hanah pressed my face into warm breasts. I sobbed. I slid into Hanah, and she over me. A weak convulsion, then sleep again snared me, as do spiders errant skeeters. After some hours came dreams.

A cackling laugh booms. Visages from Gramma Alice's Yokwat walls snap beaks. The great shadow of an overflight engulfs me. I crane my neck, but see nothing. Stars have vanished. I see only the moon. Alice points. A planet zooms up before me. An ocean world, splattered with islands. Thalassic paradise. Two moons chase around the turquoise gem, puppies in gravitic frolic. Alice shrivels. I feel the pain of losing her once again. I am naked. I look at my stomach. A great scab mars my skin.

Hanah appears, clothed in the bright regalia of Nootkan brides. Pounding cedar drums catch the cadence of voices from surrounding darkness. The chant of union pulses, like blood after a hard run. My compu-bride and I duck into our little longhouse. We have wed, after the Nuu-chah-nulth fashion. Potlatch reveling consumes the unseen village.

Our longhouse rots around us. We stand, Hanah and I, not on Yokwat's inside beach, but on African veldt, awash in grasses and acacia wattles. Jupiter and Venus hang lonely in the moonless night. Hyenas laugh in the distance. A sky-spanning crack appears, through which peek pinpoints of light. Stars, so long absent from human retinas. Talons grip the serrated edge of the growing crack. A beak too large to fully intrude pokes into the freshly repopulated void. It croaks,

"Come out, come out, little humans. Come play in the world I have made for you."

I peer through that crack with supra-human, star-piercing telescopy. Galaxies gleam, and an unfamiliar starscape, redolent with ambrosial stars, gorged upon a plenum of intelligences. The gigantic black corvid releases its grip, retiring toward eternity, flapping, complaining. Cawk. Cawk. Cawk. Cawk.

I see the retreating Mastican envelope for what it is. A gigantic clamshell.

A marvelous woman strides toward us. Deep eyes. Powerful legs. She hugs me and calls me dad. She points. We know to follow. I rise from the rock on which I sit.

I look down at my flesh.

The body is inhuman. Beside me, Hanah suffers exotic incarnation as well.

Faint cawing teases my ears.

We walk, then spin along after Zelika.

Something poked me in the chest, hard. I struggled up toward consciousness from raucous, laden dreamtime.

Hank Smelke, so recently at my table stuffing himself, his eyes now askew, leered down at me. His rifle muzzle rested against my sternum. "I thought I'd find you here, you greasy Indian shit," Hank ground.

"Hank," I said, my mind whirling.

"Where's the food?" Hank demanded.

I pointed toward our packs with one finger.

Hank pulled his deer rifle out of my chest, considering his next move.

I pressed a pretense of friendship. "You hunting, Hank?"

Hank said, "Yup." He waited a second, then said, "You." Hank's face scrunched, like rumpled aluminum foil. He threw back his head and loosed a long, bitter cachinnation. The crackbrained guffaw echoed back from facing granite bluffs as madness died in Hank's mouth, in sociopathic antiphony.

"Schulder told me about this place. He thought you would come here if there was trouble."

I shuddered. "I did not know that you and Dirk are friends, Hank."

"We ain't. We got real close recently, though. I whacked him over the head. Tied him up. Then I ate that skinny bitch of his, right in front of him. She was a gristly turd. Worst I ever tasted." Hank smiled so his gums showed, swollen and bleeding, upper and lower. "A couple days later, when it came Dirk's turn, he got real talkative. Told me a lot of interesting shit. Like about this cave and that fucksuit you are wearing. Hank poked his rifle into my shoulder.

I said nothing.

"Yah, old Dirk was a real good meal. He lasted me most of a week."

Hank looked at the sleeping women. "Looks like I'm in luck. I'm gonna get laid. And when I've had 'em and eaten 'em, I'll still get to play with that Astroforce hand job gizmo you're wearin'."

Hank poked the Winchester .30-06, clad with its rain cover and precision scope, in my face. Hank leaned down and whispered, "Some days are just plain better than others."

Hank stepped back. He took a bead on my forehead.

A blast from the dark of the cave smashed Hank's left ear through his right. The psychopath's scattered thoughts fled downslope in a tissue plume, brightening moonlit snows. A modernist canvas splattered in dark pinks and reds, trending toward black in the low light. Cannibal Hank's body slumped in a quivering heap. A black pool of viscous fluid leaked from his peekaboo skull.

I shook off shock from the blast. My ears rung. Smoke from the Browning's discharge obscured the bed of fir branches. It rose. I made out Zellie rubbing her shoulder. She clicked on the shotgun's safety, and walked over to me. We hugged. Doe and Helen joined the huddle.

I pulled Zellie's head toward mine. I said, "Thanks. You okay?"

Zellie nodded. I knew she was right. Most parents would worry that an emergent murder would fracture the fragile psychology of their adolescent daughter. I did not. Still, the event would have its fallout. Undoubtedly. Our world had turned harsh. I could not shelter Zellie from the rasp of reality.

I lifted Doe's head and kissed her. I put my arm around Zellie and Helen. I felt confident, in a way that had eluded me these last ten years. I knew I would run no more from dangers. I would run no more from myself. I am a bigamist with a remarkable daughter and a dear friend, Helen. I care for Doe. And there is Odal, who remains to me an enigma. It's not much. But it is me. It is enough.

On the fourth day, we again stood on the ridge overlooking Earthrise Deadhouse. The barn was charcoal. Wisps still rose from hidden embers. The deadhouse doors lay in the yard. Windows were smashed. I saw no intruders. We watched for a time, then hiked down. I poked the muzzle of my shotgun through the back door. Squeals and scurrying followed. Two skinny boys fled out the front door. Just scavengers. I combed the deadhouse. No others remained.

The deadhouse had been stripped. Food, tools all gone. The furniture was smashed. Why do that? Rage, I suppose. A pile of odorous brown sludge decorated the kitchen sink. Urine stained living room walls.

Doe complained, "We cannot stay here."

"Where would you rather?" I asked.

Doe opened her mouth. Then closed it. Doe threw herself into cleaning. Zellie and I tacked the doors back in place. We painted a sign in red, "Warning! Madman lives here." Zellie nailed it prominently to a tree down the north field near the formscum road. It seemed to work. Or maybe the worst of frantic foragers had perished in the psychological fires of mutual predation. As had Hank. Maybe starvation had intercepted them.

My calm deepened. Nights, we remembered stars. I did not want night-sky to fade from Zellie's memory. We drove jabs of recollected light into memory, as nails into hardwood. We hoarded the heavens in our skulls, Scrooges of precious dots. Pleiades. Dippers. The creamy smear of Milky Way. I wanted my mind replete with luminous wonder, stabs upon a retina full of black, a thousand fortunes of gems scattered across Raven's pitchy jeweler's velvet. Stars. Zellie must remember.

Odal arrived. He popped in, with a literal vengeance.

Odal said, "If I may, I would stay."

I walked up to Odal. I took one hand. I said, "Welcome, brother."

Odal told what he learned from his fleeting instant with Qadax The puddle destruction. The virulents mindlashed. Qadax catatonic. The prospect for Earth and its creatures. None of this painted a pretty picture.

I pulled Zellie and Doe to me. I asked Odal to noeform me. The alien nodded, and updated my existing doppelganger to one of his brain organelles. He noeformed Hanah as well, backing up her existence to this moment in time.

Then oddness happened. Odal laughed. A feeble, windy chortle, to be sure. But a laugh nonetheless. The first snicker in the billion year history of virulents.

Odal said, "Within me are many from the Ravenhill clan. Here at Earthrise, are others from among Ravenhills, some by genetics, others by choice."

I saw it was so, and marveled. I wondered how such union was possible. We six living creatures, counting Odal, and the noeformed mostly-dead Ravenhills, bonded. We melded our diverse lives into one. A community of mind, given to a collaborative vision of existence, of consciousness, of personhood. Diverse tributaries cascaded into a common sentient riverbottom. We felt prepared, together, to cut through eons of sentiment, to make a way for ourselves. To make a future amidst collapse of humanity's first venture.

Odal liturgized, an endeavor at which Masticans excelled, "Now we are Raven Pod, one from many." A song erupted from Odal's pinnacle sphincter, a Kwagiulth hymn of praise to the Great Spirit in the guise of Raven. Others, living and noeformed, learned the chant's pulse. RavenPod sang.

Odal said, "I have found a way forward, a way which is also a Mastican way. Alice adds that Ravenhills have found a way forward, a way which is also a human way."

Hanah added, "And a cyber way."

I laughed at the absurdity of it all. Union bound us, living and dead, human and Mastican and electronic. Nothing in common, yet now sharing all. The others saw the improbability and laughed. We brayed an atonal symphony of mirth. Life holds curves, dead ends, and surprises. It was time to laugh.

Beneath hilarity, from the incomprehensible interstices of the metaphysical, raucous cawking echoed our merriment. RavenPod intuited the rustle of inky feathers, the grip of potent talons. The weight of the noumenal settled upon a limb of RavenPod co-mentation. We, for a moment, became Enigmat's corvid temple, a sacral scramble of stolen twigs, a nest of nestled minds, his ravenry of preference.

Then we shared this vision, a waking dream:

An immense black-feathered head cocked itself comically toward our shared consciousness. The portent solemnly opened its beak. RavenPod awaited an oracular moment. Surely, our Tormentor would homilize a redemptive gem of divine wisdom. RavenPod bowed, prostrate to audit the beatitude of theophany.

The ebony demiurge burped. The gas smelled of bear grease.

Raven nestled into the tangled twigs of his ravenry, utterly amused with himself, and slept.

We understood, an hieratic flash, that everything is one, all things are connected. Unity in diversity, connection in isolation. Beyond grasping, yet at hand. Our co-mentation shimmered sacred sociality. But it was only a moment. Insight fled like rocks plummeting off cliffs, like the song of a rare migrating bird. After cherished seconds, RavenPod surfaced from its transcendent abyss.

Zellie, first to turn to the struggles ahead, asked, "What now?"

Helen answered, "We build a way forward, a way out of the Mastican envelope. We survive. Whatever the cost."

RavenPod concurred. We had chosen a path.

We knew, also, our unspoken hallowed context.

Talons scratch.
Faintly, inaudibly, we hear rasped cawing,
overhead, heartfelt, beneath being,
close at hand, yet reticent,
immanent, yet unimaginably distant,
visceral throb of unheard thunder,
silent nattering of divine drumheads,
Tinkling cascade of mirror shards,
Forbidden gifts; Prometheus unbound.
Unseen feathers rustle.
Beatific corvid guffaw.
Cawk. Cawk. Cawk. Cawk.

Raven, impenitently, toys with the human family.

BOOK TWO

TALE OF BEGINNINGS

ZELIKA'S TALE

STRAIT OF JUAN DE FUCA
SEKIU, OLYMPIC PENINSULA
EARTHRISE DEADHOUSE
2373 A.D.

I puzzle my speaking. Are you there? Do I talk to myself? I am a stranger to humans, many years now. Since Helen and Dad died. Mom too. If normal people still live, their days must mirror mine. Consumed by little tasks of surviving: picking berries, drying jerky, hauling water, fishing, salting my latrine, tanning hides, harvesting mussels, rendering oil. I speak. But to whom? I scribble, scribble. Who might read my tale?

Some smart people argue that humans are fractured upstairs; I read their books now. I have time. Odal brings books; he calls them classics. Pop. Odal appears, books in hands. Pop. He disappears, only to return with more. Where has he been? Where does he get these tomes? The Library of Congress? The British Museum? Port Hadlock Community Library? Odal handles the books with what I would call reverence, were a human doing the delivery. So, I read when not busy just surviving. When I read, I see Odal curates. These are not just any books from some especially dry garage. They are the books of humankind. Great books are the quiet underwater ravines where the long-digested sediment of human existence has settled. Layer upon layer, century after century. Only a few millennia, less than ten. Or, as Odal might joke, "An afternoon." He is not all that funny, though he is trying.

Earthrise Deadhouse is treasure to me now. When young, the place was just a house, and not the nicest I had shared. Though Earthrise is hardly more than a slumping pile of rotting lumber, it is warmer than the woods, and cooler on hot days than a rock beside the Strait. The place also serves as my library. Millennia old religious meditations, medieval blather, enlightenment exuberance, grim tales of modern hyper-population, and the skittering shallowness laid to paper during the Form period. Books entrance me. I love them. They speak to me, and comfort me. Those dead authors and I—we are friends. My dead friends think thoughts in circumstances I have never imagined, in times I never lived. Then their words roll over me. I am elevated. These odd, mostly male, misfits midwife my own thoughts, and reassure me that I am not entirely unhinged. They tell me that my view of the world has precedents, even if not fully congruent ones. I find myself mirroring Odal's reverence. I store the very best books in the driest corner of Earthrise Deadhouse. Which is, frankly, not all that dry.

But it remains elusive why I write. None remains to read. Perhaps I speak to myself, just to hear a voice. I fear my innerness lurks in mental brambles. It is hard to know what sanity means when one is alone. To whom should I compare myself? I may really be alone—the only protoplasm-and-piss human left. Odal says not.

But then, I do not always trust Odal. I cannot say I distrust him either. Humans trust for some effable reasons, and some ineffable ones. We trust when another approaches carefully, when she speaks thoughtfully, when he shares concerns we recognize as our own. We trust when others enter our stream of existence, when the person contributes time and effort, when one evidences desire to belong. We trust when it becomes customary to interact with another; we take shelter in the predictability. We trust over time, but the time involved is human scale. That is what makes trusting Odal so difficult. His time is not mine. Our clocks scratch one another—his geared to millennia, mine to days or mere hours. And then there is the face problem. Humans look in faces and find something looking back that we value or flee. The eyes speak. The smile relaxes me or chills me. Odal never smiles; no mouth, just a pinnacle orifice. Essentially, Odal has no face. Or he has three. All very confusing. And smells. I smell friends. Not odors that need tending. More basal whiffs. The stuff of metabolism and cell construction. Odal has no smell, at least none I can detect. When we talk, the exchange is human enough. Practiced from Odal's end, but, then, it has to be. The truth of the matter is that I know Odal cares for me, and I know that I would not survive long were it not for his oversight and warnings. But Odal is not my friend. At least, not yet. He seemed dear enough to Alice. Dad has affection for the weird twirler. Helen called Odal the repository of future humanity. Mom found Odal creepy. Enough of that. With my life, it would be easy to succumb to navel-gazing. I am sure I will come to feel something in particular about Odal at some point. Just not today.

Odal says Earth bakes in an oven that is only beginning to heat. But I feel no difference. I see no stars. The envelope prevents that. All planets have become conspicuous, now that teeming stars do not confuse the sky. The days, their seasons, come and go. Geese fly over, south, then north, joined by the horde of small migrators as well. It snows less often, but wilder when flakes do fly. Every day seems like more of the same. But no more crazies. I still shudder at those last desperate days at Earthrise. I still suffer the occasional bloody nightmare. Despite my humdrum, I sense change is afoot. But invisible mostly, scratching at the bottom edge of notice. I read of the human penchant for self-deception. We make of facts what we want to hear; distortion be damned. To stay functional in a terrifying world of predators and dangers, one just shelves intractable problems. Since no fix suggests itself, there is no reason to ponder. We need to believe we are good people, even when the facts are otherwise. I am certain Adolf Hitler felt misunderstood. Am I any different? I have my shotgun encounter with wacky Hank Smelke, my trigger finger itchy, his brain on a snow drift. I have that nasty episode all tucked away with a little bow on it. Hank threatened my dad and mom and Helen and Hanah and me. I ended him. Because I could. Because it seemed right at that moment. There were no moments to think it over. Just rise silently to my feet. Carefully release the safety. Point. Shoot. I am a good person. I will keep telling myself that, and hope it sticks.

Late afternoons, tasks complete, I hug my knees by pungent, salty waters. My familiar log. Rocks befriend me, stolid souls that measure lifetimes in millions of years. Creatures of intertidal sea and land, calcic or lichen-form, cling to igneous, sedimentary, metamorphic clods. Clouds billow, promising rain. Otters groom. Floating on their backs in kelp forests, they slick glandular oil over fur in sensual self-care. Mussels crowd the waterline. Sea urchins retreat, relished by the resurgent otters. The waters of the Strait roil, higher than I remember as a child. Coldwater fish wane, the salmon, the steelhead. Catfish and perch, up in the lakes, seem happy enough. I eat them. The rockfish endure here in the salt. I eat them too, when I can catch one. Deer and elk proliferate. I and hungry cougars hunt them.

I miss Helen terribly. Helen groomed my soul, in ways my mother, Doe, never managed. Mom loved me. But so much of mom lay trapped in that tangle of pain she called childhood. I suppose I will tell you, whoever you may be, about Helen and my mother. And dad, at least as much as I know. And the rest of it as well. Alone, I have hours, numerous as ants on a fallen honeycomb. When chores of living wane, I read and ruminate. Most evenings, I watch the sun creep into the Pacific, westward down the Juan de Fuca.

I am not so lonely as I feared I might be. That is not to say I do not suffer my isolation. I ache to talk. I could use a hug. I speak with what Odal says are the essences of my father and others. But not my mother or Helen. The words are those of Odal's onboards, his noeforms, but their voice is strangely breathy, the faint whistle of a pinnacle vacuole, not a toothy mouth and wet lung. But I cannot wrap my mind around all that. I had never grasped, until humanity was gone, how much I miss physical presence. Not touching. Not even sharing. Just raw propinquity. The tiny whiffs of scent, even awful smells. The quiet rustle of arms brushing torsos, of pant legs sliding past one another. The barely perceived comfort of having others with purposes and perceptions bobbing along the river of consciousness. Perhaps I write because I am lonely. That would make sense. In writing, the reader is mostly absent. In my circumstance, absent with a vengeance. But not so very different from when the world teemed with humans seeking engagement.

Anticipation touches all my hours. How does this end, for me, for humanity? Am I the last? Will the hominid line end when death takes me? Are there others? Will I ever see them? What has happened to my father, to Alice, to the Ravenhill line? Some dwell in Odal. But how? Do they grow? Are they mere simulacra? Does a noeformed human erode? Is that sediment more Mastican than terrestrial? Will the Ravenhills, ensconced in Odal, die? Can human identity persevere over eons? Should I join Gramma Alice and Daniel, swimming cytoplasm born of alien puddles? What am I to make of the visions, of Raven? I am not religious. My mother and Helen saw to that. But I cannot gainsay my experiences. Raven has touched me. Whatever that means… If Odal's account of the Maw is accurate, reality may be entirely more plastic than humans have assumed. Perhaps we live in the mind of Raven. A god who makes it up as she goes. Raven is reputed to be an occasional comic. I am not amused. But that cosmology would make sense of many things….

Still, my persistent anticipation lacks dread. When I read dismal Freud or western Buddhism, I learn that I am probably so tightly wound that I am about to explode. Freud tells me I suffer latent sexual monomania, deflected into a steamy little bucket of annoying neuroses. But I don't see that. Perhaps no one sees their own neuroses, until another points them out. I lack that human other, and so remain blindly unbalanced. Or the Buddha, Siddhartha Gautama, might have told me I am mired in unrecognized pain, mostly self-inflicted. The path out of karmic despair is compassion. If so, I am a loss. For I have no other to care for, but Odal. Caring for an omnicompetent alien exceeds my grasp. When I look within, I find calm and frequent happiness, not existential desperation. So, I do not find help in Buddha or Sigmund. At least, not much.

Bothered, I walk. I started this habit with Helen, who could walk the boots off me. With pack and rifle, I saunter and think, often missing her. I recently ended at the edge of the continent, past humps that were once the town of Neah Bay on the Makah reservation, to the raging tumult of waves at Cape Flattery. Tatoosh Island floated in the haze. The whales, humpbacks, if I guess right, are migrating. Their numbers seem to be growing, so something they eat prospers. I watched the waters. Ever rolling in waves. Once, four billion years ago, all that liquid was airborne vapor, locked in hot carbon dioxide and nitrogen. Cooling, waters rained out of the bitter atmosphere, dissolving salts from rocks over which they flowed. The brine became blood, the Earth's most astonishing transformation, eked over eons. Then, with emendations of cells and hormones, life commenced, then came to walk and talk, about when Odal was budded. I am the ocean. I have tides. I was born incoming. I die when the ocean in me recedes, when my tide ebbs. I see many others with whom I share blood. The elk and badgers and otters and fish and eagles, even salamanders.

But no humans. I seldom find primate remains any more. I did not think that a mere decade could erase so much. It is really longer. Once the Forms arrived, people never again undertook the hard work of maintaining deadhouses. The dead were consumed, ever so tidily, by the habiforms. Except for outliers like Grandmother Katherine and Alice and others of the Earthrise folks, who insisted on the human tradition of death and rot. When the panic descended as the Forms collapsed, the gaxers never buried their dead. Too much work. Too little discipline. Too much panic. The human habit of interment had died. So, the scavengers got them in their desperate hundreds of millions. Decay proceeded apace, a bonus year for carrion-eaters and the planet's bacterial biome. At eight billion, we were too many for the planet. After the forms co-opted us, our one billion was just right. Now, with only dregs remaining, we (I say "we" to give credence to Odal's assertion that there are others) are many too few.

I once worried when I traveled. Much of my kit stayed behind. On forays, I leave behind splints and bandages and crutches and a hundred other tools or stores on which I rely. Injury or illness could kill me, I fretted. I am alone. None to call. Then it happened. I turned my ankle badly miles from home as darkness fell. I could not walk. That very hour, Odal appeared. He repaired my wrenched tendons. I asked how he knew I needed help. He said I was just lucky. I knew Odal harbored no such sentiment. Another time, the Mastican appeared to warn me that my water source had become polluted in last week's rainstorm by a toxic stash some idiot left in the hills above Earthrise. Odal was watching me. If his stories were true, he has that whole invisibility thing he can do. So, I would never know. I find the tripod's surveillance comforting, though I would never tell him that. Probably my dad and Gramma Alice put Odal up to it. Once a child, always a child.

And Odal, as I have said, brings me books. I have a library to be envied in my rotting hovel at Earthrise. If there were anyone to do the envying. So, Odal may be watching over my education and sanity as well. His care seems almost parental, though one would never accuse Odal of sentimentality. He was bred for decisiveness and action by a race given to endless haggling and relational dithering. I do not understand Odal. Probably never will.

So, that is my life. At least, its essence. A lonely woman, her neighbor creatures, the planet, the alien and my onboarded relatives, books, and my wildly indeterminate future. Even death, once the one thing a person could count on, has become equivocal. There is the noeform alternative, if Odal is willing, and if I can stomach the idea. I doubt I shall.

Let me tell you how I came to be alone.

My mother, Doe Ravenhill, disappeared. That was usual enough. But, failing to reappear, that was odd. I came to learn that Doe passed at her deadhouse on tidal plains of the Strait of Georgia, near the Fraser River and Vancouver. The place was called by its First Nation's name, Tsawwassen, which means "land facing the sea." Mom, however, was seldom at her deadhouse. Mom moved around after we returned from the hills to Earthrise. She left not long after I pried Hank's sociopathic fingers from their clammy grip on this world. Doe had always been vacillating and peripatetic. Every couple months she would show up, pitch in for a time, then abruptly leave again.

When Doe did not appear for several months, I began checking her usual haunts. I paddled from place to place in my kayak. Victoria, Port Angeles, Port Townsend, San Juan Island, Anacortes, and finally, Tsawwassen, which is a long paddle from Earthrise. I found Doe's body sinking into tidal mud. Many happy insects deemed her a cornucopia. Ravens and eagles had plucked choice bits. Not much was left of her flesh, which had blackened. The skeleton was mostly intact. I sat on my haunches next to my mother's remains. I cried. My nose ran. I don't really know how long I sat there. When I came to myself again, the sun was low. I thought to bury Doe's parts, but relented. She never had religious sentiments. What was happening to her body is what happens to every body, no matter what steps others take to accelerate or forestall the inevitable. Her body posed no dangers to other humans, for, other than Earthrise, there were none. Or so it seemed. For all I knew, she had chosen that spot for this purpose. So, I left the colony of creatures she had assembled to their business.

Intense emotion wore me. I took refuge in Doe's deadhouse. My mother's letter lay on a table. I read outside in waning light.

> Zellie, I did not come to you because I know your life is with Earthrise now. So too is mine in a way, because you are there. Yet, I cannot live with Daniel and you. I am too weak, not of body, but of will. You know my story. I have never been able to focus. So, drifting . . . The Forms hollowed me out. I was vulnerable to them, like most people. Everyday living seems just too hard to me, after those years in the care of habis.
>
> Besides, I haven't long now. I have stopped eating. Drinking is a chore. Probably some cancer, like my mom. We could never tell what exactly, because the bottle seemed her big problem. Though I can never seem to make a go of living, I can decide about death. I know Odal would heal me. I know I could drag myself into Earthrise and you all would nurse me. But that seems a cheat. In this matter, I am kin to your grandmother Katherine. Death is normal for humans. And sixty to a hundred years, not a billion. That has been the harder question. I suspect Odal would noeform me if I asked.

I have found odd impressions in the mud around my deadhouse. If noeformed, something of me would be around for you, and for your father. But I cannot ask. Deep inside, I do not think I deserve that kindness, if it is kindness. I know those doubts about me come from crappy parenting. My detachment is plainly pathological.

My one happiness is that I bonded to you despite my demons. Broke the fractured attachment generational cycle. You have turned out marvelously, my Zellie. Be well. Lead, if the opportunity opens itself. You have that in you. And know your mother loved you.

Bye, darling.
DOE

I sat on the rotting steps of Doe's deadhouse. I wept. A dragonfly, clad in blue and yellow and purple and black, hovered before my face. A helicopter without rotors, humming ever so slightly. Mistook me for an especially large repast, I suppose. I worried who would cook dinner at Earthrise. I thought about my shoes. My mind shucked its moorings and drifted. Images of childhood swam past, disconnected, an affective cinema. Doe and Zellie on the run. Locations swirled. A habi in the redwoods. A deadhouse in Portland. A high rise in Seattle, long vacant. We squatted. Every city had abundant unoccupied shelter, given the population decline. And habis made life so much easier. There were men too. Always good guys, but, like my mom, not able to connect. We were entertainment, not family, to each of them. I know now, though at the time I felt rejected with each departure, that mom wanted it that way. She chose a man for his lassitude; if anything got hard, he would bail. And we would move.

Mom made each location secure for me. Given her attachment disorder, that is the astonishing part. Her own fear of connection never touched me, except circumstantially. I ate on a regular schedule. I read one good book after another. Mom had a special gift for finding people who wanted to talk about what I needed to learn. I always had people yammering at me, diverse people, a flea market of perspectives. They made me conversant, and nimble of mind. Bed was at eight. As I aged, Doe set appropriate and consistent times. I bathed daily. I de-skanked my teeth. I learned the facts of life early, and drank beer and wine, when we found some. But all moderately. With some dignity. Intelligently. Doe did for me what she could never do for herself. She nurtured me.

When mom showed up at Earthrise, during those last few years, an amazing fact emerged. Helen and my mother were friends. Never were two people more different. Mom struggled to bond. Helen bonded rapidly and permanently. Yet they were a sisterhood of two, knit by tough femininity. Mom helped Helen let life happen. Helen forced Doe to contemplate consequences. It was an unlikely friendship, but it worked.

At first light, I revisited my decision to leave mom's remains where they lay. Beside her body, I said nothing. Mom was not there, and I disliked what I had seen of funerals. As humankind's conviction faded that life survived death, at least for the predestined, the rationale for funerals grew paper-thin. There was public health to consider. There was the smell to avoid. For centuries, people who cherish no particular convictions about post-death existence nevertheless babbled pie-in-the-sky sentiments. I had said to mom all that needed saying during her lifetime. Talking to her bones would help neither of us. So, I left her where she lay. The place she preferred. Her choice was not mine to gainsay.

I tethered her kayak to mine, and paddled out into a slight headwind, across the gulf and into the Juan de Fuca. A long slog, but for me, time alone and hard work, that always centered me. I saw Earthrise in a couple long days.

At Earthrise, Helen took news of mom hard. She cried. Helen wrapped her arms around herself and crumbled to the floor. She rocked, seeking elusive comfort. I joined her. Daniel sat with us. To the extent of our knowledge, one of only four living humans had died. Our grief rang beyond mom. We were releasing. So many had died. A billion, perhaps. Now, each weighed on us. But most painfully, Doe. After a time, we spoke quietly.

Daniel said, "Is this what waits for us? Dying one at a time, until none remains?"

"There are others," Odal countered from the corner. He often rested in shadows.

"Show us," I urged.

Odal said nothing, did nothing. His way of mulling things.

Masticans wait better than humans. I suppose patience comes easier when one measures time in eons. For me, longsuffering consists in persevering two weeks, perhaps a month. I believe Odal might deliberate some matters longer than there have been humans. Which leads me to wonder how Odal views humans. Are we more than playthings? Our lifespans are Lilliputian. Odal was budded before the first proto-hominid dared its first erect step in Africa. And he is, so he says, a child by Mastican parlance. Can one care across exotic temporal incongruities? Odal is so inexpressive that one requires a generous dollop of imputed well-wishing to view him as a friend. In his world, I understand he is considered a deranged blabberer. Odal must barely get to know a human before the little creature dies. Viruses spawn a thousand iterations while a human musters just one. The generational disparity is worse with Odal, as a proportionality proposition. Could that be a purpose noeforming serves? To give Odal long enough to build a relationship with a human? If I ask Odal these questions, I am likely to confront a two-year silence. He will eventually blurt an answer at a wholly unpropitious moment after I have long-forgotten my question. So, it is hard to see how Odal's relationships with humans might prosper. Yet, here he is. And here we are.

Dad and Helen and Hanah died one after the other about a year and a half later, but in different ways and with different outcomes. I reread that sentence. It sounds so calm. These days were anything but calm for me. I find my abdominals tensing even now when I think of these events. My breath gets short. Sometimes I sweat, a trickle running from temple to cheek. It was not a good time.

When dad went, it was the day I became the last living human. I do not know the exact day, for Dad disappeared. I say I am the last. That also I do not know, because Odal is still pondering my request to meet other survivors, whose existence he promises. My solitude became silent and hard, a gemstone hidden behind my sternum. Hard and beautiful, but formed under conditions of extravagant, incessant pressure. A species in collapse. My species. My world.

At any rate, my father was not the first of my wee tribe to depart. Doe, my mother, had been first. Then Helen.

Helen had cut her foot on a shell on the beach. The tear was small, so innocuous. So begins loss. A problem insinuates itself inconspicuously—an unheard whisper, an innocuous bump, a negligible intonation. Thousands of such beginnings abort. One learns to suppress the subliminal. "Ya can't agonize over every little thing, you nincompoop!" Or so the none-too-wise saw goes. We tend to grow alert only when recognition dawns (and not always even at that juncture). How many debacles might be avoided by greater attention to inconsequential turns? But, then, what neurotic torrents would gush from elevated vigilance? Might we die of not-dying? Most of us cannot muster hyper-attention. We just wake up to find ourselves in a startling shitstorm of unknown origin.

Helen tended her laceration. Still, a rosy circle developed. The cut blackened. Pus dried. A crust formed. Dad and I gave Helen some of the store of antibiotics he had liberated from an Astroforce base years ago. A topical ointment. Some purportedly strong, broad-spectrum pills. Maybe the medicine was no longer potent. Maybe it was the wrong sort. Maybe the organism was one of those that hospitals created by ubiquitous antibiotic abuse before the Forms. Those still lingered, I suppose, making their living in abandoned sewers and cups of mussel shells. We did not know. The technical capacity to assess such matters had disappeared from the Earth.

Humans retain only what they value. When sentiments change, retention policies mutate. We once could diagnose infections. We had labs and experts and an industry devoted to such enterprise. Then the Forms swept over us. No illness. No need. So those skills lapsed. Our habits became Formic. Astroforce struggled against that tide, to no ultimate avail. So did others, with the same effect. Tribes of outliers cannot suffice as infrastructure for planetary inattention. Retaining needful survival techniques takes global effort, with people learning and forgetting, and relearning and exploring, and saving and teaching and forgetting and relearning. Sever enough redundancies and the whole popsicle-stick palace collapses. That's what happened to us. I suppose that is what Mastix intended from the outset. To strip us of our knowledge of survival, and then jerk the rug out from under us. Knock off the stragglers with a dimensional rift coffin. For Mastix, exterminating bilaterals was an armchair sport, perfected by a million genocides, woven into a subtle textile of xenocide. A science of death. An aesthetic of homogeneity. Survival for Mastix; liquidation for bilaterals. Theirs was an ironic tapestry of hatred. Extermination by strategic kindness.

Odal came to Helen. He offered to heal. As I knew she would, Helen declined. She had nothing against Odal. But she wanted to survive on human terms, not by Mastican miracles. I have tried to fathom what my Grandmother Katherine had been thinking when she foreswore Mastican meds, preferring leukemia and a painful death. And Alice too, though she let herself be noeformed. Alice could still be standing here. But she declined. A middle ground she chose. She swims in Odal's plasm, or her simulacrum does. And now, Helen…

It is hard to make much sense of the noeforms of my dad and Alice. These sequels to father and gramma obviously care about me. Which is puzzling. A bilateral hunkered in trilateral juice. Which is which and what is what? I do not know why I am so picky about the caring I receive. If something cares for me, acts in my interests, expresses love, stays involved despite obstacles to that affection, why should I care what may be its source. I am not talking about being wary of odd circumstances. One should be wary of the odd. That is a survival instinct. But everything about Earth is now odd. My primordial guts have little helpful to say about abject isolation, and finding solace in the embrace of an eight foot bacterium and his onboard passengers. Enough of this mumbling.

Helen developed a fever, and lost her appetite. Her leg blackened, then her right arm. Odal again offered help, though the dead tissues he would not be able to resurrect. Odal asked, in his whistle voice, if he might noeform Helen. She declined. Odal, as always, had no expression. He disappeared.

Helen beckoned me. "This is going to be a hard day, my young friend."

A tear crept onto my cheek. "You might recover," I said, without conviction. I just thought that was the sort of thing that a person is supposed to say to dying people. Sounds stupid to me now. Helen knew exactly what was happening, and had chosen her fate from among the available alternatives. I too knew what was to come. I am a bit embarrassed to tell you, whoever you are. At least some times, I pollute kindness with a dose of denial. Worse, sometimes in the face of trauma, I just lie, to myself, to others. It is possible to garner more comfort from plausible self-deception than from withering insight. I do not advocate denial and deflection. I am just saying. Delusion has uses.

Helen smiled. She gave me that chiding crinkle of her eyes, the gentle reproof that guided much of my teenage life. "We have had such an eventful life together, Zellie. I have cherished every moment."

I put my arms around Helen. Tears burned hot in my eyes. Hers rolled out of the corners of her eyelids, tracing a languid, accepting path to her pillow. I heaved sorrows, not just for her plight, but for the burden of loss that the death of humankind inflicts. Helen comforted me. Strangely, I was well enough. I felt bad, putting my dying friend to the task of soothing me. I guess that is the burden of she who dwells in inordinate compassion.

Helen stopped patting me, pushing me upright. "This is not the end, dear one. There is more."

"What?" I asked.

Helen shook her head. "The future is now yours. Make your choices. Take your risks. Preserve what has value. Be yourself. Now, make us some nettle tea." There was a rasp in her voice.

I placed Helen's hand beside her hip. It was limp. I set to the task. The pot. The sink. The woodstove. The jar of dried weeds. I stared at the steep.

As I poured tea, my father entered. He plopped his pack on the table. He slumped, despondent.

Helen, though weak, raised an eyebrow.

Daniel said, "Hanah is gone. I have been nursing her matrix for years, as you know. Her computational core has been deteriorating." He stopped and swallowed. "It was just a fragment of woven rare earths. It's been sputtering. Maybe too much sea air. Odal came to us. He noeformed Hanah one more time, updating her self within him. He noeformed me as well. I moved to switch to backup for Hanah. But it had failed too. When I rebooted Hanah's core, there was nothing."

I put my arms around my dad. He cried. He seldom cried. He never cried, actually. No, that's not right. He cried after Alice died on the beach. I felt dad shiver. Something sad was brewing in my father. He squeezed my arm. I squeezed him back, but his muscles lacked tension. His shoulders usually felt as though he was about to lift a big stone. Prepared. Ready for action. He felt different now. He did not feel despondent, at least his muscles did not feel that way to me. He felt—well, done.

I sat back. I looked into his eyes. He evaded me. He never did that.

Daniel Ravenhill, my father, scraped a chair across to where Helen lay. He inspected her leg and arm. He said flatly, "You are going, my dear." Dad looked into Helen's eyes. She gave a little shrug.

Daniel wiped perspiration from Helen's forehead. Fevers came and went, as did her pains.

Helen nodded. "We know what is happening to me. What about you?" she asked.

Daniel sat silently. Helen moaned, almost inaudibly.

I stirred some honey into each of the mugs. Honey was in short supply, so I added just a touch to each.

Dad growled, "Grief, I suppose."

Helen frowned. She took a deep breath, and let it out slowly. "I have seen you grieve. This is not that." She paused to gather herself. "There's something more." Helen's lips were cracking. She could not make herself drink enough to stay hydrated. She sipped a bit from the mug I held to her lips.

"Not now, Helen," Daniel said quietly.

"I do not know that I have any more laters, Mr. Ravenhill."

Dad pursed his lips. Knowing someone is dying is not the same as living the death. In the face of certain cessation, we expect an unchanged future. That is the conundrum of death. What cannot stop, stops. What cannot be, is. To now, we say never. Then, we lose.

Crows made a racket outside. I saw a murder harassing a bald eagle with a black feathered corpse ratcheted in its talons. The hubbub faded as the entourage flapped toward the Strait. Clouds, white against blue, framed a darker horizon. The wind gusted in little bursts. Trees danced jitterbug. I knew the Gulf of Alaska was sending a big blow our way. The Old Man and his stinkers, Gramma Alice would have said, with a little smile.

Daniel whispered, "I feel tired."

I said, "You have been with Hanah more than twenty years."

Dad nodded. His head drooped.

"And now, Helen is leaving," I croaked.

"Yes," he whispered.

Helen's eyes had closed. We pulled up chairs next to her bed. The sun set in a jubilation of oranges and scarlets. Little birds twittered, grabbing a last snack before heading to their nests and hollows. Darkness settled. We too slept.

Dad snored next to Helen. I woke. Helen's hand was cold. I waited for the sun to peek. After a time, Dad stretched, then saw that Helen was gone.

"Shit," he grumbled.

Daniel rose and lifted the shovel next to the front door. "Can you take care of this end?" I nodded. Dad walked around back, and began a hole next to the spot where we laid Alice. I washed Helen's face and hands. I wrapped her carefully in my best deerskin blanket. A wild rose prospered near the stream. I cut an especially beautiful blossom. I laid it on Helen's chest. Then I just sat. I cried. I daubed my face. Time passed without notice. When I got hungry, I saw Dad lying in the field grass, chewing a stem. A large pile of dirt lay at his side.

I called to him, "Jerky?"

He nodded, then called, "And some grease. Got a blister."

After meat and tea, we laid Helen in her spot. We shoveled in the hole, and patted the little mound that resulted.

"Not much to her these days. She's been wasting."

I nodded. Numb.

Neither of us had anything more to say. The loss would sweep over us as the days rolled on. We would take up Helen's tasks. Soon they would be ours. And we would go on. Without Helen. Everything about life was a bit less absent Helen. I suppose it always will be.

Dad's death was weirder. It rolled over me like a huge rock on a low incline. Slow, but certain. It began about three weeks after Helen and Hanah left us. Dad's sadness had not lifted.

"Zellie, I am gonna take some Daniel time. Think I will paddle up the outside to Yokwat, visit Hill of the Ravens and Yokwat and Alice's old shack. I need to ground myself again. Feeling rootless. Other than you, that is. You are my girl."

"Tell me more, Dad. I have not seen you talking with Hanah in Odal. Is everything okay?"

"Yes, Zellie. Hanah is well. She and I are good too. But it is not the same. She has been in my head most of my waking hours for a very long time. I know Hanah is artificial. But, to me, she was just Hanah. My lover, my friend, and my most intimate relationship. Then poof."

Dad looked at the ground.

"Sorry, Dad." I was not very wordy when my own emotions roiled. Hanah was not in my head. But she was always in my life. Since I was little.

"Things have been hard."

I nodded, and took Dad's hand. He squeezed.

I pursed my lips. "Winter is upon us, Dad. The Old Man and all."

He nodded. We just sat together. Minutes passed. Wind blustered outside Earthrise.

"I'll be okay. If things get rough, I will just beach my canoe, pull it up over me, and wait it out."

I was not convinced.

"It will only take me three days, maybe four to paddle up there."

I rejoined, "If the weather cooperates and you do not dawdle."

"Yes. There might be some dawdling."

Weather controlled so much more of our life than it once had, long ago. I lived sometimes in skyscrapers. The worst storms would pummel. Not a puff inside. But in a deadhouse, rot left cracks. The walls were more sieve than barrier. Chill brought shivers. Windstorms were breezy inside deadhouses. I (and Dad) showed greater respect for storm clouds than we once had. So, Dad's insistence on his travel plan was, in my view, reckless.

"You should wait for spring," I poked his ribs. You are not so young these days. And I will not be able to rescue you."

He laughed.

"I won't need any rescuing. It may take me a while, but I will be fine."

I was not so sure. I knew my father, the mighty Daniel Ravenhill, was depressed. Life had been sucker-punching him. But I could see he needed respite and balm of some sort.

We pulled the canoe from its alcove on one side of the cabin. Daniel's canoe was art. Carved in the old way from a single cedar log. The hollow burned, then adzed. The outside debarked, then adzed. Holes drilled to gauge thickness. Too thin and a foot goes through in a storm. Too thick and the craft rides low and cannot be handled by one person. Bow and stern rose to a flat beak and tail, like a fantastical beast. The hull was technique. Its adornment transformed handicraft into masterpiece. Charley Ravenhill, now resident in Odal, taught Daniel the skills of wood and paint.

Raven peered from the prow and from Dad's paddle: red and black and the various tans of cedar. On the canoe, sun and moon dangled in Raven's beak. Ochre reds and forest greens, mixed in the old ways from earths and pitches. Blacks of charcoal dust. Raven laughed in the precise geometrics of northwest coast sacral depiction. One could hear the avian being cawk, if one merely dared a dash of fancy. If one had ears for that sort of non-sound. Kierkegaard might have called it the derision of faith, or a light from within. Despair reveals salvation. The least tangible becomes all-gripping certitude. Veracity of nonsense—that was the only sensible approach. Kierkegaard makes me laugh, as does all the best of theology. I met some Catholic seminarians in my travels with Doe. They called their school, with no intent to disparage, training in stand-up zingers. God-talk—a moonless midnight tramp, waist-deep in what-if-itty porridge, sticky but sumptuous.

We oiled the hull inside and out, filling pores with elk grease. We built a fire on either side to melt the slather into the wood. I rewound the leather thongs on Daniel's paddle, the backup too, avoiding the jester's visage. Blisters could complicate a long haul. We pulled together some rations in bags I had made of prey skins. Daniel would eat from the ocean, but one wanted something portable at hand for the unexpected.

The unexpected is to be expected. All humans tend to invest heavily in convictions of continuity. We are inclined to yawn. We know that because the sun rises today, it will tomorrow. It is not so. There will be a day on Earth when, in fact, the sun does not rise. Every day belongs to itself. Among days, there are continuities, to be sure. But flukes and twists intrude. None predicted the Mastican arrival or the Forms. And some eventualities are too small or slow for humans. None predicted the cholera variant that killed a billion souls in the mid-twenty-first century. Or the second eruption of Mount Vesuvius. Or the Oregon tsunami horrors of the plunging Juan de Fuca plate off the American coast. Yet all happened. I cannot even reliably predict when the next storm will pummel Earthrise, though we could have done a better job of that a couple hundred years ago.

So, when a big storm cleared, Daniel left. With a warm hug and a sweet, fatherly kiss, Daniel, my last companion, paddled north toward the hazy south shore of Vancouver Island in practiced, workman-like strokes. He would paddle hard, the Raven paddle in-back-out of cold Pacific saltwater. That effort would take Daniel to the fractured outside of the island, where shelter abounded. If need be, Dad could peck his way up the coast to Yokwat during storm interludes. And coming home would be faster, with the likely winds at his back. I watched until Daniel disappeared in the sun's glare and mist.

I turned to chores neglected during Helen's illness. I replaced a leaking pipe from the cistern uphill. I turned all the jerky and rekindled the smoky fire in the bottom of its little shack. Filled baskets with fiddlehead ferns and nettles to dry. I boiled the fiddleheads to clear their toxin. I swept the cabin. I greased all the hinges and latches. I cleaned my guns and checked my bullets. An upside of American gun nuttiness is that they made enough ammo to last millennia. For a lone person, ammo for a million years waited in deadhouses everywhere. I brought cartridges home from my outings. Always old, but mostly good. I replaced my outhouse poop hole, which was cracking. It is not that easy to cut round holes in planks without fine saws. I made a note to look for better blades on my next outing. Maybe in what is left of Forks. I scraped and turned some deer hides I was tanning, and sunk a couple in a washtub of brain slurry to work its hide-softening magic. I do not know why I am telling you all this stuff, whoever you may be. I suppose because this is my life. Can't say I am unhappy. My genes speak, sometimes petulantly. I wonder about a sexual companion. My mind mulls the possibility of children. Just daydreams. Programmed daydreams from a billion years of evolution. But meaningful daydreams nonetheless.

Evenings, I read by my lamp or candles. The time is contemplative. Paragraphs meander past. I chew each. The best, I sip, like summer berry wine. I ponder my odd life in the thought-filled company of odd long-dead folk. Odal's books take me places I have never been, some to places that no longer exist, usually in centuries long past, mostly in the company of arrogant white men. There are some women, also mostly arrogant. There are even women among the greats who are people of more striking coloration than white. Like me. Probably one has to be arrogant to write. I see that I am. It seems to matter little to me that no one will read these pages. What matters is that I write. An odd exercise in futility. Is that okay? What even could transpire to convince me one way or another? A puzzle.

A big storm blew in from the northwest. These were usually howlers, screaming from the Bering across open ocean, driven by Arctic bitterness. Cold, even snowy on occasion. A doozy. Most such storms last a day or two. After three days, this one lost punch, but only a bit. It was still raining hard on the fourth afternoon. So, I stayed in.

I lit my lamp. I cracked open Mills's *On Liberty*, an exquisite exhalation on an oxymoron. A government that does not overreach. Does not crush. Refuses to stunt citizens. The rights of women and men inexorable, undeniable, impregnable. A paean sung for deaf ears, a dirge for history's kings and despots. Ultimately, Mill chanted a lament upon tyranny. Odd, because Mill himself, in India, justified British hegemony over those he took to be poor dumb brutes in sore need of a not-so-benevolent foreign despot. I forgive Mill his hypocrisy, because John Stuart was an ardent feminist and opponent of male-on-female violence. He flung opened doors through which my sex eventually strode.

I read of governments. Communist, democratic, Islamist, authoritarian, nationalist. I have never known a government myself. So I have only book-learning. I don't really get it. Such odd patterns of relating. Everyone, even people one knew well, treated as strangers. With rights. With non-personal obligations. Taxes and other impositions in their hundreds. Laws books to glut cavernous libraries, more than any human could read, much less comprehend. Stadiums, where teeming hordes bathed their itchy souls in vicarious bloodsport. Governments required so much coordination of so many strangers. Why did humans fail to reduce their numbers? Had they just forgotten the warmth of life in a circle of friends? Why tolerate relationless relating? Odal brought me a book that did the critical calculation. If all breeding couples had chosen to have only one child, the human population would have plummeted from eight billion to one or two billion in only a couple generations. And humanity could have managed two billion. They might not have been so desperate as to fall into the Venus fly trap of the Mastican Forms. So why? Governments required that people poop and pee in specific locations, walk or drive on one side of streets, but not the other, sort their garbage into colored bins, and wear masks during times of widespread illness. Governments demanded half of people's earnings, and specified how much one had to work. Why did humanity never regulate wanton breeding? I read of the botched attempt by China. The communist government there was always ham-handed and overbearing. Humans during the governmental period were amenable to vast regulatory intervention. What exempted child-bearing from scrutiny? Oddly, in the literature of the twentieth and twenty-first centuries, few thought their intention to breed was a problem. Those thinkers lived in a time when the human load turned waters into sewers and air into a garbage dump. But few stood to say, "Don't breed. We are enough." Many raised their voices for procreative liberty. Governments gave tax breaks to child-laden families. Why? Had crowding made us suicidal? Demented? Desperate for a bit of succor?

I see in myself an urge, a twinge, a curiosity about bearing a child. I suppose all women feel that. Maybe men too. But the world of eight billion was jammed with children in need of care. Most were neglected, and then matured to work the terrors that abused children wreak when grown into distorted adults. If parenting were so adamant a drive, why was any child abandoned? Why did the busy governments of Earth permit these horrors? I dwell on what was, and wonder at the inanity of my species. I suppose similar dimness hides in me, unseen for lack of relational mirrors. The human load is what made us vulnerable to the Mastican proposition. It got us off the hook for feeding and healing our innumerable offspring. Forms remediated our polluting. The Masticans solved our conundra for us. Permanently. Fatally.

Enough gritching about days gone by. The tyrannies of my life are less social than Mill's. I suffer the trouble of food and warmth. I grieve loss, at least in some part for all of humankind, but most painfully for members of my family and acquaintances. And I am locked in a lethal prison of Mastican fabrication. I would never have left the planet anyway. And I shall be long dead before Earth grows fatal to primates. Still, I would prefer not to persevere under the thumb of a regime that revels in my extermination.

There came a rustling of air in the corner, in the shadows. Drying weeds, hanging nearby, trembled, just a bit. That would be Odal. I looked up.

"Hello," I said.

Odal said nothing. That was normal. When he was ready, Odal would blurt.

But Odal did not. He just stood on his tripod legs in the corner in silence. After a few minutes, it felt odd.

So, I probed, "What's up?"

Odal spun forward a couple of feet. One eye rotated round back, another rotated into view. Disconcerting geometry.

"Daniel wishes to speak with you."

"Okay. We going to him, or you bringing Dad here?"

Odal lapsed again into silence. Odd pacing of conversation seldom meant much when speaking with Odal. So I sat back again.

Finally, the Mastican said, "Neither." I waited. Odal said, "I spin aside for Daniel."

The windy chortle of Odal's pinnacle vacuole took a different tone. Not human exactly, but more human than Odal himself. (What am I saying? This is Odal himself. The noeform thing is harder in person than in theory.)

"Hi, Zel," said noeform Daniel.

"What's wrong?" I asked. There was an unspoken agreement that noeforms do not speak as their originals, at least not during the life of the original.

"What's happened?" I began to tear up.

"I—original Daniel, that is—got caught in the last big blow that came through here. He has died."

I sat stunned. I do not remember much of what happened next. I could not speak. My face got wet and my stomach hurt.

After some minutes, I croaked, "How?"

"I—he paddled out from the outside coast to catch that fall current going north. Daniel saw the storm barreling down on him, but could not paddle fast enough to get back to shelter at shore."

I said through my tears, "That was stupid."

Noeform Daniel said nothing.

Some minutes passed with me in spasms of tears again.

I said, "Sorry. I am just angry. You have left me alone. Alone in a way no human has ever been alone."

Noeform Daniel said—I stop myself. Now this is all that remains in the universe of Daniel, my father—I had better start getting used to it. So, let me start again.

Daniel said, "I know. I am working on that."

I raised my head to peer at alien eyes, not my father's. I raised an eyebrow.

"Best not to speculate just now," Daniel said. "Still working it out with the big guy, my hotelier."

I nodded. Gentle sounds blew from Odal's top vacuole.

"The wind caught me, and the canoe started filling. So I bailed. But the bailing left more canoe to catch wind. Not bailing slowed me down. But it also froze me. It became a balancing act—little enough water in the canoe to avoid hypothermia and stay conscious, versus high enough above water to get blown seriously out to deep water for a proper drowning. Eventually, I passed out. I woke to roaring. The tumult of storm-bludgeoned rocks at Cape Flattery. The canoe and I tore down a wave, smashed against the cliff face. The canoe broke up. I crushed my face. Sank beneath the seafoam. Odal noeformed me when he arrived, but I was dead. My brain, he says, was still sputtering in the bitter waters, so he captured a last chilly noeform of me. He could not repair my body."

I said, "Sorry." I was going to say "Dad," but I had not gotten that far. Wasn't sure I ever would. Daniel would do for now.

Daniel said, "I will stay here with you."

I nodded. That was okay for a while.

But my face dried. My heaving subsided. And profound weariness slunk over me.

After an hour, I said, "I gotta go to bed. Need some time to rest and process this."

Daniel asked when he should return.

I told him three days. I knew Odal would be watching me no matter what schedule I set.

Odal tried to nod, but, lacking a neck, it little resembled human assent. More of a jerky lurch forward. The gesture sufficed for understanding.

Raven came to me in my sorrowed sleep. That he came was usual enough. That he came this night may be too much coincidence to believe. I seldom recall the details of my Raven encounters, unless I wake mid-dream. And I never know when I am just dreaming about Raven, or when Raven elicits my dream. This was an odd excursion.

I paddle Dad's canoe. Raven, the art on canoe-side, dangling son and moon in escape from some demiurge from whom he had stolen them, leads the way on the sides of my metal prow. The waters are broken, each fracture an island in a vast wooded archipelago. Waters more turquoise than are oceans most days. Two moons, one large, one small, hung over a distant green ridge. I turn to look behind me. A man, pleasant to look at, strokes strongly. Canoes string behind us. Some bear strange humaniform creatures, though most are ordinary people. A raven cawks, not the demiurge that dogs my family. Just a corvid, though larger than any I have seen. Ahead, on a low beach, stand houses of cedar planks, and many children playing. Smoke rises from cooking fires. A wisp of my hair blows across my face. I straighten it. It is older hair, like Doe's. Salt and pepper.

Then it was over. Something banged on the Deadhouse siding. I opened one eye. I hauled myself out of bed. From the front door, I spied a buck's butt. A piece of bark tossed his direction sent him bounding into the forest. Deep in my recesses, I had hoped it would be Dad or Doe or Helen or Alice or anyone. Even Odal. The world looked different from the front steps of Earthrise Deadhouse. Always in my days there, one could hope, even expect, others would arrive. Times of laughter and warmth would follow. If not today or tomorrow, then next week. Food would get cooked and eaten. Stories told. Today, the Strait looked different. Empty. No one would be coming to Earthrise. None would hug or eat or laugh. Today would be like every day for the rest of my life. Just me and my thoughts and surviving. Alone. There might be brief chats with doppelgangers, Dad or Alice or Hanah or even the other noeforms. But no humans. Loss rolled over me like a surf log. Heavy. Wet. Crushing. I sat on the steps. Watched birds. The buck poked his head out of the woods. He saw me, but continued grazing. I did not look big enough to hurt him. And he had no idea how dangerous humans are, especially when hungry or angry. I lost time. It found me through my stomach. Ate gnawed jerky. Started a stew. Threw in elk and venison, carrots, wild onions, ferns, and some sea salt. I let this cook down for some hours over the fire, ate some, and replenished the pot. I let it simmer overnight. I would feast tomorrow. Clean it up.

My inside felt hollow. Loss compounds loss. And loneliness jumps on board, aggravating stress. My time may be limited. I keep finding myself grinding my teeth. Unremediated stress overwhelms humans. Too much and we die. Daniel would say that stressed is just desserts spelled backwards, beaming that stupid grin of his. I would rather have desserts. Many of the authors I love think man is a social animal. Aristotle, for example. Man is political, by which Aristotle meant, humans must relate in small groups, the number of humans that one can see from a single vantage. Numbers larger than that confound humans. Dunbar, in the twentieth century, found the number to be 130-150 persons. More than that exceeds human comprehension. Crowds of unknown persons lead to anonymous relating, which is the agglomeration of strangers. Warmth and belonging bleed away, to be replaced by wariness and fear. Buber shared Aristotle's view, with a religious bent. People are vitally linked in small groups, fabricating identity from bonds with others and the divine. To strip a person of the other is to deny that person identity, to rob her of belonging. Humans relate as I and Thou. Rotted relating leaves only I and It. Is that what is happening to me, though I do not recognize it so far? Lacking Thous, am I stuck with It-ness? Would I be able to recognize rot in my own sense of self? Or would I just be decimated and oblivious?

I climbed into bed. I slept heavily. I woke when another bang vibrated the deadhouse. Buck was back, I thought. I opened the door. There stood a two foot tall Mastican. I was speechless. I rubbed my eyes. Slowly, I woke. This was no dream.

"I thought the envelope kept you crappers out, just like it keeps bilaterals in," I spit.

"I am not of Mastix," the creature burbled.

"Fooled me, Mr. Midget."

I sat on the steps. If the bugger was going to kill me, I might as well be comfortable. The dwarf spun closer. I held my ground.

"What do you want?"

"Nothing," it whispered or sang or whatever you call the odd vocalizations that emerge from a pinnacle vacuole.

"Well, I value my privacy. So, leave."

The Mastican stood silently on its little tripod legs. Silence ran on for minutes.

"I am of Odal," it said.

I replied, "Guessed that."

"I am Odal's bud."

"Nope. Still don't get it," I shot, getting angry.

"I am Daniel, Odal's offspring," the creature said.

"Daniel?" I asked.

The little thing made a stuttering lurch. Could have been a nod.

"My father, Daniel Ravenhill?"

"Yes, Zellie. It's me."

"This is just too weird," I said. I laid back on the steps.

"Why didn't you say you were Daniel right up front?" I growled.

"I said what seemed right," Daniel whistled.

"You freaked me out."

I started crying.

Daniel nestled on his legs. "I am sorry. This never happened to me before."

"That's for sure. Or to anyone else," I murmured. My hands trembled. I shivered. My breath came in lurches.

I sat up. "Come back tomorrow." I stood.

The creature peered at me, then popped out, just like Odal, though more quietly.

I was stunned. One thing after another. First, deaths. Now, resurrection. I wanted to scratch the itch behind my eyeballs.

I slowed my breathing, wiped my face. I relaxed muscles, group by group. I pondered. Continuity matters to me. If things were about the same tomorrow as they were yesterday, that would be fine with me. Things I don't like, I fix. If food stocks are low, I hunt and gather. If a window shatters, I find new glass. If I am tired, I nap. Keeping my world optimized has grown simpler as the number of humans has declined. Fewer competing interests. Fewer dissonances. More resources and fewer mouths to feed. Less complexity. But my social situation—that seems to have no easy remediation.

I was only just getting used to the idea of being alone, really alone. Now, poof, Dad is back, or his simulacrum. Dad who is mostly not-Dad. If Dad is back, I suppose I can expect others to show up as Odalets also. My heart raced again.

Who is Odalet Daniel? He is not my father who died. Yet he remembers much that is my Dad, if he is the noeform Odal harbors. Is that not Daniel's essence? Memory. I pursed my lips. No, a person is more than knowing and feeling. Humans are brains in bodies. This new Daniel has a body, but not Daniel's body. Daniel's corpse now feeds bottom dwellers at Cape Flattery. And the way Daniel inhabits this new body differs fundamentally from the way his brain, branching throughout Daniel's Nootkan physique, existed. What is it exactly that Odal extracts when he noeforms someone? A pattern of cognition? A soul? A profoundly intricate mesh of synaptic connections? How can what Odal copies be moved around like chunks of firewood? What are the means by which a human is noeformed? Is it a technology or a biological capacity or an artform? All of the noeforms of which I am aware are Nootkan, and most are Ravenhills. Why is that? Where lies the fascination with us?

And what is this itty-bitty Odal thing? Does Odal just squeeze off a lobe of himself? Throws in the parts he thinks his bud should have? No fetal development. No parturition. No childhood. No education. Just plop. Then "off you go." How does all this work? How can it work? A bilateral mind in a trilateral context. Three eyes informing a two-eyed brain. Three arms. Three legs. But answering to a mind built to coordinate only two of each. A human two-dimensional mind, with imputed depth from subtle cues in binocular vision. Trilateral three-dimensional cognition; three eyes creating a spherical raw experience. There must be dissonances in the conjunction of such a mind and body. The bilateral stuttering at its trilateral matrix. The trilateral taxing its onboard human bilateral. Scraping. Grinding. The bilateral down-shifting its Mastican carrier. Wham. Pop. I suppose Odal worked on this hard. This budding scheme probably predates hominids. Probably part of his big plan, about which our Mastican virulent is so cagey.

I had again begun breathing shallowly. I scratched my arm. I stretched, trying to calm down. I will be glad for company, if Daniel has not adopted Odal's conversational pace. It is plain that Odal and Dad are trying to take care of me. It must have cost Odal to bud Dad. Might even have been risky. So, I should feel grateful, I guess. But I don't. I am bothered.

I recognized the scatter of my thoughts and feelings. Exhaustion. I snuggled under my deerskins and slept. I do not know how long, but the sun had vanished during my slumber. I got up, peed, then ate jerky and dried apple slices. I drank a glass of water from my pitcher. Cool, wet, delicious in that understated way water can be tasty. I lay down again. Afternoon sun lit the room when I woke. I felt better.

I donned my boots and pack. And I walked. My Winchester hung over a shoulder. I traced the Strait northeast toward Cape Flattery. Sleep found me beneath a shallow rock overhang, one under which I had often sheltered. A small fire burned whenever I slept. Dancing flames deterred the sorts of critters that might find me delectable. Again, I slept hard, but this time woke with the sun piercing a company of giants. Not in centuries had humans logged this rain forest. Cedars towered, often more than 100 feet. The prodigious among them 200 feet. Their umbrella stole water and sun from beneath, leaving a forest floor relatively open for a walker. Corpses of evergreen ancestors lay rotting, a larder for beetles and termites. Where storms tore down cedar copses, a short-lived sprout of alder and birch would intervene while the giants reseeded themselves. Ferns and mosses cushioned the forest floor. The chitter of birds, the scramble of squirrels, the cawing of crows were a music of reverie. Occasional elk bugled brassy counterpoint. I was processing, letting the Earth heal me, reorient me.

When the sun's brilliant orb was high the next day, I reached Cape Flattery. Waves pounded its cliffs. Sixty feet below, seabirds swirled. Foam fluttered, spittle of the sea. So violent was the pounding that even the kelp forest could not root itself. Here it was that Daniel found his end. His canoe crushed to fragments. His body brutalized. I knew I would see nothing of my father. Human flesh would be battered. Would sink in the maelstrom. Would become the repast of crabs and hagfish. But pilgrimage to my father's place of death seemed necessary. To see with my own eyes. To peer at the place where he ended. To honor the man who participated in making me. The human impulse to revere is as old as the species. Here am I, the last, still burying my dead.

I retraced my steps from the edge of the continent, continuing south. Perhaps flotsam lodged in the driftwood of Hobuck Beach or the broad expanses of Shi Shi Beach. A remnant. A flake of a moment. I peered down Hobuck, looking for jetsam of human origin. Looking for a piece of Dad's canoe. I walked along the high tide line slowly, examining the drift log scramble. After a couple hours, there was Raven, jutting up on a bit of father's paddle. I sat next to the fragment. I cried quietly. I do not really know why. Dad died where he wanted, doing what he wanted. Perhaps I wept for myself. But my plight does not seem dire. For me, every day holds something new. I am lonely. But replacement Dad may relieve that pain. Maybe I weep for no more portentous reason that that I needed to cry. My emotional adapting needed a good rinse. My shoulders heaved. Things slowly calmed within. Within the hour, I was ready to walk again.

I strapped the paddle fragment to my pack. An incising stream offered a steep path up the cliff from the beach. After a few hours of the trek homeward, I chased spiders from the fire-hollowed trunk of an ancient cedar, more than twenty feet in diameter, and settled in for the night. A fire at the entrance offered dancing comfort and a bit of warmth. Not that I was especially cold. Like all the Ravenhills, the various weathers of the Nootkan coast troubled me little. It seldom snowed. Waters and cedars kept summers cool. My usual deerskins almost always sufficed. One sometimes needed another layer for rain protection. I had a long, light, well-oiled deerskin coat to repel the frequent rains. I gave it a useful hood. I found odd items in closets of especially dry deadhouses. I sometimes took one as a memento. A green hat with a blue feather. Gloves with tiny sparkles. Or boots made of seemingly indestructible synthetic fibers. My deerskin slippers were much more comfortable. My feet were hard from walking.

When the sun glowed into the trunk where I lay, I rubbed my face and peered out. There stood noeform Daniel, perched on his tripod of legs. He appeared somewhat bigger than before.

"Day three begins. Shall I stay?" Daniel asked.

I nodded.

We sat silently beneath the canopy of my giant cedar hotel, my butt nestled in soft rotting detritus, his tripod legs making a Mastican impression in the forest floor. Birds chittered. Something scratched a log nearby. Winds rustled cedars; bending branches lowed. Sprinkles of cedar frond fell, a desiccated dew of woodland detritus. Blue and white winked through our sheltering umbrella, an early winter respite from drizzle and chill. I chewed some jerky. I moved to offer some to Daniel, but then stopped myself.

"How does this work?" I asked. "I don't really understand how I am supposed to relate to you."

Daniel tripoded impassively.

"Are you doing that Odal thing with me? Should I expect an answer in a few weeks?"

"No, Zellie. I am thinking. I do not think I understand how this is supposed to work either," Daniel puzzled.

I mumbled, "I obviously need some companionship, but this is weird."

We sat in silence for a time.

"Well," I began. "Let's talk basics. I have always wanted to ask Odal, but I know I will not live long enough to receive answers."

"Okay," my companion responded.

"How do you eat? I was going to offer you some jerky. Odal never eats."

Daniel rustled on his tripod. "He eats. Mostly Odal eats directly through his cell membrane. The stuff that falls on him. In an environment like Earth, organic stuff rains constantly: bacteria, viruses, bits of plants, dead cells, poop, dust."

"And defecation?" I asked.

"The same. Masticans excrete metabolic byproducts directly through their cell membrane. The skin organ drives Mastican perception. For more than two billion of our years, Masticans have absorbed or engulfed what they preferred, and excreted or exterminated what they detested. The We is always in a Big Feast."

"So, basically," I said, "you are always eating and always crapping. Both just waft into or out of you constantly?"

"Well. We can stop either process for a time voluntarily. But absent willing something different, yes, dining and defecating constantly and simultaneously."

"So, if I gave you the jerky, you could eat it?"

"I could engulf it, out of politeness," he said.

"What?"

"I know you would be trying to care about me by the offer of jerky. So, I would engulf it. I could break it down over time into usably tiny bits. But why the effort?"

"So, that would be some lost jerky."

"No. I would suspend it in the air surrounding it, and drop it back in your stores at Earthrise."

I shuddered, "You would crap it out into my food supply?"

"Such an event neither adds nor removes any organisms from the sample. Even the air in which I suspended it would be delivered intact."

"I will never again look at jerky quite the same way, Daniel."

The Odalet rocked back and forth.

"What's that?"

"Sort of a laugh I am working on. I have not yet attempted the chortle Odal issues as laughter. For a Mastican, the process is mentally foreign and physiologically complex. There was never a need in the Mastican We. Nothing is funny. Much of humor is ignorance suddenly unveiled or perspective startlingly adjusted. Masticans, except the Pathogene, share mind utterly. There is no surprise. The perspective of one is that of all. Any ignorance is shared, and so no moment for humor arises. Laughing announces bilateral deficiency. The We finds humor disgusting."

"Wow," I deadpanned. "Let's walk home."

"That is another thing I am working on."

"Okay. Then spin along."

"Don't you find that disconcerting?" Daniel asked.

"Odal just blips in and out. He only spins in an immediate locale. Let's try it."

Daniel spun ahead as I walked. His spin would be a slight jog for me, in terms of pace.

"So, we have issue of speed. Hard to talk when you are ahead of or behind me."

Daniel added, "And spinning is not efficient. Takes too much energy. I would have to rest long before you required a break." Daniel paused. "I have been working on something."

"Yes?"

Daniel stopped spinning. He set two eyes toward their path. His hind leg reached between the front two. Daniel tipped forward, but caught himself on his "front" two legs. He repeated the sequence.

"What do you think?" Daniel asked.

"Looks awkward," I offered. "Looks like you are falling, but barely catch yourself. How does that feel to you?"

"A lot like walking. Bipedal walking is also just falling forward, then catching yourself first with one leg, then the other."

I pondered, "Yes. I suppose."

Daniel answered, "Still, the sensation is odd. My physiology wants to spin. But my mind wants to stride. I do not know if walking will work. The sensation of falling is more problematical for Masticans. Humans fall all the time, and so are accustomed to it. Masticans, given their tripod arrangement, seldom fall. So the proprioceptive alarms ring more loudly within."

We looked at each other. This was indeed my father. Adaptive. Interested. Strong. Resilient. Affectionate.

"I will keep after it. See if I improve," Daniel whistled.

I looked hard at Daniel. I pointed, "Are these two eyes moving closer together?"

"Yes."

"How is that possible?"

"I have limited control over my body configuration. I suspect that giving myself a bilateral 'front' will help with my orientation difficulties. I do not know the limits. Odal is coaching me. We will see how it goes."

I nodded, then confessed, "I doubt I will ever get used to the sphinctering eyelids."

Daniel replied, "It is worse than that." The eye closest to him sphinctered, then sank into Daniel, leaving nothing but cell wall.

I shuddered. The eye re-emerged.

"The eyes were once engulfed creatures, now long adjusted to their visual task. I could have two. I could have nine. But three conforms to Mastican psychology, and to spinning," Daniel reported. "I am also moving my pinnacle vacuole down to where a mouth would be. It is a kind of mouth, a place for taking in and expelling larger items."

I shot, "Or an ass. That too is a place for expelling."

Daniel did his laughing lunge. I peered down at the vacuole. Sure enough, it was off-center. Moving toward the "bilateral" eyes.

Daniel continued, "The human alimentary canal is a one-way design. In at the top, out at the bottom. Mastican metabolic process is less gravity-driven for they evolved floating in muck. Things are coming and going by the same vacuoles or through the cell membrane directly. The trilectical metabolism is generalized. Universal ingress and egress."

We "walked." Daniel's hind leg reached, in an impossible contortion between the other two, then pulled itself upright, lifting the others two legs off the forest floor.

"How do you do that?" I asked. "It looks like you have no bones."

Daniel answered, "I don't. Human mobility is a rope-and-pulley affair driven by paired contracting muscles fixed to bones and ligaments. Mastican mobility is hydraulic. I generate a sleeve within and pump it full of cytoplasm, or release that pressure. The process comes with the package. I do not think about how to move any more than you do. Except when attempting something new, like 'walking.' Then I have to plan and experiment."

I nodded.

"You also seem taller," I offered.

"Yes," Daniel confirmed. I have some control over that aspect of my structure as well. Eventually, I will be about the size of Nootkan Daniel. I am eating and growing. The forest here is especially nutritious. The air is filled with microscopic fragments of organic flotsam. The forest floor teems with microbiota I find delicious."

"You are eating dirt?" I frowned.

"Yes. I suppose you could put it that way," Daniel said. "But it is more than that. Masticans engulf. They engulf to eat. But they engulf to evolve as well. In the distant past, Masticans were just non-sentient, aggressive bacteria. One day, a progenitor gulped a minuscule creature with rudimentary intelligence. It was captured in a spherical plasmid. Floating and reproducing independently of the larger bacterium, it began influencing its prokaryotic host. It found smarter and smarter inclusions, eventually becoming what we would call sentient."

"Wow. That sounds flexible," I pondered.

"And dangerous. The Masticans engulfed all sorts of abilities. A telepathic creature. Another, a microbe of astounding mathematical acumen. None more important than their dimension-spanning plasmid. It made stepping-through possible. Masticans encountered the creature during a high-energy physics experiment. After a few million years of improvements, the dimensional inclusion made Mastix a threat to several galaxies."

"Including ours," I growled.

"Yes. The Milky Way is on their xenocidal agenda," Daniel whistled.

We skirted a lake created by a landslide that fell during the last Pacific plunge earthquake. A herd of Roosevelt elk grazed its outlet meadows. We stopped to watch. The bull was magnificent, an eight-by-eight, its great rack threatening eviscerations more symbolic than actual, except during the rut. Cows and calves milled. The herd noticed, but ignored, us.

Daniel said, "I tire, my dear. Let me meet you at Earthrise. Odal and I are locked in conversation."

"That is hard to picture." I raised my eyebrows.

"He gave me a telepathic plasmid. So no words, but much is said. The experience is—well, consuming. I will fill you in when the time is right."

Daniel popped out of the forest.

I shook my head. The world becomes ever stranger.

A trout jumped, launching his concentric ringlets from its landing spot. I pulled out my line and hook, put a berry on the business end, and tossed it where the beast had breached. Shortly, his head and viscera lay on the gravel beach, his slick body headed for a spit over my evening fire.

I slept again beneath my usual rock ledge. Wolves growled in the dark, smelling crisped fish bones. The pack paced at a distance because of my fire. They made haste elsewhere when I slung a shot overhead from my Winchester, just to let them know I bite back.

I rose at dawn. At Earthrise, I shucked my moccasins, sat on the front porch, and rubbed my feet.

Clouds tore overhead, though there was little wind at the house. Some front churned toward Earthrise. It would be cloudy, probably rainy. I turned inside and snuggled under my favorite deerskin with Seneca's *Epistles* 1-65. There, the acquiescence-in-fate of Greek Epictetus, his Stoicism born of slavery, met a new context, first century Roman aristocracy in the dysfunctional days of Nero. Seneca might have argued that we are all slaves to our own minds, though I am relatively certain he preferred psychological slavery to the chattel sort. Seneca had guided young Nero and cannot be blamed for that madman's preening pyrotechnics and megalomania. Seneca recommended, when sidelined, to take a step back from the main stage and do what one can. So, Seneca retired with his beloved Paulina to his villa outside Rome. In the end, mad Nero ordered Seneca to commit suicide on account of treason. Seneca protested his innocence, but eventually opened his veins. His was no easy death.

Few could be farther sidelined than me. I mulled my role in what lay ahead, if in fact anything at all lay ahead. Helen asked me to lead. Lead what? Lead whom? Alice "saw" things in me, whatever that means. Mine was not a fruitful orchard of thoughts, since I know nothing of what approaches. To all appearances, I face a lonely existence followed by an unnoticed death. We humans are not good with information deserts. We want control. Planning beckons. We yearn for elusive certitude, the sort that is generally inaccessible to mortals. If the books that Odal brought me can be taken as a message, I suppose the alien chides me. Chill out and take a nap. Let matters unfold in due course. I took Odal's oblique advice, and drifted to afternoon sleep with flame-engulfed hills of Rome and Nero's ridiculous Domus Areum tickling my mind. Apparently, I had not slept all that well the night before, with wolves at bay.

EARTHRISE DEADHOUSE
TWO MONTHS LATER

A slight pop. Morning sun shone through the window to Daniel's accustomed corner.

I said, "There you are!" I grinned over my shoulder at my only companion from the counter where I sliced jerky for a stew. I had found some wild onions the previous afternoon, which, with potatoes and carrots from my garden would be delicious.

Daniel said, "Yup. Been busy."

I raised an eyebrow, inquiring.

"Odal stuff, my dear," Daniel replied.

"Hush hush, I suppose."

"Not so much," said my father.

"Just missing you. I have gotten used to seeing you, and you are less painful to look at these days," I teased.

But it was true. Daniel had grown to five feet tall. He now had two primary eyes; the third was still there but in the "back" in his revised physiognomy. My father had gotten the knack of "walking," and so conformed in some measure to bilateral norms. He grew a little bump that passed for a nose. His pinnacle vacuole was now beneath the two primary eyes and "nose." And he had darkened some cell wall on his dome, and added stands of flagellae up there in a pretense of hair. It was fur that could rearrange itself at will, and so kind of creepy if one happened to be looking when the "hair" commenced a self-combing. A coif with a mind of its own, heeding an alien aesthetic. Daniel had become, from the cell wall out, decidedly quasi-human in appearance. A dour Humpty-Dumpty that suffered occasional flashes of my father's sense of humor.

"Is the nose better?" Daniel asked.

I looked carefully. "Needs to be wider at the bottom and smoother between the eyes at the top."

"I'll work on it," Daniel said, tipping from one leg to another in "laughter."

"You been lonely?" he asked.

"I'm okay. Just used to your company. Especially since you moved in," I responded.

"Like new furniture, just standing in the corner most of the time," he observed.

"No. It has meant a lot to me having you at Earthrise. Makes the world seem more normal, despite its ineffable weirdness."

"Seems normal enough to me too. Though I miss Hanah."

"I thought Odal updated you about the other you and Hanah in RavenPod," I asked.

"Oh, he does. And he noeforms me regularly so Hanah stays up to speed on my separate existence. But the whole thing is like getting old news. None of the vibrancy of live exchange," Daniel moped.

"I can see that must be difficult," I said.

"Just feeling sorry for myself," he whistled. "Guess I am getting more and more human."

I laughed. Daniel wobbled.

Pop. Odal stood in his corner of the deadhouse.

Daniel took a long look at his friend, now become parent. "Is it time?" Daniel asked.

"Yes, Daniel. The time has come," the alien phagocyte whispered.

I looked at both of them. "Time for what?"

Odal whistled, "Time to answer your questions."

"What questions?" I sought.

Odal responded, "The one about being alone. And those about what I am doing." His pinnacle vacuole rippled.

"Oh, those questions," I said. "The biggies."

I wiped my hands and sat. I concluded, "It is indeed about time."

Odal settled on his tripod of legs. That meant he had more than a bit to say.

"I was budded nearly eleven million of your years ago. As you know, I am Qadax's bud. I am him in every way, a mere copy. Or so the We supposed. Qadax surreptitiously ramped up my tolerance for solitude, taught me to hide it, and removed an organelle installed when Virulents are budded. A fail safe for the Puddle. You might call it a poison pill. If a Virulent is mindlashed by the We, the organelle ruptures the cell walls of that Virulent, causing instantaneous death. As you know, the We mindlashed all Virulents when the Maw fiasco destroyed Mastix. Only I and Qadax survived. He had removed his poison pill, but was insufficiently independent to weather mindlash. So, Qadax is comatose, as once was I. It was not the We that crushed me, but rather Enigmat. At Alice's Yokwat deadhouse, after an unsought encounter. My syncope lasted years. That was my second encounter with Raven, actually. The first was inside the event horizon of the Maw itself. I will tell you that story again, if you wish."

I said, "No, Odal. I remember. Haras died; you survived. The We ignored your warnings about Enigmat, whom we call Raven."

"Yes. The We went right on exterminating bilaterals in Omban, and had begun purges in your galaxy. In my survey of this galaxy, I found your primate predecessors advancing, but hid much about them. And about my far-ranging activities. Terran primates would, in a few million years, burst into visibility to the We, despite my deceptions. Then you would be killed. Qadax went along with me, but only so far. He could not break from the We. I would not succeed at rescue of any large number of humans. Or, for that matter, others of your galactic local neighbors. Six others, to be exact.

"So, I began shaping an alternative. First, I had to expand my capacity for intergalactic travel. To protect the species I had identified—seven sentiences on seven planets—each would need refuge far enough from Omban to exceed the reach of the We. That took two million years. When I was able to travel easily beyond the reach of Mastix, I selected new planets for the various bilateral species I had identified, all close enough for eventual communication with one another.

I interjected, "We will have nearby cousins?"

Odal said, "Related by sentience. The others differ in body structure and biology."

"Wow," I deadpanned. But the possibilities excited me.

"For each, I began transplanting the native biome, and accommodating conditions on the planets I selected to those who would arrive.

"When humans arrive, they will find much they have lost. Not only long-dead fragments of the world humanity remembers, but also the world human ignorance destroyed. There are carrier pigeons, and dodos, and wooly mammoths, and all manner of whales. Plants in diversity long forgotten. Species that perished entirely undiscovered by people. There are even wooly rhinoceros pairs. An earthly biome never savaged by human hyper-population.

"When humans were recognized by the We, I continued preparing those I might be able to save. Some genetic repairs. Tweaks to human intelligence. Adjustments to your immune system to meet the challenges a new planet might bring. The Ravenhills served as a lynchpin. Affection toward and connection to Enigmat. A religion. Crucial survival skills. Leadership that was not putrid. And much resilience. So, I intervened. Noeformed core members. Protected when that did not become too overt. Moved toward an exodus."

"Exodus!" I objected. "You are trapped here with us!"

Odal said, "That is so. We will need a breakthrough to exit. If none emerges, we will all die here. I and Qadax long after you, but nevertheless…"

"That was a big risk, Odal. A foolish risk," I spit.

"Not so great, Zelika. Had I been outside the envelope, I might not have been able to prepare the human survivors or terminate the envelope. That would be as fatal as cooking inside the envelope. And Qadax is inside. Were I outside the envelope, the We might be able to find me. And they would come for me with lethal intent."

I pursed my lips. "Qadax has not been much help."

"That is so," said Odal. "For now. He is immensely experienced, and acutely intelligent. A saying of mine: Qadax my tender, I his dolt."

"That I have a hard time believing." I pursed my lips.

"So too would Qadax," the Mastican youth sang. "Maybe I am in your parlance just Qadax's headstrong adolescent?"

I raised an eyebrow. *A ten million year old kid. Unlikely.*

Odal paused. He rotated one-third of a revolution on his tripod. I have never known why he does that. A tic?

Odal resumed, "There are patterns in Enigmat interventions, patterns visible to the We in a billion years of observations, then only as mathematical propositions. The Nootka, however, captured the gist of the We's assessment in its Raven cycles. Raven has a character—the Trickster. Elements of boredom, fascination with particular bilateral communities, laughter, irreverence, serendipitous interventions, dream-borne intimations, affection for the bawdy. And hunger, great gnawing hunger. I suggest that the Ravenhill clan entertains Raven. The Big Bird wants you all to play your roles. If I am right, the death of humanity in a Mastican oven will bore the Trickster. It may act to enlarge its possibilities of amusement.

"As to Earth's handful of survivors, I have been fitting them together socially as well. Like puzzle pieces. The others know of you, Zelika, though you know no more than their existence."

I shot, "Why did you choose to isolate me? I need hope in a future as much as they do."

"Your role is to maximize independence, so you can see the others from the outside, as a communal band of survivors, as well as from the inside, as beloved friends," Odal offered.

"You have been training me? Beyond the books, I mean?"

Odal said, "Yes. Tutoring. Rather expansively. You are precocious, so direct intervention is seldom required."

I was somewhat aware of these facts. Still, I had not surmised the scope of Odal's manipulations.

"I suppose I do not even want to know some of what you have been doing among humans," I said.

Odal sphinctered the eyes I could see. "That seems likely, my friend." He chortled. Or so I surmised. Odal has never quite gotten the knack of levity.

We fell silent. I rummaged my thoughts. Stirred the stew. Sucked my teeth. I sat and stared out the Earthrise window.

After a few minutes, Daniel asked, "Shall we go?"

"Go where?" I raised an eyebrow.

"To the others," he responded.

Odal opened his eyes.

There was a pop. Then we stood on a cliff's edge. On, I guessed, the east face of the Rocky Mountains. These jutted into blue, valleys white with deep snows. Faces too steep to hold drifts were encumbered with ice cliffs. In the distance, Rocky Mountain elk grazed and lazed. A few hundred feet below our perch, across a busy stream, hovels of humans stood. People washed and harvested and chopped and laughed and rested and played and ate. One urinated. Just what I would expect of any survivors. A young man waved at us. Odal waved back. Pop. I stood next to the waving person.

Odal began, "Zelika, this is Noam."

"Noah?" I blurted.

The well-muscled Coloradoan said, "Some people think I am that crabby old zookeeper. But, no, I am Noam. Hebrew for 'tender.' I am not Jewish. My mother loved to read Noam Chomsky." Noam raised an eyebrow. "Nothing? A twentieth century linguist and philosopher and activist."

"Oh, no. I have read him. I am just amazed your mother reads Chomsky for fun," I said.

Noam said, "She is that way. Fascinated with the past that is now lost to us. Odal brings her books."

"Apparently, he does that a lot," I responded.

"What about 'Zelika'?"

"Ancestral name. Keeps popping up in my family," I said, blushing a bit.

Odal said, "I will leave you two to converse for a moment. I shall speak with Daniel above." The Mastican pointed to my father. Then Odal stood cliff-top and waved. We waved back.

Noam and I chatted. I found myself diverting my eyes from his. We spoke of nothing important. His village. Work—he makes wooden and fired clay implements. We spoke of life after the Forms. I told him of my isolation.

"Odal has said that you study for us all?"

I answered carefully, "Well, I study. The utility of my work remains to be proved." I found myself blushing again, to my surprise.

Odal returned. "We must go," he said.

At cliff top, Daniel prodded, "Handsome devil, isn't he? That Noam fellow."

I lied, "I did not notice."

We flashed to deep jungle, Amazon, I believe. Sinuous ribbons, waterways of meanders, buried in greens and protrusions of hillocks, a mangrove of immense proportion. Canoes, handhewn, bore natives. A dozen or so. Probably more. These paddlers were hard to see, stealthy, slicing water deftly. Weaving in and out of the maze of snaking canals. They recognized Odal and waved. Friendly, at least to him.

We popped to a desert, probably the Gobi, given the features of the people. A rock ocean, ribboned with waves of sand. Its inhabitants rode beasts of burden unfamiliar to me, like camels, with humps and all, but not quite. Possibly wooly Bactrian camels. The group disappeared behind scrub brush.

Then came New Zealand near Parihaka, ancestral home of some Maori, a much-tattooed native people. These grinned broadly and did an odd dance before us. Then I stood in Australian outback. Orange, pink, tan. Sedimentary rocks curled in baking sunshine, now intensified by the envelope.

I asked, Are there people here? Odal pointed, but I saw nothing.

Odal said, "If they do not want to be seen, you will not see them."

Finally, the Himalayan steeps of Arunachal Pradesh. Women with rocks enlarging their nostrils, pounding grain in the shadow of a deadhouse temple, which was crumbling. Windswept granite expanses leapt thousands of feet into thin air. Wisps of cloud tore around peaks. The ladies waved to Odal, and pointed at me and Daniel. They were laughing. We all waved back, and smiled.

Then we popped back to Earthrise.

"Wow. A couple hundred people?" I guessed.

Odal said, "Fewer."

"Oh, I see. 150. The Dunbar number."

"157, to be exact," Odal whistled. "Robin Dunbar's take was a slight underestimation."

"Is that enough?" I wondered. "People?" I clarified.

"It is," Odal assured me. "After one Pleistocene glaciation, all humans lived in one region at the seaside of South Africa. They numbered 139. That was about 195,000 of your years ago, the first choke point in human evolution. One step before modern humans. Every human descends from that tiny community. Do you remember MIS6 from your reading, Zelika?"

"I do. Deep glaciation turned most of Africa into lethal desert. I did not realize that humans were so close to extinction though." I paused. "But 139," I objected, "How could you know that?"

Odal whistled quietly, "I counted."

That settled that. Odal's age always slips from comprehension. Like the Cheshire's smile.

In less than one hour I had seen all of humanity that would survive Earth. I put landscapes and smells and skies to the book-geography I had learned. A place does not seize reality in the mind until one smells its waft and tastes its dust.

Perhaps critically, I met Noam. He stuck to my mind like pitch on a moccasin. I felt warm thinking of him.

I began processing. "All these groups live in odd places. No cities. Little old tech."

"Yes," Odal agreed.

"I suppose they resisted the Forms. Like Earthrise."

Odal said, "Mostly. Two groups used Habis, but survived reversion to pre-Form ways. All dwell in shatter zones. Landscapes or peoples so difficult that governments never quite rotted out their communities. Few roads. No social security numbers. Extravagant self-reliance, arm-in-arm with pervasive cooperation. Deep emotional connections among members. And a refusal to let people who think much of themselves do much leading."

I said, "That last falls under the rubric, *Stop making stupid people famous*."

Odal said, "Yes. Humans have always been vulnerable to sociopaths. They want power, and many people are willing to give it to them. A really terrible idea."

I said, "I think it has been hard for communities to know what to do with such people. Sociopaths are often charismatic and stupendously talented. They can overwhelm most folks."

Odal proposed, "Accompany them."

"What?" I asked.

"Stand alongside sociopaths. Pair a normal person with each one. Support that normal person. Intervene with the larger group when the sociopath veers toward dangers. And teach sociopaths that they are disabled. Empathy-disabled. Compassion morons. Sociopaths cannot feel the pain they inflict, and so pose dangers. But most are bright. They will understand the risks they pose, even if they cannot care much about their outcomes."

I said, "I will have to think about this."

Silence settled for a couple minutes.

Then I made a connection. "This is Scott and his "shatter zone" peoples. Communities that refuse to be mapped or made legible to number-crunchers and bureaucrats. To governments."

Odal said simply, "Yes."

I sighed, a bit overwhelmed with all of what I had seen, with the eccentric thoughts pummeling me.

"I need some time to think."

Daniel said, "Thought you might. Back later."

I nodded. Odal and Daniel popped out.

I sat. The sun dipped behind Neah Bay's hills, shining off the Strait. The sunset shone orange and red, tickling cirrus wisps into fire-wild hair. Torched forests in north Asian Siberia painted the skies with particulate, I supposed. The planet was warming. Forests burned. Waters warmed.

I felt—I do not know what. Something unexpected. Something happening within me. Quietly, my many losses receded. Just a bit. And anticipation seeped into those vacancies.

I slept. Deeply.

EARTHRISE DEADHOUSE
TWO DAYS LATER

Daniel stood in the corner when I woke. "Hi," I yawned.

"Morning," he sang. "You ready to talk?"

"Gotta pee. And I am hungry," I responded. "Odal comin'?" I asked. Daniel tipped forward. Guess that meant yes.

When I finished my chewing and ablutions, the alien appeared.

Odal looked somehow smaller. "You okay?" I asked.

"I have budded. My volume is reduced seventeen percent. The energy expenditure in reproducing plasmids demands much," it said.

"Who's the bud?" Daniel asked anxiously. I know my father was hoping the answer would be Hanah.

"Helen," Odal said. "I apologize, Daniel. I know the mode fissure between you and Hanah troubles you. But in the next while, you and Zelika will need the tangible wisdom of Helen. She knows much of both of your needs."

Daniel sphinctered an eye.

"Is Helen here?" I asked.

Odal responded, "Not just yet. She is getting herself organized. Internally."

I nodded.

I turned topics. "So, this plan of yours. We have 157 individuals."

Odal interrupted, "No. We have 157 *members* of six different communities."

I sighed, "Point taken. Their contexts matter. So we have six groups getting together. We do not speak the same language, eat the same foods, share mores or habits or toolkits or temperature preferences. How is this supposed to work?"

Daniel said, "We have every confidence in you."

I let that sink in. "What?"

"How it works will be up to you, Zelika. You are the hub," Odal whistled.

I shot, "Historically, such a conclave would be an invitation to a bloodbath."

Daniel said, "Or an orgy. Or a festival. Or a trade fair."

I nodded, thinking it over. It was apparent that Odal's setup meant that to war was to exterminate humanity. We would plunge below the necessary number of breeding pairs.

"How are we supposed to talk?" I asked.

Odal sang, "That will be difficult the first day, less so the day after. Just work at it. You will construct a new language that all use. Your existing languages will persevere for a time, probably through a few generations," said Odal. "You will all eat what is available, since you have no choice but to do so. To the rest, you will adapt. It will rain as much as it rains. The temperature will be what it is, no hotter and no colder.

"In the end, none of you will survive without all of you. You have a minimal contingent as a breeding population, at least the smallest proven to be adequate. And you have all been through the Forms and overpopulation, even in the attenuated numbers that prevailed when the Forms regressed. So, you share much. Finally, you share Earth. You will find that common origin will outweigh many cultural differences. You share self-sufficiency and community. You will generate a mythology. I suspect Raven will be making messes for humankind to meet, wherever you settle. You will work it out together." Odal's pinnacle vacuole sphinctered shut. He settled into his tripod of legs.

I doubted, "You are quite the optimist."

Odal replied, "No. I have calculated."

"You cannot calculate people, Odal!" I spit.

Odal whistled quietly, "No, *you* cannot calculate people. Masticans are good at this sort of thing. I have measured, tweaked, and slotted every member of each community. I have fitted the cultures as well as the personalities. You can, if you wish, make it work. And something wonderful will emerge. Trust me."

"That is just it. I don't," I ground.

Odal spoke even more slowly than usual, "It is time to get over that peculiar sentiment, my dear. Examine your conception of friendship. Tell me how I am deficient."

Daniel tipped toward me.

I thought it over. I really had nothing against Odal. Our time mesh was all wrong. That was no one's fault. I have deep-seated prejudice against bacteria. Always washing my hands and face to get rid of them. I am sure that Odal does not like bilaterals all that much, given his own culture. Odal had done nothing but benefit the Ravenhills. None of us blames him for the Mastican genocide. Without Odal, that crime would have succeeded.

As I have said, Aristotle spoke of friendship. We would probably call Aristotle's sort of friendship an intimacy. Two persons inseparable. One person in two bodies. Two essences intertwined. Cicero, the Roman senator, found life without friends to be no life at all. Buber argued there is no I except in intimacy with a Thou. And his ultimate Thou is divine. With that great triumvirate of human scribblers, I agreed.

So, I decided.

"You are right, my friend," I said. "Forgive me. I have been unaccountably stingy with you." I walked over to the tall cylinder of his body. I put my arms part way around Odal. I gave a squeeze. His cell wall had a tough feel, though it gave a bit under my embrace.

I admitted, "There. That was weird. But I hug friends."

Odal twirled one full round. A tiny dance?

EARTHRISE DEADHOUSE
EIGHTEEN DAYS LATER

A cosmoform settled on the grass in front of Earthrise as the sun dipped into the Pacific. A handsome Nootkan emerged from the oval door of the vehicle. The cosmoform began grazing on my garbage. The alien tech dropped formscum as a parking place. The vehicle produced a Mastican, much to my surprise, comatose, all snug in his null field. The cosmoform placed the Mastican on a level piece of hardening scum. The human passenger, a strong man, obviously a Ravenhill, stepped onto the formscum.

"Hello, pretty lady! I am Rock Ravenhill."

"Zelika Ravenhill, sir. Are you the disappeared Rock Ravenhill from the Gaxer Accords?"

"Don't know about Gaxers."

"Are you the Rock who is noeformed in RavenPod?"

Rock looked at me dumbfounded, "What?"

Odal and then Daniel popped in.

Daniel pointed, "Look, Zellie."

In the northeast sky, just now dark enough to show, an oval of stars grew. I stared. I could not take my eyes off the porthole into the cosmos that was growing before my eyes.

Odal said to the newcomer, "Let me copy you to my version of Rock, please. To update him."

Rock put up his hands, "Hold on that crap, partner! What the hell are you talking about?"

Odal stepped back. He gave voice to noeform Rock.

Noe-Rock said, "Rock, I am Rock. This creature, Odal, made a copy of your mind when the cosmoform interpenetrated you to keep you from being crushed as you and it accelerated to relativistic speeds. I have been living a separate life in his cytoplasm since that moment. If Odal noeforms you, I will know what has happened to you since your departure."

Rock said, "Hell, that's not hard. I flew out of the solar system, reached Centauri, looked around, then came back. It's been about a week."

Noe-Rock replied, "No, Rock. You have been gone more than 170 years. Time differential, you know. The whole Einstein thing."

"Yeah. I suspected that might happen," Rock looked down. "170 years. My people are gone then."

I said, "No, Rock. We are your people. Generations have passed, but there are still Ravenhills."

Rock waved his hand. "I get it."

I tore my eyes from starlight. "Hungry?"

"What you got? I eat. But it is form food, you know. Not exactly my idea of the good stuff," Rock offered.

I stated the menu, "Elk jerky, vegetables, cooked fiddleheads, and a taste of marionberry wine, just for celebrations."

"Excellent," Rock shot, and strode toward the deadhouse.

Rock and I sat at the window, chewing. Odal and Dad took their places in their corners. Rock told his story of attempting propulsion in the cosmoform, of lost consciousness, of exploring the Centauri stars, and unconscious return.

"The weird shit began when I got back. The Cosmo thought we were at Earth, but there was nothing there. The Form poked around a bit, and flew me to a black lattice with a pulsating something inside it. Looked alive, the something or other. Residual radiation made the area quite dangerous, though the Form managed it," Rock said.

Daniel raised one of three arms, "That would be me."

"You?"

"Well, me before I died."

"You died?"

"That is a long story. The short version is that Astroforce decided to attempt to destroy that lattice with a nightmarish nuclear strike. The detonation had no effect at all."

Rock nodded. "Nor did I. I bumped it a couple of times with the cosmoform. The lattice was small. But it did not move. Had the mass of a chain of mountains, or so it seemed," Rock reported.

Odal explained, "The creature was not entirely in this universe. It straddles dimensional rifts."

"Okay," Rock said, uncomprehending. "Whatever the hell that means."

Rock continued, "I waited, wondering what to do. It was beginning to dawn on me that if I could not get to Earth, I had nowhere at all to go. I sat for a few weeks, just thinking of alternatives. But came up with less than mosquito pee. Then I fell into what I call reverie. Maybe a hallucination. Raven came, and did one of its fantastical images and bullshit lightshows on me. Do you think I am crazy?"

"If you are, then we all are," I offered.

"I just wonder. The Raven crap is so strange. I doubt myself," Rock whispered to me.

I said, "I did once as well. But no more."

After a few moments, Rock went on. "Then a talon the size of a truck appeared. It cut through the lattice like it wasn't there, and pierced the pulsing thing."

Odal said, "The plasmid."

"Okay. It pierced the plasmid. Juice leaked all over, freezing, then disappearing," Rock reported. "Then the blackness disappeared, rapidly leaving a gigantic hole in the whatever it was." Rock looked out the window. "Doesn't look so large from here."

Odal reported, "The envelope will dissipate at the speed of light. It will be gone in a few days."

Daniel pointed outside. Rock's cosmoform was regressing. Rock started to run toward it, but then realized there was nothing he could do.

Odal spoke, "This is bad news, Zelika. Somewhere, at least one Mastican has regained consciousness and is attempting to re-establish the We. The cosmoform touched that consciousness, and received its Terran suicide prompt."

Rock walked out to the collapsed cosmoform. He put a hand on its shell, now gone clammy and soft. "Thanks, my friend. I will miss you." The carcass continued shrinking. It had already begun decomposing.

"I must go," Odal said. "Zelika and Rock, please be ready to depart in approximately twelve hours. I will return for you two and Qadax."

I nodded.

"Depart?" Rock sought.

"We are leaving Earth," I said.

"Where are we going?"

"Don't know where," I reported.

"For how long?" Rock asked.

"Forever," I said.

Rock objected, "Well, I'll be damned. I just got back."

"Yup."

Rock said, "Odal?" The alien stopped his spin. "Do that copy thing, please."

Odal paused, then said, "Done."

"That was easy," Rock said.

"Yup," I said.

SOMEWHERE, FAR FROM EARTH
THE NEXT MORNING

Across turquoise waters, not far, I saw smoke. A village of shelters stood. Nothing fancy. Just a place. Good enough for now. Around me on this shore a few hundred yards from the others, stood the remainder of the Ravenhill clan, Daniel, Rock, Helen (not looking much like Helen yet), and of course Odal. Qadax stood, somnolent in the distance under a tree at the edge of the village. His null field shimmered as cedar frond bits settled on his protective field. At the water's brink, nearby, stood Noam, next to four canoes made of some glittering silver substance. The metal (if it was metal) reminded me of a salmon dancing after skittered fingerlings. I knew this event. From dreams. From Raven.

I boarded and knelt. A paddle waited. Noam gave a shove and jumped deftly into the back. I said, "Thanks."

We humans stroked confidently into cold turquoise waters. Our canoe split the surface. An image of Raven graced the bow. Rock was a bit clumsy at first, alone in his craft and out of practice. There was splashing and a bit of cursing. Two moons hung low in that morning's sky. Dad and Helen each worked their way into canoes. Their paddling bumbled. But that would improve. They would get it. We all would get it. Get everything.

We approached the village. The other five clans waited on the beach, sorted by locale of origin, looking uncertain, looking for me, I suppose. If it is as Odal has said.

My canoe ground onto the narrow sand and round rock strand. I stepped out. Noam pulled the canoe to safety. I turned to watch Rock and Daniel and Helen struggle into the village cove. Noam and Rock pulled their canoes up from the water's edge. Odal stood at the back of the group.

I looked to the people. They looked back. None knew what came next.

I began to sing. A simple song. A Nootkan children's tune. Daniel joined, mostly whistling along. Helen tried but failed. Rock opened his mouth and out came the most delicious baritone. After two rounds, others began joining. Soon, all attempted the melody. Each used words of their own languages, but the common tune. Words would come later. Finally, Odal's windy chortle rose with us, a failed attempt at song, but it was the effort that mattered, the desire to participate.

I stopped. The song faded, though some continued to sway to its now-silenced strain. I looked at them all, a small band, really. Not so many that I could not know and love each and every one. As it should be. As it will be.

I walked through the group to Odal. I embraced him, and touched my cheek to his cell wall affectionately. I walked back to the water side. I went to the Australians. I embraced a child, and put my cheek to hers. Then the New Zealanders. A hug and cheek. Then Gobi, and Himalayans, Coloradoans. For each a symbolic hug and a warm cheek. I stepped back. I held my arms wide, as though hugging the assembly in its entirety.

I said, "The People." I pointed at each person individually, all 157 of them. It took a couple of minutes. Then I swung my arms wide again, and said, "The People." Several mumbled the words, words not of their language, and a concept that enlarged their micro-worlds. Some whispered to one another. I clapped. Many laughed, and clapped with me.

I spread my arms wide again. I hugged the sky. I got down in the sand. I hugged the beach. I got up, brushed myself off, and pointing outward, I turned slowly, encompassing all that could be seen. I hugged that vista. Again, I hugged the sky.

I said, "Amity." I knelt and slapped the beach. I said, "Amity." People began saying "Amity" to one another, and explaining within their groups what they thought I meant.

Daniel "walked" to me. He pointed at Odal, then Helen, then somnolent Qadax, then himself. He said, "People?"

I looked to the assembly. Our first decision, one of billions to be made in the epoch-spanning life of a few transplanted species. And perhaps our most crucial decision. Will The People be insular or inclusive? Will we welcome or shun?

I walked to Odal, whom they all knew. I hugged him again, and nestled my cheek against him. I walked to Qadax, and opened my arms to him. I walked to Daniel, then Helen, hugging each, and rubbing my cheek against their cell walls.

I returned to my spot.

I asked, "The People?" My voice rose.

I held my thumb up, and smiled. Then turned it down, and frowned. Thumb signs are not universal, but smiles and frowns are.

I thumped my chest. I gave the assembly my vote: Thumbs Up, with my very best smile.

Most made some sort of thumbs up sign. Everyone laughed. And smiled.

I said, "The Masticans are People. At least these Masticans."

Odal spun.

Daniel tipped.

Helen, who did not yet look like Helen, did not know what to do.

And so, the end ended; the beginning began.

I sighed, not knowing if I should be comforted. As the sun sank, Amity's second moon rose again, yellow in pollen-laden air. Waves licked my toes at the water's edge. At least, I finally know for whom I write. I write for us, the human, the Mastican, the mixed, the cyber, the living and the dead. I write to tell a fragment—a pregnant fragment—of our history, from the perspective of RavenPod. From my perspective as well.

I felt something growing, something Odal had nurtured in me, in the others. Something social. Something warm. Something sober. A smaller, humbler, more compassionate view of togetherness. I like our new name for ourselves, for our planet: The People, the planet Amity. For we now embrace others not of Earth. And welcome others part Earth, part Mastix. We are no longer dwellers on a planet named after dirt, but rather members on a homeworld denominated by the quality of the relationships of its sentient inhabitants. A confederation . . . No, a community of . . . Well, I guess I would say, a community of friendship among oddballs. Given to mutual nurture. Predisposed to delight in being present for one another. Focused on recognizing what is. Will the old bastard re-emerge? The ugly hag mankind? A frenzied troop who mistook their urgencies for verities? The competitive, grasping, small-spirited, venomous, nasty little primate that once captivated human imagination? Will that moral midget skulk back into our shadows, from there to torment us? We fear that sociopathic troll hunkers beneath every bridge of consciousness. Is he gone, or merely hiding?

I trust our new circumstance, leavened by the human experience of hyper-population, will prevail. Odal says that humans were not rapacious until they over-populated. About 20,000 years ago. Before that, the human herd was stupid, beleaguered, and prone to stumbling. But not dangerously uncivil; not suicidal. Then desperation encouraged horrors, to still for a moment the grating squall of unfed mouths, of metastasizing neuroses. Misery crushed compassion. Finally, all moral exemplars were corrupt turds. How could we expect people to learn peace from such tutors? From Khans and Alexanders and Napoleons and Hitlers and Maos and Stalins and their irascible irksome ilk? Sure, there were other voices, Yeshuas and Siddharthas and Gandhis and Te Whitis, tender sparrow song in a deafening world of detonating munitions. For human billions, moral urgencies drowned in the rivers of senseless bloodletting. In those days, fun was brutal and anger genocidal. Perhaps now, here on Amity, happier stories can linger, shaping children. An architecture for extravagant cooperation. A planetary lyric for a symphony of synchronous sentience.

I learned a different story from that of hyper-population, even different than that of Formic frivolity. I sat in the school of life *after* the Forms, after the psychotic autocrats, after nuclear weapons, after gunpowder. I learned from Earthrise Deadhouse. From Hank Smelke's leer, forever frozen in a bloody snowscape. From Mom's attachment struggles. From lovely Alice and Helen and their flinty, unflinching embraces. From forests and creatures. From winds and weathers. From alien Trojan horses, and that bitter Mastican envelope. From the books of those odd people, who spoke mostly to themselves, and so to us all. I have drunk an earthy wisdom spiced with a dash of Mastix. And Raven swoops into dreams. Ever teasing. Keeping me slightly uncomfortable, ever a bit annoyed. Always intrusive, ever inaccessible.

Perhaps my fringe education is why Odal drafted me as first among equals in The People. I am to guide, not rule. I am to point and explain, then support and love. As did Katherine. As did Alice. As did Helen. The remnant will survive errors. We will recover from self-mutilations by humility, and keen strategic dissections, and laughter at the jokes we inflict upon ourselves.

What no community survives is hatred. We cannot let antipathy rot our souls, individually or collectively. For we will be consumed. Either amity will guide, or enmity will corrode. We must choose, every morning, every hour, every encounter. Friendship or alienation. The People are launched upon the path of amity. May it ever be so.

Altruism fosters altruism. Good will midwifes good will. Friendship observed woos all watchers. Community sprouts, then spreads, a verdant succulent, hardy in droughts. The People will keep life simple, but indulge extravagant mentation. We will manage our numbers, well-warned by our past inane breeding. We will care for every member intimately. We will refuse to crush non-primate neighbors. All will know every other as friend, despite unavoidable mishaps. We will apologize, and cry together. On that foundation, we will build whatever our future holds. Perhaps we can embrace the challenge of Amity, the idea and the planet. Perhaps friendship grows sacral.

Raven still toys with the Ravenhill clan. Imp. Narcissist empath. Fitful fateful fetish. Reliably unreliable, as ever. Foisting on us darkest humors. Beneath all things, yet apparent nowhere.

The People are the human remnant, and yet more.

We have clambered again from our little clamshell, stumbled into a larger world, a vast, unexpected context, in a galaxy none but long-dead astronomers ever noticed. Knowledge of matters interstellar, now lost to the apex primate of Earth. Humanity, or what is left of it, has again been lured from capsuled terror into a vast and unknown world we never imagined. Out of the clamshell. Into the breach. Onto the beach. We are far, far from the Local Cluster. Beyond the reach of Masticans. Or so we hope.

The People peer with lively minds. From first squirming in the puddles of Mastix, to humankind's transplantation so far from the Milky Way. From a gene pool, to genes that cannot be pooled. From old to new. From what was to what will be. From one life to another.

The People see:
Fledged dreamscape roiled,
Numinous talons piercing,
Clamshells pried, the meek extracted,
Hallowed pecking at psychic flotsam,
Avian derision, mana, inaudible,
Everything is connected; All is one;
We, Her ravenry, tangled hovel,
Nest of woven minds, embraced,
Sacral eremitic haven, hearing
Impalpable feathers rustle,
Cawk. Cawk. Cawk. Cawk.
Furtive divinity, afoot.

SAINT GEORGE'S HILL PRESS

On St. George's Hill (southwest of London), in 1648, poor people, under the influence of Gerrard Winstanley, tilled and built shacks on public land to feed themselves, when food prices soared during the English Civil War. They called themselves True Levellers, and sought reduction of the financial chasm between the poor and the wealthy. The king sent a representative, who found the group doing no appreciable harm. A local lord felt otherwise, and commissioned thugs to assault the True Levellers. Some were beaten. Their common meal house was burned. Leaders were tried; the judge refused to let them speak in their defense. The True Levellers, dubbed Diggers by opponents, abandoned their plots for less hostile locations. In the twenty-first century, St. George's Hill is home to an exclusive gated and closely-guarded community, consisting in 450 mansions with tennis club and golf course amenities. St. George's Hill claims to be the premier private residential estate in Europe, close to London and Britain's most desirable private preparatory schools. The median price of a residence on St. George's Hill exceeds £3,000,000. St. George's Hill, then, is the dirt upon which clash desperate diggers and entrenched elites, a metaphor barely metaphorical.

www.ingramcontent.com/pod-product-compliance
Lightning Source LLC
LaVergne TN
LVHW020713110826
845149LV00012B/2242

* 9 7 8 0 9 9 8 6 4 3 5 5 7 *